BY CARYS BRAY

A Song for Issy Bradley
Sweet Home (stories)

A Song for
Issy Bradley

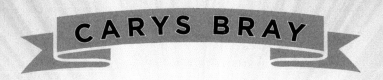

CARYS BRAY

A Song for
Issy Bradley

A NOVEL

BALLANTINE BOOKS

NEW YORK

Published in the United States by Ballantine Books, an imprint of Random House, a division of Random House LLC, a Penguin Random House Company, New York.

BALLANTINE and the HOUSE colophon are registered trademarks of Random House LLC.

Originally published by Hutchinson in 2014.

LIBRARY OF CONGRESS CATALOGING-IN-PUBLICATION DATA
Bray, Carys
A Song for Issy Bradley : a novel / Carys Bray.
p.   cm
ISBN 978-0-553-39088-9
eBook ISBN 978-0-553-39089-6
Mormons—Fiction. 2. Domestic fiction. I. Title.
PR6102.R37S66 2014
823'.92—dc23   2014024027

Printed in the United States of America on acid-free paper

www.ballantinebooks.com

2 4 6 8 9 7 5 3 1

First Edition

Title and part-title images: copyright © iStock.com

Book design by Victoria Wong

For Ailsa and Robert, with thanks

For my soul delighteth in the song of the heart;
yea, the song of the righteous is a prayer
unto me, and it shall be answered with a blessing upon their heads.

—Doctrine and Covenants 25:12

Footprints
in the Sand

NOVEMBER

*C*laire dreams she is walking along a beach with the Lord. She cannot humble herself and speak nicely, so they progress in silence. The sand is hard and damp, puddled in places; its ripples bump her bare feet. They walk until He stops and presses a gentle hand to her arm.

"Please come back. I love you."

The words whisper along the tiny hairs of Claire's inner ear. Did someone sneak into the bedroom, touch her arm, and murmur, *I love you*? She lies as still as she can, in case someone is there, hoping to talk to her. If they think she is asleep they will go away and leave her alone.

She continues to feign sleep as she listens to the morning noises. The radiators pop and clank, a kitchen cupboard slams shut, and she hears the unintelligible rumble of voices downstairs. The room feels empty, the air undisturbed. When the children breathe they puff air out of their noses like little steam engines. She holds her breath until her stomach is tight and her ears are thrumming. Nothing. No one. She tries to relax, to unfasten the tension in her muscles and soak back into the mattress. Why did she have to wake up just as the Lord started to speak? She attempts to switch her ears off, breathes deeply, slowly, and imagines herself back on the beach. It doesn't work. Eventually she gives up and occupies herself with a thought that flutters through her mind like a little biplane, trailing a banner of scripture in its wake: *"Behold, I have dreamed a dream; or in other words, I have seen a vision."*

The front door closes and Claire hides under the covers for a little longer in case anyone returns for an overlooked lunch box or a forgotten PE uniform. Once she is certain no one is coming back, she unwraps her blanket cocoon. The room tilts as she stands and she holds onto the top rail of the bunk for a moment, eyes squeezed shut. Once the ground steadies she tiptoes along the landing to her own room, drags an old pair of sweatpants off the floor, and balances against the wall as she pulls them on. Then she heads back along the landing and down the stairs, tucking her nightie into the elastic waistband as she goes. Her coat is hanging on the bottom stair post; she takes it and retrieves her pink wellingtons from the shoe tidy.

She opens the door. The fresh air is cool and smells of composting leaves, mud, and damp wood.

She walks down the empty driveway, and when she reaches the gatepost, she looks back. She doesn't have her key; perhaps it doesn't matter.

The house is tall, narrow and slightly hunched. It's the mid-terrace in a squeeze of three 1920s mock-Tudor properties. There are two windows on each of the three stories, every one crisscrossed with lead squares, making the house seem short-sighted and elderly. The front door is chunky and paneled. Its black paint is peeling away in plastic-sharp shards. Ian's new slate sign hangs next to it, inscribed in white enamel: *The Place.* He ordered it before—in the summer. And when it arrived everyone stood outside and watched him drill holes into the brick while he sang a hymn: *"We'll find the place which God for us prepared, Far away in the west. Where none shall come to hurt or make afraid, There the saints will be blessed!"* The sign is a half-serious joke.

"This is the place," Ian says as he reverses the car onto the driveway, the same words the prophet Brigham Young is supposed to have uttered on entering the Salt Lake Valley with the Mormon pioneers. The sign makes Ian happy; he grins as he passes it. Claire used to think stripping the front door and painting it red would make her happy.

She heads in the direction of the beach. It feels strange to be outside and expose her waxy skin to the weather for the first time in weeks. She keeps going and eventually reaches the undulating road that divides the marsh. The road was built on rubbish, purportedly hardcore, but contractors illegally dumped uncompacted household trash into the open cavity during its construction. As the trash set-tled, the road sank and crested, and it waves through the marsh like a tarmac sea. Claire has always called it the Bumpy Road. Even on a beautiful day like today when sharp blue sky and autumn sun-shine distract from the creep of winter, it's windy here.

At the top of the Bumpy Road there's a bird-watching viewpoint that isn't much more than a section of green fencing with peepholes. She peers through one of the holes. There's a board attached to the fence showing images of birds. She looks at the water and thinks she can see black-and-white avocets like the one pictured. It seems right to be surrounded by birds at a time like this. After all, birds have always been messengers and comforters; a dove helped Noah deter-mine the end of the flood and a raven took care of Elijah in the desert. She thinks about the selfless swallow in *The Happy Prince* and the nightingale that sacrificed itself in order to create a red rose. Several seagulls fly toward the beach and she remembers another story about birds, the miracle of the gulls. It happened in Utah not long after the first pioneers settled. Crops were being eaten by lo-custs or crickets, something like that, and the pioneers prayed and prayed until flocks of seagulls descended and ate all the pests. Peo-ple believe the Lord made the seagulls intervene and, as seagulls don't seem to be naturally helpful birds, perhaps He did. She fol-lows the seagulls and crosses the coastal road to the parking lot at the edge of the beach.

The sea is still at least a couple of miles away, but she can feel the motion of its waves in her chest as she crosses the lot, and each un-dulation brings a small, unexpected surge of happiness. Overhead a swarm of starlings whips through the sky like feathery fireworks and as she stops to watch, a swell of emotion breaks in her chest and trickles from her eyes.

She walks past a couple of cars that probably belong to the dog walkers on the track ahead and an elderly couple in a camper van, drinking from Thermos flasks. She follows a slight incline to the Sandwinning Track. There's a bright, new warning sign at the gateway: *"Caution: Ribble Estuary Cockling."* She knows the tides here are dangerous; the sea sneaks behind people, filling imperceptible dips in the mudflats, rolling in like a lake, and there is quicksand. Just last week the front of the local newspaper carried the story of another rescue.

Her wellies scuff the stony track and she hears cars whoosh behind her as they race along the coastal road. It was much quieter in her dream. To her left, in the distance, the pier needles its way from the promenade out onto the bare sand. Inland, she can see the tips of buildings and the pyramid of steel suspension cables supporting the Marine Way Bridge. To her right she can see Blackpool. And if she squints she can see the thin curve of a roller coaster. It seems like she could walk there. People have tried and some of them have drowned.

The track is sandier now, damp and sticky, gritty, like cake mix. It's stamped with a network of prints. There are wide tire marks from cockling vehicles and thinner tracks from bicycles. There are footprints, paw prints, and birds' prints, some tiny, others surprisingly large, pronged like windmill blades. As she continues, the texture of the sand changes; it is speckled with a mosaic of broken shell pieces that draws her toward the sea like a trail of breadcrumbs.

She stops walking when she sees a discarded net. It's red like the little bags that hold oranges, and half-full of tiny cockles; silver bells and cockle shells—she remembers singing the nursery rhyme to the children. She prizes one open with her thumbnails and when it unlocks like a little mouth she thinks of the children again, of trying to insert toothbrushes past pursed lips. Inside the shell is a brown jelly splotch of clam. She lifts it to her nose, smells the sea, and then drops it.

As she walks farther she can hear birds calling. It's rockier underfoot and the track is strewn with debris that the sea has spat out. The sand grows muddy and it sucks at her feet, slowing her pace. A dog barks and she glances back. In the far distance, she can see the hill summit of Rivington Pike. She remembers stories where people built towers and climbed mountains in order to talk to God. Rivington must be more than twenty-five miles away, and apart from several railway bridges the town is flat. She could have walked to a railway bridge and she has imagined doing so several times in recent weeks, but this morning's dream has made things clear. When she woke she knew where her exchange with God should take place.

The dog starts to run toward her, shaggy hair streaming in its wake like wings. It's only a puppy, an animal that's bursting with mindless affection. It jumps up and wipes sandy paws on her coat.

"I'm so sorry. Down, Bingley, down!" The man squelches through the last patch of marshy track. He tries to grab the dog by its collar while it licks the rubber of his wellies.

"Who's a bad dog? You are, aren't you? Yes, you are! Oh God. He's got mud all over your coat." He ruffles the dog's floppy ears and attaches a lead to its collar.

"Don't worry." Claire's voice sounds rough and discordant. Her tongue is thick and the roof of her mouth is sticky.

"You'd better get it in the wash, or it'll stain. You turning back now?"

"I'm heading on."

"You want to be careful out here. Got a mobile?"

She hasn't, but she nods.

"Keep looking around. Make sure the sea's not snuck in behind you; the tide's a bastard!"

She raises her hand slightly to indicate goodbye and the man does the same. She watches him and the dog walk away for a moment. He seems to sense her gaze and he stops and turns.

"Lovely day for it," he calls.

She heads on, unbuttoning her coat as she walks. Her nightie has slipped out of one side of her sweatpants, so she untucks it and lets it fall to her knees. Ian would say the beautiful weather is a Tender Mercy, a manifestation of the Lord's capacity for reassurance and comfort. She hopes so, but it's hard to know. Ian believes the good things are heaven-sent and the bad are arbitrary. She isn't sure what she believes anymore. She keeps walking in the direction of the sea and suddenly, in the squinting distance, beyond the endless corrugations of sand, she thinks she can see its shimmer. She increases her pace, forbids herself from looking left, or right, or behind, and it soon begins to feel as if she is all alone in the world.

BOOK ONE

———

All Is Well

SEPTEMBER

– 1 –

Birthday Boy

Jacob wakes up early. He isn't sure why at first and then he remembers it's his birthday, which makes his stomach tip like a Slinky. It's still dark, the thick kind that hides your hands from you. He lies quietly for a few moments, willing morning to get nearer.

"Issy, are you awake?"

He listens for a reply. The sound of his heartbeat pulses in his ears and he gives them a hard rub. The bunk bed creaks as he sits up to lean over the side.

"Issy. Issy."

Issy makes a little noise and the bed creaks. Not him this time; she must have turned over.

"It's my birthday, Issy!"

"I'm asleep."

"You're not, you're awake now. Go on, say 'Happy Birthday' to me."

"I don't feel good."

"I'm the birthday boy!"

"Shush."

"Happy Birthday to me! Happy Birthday to me!" He waits for Issy to wish him "Happy Birthday" and rubs his ears again—they are thrumming with the darkness. "I'm going to get up. Want to sneak downstairs with me?"

He climbs down the ladder and stands next to the bottom bunk. Issy's silence suggests she has slipped back to sleep, so he opens the bedroom door and creeps out onto the landing. He sneaks along the corridor and peeps his head around Al's half-closed door. There's no sign of life, so he sneaks a little farther. Mum and Dad have shut their door, and the stairs up to Zippy's room are too squeaky to risk. He turns back and tiptoes down the stairs, remembering to stand in the quiet places. He goes into the living room and switches on the television. He turns the volume down to number eight and flicks from channel to channel. It's too early for children's programs, so he finds the news. There's a clock in the corner of the screen: ten past five. He decides to watch a DVD.

His favorite cartoon at the moment is one from the Book of Mormon collection. It's the story of Ammon, who goes on a mission to the savage Lamanites. The Lamanites don't wear many clothes and they've got red and blue war paint on their chests and faces. They capture Ammon and take him to their king. The king is called Lamoni and he is fierce, with two long braids, blue earrings, and a feathery hair band. King Lamoni agrees to let Ammon be a servant, and he tells Ammon to look after the sheep. One day some wicked men come and try to steal the king's sheep. Ammon is completely brave. At first he uses a sling and some stones to shoot at the men like in David and Goliath, but eventually Ammon gets fed up with firing stones and he pulls out his sword and chops the men's arms off. Chop! Chop! Chop! Jacob slides off the sofa, steps over Issy's Cinderella beanbag, and rummages in the toy box for Al's old light saber. Chop! Chop! Chop! He chops along with Ammon and the Lamanites' arms break off like twigs. Serves them right! The servants take the arms back to the king in a bag, and he opens the bag and says, "Yes, these are arms, all right." The king thinks Ammon must be the Great Spirit, but Ammon says he is just a messenger. The king is so pleased with the bag of arms that he listens to Ammon's message about Heavenly Father. In the end, everyone is happy—except for the men with no arms, of course.

The story of Ammon is a true story from the Book of Mormon, which means it tells people something Heavenly Father wants them to know. Jacob lies down on the sofa and thinks about what he knows as the music plays and the credits roll: Stealing sheep is bad, swords are dangerous, and fighting might be OK if you do it for the right reasons.

Mum comes down just after seven o'clock.

"Hello, birthday boy. What are you doing down here?"

"I woke up and then I couldn't get back to sleep."

"You daft thing." Mum wraps her arms around him and gives him a squeezy kiss. "Let's make breakfast, shall we?"

They make pancakes. What an ace start to his birthday! Mum lets him crack the eggs. She doesn't get cross when the shells shatter into the mixture, and she does extra tosses before putting the pancakes in a dish in the oven to keep warm.

"Shall we sing a song, Mum? Shall we? I'll pick—I'm the birthday boy! Let's sing 'Here We Are Together.' "

Mum laughs. "Not that one, you always pick it! Tell you what, you sing while I finish doing this." She pours more mixture into the pan and Jacob starts to sing.

"Here we are together, together, together,
Here we are together in our family.
There's Mum and Dad and Zippy and Alma and Jacob and
    Issy
And here we are together in our family."

Mum opens the oven door and slips the new pancake into the big dish. "Lovely singing," she says in the way she always does, even when he forgets the words and loses the up and down of the tune.

"Will you tell me a story now?" He climbs onto the kitchen table and sits with his bare feet resting on the seat of one of the chairs. He sniffs the burny smell of hot oil and feels a fizz of birthday happiness in his tummy. "Tell me the story of when I was born."

"Well, once upon a time, exactly seven years ago today," Mum begins, and she recites his story while she opens the cupboards to find syrup, chocolate sauce, lemon juice, and sugar.

She jumps when the telephone rings and Jacob climbs off the table and wraps his arms around her waist as she answers it. He billows his face into her pillowy middle, closes his eyes, and squeezes extra tight. He holds his breath and pretends his supersonic strength can stick her to the spot.

"Hello, Sister Anderson. No, of course you're not a nuisance."

Jacob knows what's coming next. If he had a big sword he could chop Sister Anderson's arms off and then she wouldn't be able to use the telephone.

"Well, it's Jacob's birthday. But . . . yes, of course, just a moment. I'll go and get him."

Jacob doesn't let go of Mum when she attempts to move. She tucks the phone under her chin and tries to unfasten his arms.

"Jacob."

He holds on, even though he knows it's silly, even though he knows he will make her cross. Mum pulls the phone out from under her chin and covers the mouthpiece with her hand.

"Stop it. Let go. Now."

"But what about my presents? Has Dad *got* to go? He's already missing my party, he can't go out now as well! Am I going to have to wait until he gets back before I can open anything?"

"Let go."

He lets his hands flop to his sides and stands statue-still, pulling his saddest face. But Mum isn't having it. She shakes her head, then goes upstairs.

It's suddenly lonely in the kitchen. Jacob hears the low rumble of Dad's voice through the ceiling. He suspects Dad is going to miss the birthday pancakes and he tries to think of something to make him stay. He knows *"Please"* won't be enough, because Dad likes to follow the rules. If he is going to stop him, he will have to come up with a bigger, more important rule than the one about helping people, a rule that will trump the saying Dad always repeats when he has to disappear at important moments: *"Inasmuch as ye have done it unto one of the least of these, my brethren, ye have done it unto me."* Mum has an easier way of saying the almost-same thing: *"Do as you would be done by."* Jacob thinks about the best way to persuade Dad—*"Inasmuch as you have stayed to eat breakfast with me on my birthday, you have done it unto Jesus."* But it sounds cheeky. He wishes Dad was the kind of person who would say, "No, I'm sorry I can't come. If it's an emergency, you must call the police or the fire brigade because today is Jacob's birthday." But he knows Dad isn't that kind of man because Dad has already said, "Of course I'll come to a missionary meeting on Saturday. I'll miss Jacob's party, but I'm sure he'll understand."

Jacob looks at the casserole dish of pancakes through the glass of the oven door and decides that after he has died and gone to live in the Celestial Kingdom, when he is actually in charge of his own world, he will make it a commandment for dads to stay at home on their children's birthdays. And if they don't, he will send a prophet to chop their arms off.

Issy wakes up with achy arms. When she opens her eyes, they are full of lightning icicles. She tries to get out of bed and discovers that there isn't much breath in her tummy. She wonders if part of her has popped in the night, like a balloon.

– 2 –

Diabolical Sins

Zippy stares at the textured wallpaper on the ceiling. It's old and ugly, but Dad won't strip it in case the plaster comes off too. His voice floats up the stairs along with the smell of something cooking; he's probably talking to Sister Anderson—no one else would dream of calling at this time on a Saturday. She can't make out Dad's words, but she hopes he's saying no. She rolls onto her side, tucks her knees up to her chest, and shucks the covers past her shoulder. It's beginning to get cooler in the mornings and the air feels damp. Behind the curtains, the latticed windows are probably streaked with condensation. She slips an arm out of the covers and feels on the floor beside the bed for *Persuasion*. She opens the page with the folded corner: "*You pierce my soul. I am half agony, half hope . . .*" When she reaches the end, she sighs and takes a deep sniff of the soft, yellowed pages. Then she closes the book and places it on the pillow beside her.

The phone is sure to have woken everyone, and it won't be long before Issy slips into the room and dives under the covers in a tangle of chatter and fierce hugs. Zippy listens for the scamper of her feet on the stairs, but the house is quiet again. She yawns, rubs her eyes, and glances at the poster on the wall—"*Kindness Begins with Me.*" She made it herself, collaging the letters with strips torn out of the free newspaper, a reminder of her goal to be kind to everyone, even Alma. She isn't supposed to use Blu-tack because it leaves greasy marks, but no one has said anything and the wallpaper isn't worth protecting—it's that horrible lumpy stuff that looks like it's been spattered with sawdust. Sometimes she asks Mum what the paper is called because whenever Mum mentions woodchip she does a funny dance and sings a song about living in small houses and meeting up in the year 2000 and it's clear, just for a moment, that before she turned into Mum she was someone else, someone who knew the words to songs, someone who liked to dance.

Zippy sits up in bed and stretches. Last night's visual aid is dangling from the coat hook on the back of her bedroom door. It's a hanger, one of those white, lacy, padded ones that old people like. A little piece of heart-shaped card is suspended from the hook and it reads: *"Hang onto your values . . . Hang onto your goals . . . Hang onto your testimony . . . So some day you can hang your wedding dress on me."* All the girls got a special hanger, and a poster of a bride standing outside the Temple that says, *If This Isn't Your Castle, You're Not My Prince.* The boys didn't get anything.

Sister Campbell was in charge last night. Sister Valentine would have done a nicer presentation, but she isn't married, so she had to sit at the front of the chapel in her best dress and nod while Sister Campbell spoke. It was a shame Sister Valentine didn't have anywhere better to go on a Friday night, especially as she'd made a real effort and put lots of makeup on. She looked quite nice from a distance, but when she held the chapel door open for everyone and said, "Come in! Welcome!" Zippy could see she hadn't exfoliated before she applied foundation and her forehead was rutted like the fine side of a cheese grater.

Sister Campbell didn't help with doors and she didn't welcome anyone. She just stood at the front of the chapel and waited, her long hair in its usual braid, dangling past her bottom like the tail on a coonskin cap. Long hair can be beautiful, but there is something taxidermic about Sister Campbell's braided rope. A couple of years ago there were some polygamists from Texas on the news and the women all had long hair and high, stern foreheads; they looked as if they might break if they laughed; they looked like Sister Campbell.

Zippy hovered by the chapel doors while she waited for Adam Carmichael to sit down—*half agony, half hope*. He plonked himself in the front row beside his dad, then turned and waved and patted the empty space on the pew beside him. She hurried to the front and Mum and Dad followed.

Brother and Sister Campbell were supposed to present Standards Night together, that's the way it works, but Brother Campbell spoke for only five minutes at the end to remind the boys that porn is everywhere: online and in the Next catalog. Sister Campbell spent the majority of the night talking about the things girls need to know.

"Stand up please, girls," she said after the opening prayer.

"Before you go out every morning, you must check your clothes. You can do this by singing 'Heads, Shoulders, Knees, and Toes' in front of the mirror. Tonight you can practice in front of the young men and your parents."

Zippy's T-shirt rose when she raised her hands and she wondered whether Adam could see her bare skin. It slipped back down as she touched her shoulders, but she felt it lift again as she bent to touch her knees, and while her hands were resting on her toes Dad murmured, "You'll have to get rid of that top; I can see your back."

When she sat down there seemed to be less space on the pew and her leg ended up pressed against Adam's. He leaned in to whisper, "You look cold." And then, while Sister Campbell talked about the importance of subjecting skirts to The Sit-Down Test and The Sunlight Check, he rubbed his hand along her goose-bumped arm, which wasn't the slightest bit helpful as he had made her shiver in the first place.

"Girls who choose to be modest choose to be respected. If you check your clothes every day before you go out, you will never be *walking pornography*. I'm sure none of you want to be responsible for putting bad thoughts into men's heads. *Please* think about the men," Sister Campbell said.

So Zippy did. She thought about men; with Adam's thigh pressed up against hers and his warm fingers rubbing her arm, it was hard to think of anything else.

The quiet of the house is broken by the slam of the front door, which means Dad has gone to help whoever was on the phone. Zippy can hear Mum coming up the stairs, plod, plod, plod; a moment of quiet as she pads along the first-floor landing and then the glum sound of her feet again, plod, plod, plod.

Mum knocks first, she always does, and then she opens the door and peers around it. She looks tired and old. There are purple smudges under her eyes and gray streaks whisker the hair at her temples. Zippy has told her to dye it like Lauren's mum, but she says it's too expensive.

"Could you get up? Dad's gone out, Issy's still asleep, and Alma won't budge. Jacob's desperate to eat some pancakes. He wanted everyone to have breakfast together."

"OK."

"And after breakfast will you help Issy get ready while I go to Asda? Dad was supposed to be here, so I'd planned on him helping out, but—"

"Aw, Mum, I've got homework."

"Please."

Zippy glances at the homemade poster on the wall. Kindness leads to all sorts of blessings. Lauren calls blessings karma. She got really into it during the Buddhism topic in Year Nine and she still goes on about it; the right kind of pizza in the canteen, a treat from her mum, Jordan Banks saying "Hello"—all karma, according to Lauren. But she's wrong; when good stuff happens it's not a cosmic mystery, it's the natural consequence of good works and faith.

"OK, OK," she says. The words leak into a yawn, and while she stretches her arms high to lever the stale air out, Mum comes in properly. She drifts past the bed to open the curtains and unfasten the wet windows; a slice of autumn breeze arrows past the gaps, and the sound of seagull caws and the squawked conversations of geese seep into the room. Mum stands there staring at the changing trees in the park across the road, and it seems like a good opportunity to ask.

"You know what you did during Standards Night?" Zippy pauses, relieved to have begun and nervous about how to continue. "Well, it made me wonder . . ."

Mum turns and tries a smile, but her lips don't lift properly. She steps away from the window and fiddles her wedding ring with her thumb. "I'm sorry. I couldn't just sit there," she says.

Zippy waits for her to continue, but Mum tilts her head slightly and adopts the quizzical expression she wears on Sunday afternoons when she asks, "What did you learn at church today?"—an expression that seems to have very little to do with listening and a lot to do with deciding, as if she's making up her mind whether she agrees.

Sometimes Dad jokes that Mum could write a fifth gospel, *The Gospel According to Claire,* and he has to remind her not to look beyond the mark. Zippy doesn't want to hear an installment of *The Gospel According to Claire,* but there *are* things she would like to know, things she is beginning to feel curious about, small things such as the name of Mum's first boyfriend. But Mum rarely begins sentences with "I," and she frequently changes the subject when she is asked about herself.

"No one's perfect, Zipporah. People make mistakes." Zippy stares at Mum's hand, at her thumb as it sneaks around the back of her ring finger and flicks the diamond round and round and round. Mum's got crocodile hands; they're bumped by blue-green veins, and her skin is dry and scaly. Zippy wonders how long her hands have looked like that. Mr. McLean said in Biology that the cells of the human body are replaced every seven to ten years. That means all of Mum, except for her cerebral cortex, is literally a different person from the one who met and fell in love with Dad. Maybe that's how repentance works—a sort of gradual baptism of skin and tissue, the shedding of the old self and the cultivation of the new.

"Perhaps there *is* an ideal way to live," Mum says. "I suppose I can get behind that, but is it helpful to punish people who don't live up to that ideal? We don't live in an ideal world."

Zippy already knows the world is not ideal; Mum is just changing the subject, and two can play that game. "Well, our house is definitely not ideal. We've got that stuff on the wall—what's it called?" she asks and waits for Mum to cheer up and sing the woodchip song.

"It's called paper."

"Aw, Mum."

"I'm not talking about houses. I'm talking about people's lives."

"OK, OK." She'll ask again later, after Jacob's party, when the day is winding down and things are more relaxed. "Was it Sister Anderson on the phone?"

Mum nods.

"What's up with her now?"

"Oh, I don't know."

"I wish she'd go away."

"Zipporah."

"Well, I do. She's always bothering us. I'll be down in a bit."

Mum pulls the door closed behind her and Zippy listens to the steady rhythm of her feet as she heads down to the first-floor landing, past the other bedrooms and down the next flight of stairs, plod, plod, plod. She snuggles back under the covers, flicks *Persuasion* open, rereads Captain Wentworth's letter, and thinks *Half agony, half hope;* that's *exactly* what it's like being in love. Every gesture, touch, and word has to be weighed and measured and placed on one side of the scale: He loves me, he loves me not; half agony, half hope. Poor Anne Elliot has to wait ages to get married; she's entirely given up hope of finding happiness when Wentworth reappears. Perhaps Sister Valentine would like *Persuasion;* it might give her hope. She's getting old, and when she talks about being unmarried she does this brave, windshield-wiper grin. She did it each time someone caught her eye last night, which was quite often as she was sitting at the front, facing everyone. It made Zippy feel horribly sorry for her, so she lowered her gaze. But then she noticed the way Sister Valentine's feet plumped out of her shoes like sugar puffs, and the sorry feeling got worse. She looked up at Sister Campbell instead. No one could ever feel sorry for Sister Campbell.

"What's the worst sin you can commit?" she asked as she opened her presentation. Parents waited for their children to answer, and the silence stretched uncomfortably until Zippy plunged into it.

"Murder."

"No." Sister Campbell pursed her lips and shook her head. It was clear she was pleased to hear the wrong answer. "Denying the Holy Ghost is the worst sin, followed by murder. What sin is next to murder in seriousness?" She rapped the book she was holding into the palm of one hand and it made a thwack like a fist. "Come on!"

"Adultery?"

"Assault?"

"Stealing?"

"No, no, no." Sister Campbell was triumphant. She opened the book and began to read about the *diabolical* crimes of sexual impurity.

Mum's hand fluttered for a moment and then she raised it high. Sister Campbell stopped reading.

"Yes, Sister Bradley?"

"You know I wasn't raised in the Church, so it's possible I don't know . . ."

Sister Campbell nodded her agreement that Mum likely didn't know.

". . . but, I think that might be an old quotation," Mum continued, her hand partially raised in a way that simultaneously protected her head. "The word 'diabolical' seems a bit . . . much."

Sister Campbell flicked to the front of the book. "It was published in 1992. Not particularly old, I'd say."

Mum's hand was still shielding her head; she looked like she was expecting Sister Campbell to belt her, but she carried on.

"I do think twenty years is quite a long—"

"God is the same yesterday, today, and forever; we know that from the scriptures, Sister Bradley, don't we? Let's have an object lesson."

Sister Campbell likes object lessons. Once, she brought a dartboard to church and everyone had to take aim at a target she had Blu-tacked to the board. At the end of the lesson she peeled the paper target away from the board and on its underside was a picture of Jesus's face, smiling out through the perforations—"*This* is what you do to Jesus *every time* you sin," she said.

Last night she reached into her homemade scripture case to pull out a stick of Wrigley's Doublemint gum.

"Who would like this?"

No one said anything. Everyone suspected a trick.

"You would, wouldn't you, Zipporah?"

Zippy shook her head but then thought better of it and nodded. Sister Campbell stripped away the foil wrapping, put the gum in her own mouth, and chewed loudly.

"Mmm. Delicious." She reached into her mouth and pulled out the chewed gum. "There you are, Zipporah," she said. "Come on up and get it; it's all yours."

Zippy gave a surprised laugh and a couple of other people joined in.

"It's no laughing matter. These are the fruits of sexual immorality." Sister Campbell held the gum out and shook her hand for emphasis. "Who wants dirty, chewed gum?"

The laughter stopped. Mum whispered something to Dad, who shook his head. Mum poked him, and when he ignored her, she stood up. Zippy assumed she was headed for the bathroom, but she stepped forward and joined Sister Campbell. They stood side by side, Mum nervously fingering her wedding ring as Sister Campbell's face set into an expression hard enough to chop wood.

Mum's voice trembled and the air in the room was suddenly thinned by held breath. "I don't mean to cause contention, but . . ."

She grabbed the sticky ball from Sister Campbell's fingers and put it into her mouth.

Everyone breathed out at once.

"Yum," Mum said, her jaw working determinedly. She looked like a contestant from *I'm a Celebrity,* munching on a kangaroo testicle. "Repentance is delicious. Forgiveness tastes wonderful, too. You'd never know anyone had eaten this before. It's still lovely and minty."

Sister Campbell's cheeks went red and she held out her hand, but Mum ignored her and carried on chomping.

Finally, she removed the gum from her mouth and placed it on Sister Campbell's upturned palm. Then she sat back down beside Dad.

Sister Campbell held her hand out. "Would anyone else like a chew?"

Poor Sister Valentine was in agony. She looked from Sister Campbell to Mum and back again, uncertain as to whether it was best to emphasize the cleansing power of repentance or the diabolical nature of sin.

A horrible tickle of laughter began to scramble up Zippy's windpipe. She tried to swallow it and ended up coughing. The cough took her by surprise and caught in her throat. She tried another swallow, which led to another cough, and her eyes began to stream. Adam patted her back, but the surprise of his touch through the fabric of her T-shirt made things worse.

"Go and get a drink of water," Sister Campbell said.

Zippy left the chapel. She coughed and giggled all the way down the corridor to the ladies' bathroom. She stood beside the big mirror next to the paper-towel dispenser. She didn't feel like laughing anymore; in fact she felt as if she'd been tipped upside down and emptied of every last chuckle and snigger. She snatched a paper towel and wiped her face. It was red and blotchy. She couldn't go back looking like that, so she locked herself in one of the cubicles, sat on the toilet lid for ten minutes, and worried about how to fall in love and get married without ever making any diabolical mistakes.

"That woman," Mum said in the car on the way home.

"Claire."

"You let her say all those awful—"

"It's *her* calling, not yours."

"*You* asked her to do it. You're the Bishop, *you* called her."

"The Lord called her, through inspiration."

Mum muttered something that sounded like desperation, but Dad ignored her.

"Did you enjoy tonight, Zipporah? I did. It reminded me of being young and meeting your mum. She was a catch, you know." When Dad stopped the car at the traffic light, he let go of the gearshift and grabbed Mum's thigh.

"Catch of the century," he said and squeezed, then he leaned in and kissed Mum's cheek just before the light changed.

Zippy pushes the blankets down and frees her arms. Adam is only seventeen, so it's too early to catch him. He can't go on his mission until he's finished his A levels. He'll be away for two whole years, but she'll write to him every week to make sure he doesn't forget her. She pictures him as a missionary, riding a bike; knocking on people's doors and teaching them about the only true and living Church; converting them to the gospel; standing in the waist-deep water of the font to baptize them—dozens and dozens of them. When he comes home she'll meet him at the airport or the train station, depending on where he's been. She pictures the reunion sometimes at night before she goes to sleep. She will wear something sexy but modest, and she'll look irresistible, in a good way, in a way that makes him want to marry her. She imagines getting married, and then . . . that's where she's supposed to stop imagining, but it's difficult; it's hard to focus on eternal marriage without ever thinking about sex.

She sits up in bed and swings her legs around. The sole of one foot touches the smooth surface of the prayer rock that she leaves on the floor. She made it at Youth Night while the boys played basketball in the hall. Her rock is gray, more of a large pebble, really. She painted "PRAYER" on it and then she asked if she could go and join the boys—she'd been hoping that Adam might be shooting baskets with his shirt off again—but Sister Campbell said no. So she had to wait while the other girls painted hearts and flowers on their rocks and copied out the accompanying poem in careful, neat writing. The poem is folded up in her bedside drawer. She fishes it out from under a pile of underwear and socks. Her handwriting is hurried but not untidy. She crossed out the last line of the poem and wrote a better one when she realized she wasn't going to be allowed to play basketball. Sister Campbell was irritated. "You're making light of sacred things," she said, not realizing that you can make jokes about things and still take them seriously.

> *I'm your little prayer rock and this is what I'll do . . .*
> *Just put me on your pillow until the day is through*
> *Then turn back all the covers and climb into your bed*
> *WHACK! Your little prayer rock will hit you in the head*
> *Then you will remember as the day is through*
> *To kneel and say your prayers as you wanted to*
> *And then when you are finished just dump me on the floor*
> *I'll stay throughout the night to give you help once more*
> *When you get up in the morning CLUNK! I'll stub your toe*
> *So you'll remember to say your morning prayers before you go*
> *Put me back upon your pillow once your bed is made*
> *And your clever little prayer rock will continue in your aid*
> *Because your Heavenly Father cares and loves you so*
> *He wants you to remember to talk to Him, you know?*
> *He whacks you in the head and clunks you on the toe.* ☺

Zippy kneels down beside the bed, closes her eyes, and folds her arms. She prays for Dad and Mum and she prays for Issy, Jacob, and Alma. She prays for Nana and Granddad on their mission in Ireland, she prays for kindness, and she prays for Adam. When she has finished, she stays kneeling next to the bed and listens carefully. If you're not listening when Heavenly Father answers your prayers it will seem like He isn't there, and you'll have only yourself to blame. She listens past the sounds of her brain's workings, ignores the apparatus of her imagination, and keeps things blank and ready for answers.

Issy is prickled by squalls of shivers and spiked by goose bumps. She curls up like Mrs. Tiggy-Winkle, tries to shrink the aches by making herself small. Even though her breath is puffing quickly, it isn't blowing her tummy back up. There are clouds in her head and she can't think through them.

– 3 –

Believing

The shopping cart has a wonky wheel, but Claire doesn't have time to swap it. She hefts it up and down the aisles using her hands and the corner of one hip, briefly pausing to grab stuff, not even trying to keep a running total in her head. It wasn't supposed to be like this. She'd planned to keep this slice of Saturday all to herself, to leave the children with Ian for an hour and amble—let him settle their disputes, supervise their homework, sweep the floors, and blow up balloons for the party. She knew she wasn't going to get what she wanted the instant the telephone rang and Sister Anderson's sugary voice asked for Bishop Bradley. She had no choice but to wake him—he has to be available to everyone, at all times of the day and night. She did say it was Jacob's birthday, though, which won't please Ian if he finds out; she isn't supposed to make people feel guilty for needing help, she's supposed to make a willing sacrifice.

It's sad that Brother Anderson has cancer and she is very sorry for him, but his prognosis is good, and Ian has already given him two priesthood blessings, both of which promised a full recovery. Ian should spend today with his family. That's what families do, isn't it? She has seen them at the children's friends' birthday parties, whole families—grandparents, uncles, aunts, and cousins—celebrating together, and she has felt envious and perturbed, and somehow in the wrong because the Church is all about families, even though there won't be any extended family at Jacob's party. If her mother were alive . . . if Ian's parents weren't missionaries in Ireland . . . but everyone will be together in Eternity and that's what matters, not the fact that Ian missed Jacob's birthday breakfast to go to the Andersons, or that later, during the party, he'll be at a meeting.

Claire lifts bags of sausage rolls and chicken nuggets out of freezers and adds them to the cart, where they sit with the cheap lemonade, cookies, potato chips, and bread. All of the packaging is white—you have to pay extra for color or the plastic windows that allow you to see exactly what you're buying. Jacob is expecting party bags, but she decides to save money by buying a roll of sandwich sacks. She isn't sure what else to buy because she doesn't know much about other people's children. They are mysterious and intimidating; they ask awkward questions and keep their eyes open during mealtime prayers, they make cheeky comments about the picture of Jesus in the hall, and sometimes they swear. She quietly discourages friendships with nonmembers—it makes things simpler, easier—but the children sometimes have other ideas. Jacob was desperate for a party. He begged and pleaded, attacked her prevarications, pestered and whined until she provisionally gave in:

"As long as your dad's home, you can have a party. I'm not doing it by myself. And we'll have it early, from eleven 'til one, to get it over with."

She puts a multipack of party poppers and a bag of miniature rubber balls in the cart. She usually enjoys the supermarket. She isn't accountable to anyone here. She can wander from aisle to aisle, choosing, deciding. Here she is never wrong, always in charge, and the sound system often plays music that reminds her of her teens, allowing her to retreat into daydreams of long, post-exam summers, lazing beside the radio with friends.

"Sister Bradley! Sister Bradley, dear."

Claire's shoulders stiffen. She does not want to be called "Sister Bradley" in Asda.

"Sister Bradley!"

She turns to see Sister Anderson standing in the middle of the aisle waving a roll of wrapping paper.

"Helloooo!"

"Oh, hello. I thought—"

"Yes, yes, don't worry." Sister Anderson puts the wrapping paper in her cart. "Bishop Bradley *was* at ours, but he isn't there anymore. He drove Paul to the hospital for me. I'm sure he's got another infection, but he wouldn't go; he said I was making a big fuss about nothing."

"Oh."

"I knew he'd get himself checked out properly if the Bishop told him to—so kind of him to come round like that, at the drop of a hat. He talked some sense into Paul, I knew he would, and do you know what? When I told Paul to go and get in the car, Bishop said, 'You need a break, Sister Anderson. Let me take him for you.' Isn't that lovely?"

"Oh, yes."

"There aren't many men around like him."

"No."

"You're so lucky. If I was a bit younger . . ." Sister Anderson winks and nudges Claire with the cushioned crest of her elbow.

It's difficult to know what to say next. Of course, Sister Anderson is only joking—she must be old enough to be Ian's mother—but Claire can't laugh at jokes about eternal polygamy. "He's a keeper," she manages.

"He certainly is. He even said he'll wait with Paul at the hospital, which means I've got an hour or two all to myself to catch up with the shopping!"

"That's nice."

"Here." Sister Anderson reaches into her cart. She rearranges milk, cereal, and several cupcakes before producing a birthday card. "It's a special musical one, for Jacob. Hang on." She pulls a pen out of her handbag, writes something on the card, and drops it in

Claire's cart. "Two pounds," she says, fishing in her purse. "There. You can give it to him when you get home, on his birthday, much better than having it at church tomorrow."

Claire keeps a tight rein on her irritation as she pushes the cart to the checkout. The girl asks if she needs any bags. She does. The girl frowns and Claire starts to explain that she usually brings bags from home, but today is her son's birthday and she's got so much to do. She stops explaining when she realizes the girl isn't listening.

As she maneuvers the cart through the parking lot, Claire checks the receipt. It's hard to believe junk food and plastic toys are so expensive. She loads the groceries into the trunk and, once she's buckled into the driver's seat, finishes her checking. When she reaches an item near the end of the list—"Greeting card £2.99"— she imagines a swearword and is instantly disappointed with herself.

She takes the coastal road home so she can drive with the windows open and breathe the blasting salty air. The town runs parallel to the concrete sea defenses, long and thin, its back against the wall. The sea is out and the beach is bare, a seemingly endless expanse of dark, treacly sand. She would like to pull into one of the parking lots and escape for a while, walk and walk, pound against constraint and containment with the rhythm of her feet, but there isn't time. As she turns off the road she remembers a Relief Society lesson at church about good and bad thoughts. One of the sisters held up a toilet roll and a little basket of cotton balls. Some of the balls had the word "BAD" taped to them, others had "GOOD." The sister pushed a BAD ball into the toilet roll. "Here's a bad thought going into your head," she said. She held the toilet roll high, like a magician, then picked up a GOOD ball. "This is how you get rid of bad thoughts." She stuffed the toilet roll with GOOD cotton balls until the BAD one popped out the other end.

"There we are," she said. "Easy-peasy."

Claire begins to sing a hymn as she reverses into the driveway— the good words should fire any rude, uncharitable thoughts from her head. She imagines a cotton ball with "SHIT" written on it popping out of her ear, easy-peasy.

She keeps singing as she heaves shopping bags into the house, *"I believe in Christ; so come what may . . ."*

Jacob dashes down the hall and throws his arms around her. "Mum!"

"Hey, stop it, I'll drop the groceries! Hang on a minute, let go!" The bottom of one of the bags splits and wet, frozen packets flop onto the hall floor. She puts the groceries down and squeezes the spilled items into an unbroken bag. "Where's Issy? She's not still in bed, is she?"

"I went in," Jacob says as she rearranges the food, "and I told her to get up for my birthday. But she said she's too tired."

"Zipporah! Alma! Can you come and help, please? Well, it's only her second week; you were all shattered when you first started school. I'll go and check on her in a minute. Zipporah! Alma! Come down and help with the shopping."

Zipporah appears at the top of the stairs, pen in hand.

"I'm just doing my English."

"You didn't get Issy up."

"She said she doesn't feel well."

"Hang on." Claire pops back through the front door and to the open car trunk. She hooks her fingers around the handles of several grocery bags and sidles back into the house. "Does she feel hot? Go and check. Maybe she's coming down with something. Feel her head. If she's hot, I'll get the Tylenol. You caught all sorts in your first term. If she's just tired, tell her to get up anyway or she'll miss the party."

She drags all the shopping into the kitchen. The room is chock-ablock with cheering, chiding crafts made at Relief Society meetings, each designed to point her in the right direction: ceramic tiles, decorated woodblocks, door hangers, wall hangers, collages, and organizers. The best of her efforts is the *With God All Things Are*

Possible painting; even the children recognized the long-legged, winged creature as a bird.

She opens the fridge to store the lemonade, pausing to glance at the laminated jumble of cutesy letters beside the door: *No Other Success Can Compensate for Failure in the Home.* She allows another imaginary cotton ball to fall from her ear—"BUGGER OFF"—take that, Failure in the Home! She switches on the oven and lines frozen sausage rolls along baking sheets. As is often the case when there's work to be done, Alma is nowhere to be seen. At least the party will be over at one o'clock and then, after the cleanup, there'll be a few hours to relax. She puts the sausage rolls in the oven, grabs the Tylenol and a syringe from the top cupboard, and hurries upstairs.

Issy is curled up like a little bug, feverish and shivering. Claire touches her arms where they peep out of her princess nightie.

"Oh, sweetheart, you're not well, are you?"

"No." Her voice crackles.

Claire sucks the medicine out of the bottle with the syringe and squeezes it into the corner of Issy's mouth. Her eyes remain tightly shut and she flinches as she swallows.

"There you are. You'll feel better soon. What a shame to come down with something on Jacob's birthday. Shall I save you some cake?"

"Yes."

Claire tucks the covers back over Issy and bends to kiss her flushed cheek.

"Love you, sweetheart," she says. "Have a nice sleep. You'll feel much better when you wake up."

Back in the kitchen, she grabs a pen and begins to make a list of the things she needs to do before Jacob's friends arrive at eleven o'clock. Sausage rolls, nuggets, pizzas, cocktail sausages, party bags, hot potato. She isn't sure how she will get it all done in an hour. She makes a list of games to play and divides the party into two sections, Fun and Food, which makes the two hours seem smaller and filling them a somewhat easier task. She switches the CD player on and presses play. The flute and piano introduction reveals that the children haven't changed the CD since last Sunday. *"Dearest children, God is near you, watching o'er you day and night."* It's a good hymn to listen to in the circumstances. God loves children, He loves each of Jacob's friends and she will also try to love them, even if they turn out to be a rowdy gang of hooligans. And God loves Issy too. He will watch over her during the party and make her better. The choir accompanies Claire as she unwraps frozen pizzas and empties a bag of chicken nuggets onto another baking sheet: *"He will bless you, He will bless you. If you put your trust in Him."*

Issy's hands are cold, so are her feet. She wants Mum to come back. She wants to get up and find Mum, wants to climb into Mum's lap and nestle in the warm wrap of her arms. But her eyelids are heavy; every time she opens them they collapse shut, forcing her back into sleep. She feels as if she is falling through the mattress, down through the ceiling into the kitchen, past the linoleum and down, and down.

– 4 –

Piss Off

When Jacob's friends arrive, Al has to stand in the hallway, holding the front door open for kid after kid while trying to remember Mum's instructions about smiling at people and saying, "Come in" in a voice that doesn't simultaneously declare, "Get lost."

He spent most of the morning hiding in his room, imagining what it would be like to score a last-minute Champions League winner for Liverpool and practicing a variety of goal celebrations in front of the mirror. Mum called him several times, but he pretended not to hear. It was for her own good; if he'd gone downstairs to help, he'd have only done it wrong and made things worse. He shouldn't even be at home; today's the first day of the junior football season and he should be speeding down the wing of one of the pitches at Hightown, not answering the door to a load of bratty seven-year-olds.

It always feels weird when ordinary people come round; the picture of Jesus in the hall seems to double in size and Al feels like an outsider, someone who has grown up in the country of the house without managing to learn its language. A few of the kids' mums offer to stay and help but he says, "No thanks." A house full of nonmember women expecting forbidden cups of tea would make Mum even more pissy.

When every kid has arrived and Mum has herded them into the living room, she claps her hands and says, "Quiet, please," but no one listens. Some of the kids are singing rude versions of "Happy

Birthday," others are bouncing on the sofa, and one little monster is swinging the old light saber around his head. Mum is all sweaty and she looks as if she's going to cry; perhaps that's why she gets it wrong when she says, "Shush. Shush! Jacob's big sister, Zipporah, will be down soon, she's just finishing her homework, and this is Jacob's big brother, *Alma,* who's going to—"

"Actually, I prefer to be called Al," he corrects. But it's too late, little kids are teasing machines, weakness is their favorite smell, they can sniff the tiniest whiff of it on anyone.

"Hey, Alma!" The kids giggle. "Al-ma, Al-ma."

And Al, who has already had enough of Mum's endless pleas for help and her nail-me-to-a-cross expression, shouts, "Piss off!"

Several of the children snigger, but some, including Jacob, are shocked. Mum's face collapses for a moment, and Al realizes the most helpful thing he can do is disappear.

"I think I'll go out to the garden for a bit."

"No," Mum says. "Playing football's hardly a punishment. Go to your room, find a book, and don't come back down 'til everyone's gone home. And check on your sister while you're up there."

He stomps up the stairs and into his room. He has been telling everyone not to introduce him as Alma for ages, ever since he went to Matty's house for the first time and Matty's dad, Steve, said "Hey, Matty, I thought this Alma you were going on about was a girl!" Steve apologized and ruffled Al's hair and then he said, "There used to be an Alma in *Coronation Street*. I thought it was a girl's name, but what do I know?"

When Al got home and told Mum, she apologized so painstakingly that he was forced to say it didn't matter, when it did—it does. At least she's sorry. Dad doesn't even care; he's the one who insisted on scriptural names for everyone. Jacob and Issy got off lightly and no one minds about Zippy's name, they think it's funny; she sometimes gets birthday cards picturing that puppet with the zipper mouth that used to be on TV years ago. Dad says it's important to *"look for the positive";* having an unusual name is a *"missionary tool,"* and it's up to Al to make the most of it by telling people that Alma is the name of a prophet from the Book of Mormon. As if. Of course, Dad means Alma Senior, Mr. Humble-Goody-Two-Shoes, and not his wicked son, Alma the Younger, who got struck down by an angel.

Dad doesn't get stuff. He's one of the only people Al knows who is the same in real life as he is at church. It's as if Dad lives in the overlapping bit of one of those Venn diagrams, straddling both worlds. Other people adapt, they step from circle A to circle B, they act normal in real life and accessorize their Sunday clothes with holy words and best manners, but Dad is unchanging. He exists in a perfect egg of divine assurance. He always says and does whatever God wants him to. "Obedience is the first law of heaven," he said when he explained why he *had* to go to the missionary meeting today. Al noticed that Mum's eyes did a quarter-pipe roll as Dad spoke, but she acted like they were just skating about of their own accord when she realized she was being watched.

He picks *Bad Guys of the Book of Mormon* off his shelf. Dad ordered it specially from Salt Lake City and it seemed like it might be OK 'cause the bad guys in the Book of Mormon are pretty brutal, but it's not even a story, it's like a really long lesson, full of stuff about passing through hardships and never complaining—it's even got bloody footnotes.

Al skims a page, then puts the book down and tiptoes along the hall to Jacob and Issy's room. He pokes his head round the door and sees an Issy-shaped hump on the bottom bunk.

"Wassup, Issy-wizzy?" He leans farther into the room to make sure she can hear him. "Are you sulking 'cause it's not *your* party? Betcha are."

When Issy doesn't respond, he heads to Mum and Dad's room, where he bounces on the bed a few times. The bed isn't as bouncy as it was when he was a little kid. He tries a seat drop and the bed groans and metal mattress springs poke his butt. He gets off and sits down at Mum's dressing table. She's not got much stuff on it, just an old photograph from years ago and a jewelry box. He scowls at the photograph. It's of the whole family at the docks in Liverpool and they're all smiling, even Issy in her buggy, all except him and no wonder—he's wearing a 1990 Liverpool shirt Dad bought for a fiver on eBay because he refused to *"condone"* Carlsberg, but it was just an excuse: When the sponsorship deal changed, the shirts were *"too expensive."* Al puts the picture down. He opens Mum's jewelry box, stuffs his hand into the jumble of brightly colored beads and listens to the scratch of glass and plastic. He opens the dressing-table drawers and finds some old, empty makeup cases and a box of tampons, which he unfastens. The tampons are wrapped in orange paper and they rustle when he touches them. He takes one out and pretends to smoke it like a cigar while he watches himself in the mirror. Smoking is against the Word of Wisdom and he's promised Dad that he will never, ever do it. Steven Gerrard wouldn't smoke, only ancient French footballers like Zidane do it, but sometimes Al wonders what it tastes like and why people enjoy it so much and he thinks that one day he might try it, just to see. He stops smoking the tampon and peels away its paper. He's never seen an actual tampon. He fiddles with the pieces and a roll of cardboard comes away in his hand. There's a string dangling from the other roll and he pulls on it and the tampon pops out. He tries to put the whole thing back together but now the tampon seems too big for the cardboard bit, so he just stuffs the pieces back in the box and hopes Mum won't notice.

He gets up, goes over to Dad's bedside cupboard, and opens the drawers: socks, handkerchiefs, and folded piles of Dad's old-fashioned Temple garment underwear. Once, when he was at Matty's house, they looked in Steve's drawer and found a packet of condoms. When Matty had finished pretending to throw up they stole one and hid in Matty's room, taking turns trying to stretch it over their heads. Dad's drawers are boring and Al isn't expecting to find anything noteworthy in Mum's either, but he looks. There are socks, bras, and wormy bundles of Mum's Sunday tights in the top drawer. The bottom drawer is full of folded Temple garments like Dad's, but silky-smooth. He stuffs a hand into the glossy pile and feels something stiff and crispy underneath. He digs below the underwear and pulls out a cylinder of money, secured by a red elastic band. He unties the band and the money roll opens like a time-lapse flower. He counts sixty-two tenners—six hundred and twenty pounds.

When people find loads of money in movies they throw it in the air and laugh. Al settles for a more muted celebration and holds it at head height before letting it fall onto the bed like a shower of leaves. He's never seen so much cash. He gathers it back into a pile, rolls it, and wraps it in the elastic band. He fully intends to put it back, he does, but then he thinks about Dad refusing to pay his football association registration, about the humiliation of turning up at training sessions each week knowing he won't be allowed to play in any official matches. And he thinks about the time he really wanted to buy Matty's limited-edition Steven Gerrard Match Attax card and Dad wouldn't give him the money, so he used the emergency fiver he's supposed to keep in his blazer pocket—which was fine until Mum asked to borrow it one day when she didn't have any cash. And then he had to admit he'd spent it, and although he got a new fiver, he also got a major telling off and Dad called him a nasty thief. He curls his hand around the money. It feels good.

Before Dad put a stop to football, Al used to imagine that he'd play in the Premier League one day and make enough to buy Mum a big house with a cleaner and everything. Mum washes all the clothes; she also irons them and puts them away. There's no reason for anyone else ever to open her drawers, and that makes the money seem like a secret—but it doesn't make sense: Mum hasn't even got a job. Dad has to give her money each week to buy food and the other stuff everyone needs. He stuffs the money in the zip-up pocket of his hoodie. He'll look after it for a bit; he'll put it back later and then he'll remind Mum about his football association registration fee and his out-of-date uniform. If she acts all innocent, he'll ask whether Dad knows about the money. He won't rat her out, he'd never do that, he's on her side. He even told her so a few weeks ago when Dad was out—probably helping someone—and Brother Campbell and one of the missionaries popped round to deliver the Home Teaching message and check whether everyone was saying their prayers and reading their scriptures.

After Brother Campbell had finished lecturing them all, he said, "Would you like to assign someone to say a prayer, Alma?"

"I'll choose someone," Mum offered.

Brother Campbell shook his head. "The priesthood is like an umbrella, Sister Bradley. The men hold it and the women are protected by it. Alma should assign the prayer. He's the man of the house when the Bishop isn't here."

"I'm the adult when Ian isn't here," Mum said, and then she laughed. "Hang on, I'm also an adult when Ian *is* here! Anyway, I'm happy to ask someone to say the prayer."

"But you'd like to fulfill your responsibilities as a priesthood holder, wouldn't you, Alma?"

Al didn't care about his responsibilities, he just wanted Brother Campbell to shut up and stop treating Mum like an idiot. "Who did you want to say it, Mum?"

"I was going to ask Brother Campbell," she said.

"Brother Campbell, would you say the closing prayer, please?" Al asked.

Brother Campbell was totally owned! He had no choice but to say the prayer. And afterward, when the Home Teachers had gone, Al followed Mum into the kitchen.

"I'm on your side," he said, half expecting her to thank him.

She lifted the dishes out of the dish drainer and into the cupboard. The plates scraped each other as she forced them into a stack. When she'd finished she turned round and said, "Alma, there aren't any *sides* in this family."

Al strokes the bump of money through his pocket.

Borrowing, that's what he's doing. He heads back to his room and *Bad Guys of the Book of Mormon,* the worst of whom happens to be his namesake.

Issy is lying in a cold bath of bone hurt.

She wants Mum.

There is music—*"Happy Birthday to you, Happy Birthday, dear Jacob"*—but it is far away, like underwater singing.

There were four candles on her last birthday cake. She blew them all out at once and Mum said, "Make a wish, Issy."

She wishes now, for Mum to come. Where is Mum?

— 5 —

Happy Is the Man That
Hath His Quiver Full

Ian sings along to a Tabernacle Choir CD as he drives home from Liverpool. *"Though deep'ning trials throng your way, Press on, press on, ye Saints of God!"* His voice is loud and quite tuneful. He likes to pretend the Tabernacle Choir is accompanying him as he keeps his own time and adds extra vibrato to the longer notes like a soloist.

Driving along the dock road makes him feel small, an insignificant speck of humanity alongside the looming structures and machinery of industry. He passes the empty, crumbling acropolis of the tobacco warehouse, Goliathan container cranes, and industrial buildings. The railway line, a fire station, car dealerships, and a Chinese supermarket graze his peripheral vision, but the arc of his imagination is occupied by the docks. By soot-streaked red bricks, the crisscross of colored and corrugated metals, iron railings, concrete, and occasional snapshot slices of ships.

Ian is a pioneer. He drives a Toyota Estima, but if the situation arose he knows he would be equally at home with a covered wagon, or even a handcart. Brother Rimmer's got a handcart in his garage. He constructed it in the seventies in preparation for the trek to Zion, back when people still talked about fleeing to Jackson County, Missouri, and it seemed like the Second Coming was just around the corner; before the Brethren told everyone to stay put and build Zion in their own communities. When Ian was a small boy, Brother Rimmer used to pull his handcart to church activities and give the children rides around the parking lot while they sang pioneer songs—"*Westward ho, Westward ho!*"—and pretended to shoot Indians. The pleasure of this memory makes Ian sing louder. He wishes he'd been born two hundred years ago, when the docks were the gateway to Zion and the first Mormon missionaries landed in Liverpool. He would like to wind back time and begin his pioneer journey with baptism in the River Mersey. Imagine crossing the sea to America and embarking on the thousand-mile trek to Utah! The pioneers made enormous sacrifices and they endured tremendous trials—their persistence and faith will surely guarantee their exaltation in the highest degree of heaven, the Celestial Kingdom. His own life has been disappointingly easy by comparison. He was baptized indoors, and although the water in the font was lukewarm because the heating wasn't working properly and he shivered a bit as he changed out of his wet clothes, it was certainly no hardship. There was a party afterward with a big cake that said, "Happy 8th Birthday—Welcome Ian!" in white chocolate buttons and he felt as if his life had finally started, as if everything up to that point had been just a practice, a dry run for the moment when he would begin playing for keeps. He has been fortunate—blessed, in fact. He has barely suffered at all. He has a happy marriage, four children, a satisfactory job, and, for just over a year, he has served the Church in his role as Bishop of the local congregation, an enormous responsibility.

He was called to be Bishop on Father's Day. After he took his place on the stand, behind the pulpit, the Primary children sang a song about fathers and family with a special second verse addressed entirely to the Bishop—to him. As he listened to their singing, Ian made a silent promise always to be there for the Primary children and their families. Since that time there have been frequent opportunities to make small sacrifices, such as the ones he has made today. It's a shame to have missed Jacob's birthday breakfast and party, but these things don't begin to compare to the things the pioneers gave up. The gospel is all about serving people, it's what Jesus would do if he were here; Sister Anderson needed help and as one of His representatives on Earth, Ian gave it.

Claire finds sacrifice difficult, she often needs a little encouragement—next time he sees one of those retro *"Keep Calm and Carry On"* posters, he'll buy one and stick it on the fridge. It'd be good if they also made posters with General Kitchener pointing, *"Your Husband Needs You!"*—she could do with one of those, too! It's for Claire's sake that he tries to offset each small sacrifice by making the most of every minute he has at home. One of the apostles died a couple of years ago and in his obituary it said that although he was too busy to spend time with his children either before or after dinner, he used every mealtime wisely, talking about the gospel. It made Ian realize he had been wasting teaching opportunities, and he resolved to make mealtimes an occasion for both physical and spiritual feasting. It's good to chat about gospel-related matters at the table instead of who said what at school, or the latest episode of whatever it is the children watch on television.

They were having a family discussion about the importance of tithing last Sunday when the telephone rang. Ian answered it.

"Bishop Bradley!" exclaimed the voice at the other end.

"Hello, President Carmichael." Ian stepped out of the dining room and into the living room. "How are you?"

"I'm fantastic, Bishop!"

President Carmichael is always fantastic. His inability to be anything else cheers Ian.

"What can I do for you, President?"

"There's going to be a special missionary meeting on Saturday at the Stake Center."

"This Saturday?"

"Yes."

Ian's response—"I'll be there, President"—was automatic. Back in the dining room, he changed the subject of his discourse. "Who knows what obedience is?" he asked. Issy's hand shot up like a steeple and she held her breath in anticipation of being selected, something she'd learned during her first week of school. "Yes, Issy."

"Doing as you're told," she said.

"Well done! How important is obedience?"

"Very important," she said.

"Yes! Obedience is the first law of heaven. Do you know why? Obedience to the commandments makes us free. Free from sin and free to receive blessings from Heavenly Father. The key to freedom is obedience. Now, that was President Carmichael on the phone."

"Was he fantastic?" Zipporah asked.

"He was."

"So what did Captain Fantastic want?"

"Don't be disrespectful, Alma. He's asked me to go to a missionary meeting on Saturday morning."

"But it's my birthday party," Jacob protested.

"It's a small sacrifice when you think about it," Ian said gently.

Claire sighed, stood up, and began to stack the dirty plates. She started to walk toward the kitchen but stopped in the doorway, holding the tower of dishes like a waitress. She opened her mouth, appeared to think better of it, and closed it again.

"Let me help you with those." He got up from the table and followed her into the kitchen.

"It's no sacrifice for you," she said as she dumped the dirty plates in the sink and began rinsing the gravy away. "You just got out of supervising fifteen seven-year-olds at a party. I only organized it because you promised you'd help."

He leaned against the counter next to the sink and nodded sympathetically while she adjusted to the news.

"Nothing I say will make any difference, will it?" she asked, staring out the kitchen window and into the back garden.

He reached out a tentative hand and stroked the soft flesh of her arm.

"Right, then," she said, and she dried her hands on a towel and padded back into the dining room. "Who wants rhubarb crumble?" he heard her ask. There were shouts of "me," and when he returned to the dining room a moment later she was fine.

Ian glances at his watch as the dock road bridges, merges, and stretches into the suburbs. The missionary meeting ran overtime and he is later than promised. Claire will be upset. A spurt of acid burns his esophagus. He holds the steering wheel with one hand and rummages in his suit pocket for the little plastic box of indigestion tablets. He can't reach past the wad of missionary pass-along cards, so he tugs them out of the pocket and places them between his knees. He has promised to distribute them as part of the Church's new advertising campaign. He isn't very good with nonmembers, but the missionary meeting has inspired him to be bolder. President Carmichael challenged all the bishops to a competition to see who could give the cards out the quickest. Then he shared a story about a General Authority who sat next to Mick Jagger on a plane in the 1980s and told him he'd go to hell if he didn't turn his life around. That's boldness for you! Ian finds the box and when he stops at traffic lights he flicks it open and knocks back a couple of capsules.

He'll make up for his lateness by stopping at McDonald's. He'll buy a milkshake for Jacob and they can have a nice father-and-son chat. Afterward he'll make notes for the talk he will deliver at church tomorrow, a talk he has been mentally preparing for the past few days. He'll speak about sacrifice, he'll mention missing Jacob's party as an illustration, and he'll also tell a story about the children that will go some way toward making up for not seeing much of them this weekend. He likes to use real-life stories in his talks because they have a greater impact on the congregation. Plus, he looked up self-sacrifice on the Internet last week during his lunch hour and all that came up was a list of tattoo and body-piercing providers.

The children will pretend to be embarrassed, but he knows they'll be secretly pleased to have been mentioned. He'll tell the story of the time the tall ships came to Liverpool and he bundled the family into the car and drove them to the docks.

It felt as if they had just emerged from a time machine as they walked along the Salthouse Dock that day. The water was swimming with square-riggers and brigs, ketches and cutters. The schooners looked like they had sailed to Liverpool straight from the set of *Treasure Island*, the pylon structures of their masts strewn with bunting.

"Look," he said to the children, sweeping both arms in an attempt to conduct their reactions. "Let's imagine we're about to get on a boat to travel to America. We're going to be pioneers and we've got to leave behind everything we can't carry. When we get to America, we're going to walk a thousand miles to Utah. Imagine how exciting it would be."

At first no one responded. But everyone was hungry and he'd been clutching the shopping bag of brown-bread sandwiches. Holding the lunch as ransom proved to be an imagination activator.

"I'm sure it would be exciting at first," Zipporah said, "but I bet we'd be seasick."

"Yes! That shows you're really thinking about it!"

"Me, Daddy?" Issy called from the buggy.

"Yes, you'd come too, Issy."

"Could I take my Legos with me?" Jacob asked.

"No," Ian explained. "You'd have to make sacrifices. You know what a sacrifice is, don't you, Jacob? It's when you give up something good for something better."

"So I'd get more Legos in America?"

"No. You'd get something much better than Legos: blessings for being obedient and Eternity with your family."

Everyone waited for Alma to say something.

"I'm excited," he finally conceded. "Can I have a sandwich?"

"In a minute," Ian said. "First, I'd like it if we could sing a pioneer song."

They'd all groaned, even Claire. But it was a groan laced with affection, a groan telling him that, even though they didn't want to admit it, they were enjoying themselves and didn't mind singing on the dockside like an English version of the Von Trapp family.

"Let's do 'Whenever I Think About Pioneers,'" he said. "Just think about what they sacrificed so we can have the gospel today. After three; one, two, three."

It had been a special moment. He'd felt the reassuring warmth of the Spirit in his heart as they sang the simple words in honor of the sacrifices of their pioneer forebears. The bunting on the tall ships flapped applause at them, and although they'd sung quietly, Ian's heart filled with gratitude as he looked at the children and Claire. They probably looked like an ordinary family standing on the dockside. But they weren't, they aren't. They're an Eternal family, sealed to one another by the power and authority of the priesthood forever and ever. Like the pioneers, they'll be called upon to make sacrifices for the sake of their beliefs and, like the pioneers, they won't falter. He will describe that special, faith-enhancing moment in Sacrament Meeting tomorrow, a moment so perfect it hadn't been spoiled even by Alma's improvised second verse, which began, "I would like to have died of frostbite."

He turns the Tabernacle Choir CD down as he drives into the McDonald's parking lot. He can't remember what flavor milkshake Jacob likes—strawberry, banana, vanilla, chocolate. He reaches into the pocket of his suit jacket for his phone and realizes he forgot to switch it back on when he left the meeting. Chocolate, that's it— much better to remember than disturb Claire while she's busy tidying up. He drops the phone on the passenger seat and edges closer to the drive-through intercom.

When the girl passes the milkshake through the window he places it between his knees because the drink holder is full of scribbled-on bits of paper, empty candy wrappers, and several of Issy's barrettes. He turns the CD back up and skips to his favorite song. There may be just enough time to listen to it.

"Come, come, ye saints, no toil or labor fear,
But with joy wend your way!"

He isn't far from home when thoughts of Brother Rimmer and his homemade handcart roll back into his head. He hasn't visited Brother Rimmer for a week or two and the Tabernacle Choir's soft rendering of the fourth verse of "Come, Come, Ye Saints" reminds him of poor Sister Rimmer's death.

"And should we die, before our journey's through,
Happy day! All is well!"

Someone should visit Brother Rimmer; perhaps the Spirit is prompting *him* to do it, right now. He is never as certain as he would like to be about these things, he doesn't hear the distinct voice that some people report. When the Spirit speaks to him it's more of an impression, a prompting and, as it's always best to err on the side of caution, he takes a right turn at the roundabout and drives in the direction of Brother Rimmer's house, singing the final line of the hymn in a forceful crescendo.

"Oh, how we'll make this chorus swell, All is well! All is
well!"

BOOK TWO

The Lord Gave and the Lord Hath Taken Away

SEPTEMBER

– 6 –

Knowing

Claire knows. She knows the instant she steps into the bedroom and gauges the panting, shallow breaths. Knows when she pulls the blankets back and Issy is already diminished, half-emptied.

She kneels down as her urgent words slide off Issy's forehead and onto the floor, and when she hears herself shouting it's as if the sound is coming from someone else.

– quickly, bring a glass, *now*

– a *glass*, Alma, I said a *glass*—what am I supposed to do with a plastic cup?

She knows as she rolls the glass across Issy's thigh, as she presses harder, pushing up and down in an effort to excise the red floret-spatters. She reaches for the telephone with thick, clumsy fingers.

– all floppy and I can't wake her up

– stop asking questions and *do* something

– yes, a red rash

Her words ring, as if she is hearing them on a microphone, and she knows.

She knows when the stocky paramedic *call-me-Dave* doesn't bother with a stretcher and just carries Issy down the stairs, her limbs wilting over the frame of his tattooed arms. It's goodbye hallway, goodbye house. The front door is suddenly an exit to much more than the driveway, the street, the park, and Claire fights the urge to push ahead of *call-me-Dave* and slam the door shut; the urge to shout, "Wait! Stop! You can't take her, I'm not ready!"

She knows as she pauses in the doorway and watches the children crowd the bottom stair in a solemn huddle.

– don't be upset

– nothing to worry about

– keep trying to get hold of Dad

Jacob breaks away from the older two and dashes to the door. "When can I open my presents?"

Zipporah follows him. "Shut up," she scolds, wrapping her arm around his shoulder to soften the rebuke. "Don't worry, Mum. We'll all say a prayer, won't we, Alma?"

Poor Jacob. Poor Zipporah. And poor Alma, standing alone on the bottom stair—Claire knows he's got no intentions of praying. There isn't time to hug the three of them, before they know too, before everything changes.

IT'S BRIGHT INSIDE the ambulance; the blue overhead cupboards, yellow ceiling straps, and red and green bags of medical supplies are incongruously cheerful, like Jacob's Lego emergency vehicles.

Dave points to a blue chair beside a tinted window.

"Sit down."

Issy is marooned on the stretcher, limp and raggish, like something the tide has washed up. Dave fastens straps around her chest and legs while he talks about intramuscular injections and antibiotics. Claire picks out the word "penicillin," but she is finding it hard to hear; her ears are still ringing and her skin is tight with prickling dread. She can see the other paramedic, the woman, pacing outside the ambulance talking on a cell phone.

"We'll be off soon," Dave says. "She's just calling ahead. To let them know we're coming. So they'll be ready."

The other paramedic jumps into the driver's seat, starts the engine, and pulls away.

"We'll go as quickly as we can," Dave says. Then the sirens start, and Claire stares out the back windows as cars signal and brake and edge up curbs. Their urgency, their kindness makes her feel like crying, she wants to shout, *"Thank you, thank you!"* and she knows in the future, whenever she hears sirens, she will be transported back here.

"How long has she been unwell?"

"She was fine yesterday. She went to school—she's just started—she came home, we had spaghetti for dinner. I think she went to bed at the usual time, we had a babysitter because we had to go to a meeting at our church, there was—"

"When did you notice she was unwell?"

"She didn't get up this morning," she says. "I thought she was tired. I had to go shopping, it's my younger son's birthday, I thought she'd be up when I got back, but she wasn't. I checked on her. I *did* check on her." Her voice rises, quivers—she is protesting too much, Dave won't believe her, but she can't help it. "I gave her some Tylenol I thought it was a cold or one of those twenty-four-hour bugs they get when they start school and they seem desperately ill but they're better after a couple of hours. And then it was the party. I thought she'd sleep it off. I left her for two hours." She pauses and says it again, appalled, *"Two hours.* She's really ill, isn't she?"

Dave nods.

"She's going to die, isn't she?"

"She's very ill," he says.

WHEN THE AMBULANCE stops outside the emergency room, a group of staffers are waiting by the automatic doors in bottle-green, purple, and blue scrubs.

"We'll get her off first," Dave says. "Just wait there a minute."

The ambulance doors open and there's a draft of noise and a burst of shouted questions. Anxious, waiting arms receive the stretcher, then it disappears through the automatic doors. Claire follows, past a reception area and down a corridor to a long room lined with empty beds. The ceiling is crisscrossed by curtain tracks, but no one touches the curtains. They lift Issy off the stretcher and onto a bed, and while Dave talks to someone in bottle-green scrubs the other paramedic pushes the empty stretcher away.

Claire catches wisps of words, tiny sentence strings.

"Has she had the IM?"

"She's collapsed, we're not going to be able to do an IV."

"A central line, then?"

"I want a lumbar puncture."

"Can you intubate? We're going to need dexamethasone."

"Will someone get the mother out of here?"

A woman in blue scrubs leaves Issy's bedside and drapes an arm over Claire's shoulder. "It's all right, love," she says. "We're just going to stabilize her and then we'll move her to a ward. Why don't you go and get yourself a cup of tea?"

"I'm OK, thanks."

"You don't want to be here for this."

"Why? What are you doing?"

"Can you wait outside, please?"

"It's OK, I want to stay."

"Come on, that's right, love."

The nurse maneuvers Claire out of the room and back to Reception. The waiting area is almost empty. There's a teenager next to his mother, nothing visibly wrong, and a man sitting beside a little girl with a cut head, muttering about bloody ambulances and waiting around all pissing afternoon for a couple of stitches. Claire gets a drink and sits as far away from him as possible. She tries to sip the hot chocolate but her hands are shaking and in the end she just holds the cup.

WHEN THE NURSE comes back, the chocolate is cold. Claire leaves it on a table and follows her out to a corridor that slopes gently and appears to run the length of the hospital. They walk past murals painted straight onto the corridor walls: dolphins and sea lions and enormous, smiling blue whales. The nurse asks her what she does for a living. *Nothing.* Does she live near the hospital? *Not really.* How many children does she have? *Four.*

They pass fairy-tale paintings bordered by pink stencils: Little Bo Peep, a falling Humpty Dumpty, soldiers with glassy, hemisphere eyes, and Sleeping Beauty's castle. They pass leopards, foxes, a giant panda, and a colossal gorilla with blind circles where its glass eyes used to be. "It's a long way, isn't it?" the nurse says and they carry on past a bejeweled mine cart from *Snow White* and a sign for the ICU.

The floor is blue now, the walls are quieter and the lights lower. The corridor feels like a tunnel and Claire experiences a buildup of pressure in her head that reminds her of swimming underwater. The nurse stops to call an elevator and they stand side by side as they ascend. When the doors open, the nurse turns down the passageway marked "ICU" and Claire is flooded with the horror of knowing again.

The heavy doors at the end of the passageway are locked shut. "You'll need to press this button," the nurse says. "Just tell them who you are and they'll let you in."

The door opens to reveal a woman sitting at a desk.

"Come on, lovey," she says. "Follow me."

They pass a wall decorated with donation plaques and photographs of smiling children. Claire wonders how many of them are still alive. The nurse presses another keypad and opens a door labeled "Parents' Lounge."

"I thought I was going to . . . When can I see her?"

"They're just settling her in. Someone will come and get you when everything's ready. You can make yourself a drink while you wait."

It's cold in the Parents' Lounge. Two fans attached to the far wall drive freezing air around the room. She sits beside a fan and the cold creeps into her ears like it does when she walks on the beach. She gets up and wanders around, examining the posters on the walls and the pamphlets stuffed into various holders: Carbon Monoxide

Poisoning, Baby Bottle Decay, Pregnancy and Flu, Measles. She chooses an upright chair away from the blast of the fans and sits down again. The clock on the wall has barely moved. Time is gluey and thick. She stares and stares at the clock. Eventually, she realizes it's wrong—stopped. She chews the insides of her cheeks and spins her wedding ring round and round. Where is Ian? Somehow it will be for everyone's good that he disappeared with Brother Anderson, that he went to the missionary meeting and vanished afterward on a worthy errand. She grabs the impulse to blame him and chokes it. But she'll revive it later; she's no saint.

WHEN THE DOOR opens her stomach pitches. She gets to her feet and leans against the chair, startled by the slackness of her knees.

"Hiya, I'm Julie. I'm Isabel's nurse. You can see her now." More following, more corridors—she is lost in the maze of a sickening dream. Finally, Julie opens a door to a pristine room, brimming with beeps. Issy, at last. Lying on her back, dark hair spread over the pillow, eyes shut, a tube snaking out of her mouth and threading into a disc where more tubes grow, some clear, others blue. No nightie, just a diaper—*I'm a big girl, I don't need a diaper*—legs and trunk freckled by purple spatters, toes and fingers dark. Worse, the rash is *worse*. She is so small in the hospital bed, its sides up like a giant cot.

A woman in bottle-green scrubs waits beside the bed.

"Hello," she says. "I'm Dr. Sabzwari. Pop your bag down and give your hands a wash."

Claire steps to the sink. She washes her hands, rubs them with sanitizer, and waits for Dr. Sabzwari to speak.

"I know it's upsetting to see Isabel like this, but I'm going to explain what we're doing and I hope that'll make it less frightening. I'm sure you thought of meningitis when you saw the rash, and that's what we're looking at—it's our working diagnosis. We've done a lumbar puncture and we'll get the results soon."

Dr. Sabzwari pauses and nods her head several times. When Claire finally nods back, she continues.

"Isabel was in shock when she arrived, her veins had collapsed, so we had to put a central line in—we made a cut near her collarbone and threaded a line into a big vein near her heart so she can get fluids. We're also giving her an intravenous steroid and we're taking lots of measurements. See all the numbers on the screen? We're monitoring her heart and pulse rate, her blood pressure, her central venous pressure—that's the pressure in her veins—her temperature, and the amount of oxygen in her blood. I know it's noisy and there might be occasional alarms, but don't worry.

"Isabel's intubated, which means we've put a tube down her throat, and she's ventilated—this machine here is breathing for her by blowing gas into her lungs—and although the medication we're giving her is making her drowsy, you can talk to her; she may well be able to hear you and recognize your voice. Is there anything you'd like to ask me?"

"Her fingers and toes . . ."

"That's something we'll worry about later."

"What . . . what's the prognosis?"

Dr. Sabzwari frowns and Claire is hit by another eruption of knowing.

"She's poorly and we're hoping to see a response to treatment soon. If there's no response . . . it's serious. Is there someone you'd like to be here with you? What about Isabel's father? Does he know?"

"His phone's switched off," she says. "My older daughter will keep trying."

"I'll be in and out, but if I'm not here when he arrives someone will come and get me and I'll talk to both of you together. Please sit down."

Dr. Sabzwari points to the plastic-coated chair next to the bed and Claire sits. She looks at Issy's closed eyes and taped-up mouth.

The machines chime and bleep and the ventilator pistons air into Issy's chest.

"Why don't you talk to her?" Julie says. "Tell her a story. I bet she'd like that."

"Can I touch her?"

"It should be fine to stroke her head. I'll let you know if she isn't tolerating it."

Claire edges the chair closer, slides her arm between the bars, and touches Issy with her fingertips. Tiny fair hairs fluff the verge of Issy's forehead, bleached by hours spent outside playing in the garden and walking on the beach during the recent summer. Claire smooths them into the darker hair behind. She doesn't want to tell stories, she wants to memorize Issy: map every freckle, drink in each distinguishing feature—the curve of her bottom lip, the faint scar where her temple caught the corner of a table—learn her off by heart before her figuration is irretrievable.

She begins with Issy's favorite fairy tale, "The Frog Princess." She feels silly at first because Julie is looking at the machines, opening drawers, and unfastening little white boxes and plastic packets, but she recounts the tale anyway, and when the frog has turned into a handsome prince, she says, "They all lived happily ever after," and the words taste sour and improbable.

"You're good at that." Julie pauses to write something down. "Plenty of practice?"

"I like stories. And the children, I've got three other children, they like them too."

"I'm sure she'd like to hear another," Julie says, busy, not really listening.

Claire wonders whether Issy's ears are still capable of piping sounds to her brain. She knows she must do *something* and talking is *something,* but she doesn't think she can tell any more happily-ever-after stories. They don't fit; their neat endings grate. There must be other things she can say, and then she remembers Jacob's earlier plea, uttered in the daybreak kitchen, *Tell me the story of when I was born.* The children like true stories, they sometimes prefer them to fairy tales, and so she begins again.

"Once upon a time, I met Daddy for the first time," she says. "Daddy had just got back from his mission. I didn't even know what a mission was, but I could tell there was something different about him—he was serious and neat and I watched him sit by himself in the university cafeteria, not just once, a few times, and I felt sorry for him because he didn't seem to have any friends. My mum, your other nana, had died at the beginning of the summer. I didn't have a dad at home like you do and I felt sad and lonely, even though I had lots of people to sit with. One day I carried my tray over to Daddy's table and sat down next to him."

She remembers the way Ian stood up when she put her tray down. For a moment she thought he was leaving. Then she realized he was doing that standing-up-for-a-woman thing she'd only ever seen on repeats of *Happy Days,* and something happened as she watched him wait for her to sit down. It wasn't love at first sight, or anything like that, but she knew she liked him before he'd said a word. It was in the way his smile tilted and his ears didn't quite sit flat against his head, the way he'd combed his hair into a side part and buttoned his polo shirt right to the top. He was happy to talk, but he didn't seem the slightest bit grateful for her company and she quickly realized that she'd mistaken his self-containment for loneliness.

"I've been wondering if you'd like to go to a movie with me," he said, several lunches later. He said he hadn't seen a movie for more than two years, and when he explained where he'd been and what he'd been doing she was intrigued. She believed in the nebulous, Our-Father-who-art-in-heaven God of school assemblies and post-bereavement platitudes, a bearded Santa Claus–like figure who lived *up there* somewhere, surrounded by harp-playing angels on cumulonimbus clouds—but she'd never met anyone really religious before.

They watched *Sleepless in Seattle* because it was the only

PG-rated movie showing at the Odeon. When Meg Ryan and Tom Hanks finally met at the top of the Empire State Building, Ian reached for her hand with gentle fingers and she sat in the darkness, liking him.

Afterward he took her to a café, where she asked for a coffee and he said he'd prefer it if she had a hot chocolate. They talked for ages. He didn't kiss her when he dropped her off at the house she shared, but he did ask a favor.

"I've got some friends who need help. They've got to practice giving presentations to people. Do you think you could come along and listen?"

She met his friends at his mother and father's house. They gave her a lesson about God and Jesus and Joseph Smith. They even had a little flip chart with pictures to match the stories they told.

"I don't think you need any more practice," she assured them when they'd finished. "You're good—fluent and confident; well done!"

The friends, who were in fact missionaries, looked at her. Ian looked at her. And then she realized she'd been set up. It had seemed funny at the time. "You want me to come to your church, don't you? Why didn't you just ask?"

In the beginning there were so many things she didn't know and couldn't comprehend. The rules about tea, coffee, alcohol, and premarital sex were a cinch, but she frequently got other things wrong. The first time she went to church she wore trousers and the next time she wore a skirt that showed her knees. Once, she blasphemed as she stumbled through a recitation of a verse of scripture during a Relief Society meeting, and on another occasion she organized an unfortunate surprise by reserving a table at a restaurant on a Sunday evening. Ian's mother always let her know when she'd transgressed a boundary—"*We* don't do that," or "*We* do it like this," she'd say. Claire gradually altered her behavior and ideas so she could exchange her "I" for their "we." And, after a while, she began to belong, which made it altogether easier to believe.

"We were so worried when Ian started dating a nonmember," his mother said one day. "But you've taken to it like a duck to water."

It was hard, but in a good way, like one of those difficult diets—perhaps it wouldn't have been so appealing if it had been easy. Claire squeezed herself into the narrow tracks of her new life because she wanted Ian: reliable, dependable, family-oriented Ian. A man who would never pretend he was going on a business trip and disappear from his wife's and daughter's lives forever. It was clear that he was trustworthy, and he was also good and kind, compulsively kind: She had seen him engage in acts of kindness with the sort of last-ditch fervor she'd observed in bars at closing time.

He proposed to her outside the Temple, the place where they could be married for Eternity. They couldn't go inside because she hadn't been a member of the church for a year, so they sat on the edge of a fountain and just looked at the building. She was admiring her engagement ring when he asked how many men she'd slept with.

"Only three," she replied. And although he'd asked nicely and didn't flinch when she answered, she was soaked by a big wave of shame.

"Right," he said, and she could tell he was working hard not to mind because he swallowed a couple of times before asking, "Did you love them?"

She tried to find a way to explain it that would allow him to understand, but as she thought about it and watched his expectant face, she realized sex without love would disgust him, that it was probably beyond his imagination.

"Of course I did," she said.

"That's good." He picked up her hand and kissed it. "I forgive you. We won't talk about this again, ever. Neither you, nor I, let's promise."

His willingness to forget her sins had seemed beautiful and magnanimous, but all these years later it sometimes feels as if he has made her into someone else by drawing a ring of silence around a part of her he didn't like. And as a result she doesn't know how to talk to Zipporah about sex, how to even mention it without risking her promised silence.

The machine next to the bed beeps loudly several times in quick succession, breaking Claire's reverie. Julie leans over and presses something, and the beeps return to their previous rhythm.

"Ah, it's so romantic," Julie says. "It's like something from a film. You talked to him because he looked lonely and you ended up getting married. What were you doing at university?"

"International Studies. I thought—I had ideas about working abroad, helping people. He was doing teacher training. Mathematics; he's a math teacher. I didn't—I've never worked, I was pregnant with our oldest by the time I finished my degree."

She strokes the inside of Issy's arm, gently running her fingers up and down, up and down, like she does when they sit on the sofa together watching children's television and when Issy gets fidgety in church.

"I bet she can hear you. Go on, carry on."

"So Mummy and Daddy fell in love and we went to Prague on our honeymoon," she continues. "You'd like it there, Issy. Lots of the buildings are like fairy-tale houses, all different colors and shapes, with little turrets and castley bits, and red tile roofs. When you get better we could all go," she lies. "We'd have to go on an airplane, that'd be exciting, wouldn't it? They've got these twisty cobbled streets and little shops selling puppets. All sorts of puppets, whatever you can think of—Pinocchio, the three little pigs, footballers, princesses . . . You'd love a puppet, wouldn't you? I wanted to buy one when I was there."

She doesn't tell Issy about the beggars. About the way they knelt on the ground, foreheads resting on the cobbles, their raised, supplicating hands proffering empty tins at passersby. She remembers wanting to crouch next to them, wanting to help them to their feet, lift their faces, and make them human.

"Why are they hiding like that?" she'd asked Ian.

"Maybe they're ashamed," he'd said.

She hadn't thought so. Their groveling position spoke more of desperation than embarrassment. She stood near one of them for a while and watched. It was the tourists who gave money; the Czech people didn't seem to see him. He twitched when the coins clinked into his tin, but he didn't look up to see what he'd been given, he just muttered, *"Dˇekuji."*

Ian said he hadn't come on honeymoon to look at beggars—he hadn't wanted to leave the hotel room at all; it had been all she could do to make him supplement his soppy grin with clothes and venture outside. She allowed him to hurry her away, but they came back from their honeymoon empty-handed because he let her give every penny of their spending money to the beggars. And in the years since, she has thought about them. When she prays she sometimes feels like them: desperate and cringing, unable to meet the eyes of the being whose help she is soliciting, obliged to be grateful long before she has any idea of what has landed in her tin.

"I've never been to Prague," Julie says. "I've heard the beer's good."

"Oh, I don't know about the beer . . . Is it OK if I just . . . ?"

"The restroom is just through the door on the left."

The silence in the bathroom is strange. Her ears are pulsing and alert, primed for the repetitive beeps and steady hiss of ventilation. She turns on the taps and squeezes a handful of soap out of the grinning Mr. Soapy Soap dispenser, staring at herself in the mirror as she rubs her hands together. If there was ever a time to get on her knees and beg, this is it. There's a verse in the Book of Mormon: "For behold, are we not all beggars?" If Ian were here, he would tell her to ask the Lord to exchange the horror of knowledge for the comfort of faith. *"Don't worry about knowing, work on believing"*— that's what he'd say, and then he'd remind her that God can't perform miracles when people don't have faith. She has never understood exactly how faith precipitates the type of healing Issy requires. Faith in the face of mountainous evidence to the contrary has always felt like a trick or a trap: If she persuades herself to believe, if she manufactures assurance and puts all her eggs in faith's basket, how much worse off will she be if it breaks? Surely her shattered expectations will be harder to manage than the potentially lethal consequences of skepticism? She turns the taps off and watches as her wet hands drip into the sink. She *should* beg and plead, find the right words—words that will release the magic of healing and bind Issy to mortality before it's too late—but all she can think of is *"please."* Please, please, please . . . So feeble, she knows it won't work. She needs more, a game-changing word, one she can shout through the hospital ceiling to the deity that is preparing to steal her daughter. A word like "Rumpelstiltskin," a word that will overpower and break Him.

When she was a little girl and Dad went away, she used to ask where he was. Mum always told the truth and said she didn't know, but the question Claire wanted to ask next, "Will he come back?," remained unasked. She knew the answer and was afraid to hear it. She is similarly paralyzed now. She pulls a paper towel out of the dispenser and dries her hands and cheeks as the anesthetizing effects of shock wear off and tears finally fall. When the children were little they'd cry in the night and she would magically appear. She has allowed herself to believe that God would do the same if she ever really needed Him. She has wrapped her family in the armor of obedience, protected them with a shield of countless covenants, made and maintained like incantations, and it's all been for nothing. She wipes her cheeks again and throws the paper in the trash.

She waits outside the door to Issy's room for a moment. Maybe she doesn't *know.* Maybe she lacks faith, maybe she's wrong and there is hope; where there is life there is hope—people say that, don't they? She pushes the door open, hears the song of the machines and she knows, as surely as if she has plucked the knowledge from a tree and eaten it. She can feel it in her throat, where it congregates in a lump she can hardly swallow around. She sits down and Julie hands her a tissue. She wipes her eyes with one hand and strokes Issy's motionless head with the other. She brushes the tilt of Issy's jaw, cups the curve of her cheek, follows the swirl of her ear, and she knows.

SHE KNOWS WHEN Ian finally arrives, smiling at everyone, wearing his *I'm here now* face, bustling past her grief like Superman in a Burton suit. He puts an arm around her and, aware Julie is watching, she stands very still and tries not to mind.

"What's going on, then?" he asks, as if he's about to be called upon to remove a splinter or apply a Band-Aid, absolutely confident of making everything better, eager to jump in and rescue Issy with his priesthood power. Julie starts to explain and he nods as if he is capable of changing things, as if he's about to undo a curse like the good fairy at Aurora's christening. But there's nothing he can do, and his not knowing makes him ridiculous.

"Everything's going to be all right." He squeezes her shoulder and she wonders if he has heard a word that's been said. "I'm going to give her a blessing."

He straightens his tie, he means business: Let's get this show on the road, let's sort this problem out. Does he really think he can fix everything? Has he always been so unimaginative and stupid? He reaches into his suit pocket and pulls out Issy's glasses and his car keys. He puts the glasses down on the bed.

"For when she's feeling better, so she doesn't strain her eyes," he says.

He unscrews the lid of the vial of consecrated oil that dangles from the key ring and dabs a few drops onto his fingertips before wiping them across Issy's forehead. He closes his eyes and places his hands on her head, where they rest like a crown.

"Isabel Rachael Bradley, by the authority of the Holy Melchize-dek priesthood which I hold, I anoint your head with this consecrated oil which has been set apart for the blessing of the sick. In the name of Jesus Christ, Amen."

He opens his eyes and glances at Claire.

"Amen," she says.

She watches him close his eyes again. He stands silently and she knows he is listening for the Spirit, waiting for inspiration and guidance, and she aches for him. Once he has taken the time to listen, knowledge will puncture his optimism. He will finish the blessing, sink into the chair beside the bed, remove his jacket, loosen his tie, and they will share the anguish of knowing.

"Isabel Rachael Bradley, by the authority of the Holy Melchizedek priesthood which I hold, I lay my hands upon your head, seal this anointing, and pronounce upon you a blessing. Your Heavenly Father is mindful of you at this difficult time. He loves you and wants to bless you. Your family also loves you very much. Now is not the time for you to return to your Heavenly Father; there is still work for you to do in mortality. You have been blessed with a special mother whom your Heavenly Father loves and, according to her great faith, I bless you to be healed . . ."

He keeps talking but Claire can't keep up with his words, she can't catch them, they're flying past her ears like tiny birds, fluttering to the open door and out into the hospital corridor. He has made Issy's recovery contingent on her faith and she doesn't know how she will ever forgive him.

DR. SABZWARI SAYS it will be easier to talk in the Parents' Lounge. They sit down and Ian smiles at the doctor, as if he believes he can encourage her to deliver good news.

"I'm afraid Isabel's not responding to treatment."

Ian's smile slips. "It's early days, isn't it?"

"We haven't been able to stabilize her, Mr. Bradley. Her condition's worsening. Her brain tissue is swollen and we're beginning to observe focal seizures. We need to think about what's best for Isabel."

"I think it's best to give her more time." He looks to Claire for support. "Give her a chance to turn the corner."

"Mr. Bradley, the septicemia is progressing and—"

"You see children on television who've had their fingers and toes amputated—whole legs, hands, even arms—don't you?"

"Yes, you do." Dr. Sabzwari says it so kindly and regretfully that Claire knows she is going to follow up with something awful. "But you almost never see children at this stage of the disease make a recovery. Isabel's blood pressure is low, which means there's poor blood flow to her major organs, and poor blood flow to the brain causes brain damage. I think we're approaching the stage where we need to talk about what happens next."

Claire looks from Dr. Sabzwari to Ian. "Do you think . . . do you think we could talk about this in the morning?" she asks. "Our other children, we need to talk to them, they should be here . . ."

Ian grabs her hand and squeezes hard and she realizes he thinks she's prevaricating, holding out for a miracle too.

"Of course. We'll review things in the morning. Are you both staying tonight?"

"I'll sit with Issy for a while so Claire can have a break and get something to eat. Then I'll go home and get the children to bed. I'll bring them in the morning and hopefully . . ."

"It's good that one of you will get some rest. If there's any change during the night, we'll call you immediately, Mr. Bradley."

"I'm sure you won't need to," he says.

OTHER, BETTER MOTHERS would be able to fight the soporific, twilight hospital and stay awake. It's like Jesus's last night on Earth, when he asked the disciples to tarry with him and they kept falling asleep even though he needed the company of the people he loved. "Could you not watch with me one hour?" he asked.

Every year when Ian tells the story of Jesus's death in the special Easter Family Home Evening, Claire thinks the disciples are awful for sleeping and yet here she is, tumbling into deep, several-second pools of it every time she blinks. She would have made a poor disciple and she is an even poorer mother.

Issy's urine output is minimal and she is filling up with fluid as her kidneys fail. Her fingers are bunched like dark grapes and she's so immobile it's hard to imagine she went to school yesterday.

Claire stands and leans over the bars of the bed to rest her head on the corner of the pillow. She can smell skin and baby shampoo. She fills her nose with the lovely smell and then she sits again, resting her head against the bars. As she tries to breathe the fragrance into memory she closes her eyes and loses her battle with sleep.

THE CHILDREN SIT with Issy while Dr. Sabzwari talks in the Parents' Lounge. Claire wonders how long the doctor's shifts are and whether she has been home at all.

"So where are we up to?" Ian is wearing his suit again because it's Sunday. He looks anxious, but hopeful.

"We reviewed Isabel this morning on the ward round and we also discussed her at some length as a team. I'm afraid—"

"I saw some stories on the Internet last night about children who've come back from this, miraculous stories—there's no other way to describe them. There was one little girl who'd had her arms and legs amputated, but she was absolutely fine, doing well. She looked lovely and she had these little plastic legs with red shoes on."

"Mr. Bradley, I—"

"And I thought—those shoes, those little red shoes, Issy would like them."

"Ian, you're making it worse."

"I think if there's just the smallest chance, just one percent . . . could you, could you . . . *take* her legs? Would it make a difference?"

"Isabel's brain activity is sporadic, which means her brain has been damaged." Dr. Sabzwari nods her head slowly like yesterday and Claire nods back to signal understanding.

"We don't believe she is going to regain consciousness," she continues. "I'm so sorry. If we stop ventilation, she'll pass away, peacefully."

"Can we wait—I mean, can we just have a little longer?" Ian loosens his tie and fumbles in his jacket pockets for his little box of tablets. He pops one into his mouth and chews quickly. When he's finished, he takes a breath and holds it between puffed cheeks. Claire hears the air hiss as it escapes; she places her hand on his thigh and he covers it with one of his own, cold and slick—under his armor of faith, he's scared. She edges closer, slides her hand out from under his and puts her arm around his shoulder.

"I think the children need some more time with Issy," he says.

He knows. Claire feels him buckle; the dip of his shoulders marks the retreat of his certainty and she is relieved and terrified.

"Of course, Mr. Bradley."

"I'd like some time with her. And Claire would, wouldn't you? Oh, don't cry, come on, you've been so brave, come on—can we have a little more time, please?"

"Of course."

When they've detached the tubes, they place Issy in Claire's lap. Ian and the children huddle around the chair and Issy is surrounded by love. She is warm and malleable and Claire is certain that tiny particles of *her* are still creeping along the sluggish current of blood, hiding in parts of the brain that haven't yet been evacuated.

There is no discernible moment of death; she stops imperceptibly, like the clock in the Parents' Lounge, and Claire tightens her grip, she doesn't know how to give her up and leave her behind, how to sign the forms that will give permission for all sorts of unthinkable things to happen.

Ian bends to kiss Issy's forehead. The children are tear-streaked and stricken; he wraps his arms around them.

"OK, everyone," he says. "OK. It's OK, it's OK. We'll be OK, won't we?" They nod; Alma wipes his face with the bottom of his T-shirt, and Jacob allows Zipporah's hug.

"We'll be OK," Ian says, to her this time, and she nods like the children because there's nothing else to do.

Happy Is the Man Who Has Put
His Trust in the Lord

Ian leans back in his chair and chews the end of his pen. The *Family Home Evening Resource Book,* the Book of Mormon, and the Bible lie open on the dining-room table and pages of handwritten notes fan the spaces among the books. It's his role as head of the family to make sense of things. Tonight, during Family Home Evening, he will provide the antidote to grief by reiterating that death is not the end. He stops chewing on the pen lid to underline a note he has scribbled on one of the scattered pages: We do not mourn as those without hope. Hope—he draws a circle around the word and the squeak of the pen's fiber tip makes him doubly aware of the quiet.

It has been a peaceful day. Doors have closed gently and the hours have been interspersed with whispers and sighs, with artless strokes of arms and shoulders. The shock seems to have sunk right down into the children's feet; they have forgone their usual clomping and chosen instead to pad down the stairs and creep along the corridors. The atmosphere has been so reverent that the house almost feels like the Temple. Eternity will be just like this, but without the sorrow.

Claire has spent most of the day upstairs. When he woke, Ian made her a list:

People to call
GP—antibiotics
President Carmichael
Brother Stevens

Brother and Sister Campbell

Sister Anderson

Schools—back tomorrow but off for funeral—Monday?

Funeral director—home visit?

At first Claire disagreed about school. She wanted everyone home, a whole week off. He argued for company and distraction, for facing everyone as soon as possible and keeping busy; she understood in the end.

He sat on the end of the bed and watched while she dialed the first number, but when she realized he was planning to listen in, she cut the connection and asked him to leave the room. She said it would be easier if he wasn't there. He didn't disagree; after yesterday, he was relieved not to be involved.

When they got back from the hospital, he switched off the car engine and sagged in his seat, unable to recall a single moment of the journey. He couldn't remember whether anyone had spoken, what route he had taken, nothing. It was as if they'd been teleported home.

He didn't do his impersonation of Brigham Young; his throat was too tight to say, "This is the place." And the others were similarly immobilized. No one wanted to be the first to unclip their seat belt; they all waited, even Jacob, each reluctant to cross the threshold of the house for the first time without Issy.

Once inside, they huddled in the kitchen while Claire made hot chocolate and Ian warmed his icy-shocked hands on the hot mug. *She's not here*—he swallowed and the hurt faded somewhat, and then—*she's not here*—it started again and his whole chest hurt.

He rinsed the mugs while Claire put the children to bed. He thought about phoning his mum and dad and it was then it dawned on him: He didn't have a number, just an email address. He dried his hands and switched on the computer. He Googled the Mission President's details and it took only a few minutes for him to discover a phone number. He dialed it before he'd had a proper think about what he was going to say.

"Hello, um, President Tanner. My name's Ian Bradley, and um, my parents are serving in your mission and I—I need their phone number."

"Elder and Sister Bradley? They're a wonderful couple. Did you serve a mission, Brother Bradley?"

"Yes, I—"

"That's wonderful. Where did you serve?"

"London."

"If your parents haven't given you their number, perhaps it's because they've decided to follow Mission rules like the younger missionaries—home can be so distracting. I'd be more than happy to relay a message for you."

"I'd like to talk to them myself."

"Brother Bradley—"

"It's Bishop Bradley, I'm a bishop. And this is important, so I'd appreciate it if you could give me their number."

"Oh, I'm sorry, Bishop. If you just hang on a moment, I'll find it for you. I'm sure you understand—I didn't want to spoil things for your mum and dad. Is everything OK?"

Ian tried to reply but when he opened his mouth he was ambushed by tears. He attempted to speak through them, but his voice split and he couldn't make any words.

"Are you still there, Bishop Bradley?"

He tried again and made a series of indecipherable whimpers. There was something about *saying* that was infinitely worse than *knowing*.

"Are you OK?"

"I, oh . . . oh, I . . ."

"If you can just tell me what's happened, I'll speak to your parents for you, Bishop Bradley. I'll do it straight away, I promise. Take a deep breath. Is someone there with you?"

"Oh . . . I . . . oh . . ."

He couldn't. Something in his chest had wound and wound during the past twenty-four hours, and it was finally working loose as he tried to put everything into words.

Claire must have caught the sounds. He heard her feet on the stairs and watched as she hurried into the dining room to take the phone away from him.

"Our daughter," he heard her say.

He covered his face with his hands and cried.

"Only four. Meningitis. Yes. Thank you . . . it's kind of you. Goodbye."

There was a clunk as she put the phone down on the dining-room table and then she touched his shoulders.

"Come on, come on." She stroked him and shushed his sobs. "President Tanner's going to call your parents," she said eventually. "He didn't think you'd be able to manage it. He'll get them to call us, so you need to stop crying. Come on. Shush."

He wiped his cheeks and nodded, afraid that if he tried to speak, the inexplicable noises would begin again. She fetched a box of tissues from the kitchen and placed it on his lap. He was blowing his nose when the phone rang. She answered it for him and passed it over.

"Oh, Ian," his mum said. And that was all it took to make him cry again.

FAMILY HOME EVENING always starts with a song, but Ian forgoes it today in case the singing precipitates tears. He sits in his armchair opposite Claire, and the children take the sofa. The room feels all wrong. There's an automatic error message going off in his brain—a preset program that keeps count of the children is warning him one of them is missing. Issy's beanbag is slumped next to the toy box, cast in the dip of her shape. He tries not to look at it. He thinks about the other Church families all over the world who, no matter what has happened during the previous week, will be spending Monday evening at home enjoying gospel discussions and fun. Some people make jokes about Family Home Evening; they say it's the only fight that begins and ends with a prayer. Ian doesn't fight with his family and he wouldn't make jokes about it if he did.

Sheets of handwritten notes mark the correct page in the *Family Home Evening Resource Book*. The lesson is from the Special Occasion section: "They That Mourn Shall Be Comforted—to be used after a loved one has died." He asks Jacob to give the opening prayer and then he begins the lesson with an easy question.

"Where are Nana and Granddad?"

"They're on their mission," Jacob says. "But Dad, it was my birthday on Saturday so it's supposed to be *my* Family Home Evening. We have to look at the pictures of me when I was a baby and sing my favorite songs and *everything*. That's what's supposed to happen."

"Not this week, Jacob. We'll do it another day. How long is Nana and Granddad's mission?"

"One and a half years. So will my Family Home Evening be next week or—"

"That's enough. How much time have Nana and Granddad got left before they come home, Alma?"

"Six months."

"That's right. Haven't the first twelve months gone quickly?"

They all shrug, even Claire, as if it's something they can't be bothered to consider, and Ian knows he has to do better.

"I've been thinking about Issy, and I think Heavenly Father must have a special job for her to do, a bit like Nana and Granddad's mission, but in the Spirit World. I'm sad that we haven't seen Nana and Granddad for a year, and I'm, um, I'm sad that Issy isn't . . . that she isn't . . . isn't here. But Nana and Granddad will be home next year. We'll be so happy to see them, won't we? And do you know what? Issy's gone home to live with Heavenly Father and

Jesus, and one day, after we've finished our work on Earth, we'll all join her. We'll be so happy to see her, won't we? It may *seem* like a long time, but it will pass quickly, I'm sure—"

"Nana and Granddad aren't coming home until next year?" Zipporah interrupts. "You mean they aren't coming for Issy's funeral?"

"No, they've decided it's best not to."

"Why?"

"Well, Granddad's baptizing someone on Sunday afternoon and the funeral will probably be on Monday, so . . . missionaries don't just pop back for family occasions, they have to concentrate on missionary work, and when they do that, their families get more blessings."

Alma coughs in theatrical disagreement and Ian's fingers tighten into fists.

"It's easy to be a smart aleck and make fun of things. It takes a lot more effort to trust and have faith." He glances at Claire for support, but she is looking steadfastly at the carpet. He'd also assumed Mum and Dad would come back for the funeral. Dublin isn't far away. It would have been easy to organize, but he can't let it upset him; it's wrong to dwell on disappointments.

"It's all about the way you look at things," he tries. "Think of the pioneers. I saw a photograph of the prophet's office on the Internet and he's got a sculpture of two hands holding a little spoon on his desk. Do you know why? To remind him of sacrifices made by the pioneers. There's a story about a German lady who was traveling with a handcart in the winter and her children froze to death. When it was time to bury them, she had to dig into the icy ground with a *spoon*. No one's asking us to do anything like that. We're making much smaller sacrifices. Nana and Granddad could be here with us, or they could be helping people join the Church, helping them to be with their families for Eternity."

There's something about saying words out loud that makes them true and, having explained things to everyone, he finds himself converted. It's all right for Mum and Dad to stay in Dublin. He discards his disappointment and carries on with the lesson.

"From now on, our lives will be all about being worthy to get to the Celestial Kingdom. We've got a special, personal motivation that most people don't have, a specific goal in sight: to be reunited with Issy. We're like footballers." He looks at Alma, hoping to engage him with the sporting comparison. "Footballers train every day, don't they? We're in training for the moment when we're judged and Heavenly Father says 'Well done, thou good and faithful servant' to us."

"What if I don't get to the Celestial Kingdom? What if I'm not good enough?" Alma asks.

"You don't need to worry about that. You'd have to do something awful. You'd have to kill someone or break your covenants—you'd have to apostatize and leave the Church."

"But would I get to see her?"

Claire looks up from the carpet. "Of course you would," she says.

"Poor Issy." Zipporah's voice wobbles. "She won't know anyone. I hope she's not by herself."

"She'll be with my mum," Claire says.

Ian knows Claire won't like what he's about to say, but it's important to be honest, so he says it anyway.

"Issy *might* be with Mum's mum, provided Mum's mum has accepted the gospel. If Mum's mum hasn't accepted the gospel yet, she'll be waiting in the Spirit Prison."

"You mean our other nana who we don't know yet might be in *prison*?" Jacob asks.

"No, my mum's definitely not in prison."

"I don't want Issy to be by herself. She's only little," Zipporah says.

"She's not by herself. All our ancestors who've accepted the gospel are there. And the Spirit World's not far away, you know. It's right here, we can't see it, but it's all around us . . . it's like . . . it's like there's another dimension."

"Wow!" Jacob swivels around on the sofa, scanning the room with searching eyes. "Do you know everything, Dad?"

"No, I don't know everything. I don't have all the answers, but I promise if there *are* answers, I'll always try to find them for you."

Jacob gets up and crosses the room to sit on Ian's knee. Ian holds him carefully, resisting the urge of his arms to clasp and squeeze.

"I'm glad you know stuff, Dad."

He squeezes then. It's an action born of thankfulness and fear. Jacob giggles but he doesn't attempt to get down. He lacks Alma's prickliness, he's happy to be held, and in many ways he reminds Ian of himself when he was growing up. He just hopes he can do as good a job as his dad did.

Dad always had answers and ideas. He had huge reserves of memorized scriptures, vast gospel knowledge, and a relentless determination to flatten bumps of doubt like a lawn roller. It was Dad who challenged thirteen-year-old Ian to read the Book of Mormon, and it took him just over a year to get through it.

"You know what you've got to do now," Dad had said. "Ask if it's true. Ask with a sincere heart and real intent and you know what'll happen, don't you? Heavenly Father will manifest the truth of it by the power of the Holy Ghost. Get to it, lad!"

Joseph Smith was fourteen when he had the First Vision. Ian was fourteen when he prayed to find out if the Book of Mormon was true. He prayed every night. He was primed and ready for a visitation—if not a visitation, a revelation, some kind of manifestation, perhaps a moment of inspiration or a dream, an idea, an impression, at the very least a feeling. He tried hard. He followed the steps he'd learned at church: Desire sincerely, read and study, keep the commandments, ponder, pray, and listen. He approached the exercise with mathematical precision, praying morning and night for at least ten minutes, an allotment of time that seemed adequate without being excessive. Nothing happened. Eventually he turned to Dad.

"I wonder if you've been approaching it right," Dad said. "What've you done so far?"

"I've prayed every night."

"Good. What about the mornings?"

"Every morning too. I even knelt down and prayed in the back garden yesterday, under the cherry tree. I thought it might work better outside, you know, like the First Vision."

"And what happened?"

"Nothing."

"Nothing at all?"

"Well, Mrs. Grier must have been hanging her washing out because she leaned over the fence to ask me what I was looking for. And she offered to lend me Mr. Grier's magnifying glass. That's all."

Dad thought for a moment. "Let me ask you a question, son. Am I your dad?"

"Well, yeah."

"How do you know?"

"I just do."

"Have you seen the results of a test to prove it?"

"No."

"How do you know, then?"

"You told me."

"Would it help if I reminded you every so often?"

"No. I already know."

"How about if I wake you up in the night sometimes just to tell you? Or if I stop when I'm in the middle of an important job and phone home to jog your memory. Would that convince you?"

"I already know!"

Dad slapped him on the back. "And there's your answer, son. Right there."

Although it had been nice to talk to Mum last night, it had been Dad he'd most wanted to speak to. When Mum had finished crying

and talking she handed the phone to Dad. The first thing Ian did
was tell him about the blessing.

"I blessed her to live, Dad. I actually said it, I said she would
recover, and . . . I, oh . . ."

"It's OK, son. It's all explained in *Doctrine and Covenants,* in
Section 42. If someone is given a healing blessing and they die, they
die *unto the Lord.* If you keep reading, you'll see that when someone dies unto the Lord, death is *sweet unto them.* If something's
sweet then it's good, and it's right. The Lord wanted Issy to come
home. It was the right thing to happen. You couldn't do anything to
stop it. By blessing her to live, you ensured that she *died unto the
Lord.* There's no contradiction, nothing to agonize over. It's not
your fault."

Dad's words had breezed through Ian in a great gust of relief. He
lifted the box of tissues from his lap and put it on the dining-room
table. His sorrow was contained again, soothed and wrapped in an
assuaging bandage of scripture.

Later, when they were in bed, he told Claire that Issy hadn't
needed to stay on Earth and be tested anymore.

"She'd probably learned everything she needed to know here.
She was too good—"

"I don't want people saying she was perfect. She wasn't."

"But when children die before they're eight, they go straight to
the Celestial Kingdom, which suggests they—"

"So every child in the world that dies, *every* child that dies of
diarrhea and malaria and malnutrition, is perfect?"

He'd never considered it before. "Yes, yes they must be." He
thought about all the perfect children dying around the world, dying
at that exact moment while he and Claire lay in the dark, desperately sad, but warm, and safe, and together. He slid his hand over to
her side of the bed and rested it on the silky material covering her
thigh. When she didn't react he began to move his fingertips back
and forth in stroking circles.

"Don't change her life," she said. "Issy wasn't perfect. She wouldn't wear her glasses, she used to hide them and pretend she didn't know where they were. She drew on the walls and she howled every time she had her hair washed. She didn't sleep through the night until she was six months old and—"

"Stop it." He pulled his hand away.

"It's the truth. And I love—loved—no, love. I love all of her, every bit, I love everything, I always will. That's what you do; you love all of someone, not just the nice bits."

"But you concentrate on the nice bits, you think about them and emphasize them, you do your best to ignore the bad bits."

"*You* do."

"I do," he agreed. His eyelids were growing heavy. He'd wondered whether he might have difficulty sleeping but he was exhausted, and he felt if he just surrendered to sleep, he might wake up buoyed by a new understanding and a fresh way of framing things, something to counter the recurring pain in his chest.

"Everything happens for a reason, doesn't it?"

He waited, hoping for a quiet "Yes." But Claire didn't respond. He touched her thigh to nudge a reply out of her. She must have fallen asleep.

"It would be nice," Ian says, "if you could all just listen for a little longer." The children are beginning to get restless and he needs to hurry up and conclude while he still has their attention. "The coming weeks and months are going to be difficult. But special blessings come at sad times. We need to be on the lookout for Tender Mercies. Does anyone know what they are? I read a Conference talk about them this morning. Tender Mercies are consolations, little signs that Heavenly Father is mindful of us and trying to bless us. There was a story in the talk I read, about a soldier killed in Iraq. After his wife was told of his death, a Christmas card and message arrived from him: It was a Tender Mercy from Heavenly Father."

"Don't you think it would have been better if Heavenly Father had stopped the soldier from dying?"

"You're missing the point, Alma. Heavenly Father can't always stop bad things from happening—He can't interfere with people's agency—but he can always provide comfort."

"But if he *can* stop bad things from happening sometimes, why does he *choose* not—"

"One day we'll understand why bad things happen and it'll all make sense."

Jacob wriggles off Ian's lap. He puts his hand up above his head and waves it around as if he is competing for attention at school. "I know, Dad. I know what it's like. It's like in *Sleeping Beauty* when the good fairy comes in and says she can't undo the spell, but she can make it a bit better. It is, isn't it, Dad?"

"Well . . . I suppose it is, except we don't believe in bad spells or curses. And the priesthood is the power of God, not magic. And fairies don't hold the priesthood because they're girls—but yes, I suppose it is a bit like *Sleeping Beauty*. Now, what about the funeral? Does anyone have any ideas, anything special you'd like me to mention during the service?"

"I'd like to do one of those slide-show things with pictures of Issy's life," Claire says. "Sister Stevens is coming round later to help me."

"But it's Monday night. She should be at home with her—"

"I didn't ask. She volunteered when I called, earlier. She knows how to do it, she makes slide shows on her computer and emails them to Utah, so her parents can see the children."

"It might not be allowed." Ian gets up and pulls the *Church Handbook* from the bookcase.

"It's no big deal, putting some pictures of Issy to music," Alma says. "I've seen people do it at funerals on TV. We could have 'You'll Never Walk Alone.'" He clears his throat and starts to sing. "*When you walk through a storm, hold your head up high.*"

"Shush, I'm trying to concentrate." Ian finds the section on funerals and starts to read. No one says anything. They all wait for him to speak. He closes the *Handbook* and puts it back on the bookcase. "It's not allowed."

"You can make an exception," Claire argues.

"I can't. People will think I'm a hypocrite. They'll think it's one rule for our family and another for everyone else."

"They won't know," she says. "You didn't know until you checked. I bet no one else knows either."

"We'd be setting a precedent."

"But people are usually old when they die, aren't they?" Zipporah says. "I mean, it's not as bad for old people, is it? That's probably why their relatives don't ask about stuff like slide shows. You've hardly done any funerals since you've been Bishop, Dad. It's not like people are dying all the time. I don't think you need to worry."

"It doesn't matter what you think, Zipporah. There's a right way to do things and we're going to choose it wherever possible. We can do a slide show afterward, in the hall, while people eat. Now, for our Family Home Evening activity we're going to write in our journals." Alma groans and slumps over the arm of the sofa. Ian ignores him.

"This will be one of the most important journal entries of your lives. Claire, will you fetch the CD player, please? This is *your* history. One day your children will read your journals and they'll learn from your struggles and your faithfulness. Your journals will be like scripture to your descendants."

Ian selects a Tabernacle Choir CD. They write in their journals and it's so peaceful; if it wasn't for the empty beanbag, he could almost feel happy.

When the doorbell rings everyone jumps up, abandoning their journals to rush to the front door.

"You don't all need to go," he calls, following them into the hall. Sister Stevens is standing on the doorstep holding an enormous casserole dish and several bags of cookies tied with colored ribbon. He nods and retreats back into the living room to finish his writing. He hears Claire invite Sister Stevens in, then everyone rushes to the dining room and Sister Stevens' loud, cheerful voice disrupts the peacefulness.

"I've made funeral potatoes! You must've had them before. Never? What kind of Mormons are you? Hash browns and cheese baked in mushroom soup with cornflakes on top. You'll love 'em. They'll fill all your sad spaces. Come on, guys, we're gonna make the coolest slide show ever! Hey, Alma, you look like you could use some cookies."

Jacob's journal is open on the floor in front of the sofa. Ian picks it up. Jacob has drawn a picture of Issy lying down with her eyes closed and he has written a sentence underneath.

Issy died last night and I am sad. I am praying for a mirycul.

Alma's journal is on the arm of the sofa. It's open, but upside down. Ian sits on the sofa with his own journal on his lap in case anyone comes in. He flips Alma's journal over, glances at the left-hand page and is catapulted back to last Sunday afternoon when he said, "I don't care what you write, Alma. Just write something. If you can't think of anything, write the price of a packet of crisps. That'll be interesting in twenty years."

Crisps

Crisps from Tesco cost 50p.
At Poundland you can get 3 packets for £1. But if you nick them they're free.

He's only joking, of course, but Ian wishes he wouldn't. On the opposite page he has scrawled:

Family Home Evening sucks like a plunger and Issy's dead.

He slides along the sofa to Zipporah's place, picks up her journal and flicks through it until he reaches today's entry. She's a good girl. She has written lots.

Monday 19 September

Mum couldn't wake Issy up after Jacob's party on Saturday. Issy went to hospital in an ambulance and she died last night. It feels like I'm making it up. We went to see her yesterday and it was awful. Mum told us she was going to die and we took it in turns to sit next to her. We were supposed to talk to her but I didn't know what to say.

When you die, does someone meet you and show you around? Do they look after you while you get used to it? Do people go to bed in the Celestial Kingdom, and if they do, will someone tuck Issy in?

He puts her journal back exactly as he found it and then, even though he knows he shouldn't, he walks over to Claire's chair and thumbs the pages of her journal.

Monday 19 September

There aren't the words.

That's it. He flicks forward to double-check. When he finds nothing, it seems like she has played a trick on him. He feels slighted, but he can't say anything or she'll know he has been looking. Perhaps she needs some time. He'll check again in a few days.

He puts the journal back, steps along the hall to the dining room and stands in the doorway, watching. Claire and Sister Stevens are sitting side by side at the computer. Jacob has squeezed onto Claire's lap and Zipporah is peering over Sister Stevens's shoulder. Alma is perched on the dining-room table, throwing occasional glances at the computer, but he is more interested in the open bag of chocolate-chip cookies beside him.

"Music! That's the most important thing. What would you guys like, huh? Something inspiring, but not too churchy—no Tabernacle Choir!"

"Do a search. Type 'funeral songs' and see what comes up," Zipporah suggests.

Ian watches as Alma licks his fingers and helps himself to another cookie. His lips are ringed by crumbs and melted chocolate. When he realizes he is being observed, Alma toasts Ian with the cookie and mouths, "Tender Mercies." Ian can't tell if he is being mocked, but he smiles back anyway—even if it's a joke, it's a gentle one.

"Let's try this," Sister Stevens says.

"Somewhere Over the Rainbow" starts to play and Ian concentrates, listening to the lyrics as if it's the first time he's ever heard them, trying to work out if they're the right words to accompany Issy's life. He likes the bit about daring to dream. Dreams can come true. His dreams *are* true: He *knows* this life is the beginning of something wonderful; he *knows* human beings have the potential to become like God, to create Spirit children and populate their own planets; he *knows* families are forever. His dream—no, his *truth* is immense, eternal, and infinite: It stretches from before the beginning to after the end.

He watches as Sister Stevens puts her arm around Claire and he remembers a verse from Corinthians: "For our light affliction, *which is but for a moment,* worketh for us a far more exceeding and eternal weight of glory . . ." This is just a moment. If he could step outside himself, he would see how small his sadness is, small like the smallness of an infinitesimal number, barely there, only slightly more than nothing, so tiny it can't be measured—no more than a pinprick on a pyramid.

The verse from Corinthians continues—he concentrates for a moment, searching his memory for the words: "We look not at the things which are seen, but at the things which are not seen: for the things which are seen are temporal; but the things which are not seen are eternal."

He gazes into the dining room. Issy could be there right now and none of them would know it. He squints in an effort to see the things which are not seen, but it just makes everything fuzzy.

This song could be the right one. He enjoys the bit about troubles melting like lemon drops; everyone has troubles. After much tribulation cometh the blessings—he's definitely read that somewhere. Blessings are coming, he is certain of it.

– 8 –

The First Time

The science lab reeks of gas and bleach. Zippy stands at the back of the crowd of Year Elevens surrounding Mr. McLean's workbench.

"Before I get started, can everyone see?"

Martin Hayes is standing in front of Zippy. He's aiming the sharp end of a pencil at Chloe Ward's butt. He looks over his shoulder, sees Zippy, and steps back, motioning to her.

"Here," he says, in the careful, friendly voice people have adopted since she came back to school.

Zippy shakes her head at him. Although no one's mentioned it, she knows there was an announcement in Monday's assembly because by midmorning her Facebook page was full of condolences:

So sorry m8 x

RIP ur lil sis

hugz 2 u xx ☹

She had nineteen new friend requests, and someone had made a page, "In Memary of Izzie Bradley," which had twenty-six Likes. Lauren made several comments on the page, each one prefaced by BBF. She might as well have made an announcement: *I'm best friends with the bereaved girl, be nice to me, I'm devastated by association.*

Zippy wants to stay at the back of the class, but Martin moves and Mr. McLean notices her. "Plenty of space at the front for a small one," he calls. "You won't see anything back there, Zippy. Come on."

She squeezes past the boys and the taller girls at the back until she is standing right next to Mr. McLean's workbench. She looks down at the swirly pattern of the wood because she doesn't want to see what's laid out in front of her.

"OK, OK. Let's get started. Dissection pan. Pins. Scissors. Tweezers. Frog." Mr. McLean sounds like he's been looking forward to this all week. "The frog's been prepared for dissection, so all I've got to do is secure it. The pins go right through the tissue, like this and this, into the wax in the bottom of the pan."

Murmurs of disgust and amusement ripple through the Year Elevens. Zippy concentrates on the bench.

"First, let's just have a look at him. See how he has four toes on his forelimbs but five on his hind limbs? See how smooth and slippery he is? That's due to the mucus that's formed by cells in the skin. Now, I need to make one long cut, straight down the center of the ventral side—that's what the stomach side is called—all the way down to the cloaca, the opening his waste and sperm come out of."

There's another sniggery ripple and Martin Hayes takes the opportunity to poke Chloe Ward in the butt with his pencil. When Chloe whips around to snatch the pencil, Zippy accidentally looks up, and then she can't look away.

The frog is gray and stiff and its skin is tight and shiny.

"Right, I'm going to make the cut. Here we go."

The scissors make a rubbery sound as they cut the frog open.

"Now I'm going to make two side cuts at the top, and two at the bottom."

Mr. McLean cuts across the torso near the front legs and then the hind legs. He picks up the tweezers and pulls the flaps back. The frog is suddenly very human and Zippy's stomach scrunches—it looks like a little old man, like Jeremy Fisher in a waistcoat of skin.

"I'm going to pin the skin, like this, and this. And now I'll cut the muscle. See all the blood vessels here?"

The cutting sound is louder this time. Zippy watches as the scissors slice the tissue. She breathes slowly. The frog's spirit has left its body, it can't feel anything. But it looks so pitiful pinned to the tray with its insides out. *Breathe in and breathe out. Keep breathing.* Zippy drags her gaze back down to the workbench. The wood is stripy, flecked with imperfections and scratches. She tries to think about the wood and when that isn't enough she looks at the tiny hairs on Chloe Ward's tangerine arms, but it's no good, the dam breaks and all she can think about is Issy.

WHEN DAD ASKED her to go to the funeral directors' with Mum, Zippy said no, but he wouldn't leave it, he wanted to know why.

"I just don't want to."

"That's not a good reason. Why don't you do it for Mum?"

"Can't someone else?"

"She doesn't want anyone else there."

"Why?"

"I don't know—she doesn't want anyone except family."

"I've never seen a dead person before. It'd be like a horror film."

"When've you ever watched a horror film?"

"Why don't *you* go?"

"Well, women usually dress women and men dress men. It doesn't say anything about children, still . . . I thought Sister Stevens could help, but Mum said no. It'd be a nice thing for you and Mum to do it together."

"I don't want women doing stuff to my body when I die. My husband can do it."

"Don't be silly, you won't mind, you'll be dead."

"And I don't want to see Issy."

"It's just Issy's body, she isn't there anymore."

"I know. That's why I don't want to see her."

"It's just an empty shell. There's nothing to worry about. There's nothing scary about your sister's body."

"But I don't—"

"OK, OK. It's fine. Don't worry about it."

"I would, Dad," she said, trying to be generous in victory, "it's just—"

"No, it's not a problem. Don't worry. I'll sort something else out."

Dad picked the *Church Handbook* off the bookcase and started thumbing through the pages, his lips moving as he read stuff in his head. "I suppose I *could* go with your mum."

"That's a good idea," she said.

"I just thought that she might prefer it if you . . ."

His words dangled like a fishhook. Zippy pretended to examine her thumbnail and then scratched a pretend itch on her arm.

"Your mum's very upset." Dad sighed and flicked through more pages of the *Handbook*. "When Jesus died his friends went to the tomb to prepare his body for burial. Of course, when they got there, it was empty, but I think their intentions were clear. And I've always thought it was such a kind thing to do."

"I've never thought about it."

"I think it's what a true friend would do."

"Yeah, maybe."

"I imagine Jesus was extremely grateful."

"Yeah."

" 'Inasmuch as ye have done it unto the least of these my brethren, ye have done it unto me.' "

Dad didn't say anything else. He just put the *Handbook* back on the bookcase and left the room. But his meaning was quite clear. If she didn't go with Mum, she wouldn't be a true friend to Issy, and she would have to live with her unkindness forever.

THE FRONT BIT of the funeral directors' was like an office. A woman sat behind a desk wearing a suit and typing on a keyboard as if she was just doing an ordinary job in a building that wasn't full of dead people.

"Please sit down while I get things ready," she said. Then she picked up a phone and said, "The Bradleys are here." She didn't get anything ready. She just carried on typing with her clicky nails.

Mum sat down on the edge of a chair. She had a big shopping bag, which she put on her lap.

"What's in the bag?"

Mum opened it wide so Zippy could see inside: a little pile of clothes, a pair of shoes, Issy's patchwork blanket, the CD player from the kitchen, and several CD cases.

"We're going to have music?"

"Some people like it."

"You've done it before?"

"A few times. But the sisters were all old."

"Do nonmembers do it?"

"Dress the dead? I don't know. I don't think so. It's mostly to do with Temple clothes I think, with not letting nonmembers see them. And it's a last act of service for the person who's died. I'm sure you don't think about dying, I didn't when I was your age, but if you just try to imagine it, it's nice to think that when you die people who love you, not strangers, will take care of your body."

Zippy glanced at Mum's body. It was a bit baggy, slightly droopy in places, and she knew she never wanted to see it naked or look after it when it was dead. She gestured at the woman who was staring at her computer screen as her fingers went clickety-click, click.

"Why can't *she* just do it? Isn't it part of her job?"

Mum looked at the woman too. The woman's nails were long and straight with sharp edges and painted with sparkly purple polish.

"I wouldn't want her touching Issy."

They didn't say anything else to each other for a bit and Zippy started to feel fidgety and awkward. Eventually Mum said, "Did you have a nice day?"

Zippy pulled the sleeves of her school sweater over her hands before sitting on them. Her day had been all right. She was beginning to get used to the pitying looks and the barely concealed curiosity.

A door opened and a man in a suit stepped into the reception area. He had a swirl of white hair that curled around his head like a Mr. Whippy ice cream. He looked very serious, his hands were clasped, and he did a funny little bow.

"If you'd like to come through now," he said.

Mum sprang off her chair and Zippy followed. On the other side of the door, things were different. There was a long, green-carpeted corridor flanked by gold curtains that were pulled across partitioned segments, like a posh changing room. Zippy wondered whether there were dead people in all of the cubicles or if they kept them in a big fridge somewhere and just wheeled them out when their relatives came to visit. The man stopped by one of the curtains and did the funny bow again. Then he pulled it back a little and extended one arm. Mum stepped in first. Zippy hesitated but the man bowed and gestured again, so she followed Mum into the little cubicle.

There wasn't a window. The walls were painted yellow and decorated with a couple of old-fashioned pictures of angels in thick golden frames. The angels had wings, which made Zippy feel annoyed—angels are resurrected humans and humans don't have wings. A tablelike stand leaned against the right wall. It was covered in a long white cloth and Issy's coffin lay on top of it. The coffin didn't have a lid, which surprised Zippy because she'd imagined that it would be propped open, like in *Dracula*. The funeral directors had covered Issy with a white blanket, and from her position by the curtain Zippy couldn't see anything except the spread of Issy's hair, which made her knees wobble. She looked at the yellow walls and the green carpet and the shopping bag in Mum's hand instead.

"Take as long as you wish," the man said to Mum. Then he bowed one last time, closed the curtain, and disappeared.

. . .

"I'M GOING TO remove the stomach now," Mr. McLean announces. He pokes around the frog's insides with the tweezers and scissors. When he pulls the stomach out, he holds it up like a prize. It's prawny, a sort of tiny fetus, and a tube attached to its end curls like a little tail.

"Look at *this,* everyone."

People laugh. A couple of the lads say daft things like, "Whoa, nice stomach," and a girl giggles and says, "I'm not looking, sir, I can't look."

Zippy doesn't want to look either, but she can't help it. Mr. McLean's tweezers remind her of chopsticks and the stomach dangles from them like something meaty from a tub of fried rice. Her own stomach clenches and she runs a hand across her forehead to check for sweat. It's moist and cool and she pulls the sleeve of her school sweater down past her fingers before making a second wipe. She shouldn't have spent so long on the Internet last night; she knew she'd regret it later, but she hadn't been able to stop herself.

When they got back from the funeral directors', she wanted to know exactly what had happened to Issy. There'd been no point in asking Dad, he'd have only said, "What do you need to know that for?" and she couldn't bring herself to ask Mum, so she asked Wiki instead. The brain in the autopsy picture appeared to be wearing a polo neck of skin. She learned that the skin is cut along the crown and rolled back over the face. She tried to imagine Issy with her scalp inside out, and couldn't. She read that a cut is made from the middle of the neck to the pubic bone. The major blood vessels are sliced open and inspected, and the chest cavity is emptied of organs, which are then weighed, bagged, and, once the cavity has been lined with cotton, placed back inside, in a big jumble. When she'd finished reading, she turned off the computer, trudged upstairs, and cried herself to sleep.

"Ready for a testicle?" Mr. McLean asks.

The boys groan in unison and Mr. McLean gives a sympathetic

laugh. He rummages in the frog's torso for a moment and retrieves a bright orange thing about the size of a baked bean.

"There you go," he says. "Have a good look at that."

He leans across his desk and presents the testicle for the students in the front row to inspect. Zippy wipes her forehead again and breathes deeply and slowly.

MUM PUT THE bag on the floor and lifted the CD player out. She opened a case and crouched to place the disc in the player. She selected "Dearest Children, God Is Near You." Then she stood up and held out her hand.

Zippy's feet felt like they were stuck to the green carpet and she couldn't move for a moment, but then she took a step, and another, and another until she was standing next to Mum. She felt raw and shivery. She didn't want to touch Mum, but it seemed mean not to and so she held Mum's dry hand and they stood side by side for a little while, not saying anything. Zippy stared at Issy's face; she didn't look peaceful and she didn't look asleep. She looked like a badly made model of herself, empty of all her Issy-ness. She looked really dead.

"Right. OK." Mum unfastened their hands and took a deep breath, as if she were getting ready to start a race, or dive off a high board. "Let's get rid of the blanket and then we can get her dressed."

Mum's fingers trembled as she lifted the blanket. Zippy thought about suggesting that they go home and let the funeral people do it instead, but she knew Mum would say no.

Issy was wearing her Cinderella nightie.

"I brought her undershirt and knickers over earlier, while you were at school, and I asked if they'd put them on her," Mum said. "So don't worry, we don't have to see where they did the . . . you know." She folded the funeral directors' blanket in half and in half again, then placed it on the floor.

"Right, I'm going to get her nightie off." She bent down, rummaged in the bag, and pulled out a pair of scissors.

"You mean you're going to cut it off with the *kitchen scissors?*"

"I can't get it off by myself. And I think you're going to struggle to help, aren't you?"

Zippy nodded.

"That's why I brought the scissors."

When Mum started cutting the nightie, Zippy stepped back toward the curtain so she didn't have to watch. A new hymn started, "Lead Kindly Light," one of her favorites, a hymn full of lovely words like "encircling" and "garish."

"You like this one, don't you?" Mum said as she put the scissors on the floor next to the white blanket. "Why don't you sing along? Issy would like that."

Zippy didn't feel as if she had much choice; she had to do something. While she sang, she watched Mum lift Issy's arms and pull the nightie away. Everything was OK until the last lines of the hymn; when she sang about the smiling angel faces, her voice went all wobbly, and by the time she reached the bit about being *"lost a while,"* she was crying properly—noisy sobs that bounced off her diaphragm and bumped against the yellow walls and curtains. Within moments, Mum was doing it too and Zippy hoped that the man with the swirly hair and the woman with the clicky nails couldn't hear them.

"Oh, dear," Mum said with a juddering sob she tried to turn into a laugh. "This isn't going well, is it? You don't have to sing. No more singing. Tell you what, why don't you pass Issy's clothes to me?" She pulled a tissue out of her pocket and blew her nose while Zippy wiped her eyes with the sleeves of her school sweater.

Mum had packed a blue Sunday dress, frilly ankle socks, a flowery hairband, and Issy's best shoes—black patent with embroidered flowers. Zippy got them out of the bag and arranged them in a little pile.

"What about her glasses?"

"I've decided to keep them."

"But . . ."

"Go on."

"I was going to say she won't be able to see."

"I thought so too, but I've decided to keep them anyway." Zippy handed the dress to Mum, who unfastened the buttons, then picked up the scissors and positioned them inside the back of the waistband.

"Oh. Don't cut it."

"It'll be tricky to lift and dress her at the same time. Don't worry, it's OK, it doesn't matter."

Of course it mattered. Zippy had a horrible vision of Issy coming forth on the morning of the first resurrection with a dissected dress and her knickers showing.

"I'll help," she offered.

Mum put the scissors down. "Are you sure? You don't have to."

"No, I will."

Mum scrunched the dress until it was shaped like a ring doughnut. She handed it to Zippy and then she stood at the head of the coffin. "I'm going to lift Issy and you need to put the dress over her head."

Mum raised Issy's head and shoulders. Zippy had expected Issy's head to flop forward, but it didn't. She seemed very solid, as if all her softness had leaked out. Zippy looped the ring of dress around Issy's head, then let go quickly so she didn't have to touch her. A strip of black stitching ran across Issy's crown like a hairband.

"Don't worry about that," Mum said. "We'll cover it up in a minute. Why don't you get the socks and I'll sort this out?"

Zippy picked up the socks while Mum pulled the dress down to Issy's waist and drew the sleeve holes up her arms. She rolled Issy slightly onto her side and asked Zippy to fasten the buttons. Zippy's fingers went all fumbly as she did the job, and even though the undershirt stopped her from touching Issy's bare skin, she could sense the coldness beneath.

Mum straightened the skirt of Issy's dress and took the socks from Zippy. She lifted Issy's feet and slipped the socks on. Issy's legs looked blotchy and cold, a shade of purply-yellow Zippy couldn't name. They were still spattered with red spots and her little fingers were burgundy. Zippy passed the hairband to Mum, who put it directly over the incision on Issy's head.

Mum did the shoes next and then she asked Zippy to pass the patchwork blanket from home. Mum folded the blanket in half and placed it over Issy. It came right up to her chin. Then Mum tucked her in.

Issy looked better under her own blanket but Zippy was disappointed that she didn't look more like herself. Mum put her arm around Zippy and they stood there and listened to the music for a bit.

"One last song," Mum said, and she knelt next to the almost-empty bag, changed the CD, and returned to Zippy's side. They listened as the choir sang "God Be with You Till We Meet Again." When the song finished they were both crying, but this time the tears were leaky rather than noisy and it was easier to stop.

"Should we say a prayer or something before we go?"

"Probably," Mum said.

Zippy closed her eyes and waited.

"But I don't feel like it, so you can if you want."

She opened her eyes and stared at Mum. "Don't you think we should do it properly?"

"Go on, if you like."

"I don't know what to say."

"Neither do I."

Zippy said the prayer. But Mum didn't fold her arms or bow her head, and Zippy was pretty certain she didn't bother to close her eyes either, which made the prayer rubbish. It just sounded like a string of empty words.

After the prayer, Zippy picked up the CD player and put it back in the bag.

"I don't want to leave her here by herself all weekend," Mum said. "Do you think they'll let us bring her home?"

"No."

"I bet they would. People used to do it in the olden days."

"No, Mum."

"They did. They used to take family pictures with the dead person."

"I mean, no I don't think she should come home."

"I'm going to ask them," Mum said.

She swished the curtain back and hurried down the green carpet in search of the funny man with the white hair and Zippy chased after her because she didn't want to be by herself with Issy's body.

The bell rings for second period and Mr. McLean discards the testicle and dives back into the frog's torso. This time he emerges with something that resembles a skinny, coiled earthworm.

"The small intestine," he says as the gut swings from his tweezers.

Zippy's stomach scrunches several times in quick succession and she knows if she doesn't get out of the lab right now, she will throw up all over Mr. McLean's desk.

"Can I be excused, sir?"

"Are you OK, Zippy?" The intestine wobbles as he speaks.

"I'm just a bit—"

"Go and get some fresh air."

She pushes through the crowd of Year Elevens, looking at the floor, at the mishmash of black school shoes, not wanting to make eye contact with anyone who might either laugh or feel sorry for her. She shoves the lab door open and hurries down the corridor to the double-door exit.

Outside, she leans against the wall of the building and knocks back long swallows of fresh air. *Breathe in, breathe out.* She already feels a little better. *Breathe in.* A group of Year Sevens pass on their way to a science lesson. *Breathe out.* Some sixth-formers stroll by, heading for the sports hall. She walks over to the raised flower beds and sits on the corner of a planter. Several of Adam's friends approach, lugging heavy sports bags; they're laughing, but they quiet down when they see her and nod respectfully as they pass. Then Adam appears, bag bumping against his thigh as he jogs to catch up. He slows when he notices her and stops for a moment.

"All right?"

"Yeah."

"Good. So what're you doing here, then?"

"Just getting some fresh air."

"Right." He shuffles from one foot to the other. "And you're all right?"

"Yeah," she says again.

"I was going to send you a card."

She nods as if she knows, and briefly wonders whether he would have written "*love* from Adam," or just signed his name.

"You weren't at Youth Night on Wednesday."

"I didn't feel like coming so Mum said I didn't have to."

"I just . . . I hoped you were OK."

She attempts a smile to show she was fine and ends up pulling a face that demonstrates she wasn't.

He puts his bag down and sits on the planter beside her. She shuffles to make more space but he rests a settling hand on her arm and she observes the bones and veins hiding under his skin.

"Maybe you should go back to class? Then you won't be by yourself."

"Yeah, maybe."

"It might take your mind off stuff—better than sitting out here, thinking."

"It might."

"Good."

He slips his hand into hers and squeezes. She lifts their knotted fingers and brushes his skin against her cheek; he's warm and full of life and doesn't seem to mind her borrowing his hand for a moment.

"I'd better go."

She relinquishes his hand so he can stand and pick up his bag and then she watches his body as he jogs away. It's weird that he is made up of skin and muscle and strings of blood vessels; and it's *horrible* that one day he will die and someone might have to open him up and catalog his pieces. Does everyone look the same on the inside? It's impossible to know—it's not as if you can turn your gaze inward to follow the hairpin bends of brain tissue or stare at your sinuses.

There's no way she is going back to biology. She hopes Mr. McLean doesn't come out to see if she's all right; she doesn't want to talk to anyone, not even Lauren, not properly. When they meet up at break time she'll get Lauren chatting about Jordan Banks, that'll take up the whole twenty minutes, easily. She can't talk about this to anyone. Touching dead bodies is weird and even people at church would think it's strange to keep one in your house.

The old man with the swirly hair thought it was weird.

"Why don't you go home and have a talk to your family about it?" he suggested.

"It'd just be for the weekend," Mum said, "so she's not by herself. You can pick her up on Monday, when you come for us, before the funeral."

The man said it was something to think about. Mum nodded and pretended to consider it but Zippy could tell she'd already made up her mind.

The thing is—people are more than their bodies. Zippy isn't sure about the mechanics of it, but when Issy climbed out of herself, she didn't leave anything behind, she took all the bits that made her *her*—what's left is empty and bringing it home is pointless.

– 9 –

Miracle Boy

There are so many kinds of never. There's the never Mum uses when she says, "Never talk to strangers; it's dangerous," and there's the never Dad uses when he says, "Never play with your food; it's bad manners." But Mum talks to plenty of people she doesn't know, and Jacob has seen Dad break Oreos in half to lick the creamy bit.

Issy used to say, "I'll never be friends with you again if you don't play with me." But she didn't mean it. And sometimes she said, "I'll never eat sprouts." She did mean this, and if Mum is right, and death is definitely the end of being alive, Issy will absolutely *never* eat sprouts. However, Jacob has noticed something. "Never" is a word that doesn't always mean not-on-your-life and absolutely-no-way. Sometimes "never" means "not yet."

The house is full of sadness. It's packed into every crevice and corner like snow. There are bottomless drifts of it beside Issy's bean-bag chair in the living room. The sadness gives Jacob the shivers and he takes refuge in the garden. Like the house, it is higgledy and un-kempt. The lawn is scuffed and threadbare in places. Overgrown flower beds stream along the length of each of the old red-brick garden walls, all the way to the far wall, which is partially con-cealed by a hornbeam hedge. Randomly planted apple trees poke out of the lawn like twisted, witchy hands and clusters of green fruit cling to bent branches that are already almost bare of leaves. Wind-falls pepper the grass and Jacob kicks them as he makes his way to the end of the garden. Some of the fallen apples are rotten and they detonate, spraying pulp and larvae. Others are hard and thwack on contact like tennis balls.

Last year, Mum supervised an apple-picking operation before the trees dropped their fruit. There were bags and bags full. Mum took lots of the bags to church and Dad made an announcement in Sacrament Meeting that anyone who wanted a bag of apples could come and get one from the car trunk afterward. Lots of people wanted free apples. Mum passed them out and said, "You're welcome" a lot. She wrapped the apples that she didn't give away in newspaper and put them in empty shoeboxes in the cupboard under the stairs. When she opened up the boxes several months later, the apples were pink and yellow, and soft. "I had no idea this would happen," she kept saying, as if it was the most incredible thing she'd ever seen. She made everyone come and look. It *was* a surprise that the apples weren't Brussels-sprout green and sour anymore, but Mum said it was miraculous.

This year, Mum hasn't bothered. No one has bothered. Even the trees themselves seem to be fed up with balancing fruit in their knobbly branches, and there are so many fallen apples to kick that it takes Jacob a long time to reach the end of the garden. When he gets there he stares at the hedge, which is covered in crispy leaves that look like giant bran flakes. A few of them have fallen off, but he knows most of them will cling on through the rest of the autumn and into the winter. He knows this because last winter he and Issy played unseen in the gap between the hedge and the wall, hidden from view by the screen of lingering leaves.

It was Issy who found the dead bird. Most of it was under the hedge, but one of its wings lay on the lawn, spread out in a feathery fan. It had probably been killed by next door's cat. Issy picked the wing up. Jacob opened his mouth then closed his lips over the words he had been about to say:

"Put it down, it's unhygienic" was a sentence that belonged to Dad. Besides, he was suddenly keen to touch the wing himself. The feathers were shiny blue-black, and he had to know if they were both as sharp and as soft as they looked. Issy passed the wing to him and he touched the feathers with his eyes closed. They were soft and fluffy at the tips and coarse and strong at the base, where the shafts were thicker.

They buried the bird and its wing behind the hedge. They dug a hole with two plastic beach shovels from the garden shed. Jacob put the bird in the hole. One of its black eyes stared blankly at the sky.

"Don't get soil in the birdie's eye," Issy said.

"We have to do it properly," he replied. Although it was the first burial he had ever attended, he was pretty certain it wouldn't count if he left part of the bird peeping out from under the soil. "Why don't you say a prayer?" he suggested.

Issy prayed. She said the prayer that they all said at every mealtime, saying "bird" instead of "food." She said it quickly, like they did when they were hungry and didn't want to wait. "Dear Heavenly Father. Thank you for the bird. Please bless it. In the name of Jesus Christ, Amen."

Jacob covered the bird with soil, which he patted down with the back of his shovel. They stood in the gap between the wall and the hedge for a few moments, flanked by dark red brick and brittle hornbeam leaves.

"I think we should sing a song," Issy said.

"OK," he replied. "What song?"

"One about birdies."

"OK." He tried to think of a song about birds. " 'In the Leafy Treetops' has got some birds in it."

"No." Issy smoothed the bird's grave with the tip of her sneaker. "A good one."

"I don't know." He'd had enough. He was ready to do something else. Then Issy started to sing.

We will find a little nest in the branches of a tree.
Let us count the eggs inside; there are one, two, three.

Mother bird sits on the nest to hatch the eggs all three.
Father bird flies round and round to guard his family.

Jacob gave her a brief round of applause.

"Do you think that it was a mummy birdie or a daddy birdie?" Issy asked as they pushed themselves out from behind the hedge and onto the lawn.

"We could have checked for a willy," he said, "but it's too late now. Maybe it was a child bird."

"Oh." She looked surprised. "That *would* be sad."

JACOB THINKS HE can remember the spot where they buried the bird. At first he isn't sure if he will do anything. He stands next to the hedge, daring himself. Then he dashes back to the shed quickly, as if he is worried that something might stop him from fetching the shovel.

Spade in hand, he pushes through the hard and scratchy crisscross weave of branches and into the space between the wall and the hedge. He starts to dig. Nothing at first. He moves along a bit, his elbow grazing the wall. He disturbs more soil and he can suddenly smell clay and damp and he stops digging for a moment as he remembers.

HE DIDN'T WANT to go to the funeral. Mum was upset when he said this. As he had expected, the funeral was just more church, different from Sundays only in that they had to sit in the front row, except for Dad, who sat up on the stand as usual so he could do the service. There was an opening and a closing prayer, there were some hymns, and Dad did a talk about not being sad while tears coursed down Mum's face and sprinkled into her lap, watering her hands.

Afterward everyone drove to the cemetery. There was a deep hole in the ground. When Jacob asked about it later, Dad said it had been dug by a mechanical digger. Someone had arranged a fake grass carpet over the pile of earth that had been dug up, and Jacob stood on a corner of it, scratching the soles of his shoes along its prickles.

Dad, Al, and two of the funeral men carried the coffin from the car to the graveside. When they put it down on two planks of wood that had been placed over the hole, Mum started to make a noise. Zippy rested her hand on Mum's arm but Mum didn't stop. Dad moved away from the coffin and went to stand next to Mum. He put his arm around her shoulder and the noise continued. It was a bit like a dog howling and it sent a zigzag of fear from Jacob's heart to his willy. A squirt of wee leaked into his pants and spread in a warm circle. Dad shushed Mum but she wouldn't stop so he fished in his suit pocket and pulled out a handkerchief. He stuffed it in Mum's hand. She just stood there, so he lifted her hand and held it over her mouth for her. Eventually he let go and Mum carried on holding the handkerchief over her mouth, but the noise leaked past its edges.

Dad had to say a prayer to dedicate the grave. He said it loudly so people could hear him over Mum. It went on for a while, and Jacob wished he would hurry up. After Dad finally finished, the funeral men made the coffin go down. Someone walked up and threw a handful of soil into the hole and Mum stopped making the noise, moved the handkerchief away from her mouth, and said, "*Don't* do that."

People left quickly. Dad said Mum should say thank you to everyone. She said she was going to see them all again in a few minutes for the food, back at the chapel, but she walked with Dad toward the parked cars anyway.

Jacob moved off the plastic grass and onto the real stuff. He edged toward the hole. Issy's coffin was a long way down and it was spattered with dirt. He knelt at the lip of the grave. The earth was damp, and he could feel wet soaking into the knees of his best trousers.

He had been hoping for a miracle. Sister Anderson was always going on about them on Sundays in Primary lessons. Some miracles happened a long time ago, like Noah's Ark. Not many people seem to have thought about it, but once when he couldn't sleep, Jacob had imagined how much poo the animals must have made and how much trouble it must have been for Noah to stop them all from eating one another. It had made him realize that Noah's Ark was an ace miracle, right up there with Santa Claus's flying sleigh. There were other good miracles from the olden days, like the Feeding of the Five Thousand, Daniel in the Lions' Den, and Balaam and the Talking Ass—a miracle with a rude word in it. Dad was always saying that miracles happen all the time. Sister Anderson thought so too. She said that Brother Anderson's cancer treatment was proving to be a modern-day miracle. Maybe she was right, but Brother Anderson's head looked like an enormous egg, and Jacob had been imagining a much bigger miracle than that for Issy: one that would see her alive AND with hair.

His underpants and knees were wet and cold, and a damp, sticky smell was wafting out of the hole in the ground. It reminded him of the bag of modeling clay that Mrs. Slade kept on the side, next to the sink, in the school classroom. He looked at the soil speckles on the coffin's little silver plaque. It read, *Isabel Rachael Bradley*. He couldn't understand why anyone would want to throw dirt on Issy.

Sister Anderson crouched down next to him. "It's very sad, isn't it?" she said.

"It was meningitis," he told her.

Mum had made him say the word again and again.

"People will ask, so you must learn how to say it," she said.

He practiced until it stopped sounding like a sticky-eye infection—"mengy-eye-tus"—and started to sound more like "men-ingiantis," a band of giants who had magicked Issy into the Celestial Kingdom.

"Are you all right, dear?" Sister Anderson asked.

He wanted to say he was fine, he wanted to tell her to go away, but his bottom lip began to wobble and it wouldn't stop, even when he bit it quite hard. Sister Anderson helped him to his feet. She folded her arms around him and pulled him into her squashy tummy. Her dress was dark and velvety. His tears soaked into its softness as she patted his head gently and said, "It's such a shame."

When he had finished crying he stepped away from her and a rope of snot stretched from his nose to the front of her dress, like a bridge.

JACOB UNEARTHS A feather and knows that he is in the right spot. The feather is matted and patchy, which is disappointing, but he keeps digging. As he digs he thinks about the apples, hiding in old shoeboxes in the cupboard under the stairs. He knows that like the apples, the bird will look different when it is uncovered and he hopes the transformation will be a good one.

There are more feathers, though most of them are not feathery anymore. He digs especially carefully now. He has seen an enormous book on Egypt in the school library. There is a section about digging stuff up. There are pictures of the tiny brushes people use so as not to damage anything. The corner of his spade grazes something hard. Jacob puts it down and begins to move the soil away with his fingers. Here is the bird's back—he follows its knobbles, brushing the dirt away. The bird is mostly bones. This is not the transformation he has been hoping for. The bird's insides, and most of its outsides, have melted into the soil. Its skeleton is a browny-gray color. It's hard, but brittle, like crisps. He wipes soil from the bird's wing-twigs, which, stripped of feathers, look like dirty icicles. Lastly, he moves the soil away from the bird's skull. The eye has gone. In its place is a hole that seems far too big. His finger may even fit inside. It does.

BEFORE ISSY DIED, Mum used to read a fairy tale each night from the old, fat book that she had been given as a present when she was a little girl. Afterward she would get the Bible and the Book of Mormon picture books out and read a story from one of them too. Jacob's favorite fairy tale used to be "The Wolf and the Seven Goats."

The best bit was the part where the mother goat opened up the wolf, and her kids tumbled out of his big furry belly. "The Wolf and the Seven Goats" is just made up. But the story of Jonah and the Whale is a real-life miracle. Jonah got stuck in a whale and survived. In the Bible and the Book of Mormon there are even better stories than Jonah's, stories about people who died and came back to life, like the story of Lazarus. Jacob remembers it because there's a bit where Lazarus is *so* dead Martha says, "He stinketh," and after they read it, Mum occasionally said, "Who stinketh?" when someone farted. There's the story of Jairus's daughter too. Everyone thought she was dead and people were crying but Jesus told Jairus to believe; and when they reached the house there'd been a miracle and the girl wasn't dead anymore, she was just sleeping. *"With God all things are possible"*—that's what it says on Mum's painting of a bird with its wings spread wide in flight on the kitchen wall. Miracles are like birds, they zip through the gap between heaven and earth on hollow-boned wings. You can't catch them with traps or nets or special glue, you have to use words.

Before the funeral, the men brought Issy home in their special car. They put her in the living room and Mum sat with her for hours and hours. When Mum went to the bathroom, Jacob snuck in all by himself and stood on the arm of the sofa to have a proper look. Issy didn't look as much like herself as he had expected; she seemed smaller and a different color. He kissed her, whispered, "Wake up," and waited, but nothing happened.

After the funeral, Jacob asked Dad why he hadn't tried to resurrect Issy. Dad said that priesthood holders can't just go around resurrecting everyone. He said Heavenly Father decides if people live or die. Jacob replied that it wasn't always like that—sometimes people believed and then miracles happened. Dad said it was true, but not in Issy's case. He said, "Ours is not to question why." He said, "Sometimes believing things will turn out all right in the end is a better kind of faith than the faith that raises people from the dead."

Jacob felt cross. "So it's *all right in the end* for Issy to be dead?"

he asked. "Didn't you even try to make a miracle happen? What's the point of being in charge at church if you can't do miracles?"

Dad said he would understand it better when he was older. But Jacob understood something right then. If he wanted Issy back, he was going to have to make it happen himself.

THE BIRD'S EYE socket rings the tip of Jacob's finger. He has been praying for the bird to come back to life for a whole week. It seemed sensible to start with something little, with a small miracle, for practice.

Sister Anderson once said that faith can be as small as a seed. She brought some mustard seeds to Primary for everyone to see. They were tiny. Jacob knows that his faith is bigger than a mustard seed; it's at least as big as a toffee bonbon, maybe bigger.

He lifts his finger away from the bird's eye socket and picks up the spade to rebury it. Then he thinks. He needs to check on the bird again, maybe more than once. Each time he will have to dig it up and, if nothing has changed, bury it. As the autumn sets into winter there will be days when it is raining and days when the ground is stiff with frost. It will be much easier if he can find a safe place to put the bird.

He pushes his fingers into the soil on each side of the bird's chest and lifts gently. The head is the first thing to fall off, followed by the wing that the cat didn't damage. He is left holding a little cage of ribs and as he lifts a finger to support the spindly, dangling legs, they break off too. He thinks he might cry as a rush of salty prickles gather at the top of his nose, but he doesn't. He puts the ribs down and pulls the bottom of his T-shirt out with one hand. Then he picks the little pieces of bird up, one at a time, and drops them into his makeshift pocket. He bends to sniff the soily bones. They smell of earth. They definitely don't stinketh.

He doesn't kick any apples on his way back up the garden. If he is lucky, he will get up to his room without being noticed. Dad, Zippy, and Alma have gone to Liverpool to get the chapel ready for

General Conference. It's Mum he needs to watch out for. On Saturdays she usually cleans. According to the song they sing in Primary, "Saturday is the day we get ready for Sunday," and Mum always says that Sundays are easier to face with a clean house. But today she might just be sitting at the table in the kitchen, wet-cheeked and dribbly-nosed, staring at nothing.

Jacob approaches stealthily, ready to duck if necessary, but he can see through the window that the kitchen is empty. He opens the door, then sneaks past the kitchen table and past all the vases and jam jars stuffed with smelly flowers. He tiptoes down the hall and turns to climb the stairs. He is halfway up when he hears the toilet flush. He has to pass the bathroom door to reach his bedroom. He starts to run. The bird pieces jiggle in his T-shirt. He hears the rush of the taps and the clink of the towel ring as Mum dries her hands. He is quick. His door closes as the bathroom door opens, and he listens to Mum pad slowly down the stairs as he kneels on the carpet, behind the door, his heart jumping.

He isn't sure where to put the bird. Mum will be certain to find it if he puts it in the wardrobe. He could hide it in the bottom of Issy's toy box, but touching her stuff makes him sad. He shuffles across the carpet on his knees until he reaches the bed. He places the bird pieces on the floor and then lies down on his tummy and commando-crawls under the bottom bunk. Under the bed he discovers a couple of plastic soldiers who have deserted and one of Issy's books that must have slipped down the side of her bunk. He moves the book and the soldiers out from under the bed, and then he carefully deposits the bird bits in the far corner.

After he crawls out from under the bed, he kneels again. He folds his arms, bows his head, and says a prayer.

"Dear Heavenly Father. I have faith that you can resurrect the bird. This is a real prayer. It's not like asking for a bike or something, it's important. When you resurrect the bird, I will have even more faith. And then there can be even better miracles. In the name of Jesus Christ, Amen."

As he gets to his feet, there's a knock at the door. Mum's head appears, followed by her body and the vacuum cleaner.

"It's Saturday," she says as she moves one of the toy boxes with her foot, in search of the wall plug. *The day we get ready for Sunday.*" She sings part of the Primary song to him, trying to get him to join in.

He doesn't. He picks the soldiers and Issy's book off the floor, climbs the ladder to his bunk, and waits for the scream of the vacuum cleaner. But Mum pauses for a moment.

"Would you . . . do you think we should . . . are Issy's things *bothering* you?"

"Not really," he fibs, his tummy clenching as he stares down at the orphaned jumble of Duplos, dolls, and ponies with bright nylon hair. If he tells the truth, Mum might throw them all away; and then Issy won't have anything to play with when she comes back.

Mum's voice jellies around her words as she says, "We could sort them out, if you like."

"Don't cry," he says quickly.

"I wasn't . . ." She wipes a hand over her face, as if to make sure.

"Good. Leave Issy's things. It's OK. She might want them back—"

"Jacob, I've told you, we won't see her again until—"

"After she's resurrected, she might want them back," he explains cunningly. "Everyone gets resurrected at the end of the world. Dad said so."

Mum lets out a big puff of air. "That's a long way off."

"You never know," he says in a grown-up voice.

She chuckles at his imitation of her and switches on the machine. He watches as she pushes it back and forth, mowing the carpet. She unclips the wiggler attachment and worms it into the gap between the toy boxes. It sucks along the baseboard, uncurling and stretching like an elephant's trunk.

Then she kneels down. And Jacob suddenly feels marooned on

the top deck of the bunk, the captain of a vessel that is rapidly approaching Niagara Falls.

"Haven't you finished?" His question pierces the vacuum cleaner's greedy moan like a rescue shout.

"I'm just going to do under the bed," she calls up to him. "Goodness knows when I last did it."

She kneels on the floor and thrusts the wiggler about as if she is trying to capsize him.

"You don't have to do it today," he exclaims.

There's a sound like the clatter of homemade shakers filled with uncooked rice and pasta, and his stomach sways as the bird bones rattle up the wiggler. He wants to launch himself off the top bunk and body-slam the vacuum cleaner like a professional wrestler, but he sits still as it sucks up his hope.

"Have you got some Legos under here?" Mum starts to lie down on the floor to get a proper look under the bed.

"No," he shouts down to her. "I think it must be some . . . rubbish."

She gets up and switches the machine off.

"I'll check for Legos when I empty it later, just to make sure." She clips the wiggler down, unplugs the cord, and closes the door on her way out.

Jacob stays on his bunk for a bit, looking down at the room. Mum will probably forget to check the bag, which means he's not likely to get into trouble. That's good; it's something to feel happy about. He tries to feel happy. He pushes his cheeks up with his fingers and lifts his face into a smile but his mouth pops open and a small sob spills out. He is disappointed to find himself so far from happy. He pulls back the duvet, lies down on his tummy, and buries his head in the pillow. A series of sobs shake out of him and rattle into the pillow, grazing the back of his throat like tiny bones.

Eventually he climbs down the ladder. With God all things are possible. God helps those who help themselves and He loves a tryer:

If at first you don't succeed, try, try again. Remembering all this about God makes Jacob feel ever-so-slightly better. He drops the stray soldiers in his toy box but he keeps hold of the book that was under the bed. It's the story of Jack and the beanstalk. He opens it to the middle page, which is a special fold-out picture of the beanstalk, its tip hidden by clouds. He knows that "Jack and the Beanstalk" is not a miracle. It's just a fairy tale. No one could get some magic beans. It could *never* happen: absolutely-no-way. Fairy-tale nevers are not the kind of nevers that Jacob is looking for. He is in search of nevers that can be slipped under, scaled, or tiptoed around. But even though he knows that fairy-tale nevers are impossible to bend, he wishes he had a beanstalk. He wishes Sister Anderson would bring magic beans to Primary instead of mustard seeds. He wishes he could plant the magic beans at the bottom of the garden, behind the hedge, and watch an enormous stalk twist and stretch skyward. And even though Dad says heaven is not actually in the sky, he wishes he could climb the stalk right up into the clouds and find Issy. That would be ace.

— 10 —

Yer Ma

Normal people are heading to Liverpool to watch the Derby but Al, Dad, and Zippy are on a cleaning mission, bombing down the dock road toward the chapel, which must be spick-and-span before General Conference. Al doesn't see why they should clean the chapel. It's not as though they even live in Liverpool—they go there only for special meetings and activities that involve the whole area. There aren't any proper cleaners, which means everyone gets to share the *blessings of service*. It would be nice to have a break from the *blessings of service,* what with Issy and everything, but Dad says he can't ask people to clean the chapel if he doesn't also do it himself. Cleaning is a total waste of time—at four o'clock when the first of the General Conference broadcasts is relayed, the lights will be out. Everyone will watch the prophet on the giant screen and no one will know whether there're crumbs on the carpet or finger-prints on the glass bits of the doors.

It's boring in the car. Dad prefers the Tabernacle Choir to Radio 5 and Zippy's sitting in the front so there's no one to talk to. Al's got his iPod Shuffle with him but he's saving it for later. He's got only a few songs on it 'cause Dad does spot checks and deletes things that don't meet Church standards. He even deleted a load of songs by The Killers; it didn't make any difference when Al objected that Brandon Flowers is a member of the Church. In fact, according to Dad, it's worse for a member of the Church to write songs about smoking and taking girls' clothes off, as those who have received the greater light will receive greater condemnation for their sins.

"Where's your suit jacket, Alma?"

Al locks eyes with Dad in the car mirror. It's too late for them to turn back so he tells the truth. "I left it at home."

"Oh, Alma."

Dad shakes his head and pulls his disappointed face, the one with the tight dog's-arse lips. Al looks away. Sometimes he likes to imagine he was adopted and a dead ordinary relative is searching for him: someone who likes football, someone who hasn't thought about God since they were forced to say the Lord's Prayer in assembly. He glances back at the mirror and can't help picking at Dad's disappointment.

"We're *cleaning* the chapel, Dad. I'm not wearing my jacket to clean the chapel."

"No one's asking you to. You need it for later, for Conference. It's disrespectful to listen to the prophet without your jacket."

Al shrugs. His hoodie is scrunched up in his lap. Perhaps he'll wear it disrespectfully while the prophet speaks. He'll also wear it if he gets cold and if he gets a chance to sneak off. He'll use it to cover up his white shirt and tie so people don't think he's a weirdo wandering around Liverpool on Derby Day in his best clothes. Mum's money is stashed in the hoodie's zip-up pocket. It's been there since he borrowed it two weeks ago. He's definitely going to put it back, but he's waiting for the right moment. He rests his hand on the pocket and grasps the roll of notes through the material. Having the money makes him feel better. He's not got any plans to spend it, but just knowing that he could lifts his mood and counters the ache that's cased his stomach since Issy died.

THERE ARE ONLY half a dozen cars in the church parking lot. Al recognizes Brother and Sister Campbell's old Saab and President Carmichael's Jag; the others must belong to people from Liverpool. He watches as Zippy examines herself in the mirror—she's nuts if she thinks Adam has come with his dad; he's probably playing rugby for school. President Carmichael likes sports; he always takes the annual church Dads vs. Lads football match seriously, and he's one of the few dads who doesn't have to resort to leg-breaking tackles to keep up. In fact, last year President Carmichael scored a late equalizer for the Dads and when the ball hit the back of the net he removed his T-shirt and his garment top and swung them around his head while he ran the length of the sideline. Brother Stevens pumped the air and shouted, "Go, President!" in his loud American voice, but the spectating families went dead quiet. Mum was sitting on a picnic rug with Jacob and Issy; Al caught her smiling. Sister Campbell didn't find it funny, though; she pulled her braid over her eyes, and Dad just stood in the goal at the other end of the pitch, totally bewildered, as President Carmichael sprinted toward him, half-naked and whooping wildly. People aren't ever supposed to take their garments off unless they're having a bath or something, but President Carmichael didn't seem at all embarrassed at having broken the rules in front of everyone. He rolled his things back on and jogged to the center circle for the restart. He's definitely not the kind of man who would make his son miss out on sports to clean the chapel.

As they walk into the building, Al is gutted to hear the distant drone of the vacuum cleaner. Vacuuming has to be the least crappy of all the cleaning jobs. You can vacuum with your iPod on and everyone leaves you alone to get on with it. He watches as the appliance shoots into view at the far end of the long corridor, propelled by Sister Campbell, who is launching it at the baseboards, her braid swaying like a pendulum. Brother Campbell follows, waving a duster and a bottle of window spray.

"Alma Bradley, just the man!" Brother Campbell flicks the duster like a linesman's flag. "The men's toilets need a good clean. Sister Campbell was all set to do it, but I thought she should be saved from such an experience!"

Al watches Sister Campbell smash the Hoover into a small gap between several stacks of chairs. She is quite clearly not in need of being saved from anything.

"Go and have a look for some bleach in the cleaning cupboard. I'll come and help you in a minute." Brother Campbell waves the duster again as if to say, "Play on."

Al looks at Dad and considers protesting. Surely it's dangerous for kids to be in charge of bleach? Dad stares back, practically daring him to complain. They hold each other's gaze for a moment before Al capitulates. He ties his hoodie around his waist and they head for the cleaning cupboard.

The bleach is in a huge container, much bigger than the containers in the bathroom at home. Dad reaches and passes it to him.

"Don't get it on your clothes. I didn't think we'd be doing this sort of cleaning; we're not exactly dressed for it."

"I could do something else."

"Do what Brother Campbell says for the moment."

Al lugs the bleach to the men's toilets. They reek of pee and the floor is stained and wet around the urinal. He wonders if it's always this dirty; maybe he's noticing only because he's got to clean it up. He puts the bleach down next to the sink. He may as well pee before he cleans. He stands farther back than he should because of the wet patch, takes aim, and squirts on target. It's only as he's finishing that he joins everyone else who's stood back to avoid standing in the wet, and dribbles on the floor.

He washes his hands and waits for a moment. When Brother Campbell doesn't appear, he steps out into the corridor where he can hear the vacuum humming in the distance, probably on the parallel corridor that runs along the other side of the hall and chapel. He unties the hoodie from his waist and slides it over his head. The back door is still open. It would take only a few seconds to sprint to the end of the corridor and outside to freedom. He'll get in big trouble if he runs away, but what's worse, a major telling off or cleaning the toilets?

He runs. And when he passes through the open door he keeps running. He runs through the lot at the back of the building and out onto the street. He turns right and keeps running until he reckons he's gone far enough to safely stop. He's barely out of breath, pleased with himself and slightly surprised at his own daring. He's going to be in trouble, but when it comes down to it, all Dad's got is the disappointment speech and, having heard it so many times, Al is almost immune to its particular hurt.

He decides to walk straight down Queens Drive. That way, when he's had enough, he'll be able to turn round and retrace his steps. He walks past houses and a school and a small row of shops: laundromat, newsagent, Bargain Booze, and a betting shop. The betting shop is packed; people are probably betting on the match. He looks through the window at several televisions and wonders whether they'll show the footie later. He never gets to watch live football. Dad says TV extras are too expensive so Al has to settle for recording the highlights on *Match of the Day*. He'll return to the betting shop in a bit, after kickoff, to check on the score.

He carries on down Queens Drive until he reaches a big square of grass where some lads are having a kick-about. There's five of them, all wearing Everton shirts. A little lad with dark hair is the best player, the others are OK but he can tell they don't play regularly, they're probably here 'cause it's Derby Day. He sits on a graffitied bench and watches their game.

AL USED TO dream of being a professional footballer but right in the pit of his stomach, in the part that's so deep and airless a visiting canary would snuff it, he knows it's too late. He's missed his chance. It was only a small chance and probably wouldn't have come to anything, but still.

At first Dad thought football was a good idea. He said if the Devil made work for idle hands he'd probably got plans for idle feet too. Al trained with Sefton Rangers. Matty's dad, Steve, gave him lifts 'cause Dad was usually busy with church. Traveling with Steve was brilliant. He told jokes and called everyone *"mate"*; sometimes he farted in the car, shouted "Gas attack!" and made all the windows roll down at once. When Sefton Rangers started to play competitively, Steve drove Al to Saturday-morning matches. The first time they edged along the narrow track that led to the pitches at Hightown, it was like entering a different world. At the end of the track hundreds of cars were directed onto the corner of an enormous expanse of grass and sardined into tight rows. Al watched as parents, kids, and dogs burst out of the cars hauling wellies, umbrellas, and camping chairs. He'd never seen so many pitches, players, and parents; he realized he was part of something massive and it felt really good.

Dad came occasionally, when he didn't have to attend meetings or help with service projects, but he looked bored standing on the sideline. He didn't really talk to the other parents and he never cheered or shouted when Al set someone up or scored. At halftime, when the players were all swigging from their water bottles, Steve used to say, "Let me get you a tea, Ian, *mate*." And Dad, who's not really anyone's *mate*, would stand there awkwardly with his hands in his pockets and say, "No thanks. I don't drink tea." Al used to worry that Steve might ask, "Why not?"—a question that would give Dad the perfect excuse to do some missionary work by explaining about not drinking tea or coffee because of the Word of Wisdom. But Steve never asked, he just dashed down to the burger van so he didn't miss the start of the second half.

It was at the end of last season that Al was spotted. The Everton scout had come to look at another boy, but he noticed Al as well. Dad wasn't there, so the scout spoke to Steve and gave him the letter. Steve explained it all in the car on the drive home. Al had been invited to go to Finch Farm, the Everton training ground, so they could have a proper look at him and decide whether they were interested. Steve blathered all the way home, ricocheting between excitement and restraint. "It's the dog's bollocks, this is! I'm thrilled for you! Don't get your hopes up, though, eh? They're just having a look."

Later, when Dad read the letter, he said absolutely not. It was one thing playing football for a hobby, but it was another to consider it for a career. Football was absolutely not conducive to living the gospel.

And that was that.

After Sefton Rangers played their last match of the season, Dad said he couldn't afford to pay the registration fee anymore and Al knew he was stretching the definition of *"afford"* to include the cost of *the eternal consequences of football-related immorality*. The club wasn't insured for unregistered boys to play in league matches, but Al was still allowed to come to training. The new season started two weeks ago. He thought he'd take his mind off missed matches by practicing skills in the back garden, but whenever he steps out there he remembers Issy won't be following, which makes the hurt in his stomach worse.

A FAT LAD in jeans stops playing football and saunters over to Al's bench, squeezing his hands into his front pockets in an attempt to look hard. "What're you lookin at?" he says.

"Just the footie."

"You play, then?"

"Yeah."

"For a team?"

"Used to."

"Who?"

"Sefton Rangers."

"Never heard of 'em."

Al would be surprised if the fat lad had heard of any of the teams in the Hightown Junior League; he's probably never watched an amateur game. He looks like a member of the Couch Potato Brigade.

"Who d'you support?"

"Liverpool."

The fat lad spits on the grass and the others stop playing and wander over.

"Looking for a win for the Pool today, la'?" one of them asks.

"Yeah."

"Why don't yer have a look for some rocking-horse shit while you're at it?"

The lads laugh and high-five one another.

"You any good?" the littlest lad, the one who can actually play, asks.

"I'm OK."

"Bit of a posh git, aren't yer?" The fat lad gives Al a measuring look.

Al doesn't say anything. He reckons they'll let him play in a minute, when they've finished ribbing him.

"What yer dressed up in posh trousers for?"

"Wedding," he lies. "Got bored."

"Yer might be posh, but I reckon yer ma's a big prozzie. I bet Rooney's had her." The fat lad raises his arms and celebrates his joke like a goal while the others laugh.

Al doesn't react. It's OK, it's just a sort of test. All he has to do is wait.

"I bet yer ma's so massive that when she goes to the cinema she sits next to everyone."

There's more laughter and the fat kid jogs on the spot, warming up for his next joke as his belly wriggles under his football shirt.

"All right, stop mucking about, Danny." The little lad takes charge. "Yer wanna play, then? Three on three?" He doesn't wait for a response; instead he kicks the ball to Al and Al knocks it straight back. "What's yer name?"

"I'm Al. You?"

"Joe. Get on the end of this, Al."

Joe whacks the ball forward with the inside of his foot. Fat Danny gets a slight head start, but Al knows he can beat him and he sprints along the grass, wishing he was allowed to wear trainers with his church clothes.

"Yer ma's muggin," fat Danny puffs.

Al ignores him and keeps running. They reach the ball at the same time and Danny extends his leg for a sliding tackle.

"What's Al short for, then? Al-Qaeda?"

Al jumps over Danny's leg and executes a practiced Sombrero flick. "Watch and learn," he calls as he reclaims the ball, dribbles along the wing of the makeshift pitch, and shoots between the coat-posts of the goal.

"Goooooooooooooal." Little Joe shouts it like a Spanish commentator, as if it's the goal of the season, and Al can't stop his mouth from relaxing into a smile as they jog back to the center of the pitch.

"How about you and me against the others?" Joe says as he lobs the ball to fat Danny for the restart.

Danny tries a bit of fancy footwork. It takes only a moment for Al to dispossess him, then he pounds along the grass, nudging the ball from foot to foot, gulping the cool autumn air, savoring the way it slices past his throat and into his chest. His lungs are pumping and his nose is full of the best smell in the world—football. It reeks of grass and the wet-potato-skin smell of soil; it's a smell that creeps up your nose at the end of August when the mornings get nippy and the rot of summer starts to soften the ground, a smell that sends your thoughts deep into your feet where there's no room for God, no space for Eternity. Right foot, step over, left foot, scissor dribble—he would play footie all day every day if he could, and at night he would go to bed brimming with uncomplicated, bone-deep contentment. He chips the ball to little Joe and dashes forward to get on the end of the one-two.

"Goooooooooooooal," Joe howls.

Fat Danny grabs the ball, puffs back to the approximate center of the pitch, and kicks off again. One of the other lads passes back to Danny but Danny can't block Joe's tackle and the chase is on for another goal. Joe passes to Al, who races along the wing. Danny tries to keep up. He looks like a sweaty tomato, utterly pooped except for his gob, which seems to run on Duracell batteries.

"Yer ma's so poor, when she goes to KFC she has to lick other people's fingers."

Al flips Danny off and leaves him standing.

"Yer ma's so fat, she doesn't need the Internet—she's already worldwide." Danny wheezes as Al and Joe celebrate another goal.

They all jog back to the center together and Danny flops onto the grass, where he lies on his back, panting.

"Shall we swap things around?" Al asks. "Let's start from scratch and pick teams."

One of the lads checks his watch. "Sorry, mate. We're gonna have to go. We're meant to be watching the match at mine, kickoff was ten minutes ago."

"Aw, you could've said," Danny complains. "Someone get me coat for me."

Al watches the lads retrieve their coats. When they come back they heave Danny to his feet and Al wishes they weren't going. He doesn't want them to walk away and leave him standing, so he heads off first.

"See ya, then," he says.

As he reaches the pavement, someone calls after him, and when he turns, Danny and the others start singing:

> If I had the wings of a sparrow,
> If I had the arse of a crow,
> I'd fly over Anfield tomorrow,
> And shit on the bastards below,
> Shit on, shit on,
> Shit on the bastards below.

"Jog on, Al-Qaeda," Danny shouts.

Al gives Danny a wave and heads back up Queens Drive. His

stomach aches. He pretends it's just the adrenaline crash at first before conceding that he's sad. Everyone is, even Dad, it's obvious 'cause he's left all his normal words at Cliché Converters—he can't stop saying crap like *"This life is but a moment"* and *"Time heals all wounds,"* as if he thinks everything will be better once Issy is forgotten. Al isn't going to let time heal anything. He isn't going to allow himself to forget, in fact he's glad his stomach hurts because it's evidence of his ability to remember and he deserves to be punished by memory.

Issy's first word was "Ma." Everyone thought she meant "Mum," but Al knew she was saying the second half of his name, and when he came into a room and she called "Ma, ma, ma," and waved her tiny, starfish hands, it made him feel happy. It wasn't like she was anything special—she always had dribble on her chin and half the time she stank of poo—but she noticed something good in him, something no one else could see, and so he didn't mind her; he thought she was all right. As soon as she started to walk she began to follow him around. He pretended it was annoying; sometimes he would jump over the stair gate and sprint upstairs just to hear her call his name from the bottom step: "Al-ma, Al-ma!" Once she was old enough to be out in the garden without Mum following her around saying "Careful, Issy!" she watched him play football, and when he practiced free kicks and precision shots against the apple trees she retrieved the ball for him like a little dog. Sometimes he tested her, but she still liked him. Occasionally he kicked the ball at her and watched as she tried dead hard not to cry. Sometimes he said, "I don't like you," and then, just as her face folded, he said, "I don't mean it." He can't remember being nice to her; he knows he was, but he can't remember it at the moment. All the mean stuff has risen to the surface and it's floating there like shit in the sea. He wasn't nice to her even while she was ill in bed—*dying* in bed—he was too busy being a smart-arse to notice how sick she was. He is a first-class shit. What he would like most in the world, besides her not being dead, is to go back in time and say something nice: Thanks for collecting the ball for me. I like you. I'll miss you.

WHEN HE GETS to the betting shop he stops and looks through the window. There aren't many people there now, they probably prefer to watch the match in the pub—betting shops and pubs, two places he's never supposed to set foot in, even when he's older.

The match is showing on several TVs. It doesn't matter that he can't hear the commentary, he's just happy to watch. He reckons Liverpool can win, even with Gerrard on the bench. He leans closer to the window as Rodwell and Suárez clash in what looks like a soft tackle. The replay confirms there was no malice in it, but when the camera pans back to the action, Rodwell's getting a red card.

Rodwell's only a teenager and he's local; he trained at Finch Farm and played his first match for the Everton Reserves when he was just fifteen, which means he's brilliant, even though he's a Toffee. Al is sorry for Rodwell for a moment, but the feeling doesn't last long: Rodwell's parents probably took him to matches and cheered when he played well, they probably let him practice on Sundays. He thinks of his own Sundays—three hours of church followed by a whole afternoon of time-wasting and reverence, and the thought sends him straight back to the Sunday before Issy died.

He was sneaking out of the house, a tennis ball hidden in his right armpit, just centimeters from freedom, when Dad poked his head round the kitchen door.

"Alma, just the man. Let's do your interview now."

He followed Dad back to the living room, wishing bodily harm on the individual who'd decided that righteous fathers must interview their children once a month.

Dad closed the door behind them. "Sit down." He gestured at a chair in a way that made Al feel like a visitor.

"Let's start with a prayer. You say it, please." Dad bowed his head and folded his arms.

Al didn't fold his arms and he kept his eyes wide open as he said, "Dear Heavenly Father. Thank you for this sunny day. Thank you for this interview. In the name of Jesus Christ, Amen."

"Amen." Dad opened his eyes. "So, how are you?"

"Fine."

"How's school going?"

"Fine."

Dad didn't respond but Al was wise to the silence. He knew not to jump into the pause with both feet and reveal something. He waited it out while the clock ticked and the tennis ball bristled his armpit. "Think you can elaborate on 'fine'?"

"Not really." The tennis ball's furry nylon coating was beginning to make him sweat.

"How's your testimony?" Dad leaned forward, resting an elbow on each of his knees, pushing his palms together like a praying mantis.

"Fine."

Dad frowned and Al realized he'd said too many "fines."

"How do you feel about Joseph Smith?"

"Fine." A laugh quivered in his windpipe and he covered it with a cough. "Good. Yeah, good."

"You know Joseph Smith was only a little older than you when he had the First Vision? How does that make you feel?"

Al pretended to consider the question. "Well . . ." he said, trying to sound thoughtful.

"Pretty impressive for a young boy, wasn't it? Especially when you think of what so many fourteen-year-olds are up to nowadays." Dad sighed and leaned back in the chair.

"Did you know Steven Gerrard had a tryout with Man U when he was fourteen, Dad?"

"Everything's OK at school? You've had a good first week back?"

Al nodded, concentrating on his armpit, which had launched into a series of clenching spasms.

"Anything you'd like to say to me? No? Well, I'd like to share my testimony with you."

Al looked at the carpet as Dad bore testimony of the truth of the gospel. He said it was the best thing in his life, a shining beacon in the darkness, and he didn't know where he'd be without it. Al knew where he'd be without it—playing football in the garden.

"I'll offer the closing prayer, then," Dad said finally. During the prayer Al stared at the framed cross-stitch picture above the mantelpiece: *"Families Are Forever"*; or in other words, *"You'll Never Escape."*

After he had finished praying, Dad stood and extended his right hand. Al tried to grasp it with his arm pressed flat to his side, but Dad insisted on a hearty up-and-down shake, which made the ball pop out of his armpit and drop to the floor, where it bounced several times.

"Would you believe me if I said it was a hairball?"

"It's not exactly difficult to remember the Sabbath day and keep it holy." Dad picked up the ball and tried to stuff it into the pocket of his trousers. "Off you go."

Al walked around the garden for a bit, thinking of other things he could have said when the ball fell out of his shirt. Things like, "My balls just dropped." He sniggered to himself and wished Matty was there to share the joke. He thought about fetching a proper football from the shed, but decided against it, kicking a few of the early fallen apples against the wall instead.

He was about to head indoors when Issy appeared. She was giggling. She lifted the back of her Sunday dress and produced the tennis ball.

"How'd you get that?"

"Daddy left it on the chair after my interview. He went upstairs to look for Zippy."

"So you nicked it and stuffed it down your knickers? High-five!" They smacked hands and he gave the ball a precautionary wipe with his shirt tail. "Go and stand over there, near the wall. I'm going to see if I can kick it right at you. You can dodge, but you mustn't move until the ball's left the ground, OK?"

He chipped the ball with the inside and then the outside of each foot while she chattered as she dodged shots and retrieved for him. Someone in her class had done a wee on the floor during their first-ever PE lesson, she'd been talking about it all week, and he half-listened while he refined his touch, wishing he had a goal so he could practice free kicks properly. Neither of them noticed Dad watching from the kitchen door.

"Bring the ball here."

Issy picked it up and carried it to Dad.

"I've already told you once today," he said. "I shouldn't have to tell you again. Alma, no football training for you this week."

Al kicked the ground and dislodged a tuft of grass. Dad wouldn't be happy until he'd trussed him up and sacrificed every last bit of him, like bloody Abraham.

Issy rushed over and wrapped her arms around his leg in a consoling hug, but he shook her off and shoved her back toward Dad.

"It wasn't me. It was her," he said.

She stumbled when he shoved her and Dad picked her up, as if she was in danger and needed protecting. "You're accountable for your own actions, Alma," he said. "You didn't have to break the Sabbath. It was your choice and you can accept the consequences."

Issy didn't look back as Dad carried her into the kitchen. If she had, Al would have mouthed "Sorry," or at least winked. That's what he likes to think, anyway.

It'd been shitty to snitch on her. He'll always regret it. It'll stick with him in the same way missed penalties and own goals stick with footballers. He knows it serves him right, he deserves it, just like Gerrard deserves to remember the penalty he missed at Blackburn last season.

Penalty for Liverpool!

The staff in the betting shop stop what they're doing and watch

as the Everton players pantomime indignation and the ref points to
the spot, blowing his whistle to shut them up. Kuyt is going to take
it. He never misses, he's bound to score, and with Everton down to
ten men, the floodgates are sure to open for an epic Pool win. Al
wills Kuyt to do it. He can barely look as the Dutchman takes a
run-up, then kicks the ball. Crap. It's a rubbish penalty, a pathetic
miss, straight at the goalie. Al could have done better himself—
come on, Liverpool—he can't believe they're throwing it all away
on the day he's finally watching them play in real time and he suddenly wonders whether they'd do better if he wasn't watching, if
he's actually jinxing it 'cause he shouldn't be standing outside the
betting shop, he should be cleaning up pee but he's run away, like
Jonah. Perhaps if he goes back and does what he's supposed to do,
Liverpool will win.

He heads up Queens Drive again, stroking his hand over the roll
of cash in his hoodie pocket, thinking about all the things he could
buy.

When he reaches the chapel he jogs down the side of the building
and into the parking lot so he can sneak through the back door. He
hurries along the corridor, opens the door to the hall, and there's
Dad, pushing a massive two-sectioned broom along the waxy floor.
The broom is open like a giant mouth and its jaws are stuffed with
dust bunnies and old bits of dried-up food. Dad ignores him, so he
stands next to the stage for a bit, looking around, trying to pretend
he's there for a reason. Eventually he turns and heads for the door.

"Where have you been?" Dad's voice fills the echoing space.

"Nowhere."

"Have you been playing football?"

"No."

"Alma, you've got dirt all over your trousers." He looks down.
Shit.

"Don't you think your mum's got enough to worry about at the
moment without having to do extra washing because you can't do

as you're told? It wouldn't hurt for you to think of someone else first, would it?"

Dad turns to push the broom along the next section of floor and Al wants to say it wouldn't hurt for him to think of someone else first either, but although the words are straining at the gate of his mouth, he can't let them go.

Dad pretends he has to do all this *stuff* 'cause he's the Bishop, but he does it 'cause he wants to. He's got a choice—he's an adult. He goes to meetings all the time and he enjoys it, he stays behind after church for hours and he likes it—it probably makes him feel important when everyone lines up outside his office to tell him their problems and ask for help. He could have canceled his meetings when Issy died, he could have told everyone he was taking a few weeks off, but he wants them to think he's a hero, carrying on in the face of adversity. He can't even do easy things to cheer Mum up.

When the hearse arrived last Saturday afternoon Dad was angry. He waited until the men had left Issy's coffin in the living room and then he started right in, he didn't even bother to close the door, so Al eavesdropped from the landing.

"We don't do this, Claire."

"Don't tell me what 'we' do."

"Well, we don't."

"I want to."

"We concentrate on the resurrection. That's why we don't have crosses everywhere. I shouldn't have to tell you, you know this—the empty tomb, that's what we think about, not the body left behind."

"Stop telling me what to do."

"I'm not, I'm trying to explain—"

"Is there something in the *Handbook* about not doing it?"

"No, I don't think so, I just think—"

"Then you can't tell me not to."

"You didn't even ask what I thought. And what about the children?"

When Mum started talking again Al had to concentrate 'cause her voice was quiet.

"I *never* ask for anything, ever." She sounded like a bag of wasps. "But I'm asking for this. Actually, Ian, I'm not even asking."

Dad sucked it up and Issy stayed in the front room until the funeral. Jacob didn't seem to mind but Zippy spent the whole weekend upstairs sulking. Al hadn't been at all sure what to make of it. Part of him wanted to laugh because it was so weird. He actually made a little chuckle as he watched the men carry the coffin through the front door from his vantage point on the landing, but it was the kind of chuckle you do when you're hunting for a reaction and you can't find the right one. The coffin had been on a wheelie stand and there was a sort of tablecloth thing dangling over it, like a skirt. It'd looked like something a magician would use, a levitating prop, or one of those platforms ladies lie on before they're sawn in half.

Dad stops pushing the broom and tucks his tie into a gap between his shirt buttons. "There'll be a dustpan somewhere in the kitchen. Do you think you can go and get it without doing another disappearing act?"

He fetches the dustpan and works alongside Dad, sweeping up little piles of muck and depositing them in a trash bag. When the whole hall has been swept clean, they start to unstack the chairs that line the walls at each end. There will be so many people at Conference that the screen between the chapel and the hall will be opened and latecomers will have to listen to the prophet from the basketball court.

They're just finishing up when President Carmichael pokes his head round one of the doors. "Bishop Bradley and Alma," he calls. "How are you?"

"Fine, thank you, President," Dad replies. "How are you?"

"Fantastic!"

Al tries to catch Dad's eye to share the joke, but he won't join in.

"Can I borrow Alma for a moment, Bishop?"

"Be my guest," Dad says.

Great. Another interview. That's all Al needs. President Carmichael waves him through the door and ushers him down the corridor to his office. Even though President Carmichael doesn't live in Liverpool, his office is here, next door to the Liverpool Bishop's office but bigger, nicer. The desk is chunky and the chairs are soft.

"Sit down, sit down."

President Carmichael sits in the leather swivel chair behind the desk. On the wall above his head are three framed pictures: Joseph Smith looking windswept and poncey; the prophet—way younger than he is in real life; and Jesus with hair like Cheryl Cole in the L'Oréal ad.

"How are things with you, Alma?"

"Fine."

President Carmichael grins, as if he's used to doing interviews where people say "Fine" to every question. He taps his hands on the desk for a moment, then reaches into his suit pocket. He gets his phone out and flicks a finger across the screen.

"I don't know many lads who'd happily spend their Saturday afternoon cleaning."

"Neither do I."

President Carmichael laughs and holds up the phone.

"Now it's time for the classified football results," he says, and Al can tell he's about to read the score like James Alexander Gordon on the radio. "Saturday the first of October, Barclays Premier League: Everton zero, Liverpool two." He turns his phone off and puts it back in his pocket. "I thought you'd like to know. Do you think I've got a future on Radio 5?" He opens a drawer in his desk, digs around, and produces a four-finger KitKat.

"There you go."

"Thanks." Al picks up the chocolate. He knew Liverpool would win if he came back.

"Go on. I bet you're starving, boys are always starving—mine are, anyway. What're you going to do during the Relief Society session of Conference?" Al's mouth is full. He shrugs.

"Is Jacob coming along with your mum? You can wait here together until the Relief Society session's finished, if you like. Save you
from having to watch girls' stuff. Me and your dad are presiding,
but there's no need for you and Jacob to be there. I've got *The Princess Bride* on my laptop, it's got to be better than listening to old
ladies, hasn't it?"

President Carmichael is a real person, that's why people like
him—Dad would never acknowledge that anything to do with
church could be the tiniest bit boring. Al stuffs the last stick of Kit-
Kat into his mouth, wads up the wrapper, and goes to put it in his
hoodie pocket. Then he remembers the money and keeps hold of the
paper. He's seen *The Princess Bride* a billion times, so has Jacob,
they've seen it so many times they can quote parts of it to each
other. It's a bit babyish, but it's definitely better than watching the
Relief Society Conference or hanging around in the corridor until it
finishes.

"Be good to your parents, eh? All this . . . everything . . . it's
hard for them. Come on, let's find some hymnbooks to go on the
extra chairs in the hall; some people like to sing along with the Tabernacle Choir."

Al feels a rush of cheerfulness as they leave the office; he isn't in
trouble, Liverpool won, and the inside of his mouth is sticky with
chocolate. He gives President Carmichael a burst of his best Tabernacle Choir impersonation. "Laaaaaaaa, la, la, la."

To his surprise, President Carmichael joins in and they head
down the corridor together warbling like a pair of *X Factor* rejects.

He has to sit with the family during Conference. Mum calls it
"sitting as a family" and she makes a big deal of it 'cause Dad usually sits up on the stand during church meetings. Al ends up right in
the middle, squeezed between Jacob and Zippy.

It's getting dark outside and the lights in the chapel and hall have
been switched off so everyone can concentrate on the massive
screen. The chapel is full and people are sitting on the first couple of

rows of chairs in the hall; tomorrow the hall will be full too 'cause more people come to the Sunday sessions of Conference.

"Alma, take your hoodie off. It's about to start."

Al lifts the hoodie over his head and bundles it into his lap. An American announcer welcomes everyone and the camera pans over Temple Square in Salt Lake City, which always looks sunny and sparkly clean. Then the Tabernacle Choir start to sing "The Morning Breaks," the song they always sing at this session of General Conference. Dad gets his hymnbook out to join in, and the camera switches to show thousands of people sitting in the Conference Center. They aren't singing, they're listening to the choir, but Dad doesn't notice, or perhaps he doesn't care. *"Lo, Zion's standard is unfurled!"* he sings.

Jacob tugs Al's sleeve. "I'm Miracle Max," he hisses.

"What?"

"I'm Miracle Max from *The Princess Bride*."

"Oh, right."

"Doing miracles is what I do," Jacob whispers, trying his best to sound like the crazy old man from the movie.

Al sniggers. "OK," he says. "In that case, I'm Inigo Montoya. *You killed my father, prepare to die.*" He delivers the line in his best Spanish accent to make Jacob laugh.

"Shush." Zippy pokes him. "Don't be immature."

He'd rather be immature than super-holy. Zippy probably thinks the prophet will say something amazing once the choir's stopped singing, something like "Get ready for the Second Coming . . . tomorrow!" instead of his usual snore-ful stories.

He pokes Zippy back. Dad frowns and shakes his head, but he doesn't stop singing.

"The dawning of a brighter day, the dawning of a brighter day." Mum isn't singing, she's just staring straight ahead. She looks like she's been whacked in the face by a football, sort of concussed. Al twists the hoodie bundle in his lap until he can feel the roll of cash through the zip-up pocket. Maybe the prophet will say something

amazing, something so bloody brilliant and wonderful that it will make everything better. If the Second Coming *is* just around the corner it'll be followed by the Millennium and then Issy will come back . . . *if* it's true. He watches Jacob rest his hand on Mum's lap; she doesn't seem to notice, and as the song slows to its conclusion and Dad's voice gets louder—*"Thus Zion's light is bursting forth, to bring her ransomed children home"*—Mum closes her eyes. She does it in such a deliberate way, it's as if she's closed her ears too and it's like she's not sitting with them anymore.

The opening prayer begins, and although he usually keeps his eyes open, Al squeezes them shut 'cause he feels like he did when Kuyt stepped up to take the penalty earlier; he's willing something good to happen but he can hardly stand to look.

BOOK THREE

Then Hezekiah Turned His Face Toward the Wall

OCTOBER

– 11 –

Waiting

Claire can bear to be up only when they are out. She hides under the warm puff of Issy's duvet, eyes squeezed shut as Ian's panicky voice floats up the stairs.

"Have you got your lunch, Zipporah? I made some sandwiches. They're on the side in the kitchen. Well, I didn't know you don't like tuna. Do you need some bus money? Sorry, it's all the change I've got. Can't you get off a stop early? Jacob, come on, hurry up. Where's your helmet, Alma? Don't be silly—you'll look a lot worse with your brains on the road. Jacob, *come on.*"

The front door closes and Claire remains under the cover in case one of them comes back for something. When the quiet has settled she climbs out of bed and inches down the stairs like an old woman, one hand on the banister, the other braced against the wall, dragging the ugly lump of her grief behind her.

The kitchen smells of toast and decomposing flowers: roses, delphiniums, chrysanthemums, carnations, and lilies; they've been stuffed into vases, jam jars, and plastic beakers, two especially large arrangements languish in buckets. The stink of the lilies turns her stomach; something sour and rancid lurks under their sweet pungency. She ought to throw the flowers away, they are long past their best, but to remove them would be to admit something, to mark a conclusion. She sits at the table trying to ignore the incongruous optimism of the homespun crafts and knickknacks. *"No Other Success Can Compensate for Failure in the Home"*—the laminated jumble of cutesy letters is particularly inapt.

There have been so many failures. When the children were younger they were all hers—impatience, disorganization, boredom, tiredness—but as the children have grown older, the tent of Failure in the Home has marqueed to also include their inadequacies—untidiness, disobedience, irreverence, breaking the Sabbath, and a multitude of other discouraged behaviors and sins of omission—all evidence of her spectacular Failure in the Home. She shuffles over to the sign, pulls it off the wall, and drops it in the trash, wondering what to get rid of next.

So far this year, the sisters have made felt flowers, sugar-cube Temple sculptures, Daughter of God fridge magnets, Temple marriage clocks—♥ *For Time & Eternity* ♥—oatmeal-bath sachets, and wooden wall signs. She'd been looking forward to the wooden wall signs, she'd been thinking about painting her sign with something kitschy and self-deprecating like *"God Bless This Mess."* But when she arrived at the chapel, Sister Stevens had already stenciled a quote onto each rectangle of wood.

Claire hates her sign. She brought it home from the Relief Society meeting and hid it in the musty cupboard under the sink, punishing it with darkness and a top note of shoe polish and bleach. Ian found it; perhaps he inexplicably decided to clean his own shoes and saw it lying there purposelessly. She followed the racket one Saturday morning and discovered him kneeling astride the sink pushing a gyrating drill bit into the window lintel.

"Pride of place." He grinned and blew her a kiss.

Because Sister Stevens stenciled the letters, the sign is the neatest of Claire's homemade efforts. The characters sweep and loop in even calligraphic curls:

"Home is where women have the most power and influence; therefore, Latter-day Saint women should be the BEST home-makers in the world."

Sometimes Claire sneers at the sign, occasionally it makes her feel like crying; she is definitely not one of the best homemakers in the world—there is evidence of this all over her kitchen, all over her life. The BEST homemakers in the world buy supplies for their children's birthday parties ahead of time, they check on their children and notice when they are seriously ill. She pushes the chair to the sink, climbs up, and reaches for the sign. It is solid and heavier than she remembers. She steps down and puts it on the table. She would like to deface it, to replace BEST with a word like "stressed" or "depressed." If she was clever she'd be able to think of something funny, a way of changing the words around to make it say something entirely different, then she could hang it back up and take pleasure in everyone's obliviousness. Instead, she unlocks the back door, takes the sign outside, and stuffs it in the trash can.

As she comes back indoors, she notices Issy's goldfish and can't remember when she last fed him. She hunts for the little pot of food and discovers it behind a jar of flowers. After she's fed the fish she thinks about feeding herself. The fridge is littered with foreign casserole dishes, plastic-wrapped and crusted with leftovers.

They must be passing a sheet around in Relief Society—*"Sign here to make a meal for the Bradleys."* The sisters choose recipes rich in calories and comfort and leave them on the doorstep alongside Tupperware tubs of treats: chocolate brownies, cookies, cupcakes. They don't ring the bell. Claire imagines them tiptoeing up the driveway, arranging their offerings, then dashing away before she can assault them with her sadness on the doorstep. There's nothing she'd like to eat so she closes the fridge and sits down.

Sympathy cards are stacked in a zigzag pile on the table; the mantelpiece and windowsills are full. The postman slides fat bundles of commiseration through the letter box every day: heartfelt wishes and bad poems in muted, floral pastels. People write little notes inside the cards. She is longing for a note saying *"I'm so sorry"*; she is sick of explanations and justifications.

"You must be a very special family to have been given such a
challenge."

"Bless Issy for coming into your family and giving you a heavenly destination to work for."

"Heavenly Father knows there are important lessons for you to
learn from this experience."

What is she meant to learn from this experience? Ian would answer the question with a list of virtues like the ones written on the
Sunday-school chalkboard each week, irrespective of the lesson
topic: patience, faith, long-suffering, endurance . . . It's easy for
him, his thoughts traverse a one-way system, there's no room for
roundabouts of doubt or recalculations; once he settles on something it's true and she mostly likes this about him, it's what makes
him so steadfast and loyal. When he decided he loved her she knew
he wouldn't ever change his mind; loving her became a fact of his
existence, as veritable and infallible as scripture. He's a man who
sticks to the road of his experience, he doesn't look left or right or
back; he never rubbernecks or pulls over to glory in the wreckage of
other people's lives, he never gossips or points fingers; he calls encouragement as he passes those who've broken down, he throws a
towrope to people in difficulty, but he always keeps to his desig-
nated route. There's one truth, one way, and Ian is following it. It's
true she has caught him once or twice staring into the distance,
hands clenched, blinking back tears, but, with the exception of that
first night, each time she has reached out to touch the hem of his
unhappiness he has wiped the feelings from his face and pulled
away. She wishes he'd come to a halt. Pause. Just for a while. Why
can't everyone just stop? Even the children adhere to their routines
in a way that suggests their feelings are superficial. She has wondered if Zipporah is hiding her grief in her bedroom, whether Jacob's tiptoeing and whispers to no one in particular are a symptom
of cheerlessness or conciliation, and as for Alma, he has dressed
whatever unhappiness he feels in a coat of jokes.

"It's no wonder Sister Valentine is so fat," he said as they tackled one of her monster meals, last week, before Claire retreated upstairs.

"That's unkind," Ian chided. "Perhaps she can't help it. You don't know, it might run in her family."

"*No one* runs in her family." He looked around, waiting for someone to laugh; when they didn't, he carried on.

"The best thing about this is the food. What? I didn't mean I was glad or anything. Wow, that went over like a fart in church."

Ian told him not to say "fart" at the table, so he got up and went into the kitchen and said it there. Ian told him to sit down, but he was incorrigible.

"If a rat catcher is called a ratter, what's a bug catcher called?" he asked Jacob.

Sadness that's so easily disguised can't run deep. None of them are sad like she is, no one else's grief is immobilizing. The way they are carrying on—going to school and work, pretending everything's OK—sickens her. They are allowing the momentum of routine to push them onward, ever onward, as if they are marching to the chorus of a relentless hymn.

There is a smack as another bundle of sympathy lands on the mat in the hallway. She gets up, retrieves a handful of envelopes and a small package, and shambles back to the table. She opens several cards, the verses are absurd and twee.

> *"God's garden is full of beautiful flowers,*
> *Sometimes he plucks the best ones for himself*
> *And puts them where he can enjoy them, always."*

> *"No longer here*
> *But ever dear*
> *And always near."*

> *"Although today is full of sorrow,*
> *God will make things right tomorrow."*

She dumps the cards in the pile with the others. There are two envelopes left. One looks like a letter and the other is the small package. She opens the package first. It contains a book and a note from Sister Stevens.

Dear Claire,

I ordered this from Salt Lake as soon as I heard the news. It finally arrived. Hope it helps,

Ashlee x

The book is small and slender. It's called *Angel Children* and Jesus is pictured on the cover, holding a small boy, his right hand outstretched. He looks like the Child Catcher. She flicks through the pages, glancing at the chapter headings: "Faith and a Time to Die," "Faith Sufficient to Heal is a Gift," "Overcoming the Challenge." Her eyes are drawn to a quotation near the end of the book: *"And the prayer of faith shall save the sick."* She cracks the narrow spine and begins to read about King Hezekiah. Isaiah tells the king to set his house in order as he is about to die, but when Hezekiah prays the prayer of faith, God allows him to live for an additional fifteen years. Claire remembers not praying in the hospital, not believing her words would work: *"the prayer of faith"*—was it so simple? She keeps reading. Hezekiah's story is followed by that of an ordinary man whose son is sick. The man prays for his boy's recovery, he absolutely refuses to give him up to death, and Claire wonders about the apparatus of such a refusal—how does one go about refusing God? The boy's life is saved, but when he grows up he becomes a great sorrow to his parents and they decide it would have been better if he had died when he was a child. She slaps the book against the table.

The remaining envelope contains a letter.

Dear Sister Bradley,

I went to the Temple yesterday. I was sitting in the Celestial Room, contemplating Eternity, and I saw something out of the corner of my eye. When I looked, there was nothing, but then I saw it again, flickering, and I knew it was a spirit. The Holy Ghost whispered to me that it was Issy. I know she is nearby, watching over you all at this time, and if you stay faithful you will see her again.

Gospel love,
Sister Anderson

Claire tears the letter in two. Perhaps someone might have noticed how ill Issy was if Ian hadn't disappeared to coax Brother Anderson to the hospital. Why would Issy appear to Sister Anderson and not to her own mother? Clearly she wouldn't, she just wouldn't. She wads each half of the letter into a ball and stares at the empty space above the sink.

AT FIRST SHE tried to carry on. She walked Jacob to school and survived the playground, feeling like a member of the royal family as she greeted people and collected flowers. Things quieted down in a matter of days—once people had expressed sympathy they didn't have much else to say. Grief enclosed her like an invisibility cloak, and with no one to talk to, she thought about the empty chair in Issy's classroom and wondered whether her teacher had removed her name badge from her desk and unpeeled the little sign above her coat peg.

On the walk home, she meandered around the park scuffing through piles of fallen leaves, thinking about where she was in relation to memories of Issy, which were everywhere, poking her from all directions—she couldn't stop them, it felt wrong to try. At home, she couldn't pass Issy and Jacob's room without entering it. She opened drawers, searched for Issy's scent on things, and her sadness fastened itself to ordinary objects: unfilled slippers, abandoned toys, and empty clothes hanging in the wardrobe, waiting. It began to feel as if these objects ought to leave of their own accord, disappear quietly in order to save her feelings. She hovered in the bedroom, haunting the vestiges of Issy's life, and watched from the window as the hedge sobbed leaves and the breeze huffed them into every corner of the garden.

Things changed after General Conference weekend. She experienced the newly familiar horror on waking that Monday morning, but it also felt as if there was something heavy in her chest, pressing her into the mattress, and she longed to fall back into the oblivion of sleep. Her legs ached as she stepped into her clothes and she could hardly lift her arms as she hung out the washing. When she dropped Jacob off at school the Reception teacher stepped into the playground holding Issy's PE uniform.

"Mrs. Bradley, I—this—I didn't know—do you want it?"

Claire took the bag and walked home with it pressed to her chest. She carried it straight upstairs and hung it on the hook on the back of Issy and Jacob's bedroom door. Then she stood at the window and looked out at the garden as she thought about the story the prophet had told at Conference.

The prophet usually tells stories about himself. The stories are heartening and refreshingly straightforward, replete with uncomplicated goodness: hospital visits, Christmas presents for the needy, small acts of kindness—the things Claire values, the things she believes are at the heart of religion. But the story he told this time was different. When the prophet was just a boy he left a five-dollar bill in his pocket. He realized his mistake only after his clothes had been sent to the laundry. He was worried about losing the money so he prayed and pleaded with Heavenly Father for its safe return. The clothes came back and the five-dollar bill was miraculously intact; the prophet's prayers had been answered. When the broadcast ended and the chapel lights were switched on, Claire looked around at people she considered to be friends, hoping one of them might whisper, "It must be hard for you to hear about the miraculous rescue of a five-dollar bill," or even dare to murmur, "Maybe the prophet was mistaken and it was just good luck that saved the money." But no one said a thing, she didn't encounter so much as a sympathetic eye roll, and although she thought the story might bother Ian too, she was wrong. "You're not criticizing the prophet, are you?" he asked.

She watched through the bedroom window as the breeze buffeted the clothes she'd pegged on the line and stared at the fallen apples, unfazed by the waste. She imagined the prophet as a little boy, panicking about the money, praying that everything would be all right. It was easy to feel sorry for him, to understand his need, but it wasn't an answer to prayer or a miracle—God would *never* exercise His power to save money, even for a child. He wouldn't.

She was weary, utterly tired of trying to get everything straight in her mind: faith, miracles, prayers, blessings . . . She turned away from the window and crossed the room to lift Issy's covers, and for a moment she could smell Issy's skin and hair. That was when she decided.

She popped downstairs briefly to fetch Issy's glasses from her handbag. As she passed the telephone, she bent down and unplugged the cord. When she got back upstairs she changed out of her clothes and into her nightie. Then she climbed into the bottom bunk where she lay, holding the glasses. She unfastened them and ran her fingers along the arms where they'd hugged Issy's head from temple to ear. The vacant round lenses gaped *"Oh"* at her, as if they were aching to be animated by the arcs of ears and the underscore of a smile. She positioned them on the pillow next to her. Then she closed her eyes and fell asleep.

When the front door burst open, she jumped. She heard footsteps racing down the corridor, followed by the fling of the living-room, dining-room, and kitchen doors. The feet attacked the stairs and dashed along the landing to her bedroom, then up the second flight to Zipporah's room before pounding back down to open Alma's door, the bathroom door, and finally the door to Jacob and Issy's room.

"You're here!" Ian was out of breath. His hands braced the door frame. "You're here! I was so worried. What's going on? Are you all right? I had a call asking why no one had picked Jacob up. I tried to get through, but the phone just rang and rang. I thought—"

"I unplugged it."

"What?"

"I don't want to talk to anyone."

"You can't just unplug the phone! Jacob was waiting. He didn't know where you were. I had to leave work. What are you doing?"

"Resting."

"In here? Why? Are you ill?"

"No."

"Come on, you'd better get up."

"No."

"Come on." He stepped into the room, slipped his hand under the blankets and searched for her arm. His fingers squeezed hard. "Stop being silly."

"Get off. You're hurting me."

"You shouldn't be here." He grasped her and tugged until she was half hanging out of the bed. She closed her eyes and allowed herself to go limp. He'd never touched her like that before, never. He yanked her farther until her head and back touched the floor, then he leaned in to move her legs out of the bunk. The covers slid away, Issy's glasses must have slipped onto the carpet, and when Ian tried to grab her ankles there was a crack as the glasses shattered under the sole of one of his sensible shoes.

Upturned and frightened, Claire kept her eyes closed while he determined the source of the noise. She heard his intake of breath when he realized and the creak of the floorboards as he knelt down to pick up the pieces, but she didn't open her eyes because she knew if she watched she would feel sorry for him and she wasn't ready to forfeit her anger.

"I've broken Issy's glasses," he said. "We can get some new ones, can't we? They'd let us, wouldn't they? In the shop, they'd let us buy some without her . . . They're in pieces. Look what you made me do."

She didn't move, she lay perfectly still with her back on the floor and her legs in the bed. He waited for a moment and then she heard his feet on the stairs.

She kept her eyes closed as she maneuvered her legs out of the bed and onto the floor. She knew she'd done something terrible by not collecting Jacob and by refusing to get up when Ian asked. She felt ashamed, but not enough to go downstairs and apologize. It was something of a revelation to realize that her daily life was fueled by expectation and its structures were fragile and easily transgressed. She scrambled onto all fours and climbed back into the bed.

She didn't join the family for dinner. She didn't wash the dishes or bring the laundry in off the line; she lay in bed rehearsing years of tentative, often reluctant, obedience and pondered the dimensions of a proportionate punishment.

"CONGRATULATIONS ON YOUR eternal marriage! Now you can get on with the things that really matter." Although she laughed at the note that accompanied Ian's parents' baby-quilt wedding gift, Claire was pregnant before finals. Swept away by everyone's happiness, she read baby magazines and allowed the older sisters to fuss and stroke her belly in the church corridors, listening as they offered unsolicited advice about breastfeeding and suitable baby names.

Ian's parents were at the hospital within an hour of Zipporah's birth. "You're a lovely girl, aren't you?" his mum cooed as she held her first grandchild. "Yes you are! And you'd like a little brother, wouldn't you? Yes you would!"

"Give us a chance, Mum," Ian laughed.

People at church began asking Claire when she was going to have *"the next one"* before Zipporah was three months old and she didn't mind because she thought it would be a good idea to have two children quite close together.

When Alma was born, Ian's mum was ecstatic. "Hello, future missionary," she said as she held him in the hospital. "You'd like a little brother too, wouldn't you? Yes you would!"

That was when Claire realized she wasn't going to get away with just the two.

Alma was busy blowing the roof off her life with his noisy toddler tantrums when Ian's mum asked whether she had started trying for *"number three."* Claire explained that she didn't want any more and Ian's mum said, "I'd have had at least half a dozen if I'd been able . . . I always think it's a shame when women don't throw themselves into motherhood. After all, it's what they'll be doing for Eternity. They may as well get the hang of it now."

"I'm not sure I want to keep reproducing for Eternity," Claire confided. "I don't think it's my thing. I mean, I love the children, but I don't want to do this forever."

"But it's exactly what you'll be doing! You'll be populating whole worlds—not by yourself, of course; Ian's other wives will help."

"His other wives?"

"In the Celestial Kingdom."

"There'll be other wives?"

"Of course. Polygamy is eternal—just because we don't practice it now doesn't mean we don't believe in it. It's in *Mormon Doctrine.* We gave you a copy before you got married. Where is it? I'll show you."

Claire fetched the book and listened as Ian's mum read aloud from the section that dealt with the Ennobling and Exalting Principle of Plural Marriage. She learned that the Holy Practice would commence again after the Second Coming and she felt nauseated for the remainder of the afternoon.

"It's just the way it is, Claire," Ian said when he got home from work. "It was that way in the Old Testament and it's that way in nature. You won't mind in the Celestial Kingdom, you'll be perfect, so you won't feel jealous. It's silly worrying about it now."

"You said polygamy was in the past. I asked you about it before I joined the Church and that's what you said."

"It *is* in the past."

"You said it all ended more than a hundred years ago."

"It did."

"You didn't tell me the truth."

"I answered the question you asked."

She thought about it for days, humbly at first, and then with growing indignation. She couldn't believe in it, but that wasn't enough, she wanted to stop him believing in it too. She bought unauthorized underwear that exposed her thighs and belly and wore it before bed so he could enjoy removing it. She did things she had previously heard him describe as *"immoral"* and *"impure."* He was startled, but she quashed his objections. She maintained a heightened level of attentiveness for several weeks until life caught up with her and she couldn't muster the enthusiasm for perpetual sexual acrobatics, no matter how eternally binding. She resolved not to think about polygamy and retreated to their familiar, hokey-pokey sex that was nice because it was comfortable, and she knew all the words and moves by heart.

Not long after, Ian asked about having another child. The decision was mostly hers, he said, but the Lord would show her the way. The Lord kept quiet, giving Claire the impression that He wasn't especially bothered. Ian was. He explained his theory that *"replicating"* was the best way to describe the creation of two children; *"multiplying and replenishing"* required three or more. She agreed to have another, deriving a secret glee from her body's refusal when nothing happened. Ian was patient. "The Lord's time isn't our time," he said. But his mum wouldn't leave it alone, she tugged and worried at it like a dog on the end of a shoe. She gave advice about ovulation and offered to babysit Zipporah and Alma overnight, if it would help. Eventually, once Alma had started school and Claire had begun to daydream about part-time jobs and separate bank accounts, she got pregnant again.

Not long after Jacob was born, Ian's mum started to say things like, "Three is an awkward number," and, "Alma's got that middle-child problem, hasn't he?"

Claire prayed about it and made a deal: *"One last time, but I want a girl."* As she lay on the bed in the scanning room, it felt as if her whole life hinged on the revelation of the baby's sex. She knew she wasn't like the other women at church; she didn't have spiritual experiences, unless she counted the way she felt when she walked on the beach. She never knew what to say in Testimony Meetings; she couldn't muster tearful declarations and statements of absolute truth like Sister Stevens: "We were on vacation in Disneyland and I couldn't stop crying because we have the *gospel*—we were the happiest *people* in the happiest *place* on Earth." She couldn't speak like Sister Campbell either: "I *know* the Church is the only true Church on the face of the Earth. I *know* Joseph Smith was a prophet of God. I *know* we have a living prophet who converses daily with Jesus Christ and leads the Church by revelation." Whenever possible, she avoided bearing testimony, and on the occasions when she was compelled to as the Bishop's wife, she simply stated that joining the Church had made her feel a part of something good. The sonographer said, "You're having a little girl," and Claire felt like Hannah in the Old Testament, as if she had prayed Issy into existence.

After Issy was born, Claire caught Ian's eye in the hospital. "No more," she mouthed and he nodded and said he loved her hugely, more than she could imagine. But love isn't measured by size or weight; she learned that after Issy was born. Love is measured in ways. It isn't a case of more and less. It's this way and that way, gladly and carefully, freely and gratefully. That's how it was with her last baby: her lovely, make-the-most-of-it child. Each of Issy's firsts was also a last: a joy and a relief, a beginning and an ending, all of Claire's own choosing.

IAN RETURNED A few hours later with food on a tray. He stood in the doorway and cleared his throat. "Will you get up now?"

She pulled the covers over her head and mumbled, "I don't think so," into the duvet.

"Are you going to get up tomorrow?"

"I don't know."

"What's wrong, Claire?"

She tugged the covers down a little so she could see him. He'd removed his tie, undone his top button, and his shirt was partially untucked; he looked forsaken, like an unmade bed.

"You didn't even come down for Family Home Evening. What's happened today? Has something upset you?"

Of course she was upset, but the upset was sharper than Issy's returned PE uniform, less fathomable than the prophet's story, and heavier than the weight she'd felt in her chest when she woke that morning.

"Jacob needs to go to bed." He stepped into the room and placed the tray on the floor, as if he might tempt her out like an animal. He'd folded a piece of kitchen towel in half to make a napkin and put a rose from one of the sympathy bouquets in a glass of water. He sat down in front of the wardrobe, his knees pointed straight at the ceiling, and his trousers rode up past the tops of his socks.

"I know it's difficult. But you, you've got to—"

"It's not the kind of sadness that just dries up."

"I know . . . but will you get out of bed, please?"

"I don't want to."

"I don't either, in the mornings, it's . . . I think one day it won't be such an effort. I *know* it's going to get better, it's just going to take some time." He stretched his legs out in front of him; his feet almost reached the bed, there were holes in the heels of each of his socks, and she felt glad his mother was on the other side of the Irish Sea. "I'm sorry about the glasses. Do you need a blessing? I'll phone President Carmichael and ask him to come and assist. I know it's Monday, but I'm sure he wouldn't mind."

She couldn't talk past the sudden lump in her throat. She thought about the little business cards in the pocket of his suit jacket, tracing his Priesthood Line of Authority: *"Ian James Bradley ordained a High Priest by Ronald Bradley, Ronald Bradley ordained a High Priest by James Poulter,"* and on, and on, until it reached Brigham

Young, then Joseph Smith and Peter, James, and John, who came back to Earth in 1829 to restore the priesthood, and finally back to Jesus Christ. Ian had the cards made specially, so the men he ordained could verify the source of their authority to bless and bind on earth and in heaven. All that power, passed down by the laying on of hands like a sacred Midas touch. It *should* work—she'd thought about it a lot since the blessing in the hospital; unworthiness on Ian's or Issy's part would affect the outcome of a blessing and invalidate the promises made, but they were both eminently worthy. Lack of faith may also cause failure and her own lack was a fact; from the moment they arrived at the hospital she hadn't believed in anything except the evidence of her eyes. She wished she could go back in time to sit next to Issy's bed and say, "I do believe, I do, I do!" like one of Peter Pan's Lost Boys. But even as the thought took hold, she couldn't imagine having enough faith to support the magic of healing.

"I don't want a blessing," she said. "It won't help. It won't work."

"You don't mean that."

She considered telling him that she *did* mean it but pulled the covers back over her head instead.

"I don't know what else to do to make it better," he said. And then he got up off the floor and went downstairs to tell Jacob to go up to bed.

CLAIRE REALIZES SHE is crying. She used to know when she was about to cry, but it's not like that anymore. There's no anticipation, no winding mechanism. She is full of tears and every so often they just slop out. They drip onto her hands and onto the balled-up pieces of Sister Anderson's letter. It's only when she gives the pieces a further scrunch that she notices the envelope, propped next to the pile of sympathy cards. Ian has dotted the "i" in her name with a heart like she used to when they first met. She tears it open, embarrassed for him and his stupid, ineffectual optimism. Inside she finds an article from the online version of *Ensign* magazine that he must have printed off specially. Several sentences have been highlighted.

"Mother, Do Not Mourn," she reads. The story is about a bishop's son who was run over by a freight train. *"The boy's mother felt no relief from sorrow during the funeral and continued mourning after the burial."* She reads this sentence several times, partly because Ian has colored it bright yellow but also in an attempt to grasp its significance. Are funerals supposed to relieve sorrow? Is burial meant to signify the end of mourning? Is Ian implying that she is not following the correct pattern of grief? She reads on, warming to the boy's mother. *"The boy's mother lay on her bed in a state of mourning."* This part of the story has also been highlighted, so she reads it again. It's a realistic detail and it makes her feel slightly more charitable toward Ian, who probably stayed up late, looking for helpful stories in the *Ensign* archive. The feeling doesn't last long.

"While the mother lay on the bed, her dead son appeared to her. He told his mother not to cry. He said that he was all right and assured her that his death was an accident. 'Tell Father that all is well with me, and I want you not to mourn anymore.'"

So that's his point. Nearly three weeks of mourning is enough. Time to move on. She scrunches the paper into a ball. Other people's stories are suffocating her, she is sick of their assurances, their miraculous interventions and happy endings. She stuffs the balled-up papers in the trash bin and shuffles up the stairs.

The room smells of musky, unwashed woman. She picks a furry white bear out of Issy's toy box and gets into the bed. She holds the teddy up to her nose and waits. She isn't expecting much, she's not a greedy person. All she wants is a small sign, an ounce of reassurance that Issy still exists somewhere outside of memory.

She is still waiting several hours later, and when the front door opens and voices fill the hall, she tugs the covers over her head and goes to sleep.

– 12 –

Happy Is the Man
That Findeth Wisdom

Ian presses "enter" in the darkness of the twilight house.

My wife won't get out of bed, she's always down . . .
Is **my wife** lazy? She **won't get out of bed** . . .
My husband **won't** grow up. He stays in **bed** . . .
Why **won't my wife** sleep with me? . . .
My dog **won't get out of my bed** . . .

He clicks on a couple of pages that seem relevant but they're written by people whose wives are suffering from depression. He decides to search the *Ensign* archive instead and types "emotional problems." The first page of results isn't any help:

Fortifying the Home from Evil
Women Are Incredible!
Temple Worship

He finds what he needs on page 2: "Solving Emotional Problems in the Lord's Own Way." He grabs a pencil from the pot next to the computer and makes notes as he reads.

—If you have a miserable day (or several in a row) <u>stand</u> and
  <u>face them</u>.
—Things will get <u>better</u>.
—Counseling = spiritually <u>destructive</u> techniques.

—<u>Do not</u> delve, analyze, or dissect. Harder to put something
   back together than to take it to pieces.
—Solve problems <u>the Lord's way.</u>

He folds the piece of paper and stuffs it in his trouser pocket as
the computer shuts down. The house hums its night noises and he
clasps his hands together and says a quick prayer. He listens past the
night noises, following the line of his radius from perimeter to
center, and there, right in the middle of himself, where things are
very quiet, he discovers a verse from Hebrews: *"For whom the Lord
loveth he chasteneth, and scourgeth every son whom he receiveth."*

He stands, pushes the chair back quietly, and tiptoes up the stairs
and along the landing, feeling his way to the bedroom, which is
dimly lit by the streetlight outside. He takes his clothes off, hangs
them on the half-open wardrobe door, and stands at the side of the
bed for a moment, a ghostly figure in the yellow gloom, covered
from neck to knee by Temple garments. The blankets are rumpled
and a quick flick of the duvet exposes Jacob, his little body spread
wide in the fling of sleep. Ian is suddenly aware of the way his love
for his youngest son fills him from his toes all the way to the back
of his throat and he knows if he, with all of his imperfections, can
love like this, it is impossible to imagine how much Heavenly Father, who is perfect, must love His children.

After he has straightened and tucked the duvet around Jacob,
Ian kneels beside the bed. He folds his arms, closes his eyes, and
begins his evening prayer. The worn carpet is scratchy against his
knees. He shifts and settles, taking care not to rest his whole weight
on his heels in order to avoid the pins and needles that frequently
accompany long prayers.

"Please bless Claire," he murmurs. "Bless her with . . ." He
searches for the right word. "Bless her with patience and . . ."

He pauses as he tries to calculate exactly what it is that Claire
needs.

· · ·

THE FIRST MORNING without her was the worst. Ian waited until seven-thirty before he went into Jacob's room.

"Are you going to get up?"

She was lying on Issy's bunk with her head under the covers. He was pretty certain she heard him, but she didn't respond. He waited, hoping she might say something, give some sort of approximation of the likely duration of her leave, and although he felt like pulling her out of the bed, he didn't; he'd learned his lesson and he had the pieces of Issy's glasses wrapped in a handkerchief in his drawer as a reminder of his miscalculation.

There were clean, ironed shirts that first morning because Claire had taken care of them on the weekend, but there was a basket full of dirty washing in the bathroom from the previous day and, because he suspected that Claire was going to ignore it, he delegated the laundry to Zipporah. He supervised the breakfast and hurried everyone up, not even thinking about packed lunches until he popped into the kitchen to snatch his sandwiches off the side where Claire usually left them. The bread box was empty so he grabbed a loaf from the freezer. He slapped jam between pairs of stiff slices and tossed them at the children. Once Alma and Zipporah were on their way, he hustled Jacob into the car and dropped him off at the primary school's Early Drop-off Club before driving across town to work.

It would have been more convenient for Zipporah and Alma to attend his school but Claire had been keen for that not to happen. "They need to be by themselves sometimes," she'd said. "We're always with them, at home, at church. Let them make their own way through high school." And he'd acquiesced because she didn't usually express strong feelings and it felt nice to let her have a say.

He was just in time for work. After supervising registration he taught decimal numbers to Year Seven; it was a relaxing start to the day. He'd taught them only twice before Issy died; they weren't watchful and quiet like the older students, who seemed to be gauging his sadness and looking for signs of weakness. At lunchtime he braved the waft of coffee in the staff room, a wedge of pass-along cards stuffed in his pocket. He blessed his jam sandwiches and ate them slowly, hoping for a missionary opportunity. Dave Weir sat beside him and tried to sell him a ticket for the raffle at the PE department's Race Night. Ian handed over the money but refused a ticket. When he tried to articulate his position on gambling, Dave said, "It's cool—never apologize, never explain." As he left the staff room Ian put the missionary pass-along cards—"Three Ways to Become a Happier Family," "Finding Faith in Christ," and "Truth Restored"— on the windowsill beside the leaflets about student exchanges, dyslexia, and teenage pregnancy. During the afternoon he lost himself in number lines and quadratic equations, and before he knew it, it was time to race to collect Jacob from After-School Club.

Wednesday followed a similar pattern. He learned a thing or two about sandwich preferences and homework supervision and he survived on less sleep than usual because Jacob was up in the night, but he managed, that was the main thing.

"Long-suffering"—the word finally comes to him.

"Please bless Claire with patience and long-suffering."

He pauses for a moment to add, "Me too," and, having settled on the right words, continues with his prayer.

"Please bless Jacob with understanding and bless Zipporah as she continues to develop the qualities to attract a righteous husband."

Ian's knees are complaining; he moves and one of them crunches. The answering of prayers must be a triaged procedure, he thinks, with the most urgent pleas floating to the top of the queue for immediate attention. He has always been happy to wait his turn but tonight, beset by a sense of urgency, he searches for words that will elbow his entreaty to the front of the line.

"Please bless Alma," he says. "Bless him . . . bless him with . . ."

· · ·

BY THIS MORNING, things were running a little more smoothly. They were eating breakfast when Jacob asked how long it would be before Mum got out of Issy's bed.

"Well . . ." Ian struggled for an answer, "she can't, she can't find . . ."

"What? What can't she find?" Alma asked.

"She can't . . . It's very difficult . . ."

"I've just got to do something." Alma dashed out of the kitchen and pounded up the stairs to his bedroom and Ian was grateful for the interruption.

When they got home from work and school there was a casserole dish on the doorstep—Sister Campbell's shepherd's pie, made with instant mashed potatoes, ground wheat, and several tins of baked beans.

"This is pukable," Alma moaned. "I'm going to cycle to school by fart power tomorrow."

"Don't say 'fart,'" Ian scolded.

"I saw this bloke on the way back from school, right? He was about 400 pounds. He was wobbling down the road and his legs were rubbing together, all the way down to his shins—friction burn—ha ha! He was wearing this T-shirt and on the back of it, it said, *'Imagine there's no hunger. —John Lennon.'* So I cycled past and I shouted, 'You don't need to *imagine* it, mate!'" Alma put his fork down and sniggered. "If he ate Sister Campbell's shepherd's pie his massive guts would blow right out of his butt."

"That's enough. Don't be so unkind and ungrateful." They ate in silence after that. There was a long hair in Ian's portion but he couldn't complain—the last time he cooked was on his mission, if you could call that cooking. When he got back he lived at home, so his mum did it all, and then he married Claire so there'd never been any need.

After dinner he needed to go Home Teaching but he didn't want to leave until he knew everything was in hand. Zipporah was finishing the dishes, Alma was outside getting the washing off the line, and Ian was sitting at the kitchen table listening to Jacob read, pleased with himself for organizing things so well, when he heard a strange noise coming from the garden. He told Jacob to keep reading to Zipporah and went outside to see what was going on.

It was Alma, sitting on the grass next to the washing basket, crying loudly. Half the washing spilled out of the basket in an untidy jumble and the rest was still on the line. Alma's face was buried in his hoodie and his shoulders shook as the back garden filled with undulating, high-low howls. Ian couldn't recall a sorrier sight. He hurried over and sat down on the grass.

"Don't cry."

Alma didn't look up from the pillow of his hoodie.

"When I feel—when I'm upset—there's a thing that sometimes helps me to feel a bit better." He reached out to pat Alma's back a couple of times. "I know you miss her, especially out here, perhaps? What makes me feel better is when I do something for someone else. It's called *'losing yourself in service.'* You forget about yourself by making other people feel happy."

Alma's sobs rolled on, so Ian increased his volume.

"I've been thinking that BROTHER RIMMER could do with some HELP. I went to SEE HIM, the other Saturday, the day when Issy . . . He's getting ON A BIT and he can't do everything he used to. His lawn needs MOWING." He paused to rub the curl of Alma's heaving back. "And perhaps he'll give you a few POUNDS for your MISSION FUND if you do a good job."

Alma's sobs suddenly decelerated and Ian mouthed a silent "Thank you" to the heavens for helping him find the right words.

"I'll see Brother Rimmer later, when I go Home Teaching. I'll tell him you'll help on Saturday, instead of going to the Work Day at the chapel. OK?" Alma's face was still buried in the hoodie, but he moved his head up and down a couple of times, which seemed to indicate "Yes."

"Great. Don't forget to bring the rest of the washing in," he called as he hurried back to the kitchen.

.   .   .

FAITH. THAT'S WHAT Alma needs.

"Please bless Alma with faith."

Ian yawns and leans forward, resting the shelf of his folded arms on the mattress.

"Please bless Mum and Dad in Ireland. Help them to bring many souls to the gospel. Please bless everyone at church."

He pauses to remind himself that charity is the pure love of Christ and continues, "Bless the Andersons . . ."

HE WENT HOME Teaching with Brother Stevens. They visited the Andersons, Sister Valentine, and Brother Rimmer. Ian hadn't had a chance to read the Home Teaching message, so Brother Stevens gave him a quick summary in the car on the way to the Andersons' house.

"A young man is dying and the prophet is at his bedside—oh, I'm sorry, Bishop, this is kinda close to home."

"Not at all."

"So the man asks the prophet what will happen to him when he dies, and the prophet reads him some verses from Alma chapter forty that explain it all. The man dies happy—yadda, yadda, yadda—the Book of Mormon promises incomprehensible joy and never-ending happiness, et cetera—it's the most correct book on the face of the Earth, and so on. It's pretty straightforward. We could change it a bit for the Andersons—with his cancer and everything, it might be kinda insensitive."

Ian turned into the Andersons' road, signaled, and pulled over outside their house. "I don't think so," he said. "The prophet chose October's message, it might be just what the Andersons need to hear."

The visit was a short one. Brother Anderson wasn't feeling well and Sister Anderson interrupted the message to ask if Claire had received a letter. Ian said he hadn't had a chance to talk to Claire—she'd been so busy.

"I wrote to say I saw Issy at the Temple."

There was something pink and marshmallowy about Sister Anderson's face and Ian was tempted to test the veracity of her claim
with a series of skewering questions. It wasn't that he thought such
a visitation was impossible, but it seemed both unlikely and hurtful
that Issy would choose to appear to Sister Anderson. He wanted to
say that communications from the Spirit World shouldn't be chatted
about as if they are everyday occurrences, but Sister Anderson's eyes
were dribbly with emotion and he had to remind himself that everyone is given a gift by the Spirit of God: Some are given the gift of
faith, some are given gifts of knowledge or healing, and others are
given the gift of the discerning of Spirits.

"Thank you for telling me," he managed.

Sister Valentine was pleased to see them; she listened to the message carefully, and when Ian asked if there was anything they could
do for her, she nodded.

"I had a dream," she said. "I dreamed I was kneeling at the altar
in the sealing room at the Temple. A man was kneeling opposite me
and we were holding hands—our reflection stretched on and on
forever in the sealing-room mirrors. The man was older—when I
say older, I mean about your age, Bishop." Her voice shushed to a
whisper. "I know it was only a dream and you have to be *careful*
when you talk about the Temple, don't you? But I was there, and
the man was there, and our eyes met across the altar . . . what do
you think it means?"

Brother Stevens was happy to offer an interpretation.

"Gosh, I bet I know what it means, Sister Valentine, I bet you're
gonna get married! I bet you're gonna get married to the guy in your
dream!"

"Do you think so?" Her eyes filled with tears, which she pre-
vented from falling with fluttery, hand-flapping motions. "Do you
really think it means that?"

"Sure," said Brother Stevens, "I think that's exactly what it
means."

"What about you, Bishop? What do you think?"

Ian had been thinking unworthy thoughts as Sister Valentine spoke. He knew it was uncharitable but he couldn't help it: *"Issy died eighteen days ago, I don't care about your ridiculous dream."*

"I think Brother Stevens is right," he said.

Sister Valentine beamed. "Oh, Bishop!" she said and she stood in her doorway and waved as they drove away.

Brother Rimmer's blue-and-white-striped pajamas hung from his enormous waist like a circus tent. He offered Barleycup and Brother Stevens said, "Sure, we'd love some," so Ian had to drink it, even though it tasted like mud.

"I'll put the lad to work, Bishop," Brother Rimmer said when Ian asked him about Alma. "There's nothing like a bit of graft to cheer you up."

Ian dropped Brother Stevens at home after the visits.

"Goodnight," he said. But Brother Stevens didn't get out of the car.

"How are *you* doing, Bishop?"

"Oh, I'm fine."

"And is Claire OK? Only, Ashlee's tried to call her a few times during the day and there's never anyone at home. Jacob said she was in bed when Ashlee phoned yesterday, but it was only five o'clock."

"She's got a bit of a cold."

"Oh, poor Claire."

"All bunged up . . . and a sore throat."

"Give her our love, won't you?"

When Ian got home he felt terrible for lying and it suddenly occurred to him that he was going to have to do it again on Sunday if Claire didn't get out of bed. The situation had the potential to morph into a deception of huge proportions, and that's why he'd stayed up late looking for answers on the Internet.

"PLEASE FORGIVE ME for being untruthful and please bless me to carry on. In the name of Jesus Christ, Amen."

Ian waits beside the bed, hoping for an immediate answer. All he hears is an echo of his own words—"Carry on, carry on, carry on"—and it is enough to keep him going; if he doesn't get into bed he will fall asleep on his knees.

He climbs in carefully and Jacob shifts and rolls closer as the mattress dips, air beating out of his mouth in shallow, sour puffs. Ian remembers how it was when the children were babies and their milky breath blew through bare gums, he remembers Issy occasionally lying between him and Claire when she wasn't well or she'd had a bad dream, and he reaches for Jacob's hand, trying to find the right tightness of grip, one that won't wake him but will hold him fast to mortality.

Jacob persistently arrows toward the center of the bed, no matter how often Ian gently repositions him, and at five o'clock, when there's no longer any point in trying to sleep, Ian climbs out, pulls on yesterday's clothes, and tiptoes down to the kitchen. He makes the sandwiches and loads the washing machine. The kitchen smells strange, like rotting and something else, something burned. It's probably the sympathy flowers; their crispy petals dot the countertops like confetti and the ribs of the leaves are showing. He opens the back door and carries the flowers out to the green garden-waste bin, bunch by bunch. He puts the empty vases and buckets next to the sink to wash later and wipes the countertops clean. The room feels empty and bereft.

When the children come down, he tells them to sit at the kitchen table.

"Mum isn't feeling well at the moment. She's very . . . tired because of everything that's happened. If people ask where she is, you can say she's not feeling very well, but I don't want you to say she's in bed—we'll keep that bit a secret in case people think she's lazy, which she isn't. Understand?"

They all nod.

"Now, what cereal do you want?"

"Shreddies."

"Oh, I forgot to buy a new box on the way back from Home Teaching."

Jacob starts to cry and Alma calls him a big girl.

"I'm a girl," Zipporah says. "And I'm not crying, so what's your point?"

"A proper girl would've done a better job of washing the clothes."

Ian's head is fuzzy from lack of sleep and he's not up to refereeing a fight so he tells them to eat in silence or leave the room.

Later, as Zipporah is leaving for the bus, she turns and says, "Dad, can I stay at Lauren's tonight?" She looks like she is expecting a firm "No," and Ian is about to refuse when he realizes he'd rather not. She's been so good about keeping up with the laundry and the washing-up, and if Claire doesn't get out of bed next week and the Relief Society meals stop coming there'll be the cooking to do too. She deserves a little break and her expression when he says "Yes" is priceless, he feels like a genie granting a wish. "Remember who you are and what you stand for," he adds as she hurries up the stairs to pack some clothes. "The Spirit goes to bed before midnight and so should you!"

When it's time for him to take Jacob to school, he rushes back into the kitchen to collect the sandwiches. That's when he notices Issy's fish, floating sideways near the surface of the tank. He bows his head; it's too much, there's been more than enough sadness— he'll have to dash to the pet shop during his lunch hour.

IAN GRABS THE envelope from his pigeonhole as he passes. It's too fat to be another sympathy card, and although he's in a hurry to get to the pet shop, he's curious. He pushes his thumb past the seal and pauses as he notices a scrawled message below: *I think these belong to you.* His thumb catches, changing the direction of the tear from horizontal to vertical, and the pass-along cards from the missionary meeting spill onto the floor. He kneels to pick them up, stuffing them into his pockets: "Three Ways to Become a Happier Family," "Finding Faith in Christ," and "Truth Restored."

He catches a glimpse of himself in the mirror as he pulls out of the school parking lot—red flushes streak his cheeks like war paint; it's unsettling to think that his missionary work may have offended one of his colleagues, but every man who has been warned *must* warn his neighbor, even if the effort leaves him raw and rebuffed.

He doesn't have time to be fussy about the fish. The one he picks is almost the right color. It seems a bit bigger than Issy's but he can't afford to waste any more time over it or he'll be late for Year Nine Trigonometry.

"Do you need a tank or any food?" the boy at the register asks.

"No thanks." Ian pays and dips his hand into his pocket.

"Can I help you with anything else?"

"No, but I can help you," he says as he presents the boy with "Three Ways to Become a Happier Family."

"YOU'VE GOT SOME felt tip on your hands. Go straight upstairs and give them a good wash before you have a cookie."

Ian watches from the doorway as Jacob trundles up the stairs. When Jacob disappears he rushes back to the car, flips the glove compartment open, and grabs the fish bag.

He dashes into the kitchen, unknots the bag, and slides the new fish into the tank. He tries to take the dead fish out but it's slippery, and when he finally grasps it, it shoots out of his hand like a bar of soap.

He is on his hands and knees with the slippery, cold fish pressed flat under one palm when Jacob appears to collect his cookie. Ian curls his fingers, scraping his cuticles against the floor until the fish is enclosed in his hand. Making sure not to squeeze, he stands, slowly. "I forgot to wash *my* hands," he says. "Silly me. Back in a minute."

In the bathroom he opens his hand and lets the fish fall into the toilet. He unravels a stream of paper, which he balls up and drops on top of the fish. Then he flushes and it is gone.

After he's washed his hands he steps out onto the landing and turns to glance at Issy and Jacob's room. The door is half-closed, he can see the bump of Claire's body under Issy's duvet, and it suddenly occurs to him that maybe she can't get up, maybe she really is ill. He tiptoes to the door and pushes it wide open, it squeaks, but she doesn't move, so he stands there and watches the covers for evidence of respiration, as he did when the children were babies. He thinks there is movement—yes, there is, one breath, and another, she's OK.

He tiptoes away and sits on the top stair. His mother warned him about marrying a nonmember, but he wouldn't listen. If people find out about this, he could be released as Bishop. This trial is not the kind of trial he understands. He knows what to tell himself about death, but this is something else altogether. Pioneer women didn't refuse to stop walking, they didn't lie down on the plains when their children died. He digs in his pocket and pulls out last night's list. He has to keep going. There's the dinner to sort out. There wasn't any food on the doorstep when they got home and Zipporah is going straight to Lauren's house from school; they'll have to manage with the leftovers in the fridge tonight. The bathroom looks a bit rough and there's the ironing to do before he can even think about getting to bed. Tomorrow is the Work Day at the chapel and he's got a pile of math homework to mark. He is so tired. He looks back over his shoulder at Jacob and Issy's room. He'd like to sleep too, but someone's got to *stand and face this*.

— 13 —

Dirty Sandwich Licker

No one has touched Zippy since Issy died. Not properly. Dad sometimes pats her shoulder and Jacob occasionally climbs onto her knee, but no one has hugged her, no one has wrapped their arms around her and asked if she is all right. So when Lauren's mum opens the front door and steps forward with outstretched arms it's lovely but it's also a bit sad, and Zippy has to try really hard not to cry while Lauren's mum rubs her back, as if she is trying to alleviate sadness in the same way women at church rub the backs of their babies to alleviate wind.

"I thought about popping round to yours," Lauren's mum says as she lets go and ushers Lauren and Zippy indoors.

"And I would have, but I wasn't sure . . . your mum's so quiet. I didn't know what to say."

Zippy is glad Lauren's mum didn't pop round. Lauren's mum isn't married and she's got a tattoo on her ankle. Her hair is yellow-blond and she says "Oh God" all the time. She even adds extra syllables: "Oh Go-o-o-o-d," and Zippy can imagine Dad's face if Lauren's mum came to the house with a big helping of condolence and a side order of blasphemy.

"I'm glad you've come, Zippy. I told Lauren there was no way she was going to this Jordan Banks's party on her own. You'll stick together and be sensible, won't you?"

Zippy nods; she always avoids addressing Lauren's mum directly because it feels weird calling her Mel. Every adult she knows is either Mr. or Mrs., Brother or Sister. Lauren's mum is the only person who wants to be called by a first name and Zippy can't get used to it.

"Come and sit down. This'll be nice, won't it? Give you a chance to have some fun."

She's horribly nervous; she hasn't been to a party with nonmembers since she was in junior school—when she asked Dad, she wasn't expecting him to say yes.

She sits next to Lauren on the brown leather sofa. Lauren's house is always tidy because it's just Lauren and her mum, and everything matches too, like in a catalog.

"I'll leave you to yourselves, make yourself at home, Zippy."

"Sorry about that," Lauren says. "I told her not to make a fuss, but she said it'd be worse if she didn't say anything."

"'S OK." Zippy flips her shoes off and lifts her feet onto the sofa.

"What are you wearing tonight?"

She opens her backpack and pulls out a Primark T-shirt and a pair of boot-cut jeans.

"Oh. You can wear something of mine. There's this makeup tutorial we can watch and I'll do your hair too, if you like."

ZIPPY CATCHES ANOTHER glimpse of herself in the mirror above the fireplace in Jordan Banks's living room and tries not to stare. The girl from the YouTube makeup tutorial promised soft, smoky eyes, but Lauren didn't follow the instructions.

"It's difficult with blue eyes and dark hair," she said. "Browns are OK for every day, but I reckon blues are better for parties."

Zippy's eyes look enormous: boggly and metallic-bright like an insect's. Her hair is different too—Lauren backcombed the front section, dragged it behind her ear, and secured it with a flower clip. She is wearing Lauren's clothes: a little blue dress, a cardigan, leggings, and Ugg boots.

It had been lovely not to think, to follow Lauren's persuasive lead and allow herself to be fussed over and tended, ministered to. But if Dad could see her now he would say she looks worldly and immodest, he would be furious, and she isn't sure whether she likes the version of herself that keeps darting past the mirror. It feels as if she is hiding inside someone else's body, as if her eyes are cameras set to record an experience that is happening to someone else.

Music thumps out of an iPod dock in the corner of the room. A few people are half-dancing, others are jammed onto the sofa, vying for space, laughing, and some are sitting on the floor slotted around the perimeter of the room, like the edges of a jigsaw. Zippy recognizes plenty of sixth-formers and lots of them have said hi, but she doesn't know anyone properly, there's no one she can chat to or sit with, and even if there was, they might feel awkward—what to say to the girl whose sister has died?

She checks her watch. She has been wandering between the living room and dining room for almost three minutes since Lauren went upstairs with Jordan Banks. If she had the energy, she might manage to be cross, but everything seems so immaterial. What's the point of being angry about something that won't matter in the morning? She looks for something to do, something that won't make her look lonely and friendless. If she had a phone, she could at least stand in a corner and play a game or pretend to text people. Instead, she studies the bookshelf and stretches something that would ordinarily take seconds into minutes. Jordan Banks's family owns fifty-one books. She has read very few of them, just the Roald Dahl stories that came free with boxes of cereal a few years ago. The rest of the books are by Stephen King and there is also a slim, modern translation of the New Testament. Dad says that Stephen King isn't uplifting; he also says that modern translations of the Bible are useless because they are diluted, like a game of telephone. If she was by herself, Zippy would slide the book off the shelf and have a go at reading the familiar stories in modern English.

When she has stared at the books for far too long, she plods back into the dining room. The table is buried under a flock of bottles and there are stacks of clear plastic cups on the windowsill. She squeezes past several people and helps herself to a cup, looking for something that's OK to drink. She isn't sure what's alcoholic and what's not. There's Coke, which some people at church drink, but she's never tried it. Dad says people who drink Coke aren't obeying the spirit of the Word of Wisdom, and when it comes down to it, it's pretty easy to avoid Coke, much easier than never imagining what it will be like to have sex. She looks for lemonade, but she can't trust any of the clear drinks. One of the sixth-form lads, Will something-or-other, picks up a bottle and fills his cup with a drink that's yellow and fizzy. He notices her watching and angles the bottle toward her cup.

"No thanks," she says.

"Oh yeah. You're Muslim, aren't you?"

"Mormon," she mutters.

Will's wearing a cardigan and big glasses that he probably doesn't need. At least he's talking to her, even though she'd rather not talk about religion because whenever she has to stick up for the Church the words come out wrong. Dad makes it all sound sensible and logical, yet when she borrows his language and ideas, it always sounds absurd.

"Oh, right, a Mormon," he says. "You shouldn't be at a party, should you? It's not allowed, is it?"

"I'm allowed."

"Sorry, I must've got mixed up."

"I think it's Jehovah's Witnesses, the no-parties thing." Zippy's face grows hot under its glaze of makeup. She's embarrassed to have been mistaken for a Jehovah's Witness. Dad says they don't let people have blood transfusions and they believe only a few people can get to heaven. She doesn't know much about them, but they sound weird and she doesn't want anyone to imagine that she's got anything to do with them.

"So what do you want to drink?" Will starts lifting other bottles off the table, reading out names she doesn't recognize.

"Something nonalcoholic," she says.

"A small one won't hurt. Here"—he lifts a white bottle—"try some of this with a bit of Coke. You'll like it."

Zippy looks beneath the bottle's palm tree and sunset picture and catches the word "rum." "No, it's OK, thanks. I'll get some water."

She presses through the crowd, past a kissing couple—"Excuse me, sorry"—and down a step into a long, narrow kitchen. The light is off and there's another couple embracing near the back door; she tries not to look at them and heads straight for the sink.

"Zippy?"

She puts the cup down on the draining board and turns slowly because she doesn't know what to say. It's Adam standing by the back door, practically wearing a girl—she is hanging from his neck like a long scarf, her mouth fastened to his collarbone. And he is holding a green glass bottle.

"What are *you* doing here?"

"Same as you, probably," she says, even though she hasn't come to Jordan Banks's party to drink beer and get off with people.

"Are you by yourself?"

"With Lauren."

"Where is she?"

"Upstairs. With Jordan."

Someone else follows Zippy into the kitchen, switches on the light, and walks to the far end of the room to open the fridge. The girl detaches herself from Adam's neck and turns around. She is blond, tall. Adam rubs his forehead with the heel of his hand, and when the girl looks from him to Zippy her eyes slice a dislike so sharp it hits Zippy like a pair of throwing stars.

"Back in a minute," Adam says to the girl. He puts the beer bottle down next to the sink and nudges Zippy to the back door, which he opens, making an after-you gesture.

She steps into a long, paved garden. It's cool outside, it smells of damp leaves and wood smoke, and the sky is bare black, dotted with occasional stars. Tubs of dying flowers run along the fence that splits the garden from the neighbors. Adam follows her out and strides past her to a wooden bench that leans next to the back fence. He sits down and pats the slats beside him. When Zippy sits, her little dress rises up past mid-thigh, utterly failing the Sit-Down Test.

"Zippy, you're a *nice* girl."

Adam's words hang in the air for a bit. He leans back and rests his hands on his legs. His hands are lovely, he's got piano fingers; he can play loads of nice songs, he likes Coldplay and Iron and Wine, but his dad prefers him to practice hymns in case he gets sent somewhere foreign on his mission and there aren't any pianists. He likes the old hymns that no one sings anymore—"A Mighty Fortress Is Our God" and "Cast Thy Burden Upon the Lord"—he says they've got better harmonies. Sometimes he sits and plays them after church while everyone's chatting and Zippy watches him. She watches him on the sports field at school during rugby practices too. He wears a number 8 shirt and he pushes at the back of the scrum, grabbing the other lads and pulling them over. No one at the party would believe that he sometimes sings hymns. She glances at his fingers, happy that a part of him is hidden from everyone except her.

"You shouldn't be here, Zippy."

She wonders how much beer he's had; she's seen drunken people only on television, where they fall over in the street, pull angry faces, and laugh at stuff that isn't funny. Adam looks like himself; when he walked to the bench he walked in a straight line, so he can't be drunk, and he's mistaken if he thinks she's going to let him tell her off.

"Neither should you."

"Well, that's me told."

"Yeah, consider yourself told, Carmichael." She gives him a light punch on the shoulder, glad of the chance to make a joke out of things, uncertain how else to respond to their mutual misde-meanors: her immodest clothes and his consumption of *beer* while that girl slithered all over him. "Don't let me ever catch you at it again," she teases.

"You won't," he says.

"Good." She places a tentative hand on his shoulder. "No one's perfect. Everyone makes mistakes. I won't tell my dad or anyone about the beer . . . or the girl." She moves her hand to her lap and waits for him to thank her.

"Right," he says.

"Maybe you shouldn't go to parties. And maybe I shouldn't ei-ther," she adds quickly. "But you—you need to think about prepar-ing for your mission."

"I think about it all the time."

"That's good."

"Some people don't go, you know."

"Yeah, sad, isn't it?"

"And loads of lads muck about before they go."

"Oh, I don't think they do."

"My brother, right? He was drinking and doing other stuff—*everything*. Then he repented and off he went. When you get back from your mission everyone expects you to get married straight away, so the only time to muck about is before you go."

"That's just your brother, not loads of lads. It's no reason for *you* to muck about and break the commandments."

"Do you seriously think *anyone* keeps all the commandments?"

"People try." Zippy slips her hands under her thighs, hiding them from the spiky cold. "I try."

"Do you know what Brother Campbell said once? He said proper kissing before marriage is wrong; if you kiss someone in a way you wouldn't kiss your mum, your dad, or your sister, it's a sin. What a load of bollocks!"

Zippy squirms. You aren't supposed to criticize leaders, even if the criticism is true. She pulls her hands out from under her thighs and rubs them together nervously.

"I've been thinking—it's the best thing about Critical Thinking, you get to think for homework. Are you going to do it next year?"

"No, Dad says it's Atheism for Beginners masquerading as an AS level."

He snorts. "Bishop Bradley's so serious, no offense—he is, though, isn't he? So, here's what I've been thinking . . . if you weren't already a member, would you join the Church?"

She has thought about this before. "No," she confesses.

"Me neither."

"But I've worked it out—that's *why* we've been born into it, see? Heavenly Father knew we wouldn't find the truth any other way. It's pretty amazing that out of all the billions of people in the world, we've got the truth."

She stares up at the vast black sky. "Look up. See? The universe is so big and like, *incredible*. Do you ever . . . do you think we knew each other before we came to Earth? In the preexistence? Sometimes I like to think—I think we were probably friends. And now here we are, together." She pauses and risks another pat on his shoulder while he's looking at the stars. "We're being tested to see if we'll choose the right. If we make mistakes, we can repent. Sometimes when I think about how amazing it is my head goes all spinny. Brother Campbell's got to be wrong about kissing, my dad's never said anything like that—and you're right, he *is* really serious—but he says kissing's fine, as long as you keep your hands to yourself."

"Yeah, well, Brother Campbell was reading it out of a book by a General Authority. No offense to your dad, but he's only the Bishop."

"Your dad's the Stake President and I bet he's never said any-thing about not kissing."

"He never talks about stuff like that."

"Lucky you. My mum and dad did it together. Mum sat there

wringing her hands while Dad talked about the Sacred Powers of Procreation; it was like a Family Home Evening lesson just for me— they even started with a prayer."

Adam shakes his head.

"I was so embarrassed," she says. "I kept laughing, but it wasn't funny. That book of Brother Campbell's was probably really old."

"Would you seriously marry someone you'd never kissed?"

She looks at Adam's mouth and thinks she'd marry him no matter what, even if he'd never held her hand or said he loved her. "Course not," she says.

"Then he started going on about licking the butter off sandwiches."

"Who, Brother Campbell?"

"Yeah, he reckons if you kiss a girl and you *don't* marry her, you've licked the butter off another man's sandwich."

"It's just the Campbells, they're weird. Sister Campbell thinks girls who've, you know, *done it* are filthy."

"It *is* different for girls," he says.

"What do you mean?"

"It's just different."

"How?"

"Well, think about my finger—how many germs are on my finger? Not many, right?" He holds his hand up and wiggles his index finger at her. "Now think about how many germs are in my mouth." He turns sideways and opens his mouth wide. When he breathes out his breath smells bready and she wonders if it's what beer smells like.

"So my finger is a bit like . . . and my mouth is, well, you know . . . And it's not as bad for a bloke, is it?"

Zippy becomes aware of the workings of her heart as it flushes indignation along miles of capillaries. The feeling folds her in half and she reaches for her feet in an effort to curl her body around it, sliding her hands into Lauren's Ugg boots as she pretends to adjust her socks. "You *really* think that?" She straightens; maybe he has drunk too much beer, perhaps drunken people fall over their thoughts before they fall over their feet. "Adam, you sound like Angel Clare."

"Who's she?"

"Oh, no one."

"This is a weird conversation."

She stares straight ahead, at the back of Jordan Banks's house. People are talking and laughing in the kitchen. Looking at them move behind the window is like watching a reality show on a flat-screen TV. No one in the kitchen has the gospel, none of them know where they came from, why they are here, and where they are going after they die; this thought usually cheers her and makes her feel extraordinary.

"So, have you already . . . ?" She's glad that the light from the kitchen window is mostly shining over the part of the garden that is nearest to the house and she and Adam are swathed in shadows.

"No." He shakes his head and his shoulders rise defensively as he adds, "Not yet."

"Is there someone you'd like to . . . ?" She can't finish the sentence. Why does he think it doesn't matter if he breaks the commandments?

"Why are you here? Is it to do with Issy?"

"No."

"Don't do anything stupid while you're upset."

Zippy bites the insides of her cheeks and digs her nails into the palm of one hand.

"People reckon when bad stuff happens you get some kind of spiritual experience," he continues. "Like a sort of consolation prize or something, you know—*'after the trial cometh the blessings.'*"

"It's not like that. You just feel really upset all the time. It's actually pretty hard." Her voice wobbles and ducks under her windpipe and it takes her a moment to catch and reclaim it.

Adam sighs. He puts his arm around her shoulder, pulls her

close, and she leans against him awkwardly, holding her face away from his body.

"Oh, come on." He slides his hand up to her head and angles her jaw with his fingertips until her cheek meets his chest. She holds her breath for a moment, afraid to swallow in case it sounds like a gulp. She can hear his heart through his T-shirt; she would like to turn her head, press her mouth to his chest, and eat every beat.

"I'm trying to be good," she continues. "It's not easy, is it?"

"No."

"Sometimes I think about things I shouldn't."

Adam's chest dips and she can tell he is amused.

"Everyone does," he says.

"But I'm trying."

"I know. You're a good person. You *believe.*" He leans his head down to meet hers and strokes her crown with the slope of his jaw.

" '*We believe all things, we hope all things* . . .' " she cites, warming the fabric of his T-shirt with the puff of her breath.

"Don't quote the Articles of Faith at me."

"Sorry."

"You should go home."

"OK."

But she doesn't move. She wants to memorize this moment so she can retrieve it—hang it up in her imagination and take it out every so often to rewear the imprint of his chest against her cheek, resmell his skin, and relisten to the low thud of his heart. Dad says teenagers don't feel proper love; he says it's just infatuation. But he's wrong. She knows what she feels is love, she can tell because it's not just a shivery, upside-down, flip-flopping feeling, it's also fierce and determined, and it won't change, even after all the silly stuff he's just said.

"Come on, then." He lifts his arm away and stands. "Up you get." He extends his hand and Zippy clasps it, allowing him to pull her to her feet. "I'll find Lauren for you, if you like," he says.

She nods. He's still holding her hand and she doesn't want to say anything in case it makes him let go.

His thumb strokes her ring finger. "Is that a CTR ring?"

"Yes." She unfastens her hand and hides it behind her back.

"As if you need reminding to Choose The Right."

He reaches out to touch the flower clip behind her ear. She inches forward and so does he and then he is somehow hugging her. His arms lock behind her and his hands press her to him and she can feel each of his fingers stamping their warmth through the fabric of her borrowed cardigan and dress. She wedges her cheek against the bump of his pectoral muscle and clamps her arms around his waist. His belt buckle digs into her stomach and she clings to him until she feels soft everywhere, until her knees are melting and she wants to spread herself all over him like honey on toast. If she could, she would climb right inside his skin and wrap herself up in him. She closes her eyes and forgets all about finding Lauren and going home.

ZIPPY LIES ON the roll-out bed, staring at the ceiling as Lauren describes kissing Jordan Banks.

"He was so good at it I was practically having snogasms." Zippy isn't exactly sure what Lauren means, but she makes agreeable noises in the right places. She doesn't say anything about Adam— what happened between them is private.

She's glad when Lauren stops talking and falls asleep because it means she can cry in peace. The covers are scratchy, they don't smell like home, and she isn't sure why she is crying, whether it's because Issy is dead and Mum is hiding upstairs like Mrs. Rochester, or because of what happened when Adam stopped hugging her in the garden.

"You're nice," he said, and then he bent down and kissed her. Perhaps he had intended only one small peck at the verge of her lips, but she didn't want one of those Brother Campbell-approved kisses, so she turned her head until their mouths bumped and Adam made a noise like a sigh and kissed her properly. His lips were warm and soft and cautious at first. When he slipped his tongue into her mouth he tasted like bread and himself—remembering it makes her stom-

ach scrunch and reminds her of something Dad always says to illustrate that obedience is freedom: *"Kites have to be tethered before
they can fly."* While Adam was kissing her she felt grounded for the
first time in weeks, as if her gravity had been switched on again and
her feet were suddenly heavier than her grief; she felt back within
herself, completely alive, grateful for the drum of her heart, the thud
of her blood, and, somewhere inside, she was *flying*.

When he pulled his lips away she tried to think of a way to make
him carry on. She remembered the blond girl in the kitchen standing
with her mouth on his collarbone; her own lips wouldn't reach that
high—she'd get a mouthful of T-shirt if she tried to kiss him there—
but it didn't matter because he wasn't stopping, he was just bending
down to kiss her neck, and she couldn't stand there doing nothing,
so she grabbed one of his hands, lifted it to her mouth and kissed
the pads of his thumb and fingers, right on the spots where they
touch the piano keys. And when she'd kissed every one, she started
again, and again, and carried on until he slid the tip of his index
finger into her mouth. She explored it with the end of her tongue
and he pushed it farther, demonstrating that he didn't mind the
germs in her mouth, and she began to suspect he hadn't been thinking properly when he said the horrible stuff about girls. She licked
his finger and then she sucked it, which he seemed to like because
the harder she sucked, the more fiercely he kissed her neck, which
was lovely: a combination of cheek and lips, of rough and soft,
grazing her neck, her collarbone, and then, as he slid her cardigan
and the strap of Lauren's dress to one side, her shoulder. She wasn't
sure whether he should be doing that, whether it was breaking the
Law of Chastity, but when he nibbled her skin her stomach skipped
and she responded by testing his finger with the blades of her teeth.

"Whoa, Zippy."

He took a step back; he was breathing heavily and she realized
she was too. He *definitely* liked her. He couldn't kiss her like that
and not like her. Maybe he even *loved* her—she felt as if she might
burst into song, the way they do in musicals and Disney movies. It

was suddenly easy to imagine what it might be like to take all her clothes off in front of a man and let him touch her everywhere, not minding at all about being modest. It was easy to envisage how she might one day walk the tightrope between sin and love without falling off, how it could be wonderful and not wicked.

She wanted to say *"I love you,"* the words were right there, all warm and ready in her throat, when it occurred to her that the only thing better than being kissed by Adam would be for Issy to be alive, and remembering Issy made her sad, so she made a little joke.

"You've got to marry me now, you dirty sandwich licker."

Adam's eyebrows shot up and he pulled a horrible face, as if marrying her was the worst thing he could possibly imagine. Then he hurried over to Jordan Banks's back door and held it open.

"It was a joke," she said as she stepped into the kitchen. He didn't respond. He pushed past the dining-room crowd and went straight upstairs. She followed him as far as the hall but stopped beside the bottom stair. A few moments later, Lauren came down.

"Adam said you want to go. Are you OK?"

She nodded and dawdled as they approached the front door, glancing over her shoulder, hoping he would reappear on the stairs.

The roll-out bed isn't even a little bit comfy but it doesn't matter, there's more important stuff to worry about. Maybe the blond girl was waiting upstairs for Adam, perhaps he wrapped his arms around her, told her she was nice and broke all sorts of commandments. What if he dies unexpectedly, before he has repented? He won't go to the Celestial Kingdom, he'll have to wait in the Spirit Prison until he is judged and then he'll have to spend Eternity in one of the lower Kingdoms, without a wife or any family, forever. She scrubs at her cheeks with her pajama sleeves, she's got to stop thinking about miserable stuff—Adam's not likely to die for a long time.

She rolls onto her side and hugs a big dollop of duvet. She has ruined everything with her scary, desperate joke—*all agony, no hope*. He'll never love her now.

— 14 —

Stupid Twat

Cabbage and fish—the smell gusts out like a big fart when Brother Rimmer opens the front door.

"Well, you've got a face like a line of wet washing, Alma Bradley."

Course he has—last Saturday he had to clean the chapel and today he's stuck being an odd-job man. Al shouldn't be here at all, he should be playing football with Matty and the rest of the team.

Brother Rimmer tuts and shuffles back carefully—he could do with one of those reversing alarms: beep, beep, beep. He is the widest person Al knows: normal at the top, with a droopy neck and sloped shoulders, but his waist, oh, it's *tremendous,* as if all of his fat has slipped down to his middle, where it hangs like a massive ring doughnut.

The hall is decorated with jagged-edged pictures of the prophets torn out of the *Ensign* and Blu-tacked to the wallpaper. Mum says Brother Rimmer is a *character.* On Fast and Testimony Sundays he likes to wobble up to the pulpit and say weird shit. Once he said if everyone prayed at the same time they'd generate enough energy to power a lightbulb.

"Come in, come in."

Al follows Brother Rimmer into the living room.

"Sit down there, lad."

He perches on the edge of a grubby pink velvet sofa with tassels along the bottom. Brother Rimmer lifts his colossal cardigan out of the way and sits on a swivel chair next to his computer.

"I bought this after Sister Rimmer died," he says, "with the compensation money." He pats the computer as if it's alive.

Sister Rimmer had a hip replacement and then she died. Brother Rimmer sued. Everyone knows because he often mentions it in Testimony Meeting, although he never says how much money he got.

Next to the computer is a special keyboard with wide white keys that looks like it was designed for partially sighted people, but Brother Rimmer probably needs it for his fat fingers.

"This computer has given me a whole new lease on life," he says as he switches it on, like he's in an ad or something. "Did you know that the Interwebs were created so people can trace their ancestors and do their Temple work?"

Al knows he should let this pass, but he's fed up. "They told us at school that a bloke called Tim Berners-Lee invented the Internet."

Brother Rimmer chuckles. "I expect the Holy Ghost prompted him to do it—Tim whatsit *and* God." He taps his nose with his finger as if he has just revealed a Top-Secret Fact. "Do you want to see my family history?" He opens a Word document. "Look here," he says. "Look what I've found out. I'm related to the royal family and they're related to Jesus through the kings of Scotland, see? And the kings of Ireland and the Viking kings, are you following me? And here we've got the kings of Israel. If you go back further, I'm related to Noah and then Adam. There you are, lad. What do you think of that?"

"I don't know."

"I like to surf the Interwebs and find things out. Just because I'm old doesn't mean I've forgotten how to use my noodle."

Al sniggers.

"So, shall we get to work, then?" Brother Rimmer heaves himself to his feet and motions to Al to follow him. He heads into a poky kitchen with funny, old-fashioned, boxy units in a horrible shade of green, then he opens the back door to reveal a large gar-

den, covered in knee-high grass, dandelions, and other flowers Al
can't name. It's going to take hours and hours to mow.

On the left side of the garden there's a garage with a rusty-looking
up-and-over door and a window and door in its side.

"Is that where you keep your lawnmower?"

"Oh, I've changed my mind. I'm not too bothered about the
grass. *'And God said let the earth bring forth grass'*—who am I to
argue? There's more important things to be getting on with."
Brother Rimmer waddles out into the garden.

"Come on," he says. "Keep up!"

When he reaches the garage he pulls a set of keys out of his cardigan pocket. He fumbles for a moment before slipping the right
one into the lock. The door opens and there is a warm waft of wood
and something sharp and tangy that reminds Al of the stuff people
paint on their fences. Brother Rimmer turns on the light and steps
inside.

Al follows. He scans the space: ancient lawnmower, a couple of
toolboxes, a high-backed armchair, and several shelves loaded with
canned food—mushy peas, corned beef, and peach slices. In the
middle of the garage something is covered by a massive sheet.

"Put the wood in the hole, lad."

"What?"

"Close the door!"

"Oh, OK."

Once Al has shut the door, Brother Rimmer swoops the sheet
away, as if he's doing a magic trick, and Al is disappointed. Underneath there's just a wooden *thing*. A sort of big box on wheels.

"Well, what do you think of that?"

Al can see he's supposed to be impressed, but he isn't.

"It's a handcart, Alma Bradley, a genuine, handmade handcart.
I built it myself and you and I are going to restore it." Brother Rim-
mer sinks into the armchair. "You aren't the most miserable person
I've ever seen, but you look like him. Come on, lad! Open up the big

toolbox. Unclip it just there. You want the sandpaper sheets. The thickest one, that's right. Now rub along the wood in the same direction as the grain. Look for the grain—it's like a tide—see which way it's going, and rub."

Al brushes the paper along one of the cart's long arms. The scratchy noise makes his hair stand on end.

"That's right! Take your jacket off and put some muscle into it. Here, give it to me, I'll look after it for you. Know why I made the handcart?"

"No." Al's arm is already beginning to ache.

"It'd certainly come in handy if the prophet said it was time to return to Zion, wouldn't it, eh? We used to talk about it a lot, when Sister Rimmer and I first joined the Church—the gathering of the saints."

"But they had planes when you joined the Church, didn't they? So you wouldn't need a handcart."

"Course they did, I'm not that old! But all sorts'll happen in the Last Days. What if you needed to flee and there weren't any planes left? I'll tell you what you'd do; you'd pack your belongings and your Food Storage in this old girl. Then you'd pull her to Liverpool, where you'd hop on a boat to New York and trek to Utah, just like the pioneers.

"Keep rubbing, that's right. Once you've done that arm, come round here and do this one. Not long 'til the Second Coming now. Have you been watching for the signs of the times?"

"No."

" *'No man knoweth the hour,'* but the righteous will recognize the signs. Do you know what it says in my Patriarchal Blessing? It says I'll live to see it. *I'll see the Second Coming!* How about that, then?"

Al shrugs. People have been waiting for the Second Coming for two thousand years. It probably won't happen. It's just something to talk about, like England winning the World Cup.

"Every nation will gather in Jerusalem to see Jesus appear on the

Mount of Olives and destroy the wicked people who don't believe. He'll roast them like crackling and then he'll bring peace to Earth. And I'm going to see it all. Have you had your Patriarchal Blessing?"

"No."

"Why not?"

"I dunno."

"So you don't even know which of the ten tribes you're from? You should get it, lad. It'll set your whole life out on paper and let you know what's to come. Once you know what's coming, there's no need to be scared. *'If ye are prepared, ye shall not fear.'*"

"The stuff about people being roasted sounds pretty scary to me."

"Course it isn't, it won't be happening to you. Do you know your Articles of Faith?"

Al had to memorize all thirteen Articles of Faith when he graduated from Primary to Youth. Mum bought him a packet of football cards for every article he memorized, but he can't remember any of them now.

"Give us number ten."

He clears his throat. "*'We believe . . .'*"

"Good guess! They mostly start with 'We believe,' so you were pretty safe there. *'We believe in the literal gathering of Israel and in the restoration of the Ten Tribes; that Zion will be built upon the American continent; that Christ will reign personally upon the earth; and that the earth will be renewed and receive its paradisiacal glory.'*"

"Oh, yeah."

"*'Come to Zion, Come to Zion! For your coming Lord is nigh!'*" Brother Rimmer sings the words of the hymn in a thin, reedy voice. "Do you know where the ten tribes are?"

"No, um—are they lost?"

"I've been researching it on my computer and guess what? They're inside the Earth."

Al stops sanding. "What? Alive? And inside the Earth?"

"That's why no one's found them. Airplanes aren't allowed to fly over the North and South Poles. You know why? It's where the openings are. And it's why you can't see the Poles properly on Google Earth."

"Maybe you can't see properly 'cause everything's, you know, dead white?"

"There's an expedition planned for next year, to the North Pole, just above the Arctic Circle, where the sea isn't level anymore. They're going to search for the opening. I've made a donation."

Al shakes his head. Real life isn't exciting enough for some people. You can tell them amazing things, true facts like Zidane was never caught offside in his whole career or Beckham scored a goal against Chelsea that traveled into the back of the net at 97.9 mph, and they don't care.

"You shouldn't send money to anyone; you have to treat people online like you'd treat them in real life—that's what they say at school. If someone knocked on your door selling stuff, you'd tell them to go away, wouldn't you?"

Brother Rimmer laughs. "Course I wouldn't," he says. "How do you think I joined the Church in the first place? The missionaries knocked on my door and I said, 'Come in.'"

"Oh."

"I'd never met anyone from America before. America was *big* back then and people actually liked it—Elvis Presley and the Everly Brothers, Oldsmobiles, Cadillacs—very exciting. Sister Rimmer and I weren't much older than the missionaries. When you're a convert, like me, you never forget *your* missionaries. Elder Nielson—could've eaten an apple through a barbed-wire fence with those big white teeth—and Elder Riter.

"Sister Rimmer wasn't having any of it at first. But then she read the Book of Mormon and when she prayed to find out if it was true, that was that. We joined the Church right away. We hadn't been members long when Elder Riter gave Sister Rimmer a blessing because we hadn't had any children." Brother Rimmer pauses to clear his throat.

"Keep rubbing, that's right. When you get to the end, swap to the fine paper. Sister Rimmer fell pregnant. And we had our daughter."

Al fetches the finer paper from the big toolbox. "I didn't know you have a daughter," he says.

"Our Andrea died. She drowned."

Al's hand drops to his side; he should say something nice to Brother Rimmer but he can't think what, he can't even borrow something nice that someone said to him when they heard about Issy 'cause they all spouted crap.

"She was about your age. We never had any others. Only her."

Al rubs the handcart's arms again so he doesn't have to watch Brother Rimmer's neck wobble sadly as he swallows.

"Everything happens for a reason."

Al rubs harder. He hates it when people say that. It makes it seem like Heavenly Father goes around killing children in order to teach their families a lesson.

"People are never the same after something like that. It happened to the pioneers all the time, you know. Have you seen pictures of Joseph Smith's wife, Emma? She's that miserable, you'd think they dropped a stitch when they knitted her face. But five of her children died, didn't they? It leaves a mark. Changes people forever."

Al thinks of Mum and hopes Brother Rimmer is wrong.

"Right, then." Brother Rimmer hefts himself to his feet. "I bet your stomach thinks your throat's been cut. Piece of cake and a drink?"

"Yes please."

Al watches through the garage window as Brother Rimmer shuffles along the bottom half of the garden before disappearing into the house.

He puts the sandpaper down in the bed of the handcart, rubs the wood dust from his hands, and takes a little stroll around the garage. On the floor, next to the big plastic toolbox, is a smaller box, old and rusty, shaped like a little house with a handle on its roof. Al nudges it with his toe, then he bends and tries to flick the clasp up but it seems to be rusted shut. He tries again; this time it snaps open. He glances out the window; there's no sign of Brother Rimmer.

Inside the box there's an old *Ensign* from 1973. It's a special issue, "The Church in Europe." Al flips to the middle page and a series of profiles titled "The European Saints." It's weird how members of the Church call one another saints. Al is drawn to a picture of a large man in a brown tartan suit. It takes a moment for him to realize that it's Brother Rimmer. He puts the magazine down and has a look to see what else is in the old toolbox. There's a handkerchief with fancy initials sewn into one corner and a small, old-fashioned teddy bear with movable arms and legs. Underneath the handkerchief and the teddy bear, at the bottom of the toolbox, there's an envelope. Al slips it out and, as it's resealable, he opens it. Inside there's a wad of cash. He grabs a corner of one of the notes and pulls it out. A fifty.

What is it with grown-ups and money? Does Brother Rimmer think he won't get a chance to go to the bank before he sets off with his handcart? How can he be so dense? Anyone could break into the garage. It would be easy to smash the window and climb in.

Al slides the note back into the envelope and darts to the window. There's still no sign of Brother Rimmer. He puts everything back in the box and closes the lid.

He'd like to think the money is a Tender Mercy. Unfortunately, it's almost certainly a *temptation*. And although it says in the scriptures that no one will ever be tempted beyond what they can bear, he isn't sure he can resist.

HE WAS BRINGING the washing in on Thursday evening when he was punched by a thump of dread. His hoodie was hanging on the line and he had no idea how it had got there.

At breakfast Dad started to say Mum had lost something:

"She can't find . . . she can't find . . ." and it occurred to Al that maybe Mum had gone to bed because she couldn't find the money, a problem he could easily fix, and so he dashed upstairs, dragged the hoodie out of the bottom of his wardrobe, and chucked it on his bed as a reminder to put the money back later that evening when Dad would be out Home Teaching and there was no chance of getting caught.

And yet there it was, dangling from the washing line. He didn't dare reach for it because one of two things was suddenly true: either Zippy had emptied the pocket, or the money was still there. He was so scared he actually prayed. He didn't get down on his knees or anything, he just closed his eyes and whispered, "Please don't let the money be in my pocket, Heavenly Father." And then, sensing that a polite request might not be enough, he offered some inducements. "I'll read the scriptures every day, for a week . . . I'll be nice to Jacob . . . I won't swear . . . I'll try not to wind Dad up . . . I'll sing the right words to the hymns: I'll sing 'We Are All Enlisted' instead of 'We Are All Conscripted' . . . I'll go upstairs and talk to Mum . . . I'll do all of it, *if* the money isn't there."

As soon as he opened his eyes and allowed himself a proper look at the pocket, he knew. He unzipped it slowly, edging his fingers inside until they nudged the wet roll of cash. He pulled it out, slipped the red elastic band away, and tried to separate the notes. It seemed like the most sensible thing to do—if he didn't separate them they might stick to one another and become inseparable as they dried. His fingernails were blunt and he made a little rip in one mushy corner. Perhaps if he waited until the notes were slightly drier he could peel them apart and let them dry in the air. But how would he hide them while they dried? It wasn't as if he could pin them to the washing line. What the hell was he going to do? He wrapped the band around the money and zipped it back into the pocket. His hands were shaking and he felt sick. It was all Mum's fault for going to bed. And Zippy's fault for being a busybody—who'd asked her to nick his hoodie and lump it in with the washing? He was furious with them both, but he knew someone else was also at fault: him. What if he hadn't taken the money? Maybe missing it had been Mum's final straw. Perhaps she'd been looking for it on Monday and that was why she was in bed when they got home from school. He imagined her opening her drawer in order to touch the money and feel its possibilities; he pictured her frantically dragging Temple garments out like a magician with a long string of handkerchiefs. She probably searched the house from top to bottom, same as the woman in the parable of the lost coin—poor Mum.

Al's knees folded as suddenly as a Wolverhampton Wanderers defense and he ended up smack on his butt under the washing line, crying. Once he started, he couldn't stop; it was well embarrassing when Dad came out but then Dad said he could earn some money from Brother Rimmer and, as long as he ignored the bit about putting the earnings in his mission fund, it seemed like one of those Tender Mercy things 'cause he suddenly had a way to replace any spoiled notes.

After Dad went Home Teaching, Al dragged Jacob outside to play football but Jacob found a dead wasp and scampered off into the house with it. Al stayed outside for a while, dribbling the ball up and down the garden, slaloming around the fallen apples. The exercise forced the anxiety about the money into his feet, and after he'd booted it about for a bit and given it a good kicking, he had an idea.

When he was slick with sweat and nicely tired he went back indoors and annoyed Jacob until he retreated to bed. Zippy told him off for setting a bad example. "You're meant to be the priesthood holder while Dad's out," she moaned before flouncing upstairs to read soppy books. He didn't expect her to reappear until morning and there wasn't much chance of Mum coming down either, so he was safe.

He switched on the TV, loud enough to provide some background noise, but not so loud that he wouldn't hear if someone came down the stairs. He sneaked along the hallway into the kitchen, delved into the washing basket, retrieved the hoodie, and got the wet money out of its pocket. He found a spot on the kitchen countertop that wasn't sprinkled with dead flower bits, placed the wad there and unfastened the elastic band. He'd overreacted, all was not lost; he just needed to hurry the drying process before he attempted to separate the notes again.

He opened the microwave and placed the pile of money on the turntable. He wasn't sure how long to nuke it for. He'd seen Mum put baking potatoes and frozen chickens in there for ages. He keyed in five minutes—he reckoned it'd be plenty.

While the turntable revolved he rehearsed his plan. Once the notes were dry he'd stick them under something heavy, to press out the wrinkles. Hopefully the small tears he'd made when he first tried to pull them apart wouldn't matter, but if there was a problem he'd replace any damaged notes with money he earned at Brother Rimmer's and then he'd roll them up again and slip them back into Mum's drawer.

He watched the notes revolve until he heard a little snap that sounded like the microwave popcorn Mum occasionally bought for a treat. He looked for the STOP button and he couldn't find one, there was no bloody STOP button. The microwave carried on whirling the money round and round, practically mocking him—ner-ner ner ner-ner. When he saw something spark he grabbed the door, pulled, and it opened to reveal a small lick of flame rising from the pile of notes. He didn't panic—he'd sat through too many boring Family Home Evening lessons on emergency preparedness—he flipped up the arm of the tap, grabbed a tea towel, soaked it, bunched it into a ball, and lobbed it on top of the money. Then he panicked.

He dashed out into the garden, kicked several of the apple trees, and shouted every swearword he knew. The lawn was littered with fallen apples, which he crushed, kicked, and chucked at the hedge, enjoying the whack as they broke through the branches and smashed into the wall behind.

Back inside he wedged the kitchen door open to get rid of the burny smell. Then he lifted the tea towel out of the microwave, rinsed it under the tap, and chucked it in the washing machine, hoping Zippy wouldn't notice it in the morning when she loaded the machine. Finally, he had a proper look in the microwave. The money sat in a puddle of water and tiny black flakes, and when he lifted it out he could see there was a small burn hole right next to Charles Darwin's nose that pierced almost every note.

He left the notes on the side while he wiped the water and flakes out of the microwave with thick wedges of paper towels. When he'd finished, he closed the back door and rolled the wet, burned paper into a soggy cylinder, which he fastened with the elastic band. The hoodie lay on top of the pile of clean washing. He unzipped the pocket and put the money back before tying the sleeves around his waist. On his way to his room he paused at the under-stairs cupboard, unfastening the latch to reveal shelves of canned food and backpacks stuffed with sleeping bags, camping equipment, spare clothes, and matches. He wasn't sure if the food storage and emergency supplies were for the Second Coming or just a matter of common sense, it depended on whether he listened to Dad or Mum; either way he reckoned he was safe to help himself to a four-pack of Mars bars from the nearest backpack: It wasn't the end of the world, but it felt like it.

Upstairs, he knelt beside his bed, folded his arms, and bowed his head. He tried to picture someone there, someone who cared about what had just happened, but he couldn't hear past the voice in his head. It jabbered on as he chain-ate the Mars bars. It wasn't the *"still small voice"* everyone goes on about at church; it was loud and goading, and it was saying, "You stupid, stupid twat."

WHAT AL'S ABOUT to do is only swapsies, it's not stealing, he's not a complete shit. Mum's money may be worthless now, but if the Second Coming ever happens and Brother Rimmer makes it through—not likely, as it'll probably resemble a Zombie Apocalypse—he'll also have to get through Armageddon, and after that people won't mind a little fire damage on their notes, will they?

Al empties the toolbox and helps himself to twelve fifty-pound notes. He considers taking a thirteenth but decides against it—that would be stealing, he'll earn the twenty-quid difference. He unravels Mum's cash and tries to flatten it before stuffing it into the envelope, where it curls and bunches. Never mind, once everything's back in the box it's impossible to tell.

When he hears Brother Rimmer's back door close, Al nudges the toolbox back to its original position and opens the garage door. Brother Rimmer waddles through the long grass carrying a tray.

"Here, let me, I'll take that for you."

Brother Rimmer shuffles back to the armchair and Al puts the tray down on the floor. He passes a steaming mug and a plated slab of cake to Brother Rimmer. Then he sits down next to the tray, even though the floor's covered in wood dust, picks up his mug, and has a sip. Ugh—Barleycup. At least the cake is chocolate and Brother Rimmer has cut big pieces.

"Have you ever done anything really brave, Alma Bradley?"

"No." Al's mouth makes a sticky noise when he speaks.

"Do you wish you had?"

"Not really."

"Don't you want to do great things?"

"I'd like to play for Liverpool." He takes another bite of cake.

"I mean eternally significant things."

"I dunno," he says with his mouth full. "Not really. I just want to do normal things."

"Have you heard of the Sweetwater River Rescue?"

Al shakes his head.

"In the 1840s three young men, a little bit older than you, carried members of the Martin Handcart Company across the Sweetwater River. It was waist-deep and there were chunks of ice floating in it. The boys all died later as a result of their efforts, and Brigham Young said their salvation was assured by their bravery. Think of that—one brave thing and BAM! Your salvation's assured."

"I've never done anything brave." Al licks the chocolate off his fingers. It's not so bad, this, sitting here eating cake and listening to Brother Rimmer spout weird shit. He can think of much worse things, like cleaning urinals and watching endless hours of General Conference. "What about you?" he asks. "Have you ever done anything dead brave?"

"Not so as you'd know." Brother Rimmer slurps his Barleycup and stares at the bare garage wall.

Al stands and brushes the crumbs off his sweat suit bottoms. He gets the sandpaper out of the handcart and starts sanding where he left off. He'd been certain that Brother Rimmer was about to tell him an amazing story of bravery. It's hard to work out what adults are going on about sometimes.

"I was there when Andrea drowned," Brother Rimmer says.

Al concentrates on following the grain of the wood.

"I couldn't save her. Never been much of a swimmer." There's a big clink as Brother Rimmer puts his mug down on the concrete floor. "Faith is an act of tremendous bravery, Alma Bradley."

Al stops sanding again and glances at Brother Rimmer, spilling out of the armchair—a big dollop of sadness. Al doesn't understand faith. He isn't sure whether faith is brave or stupid; sometimes they go together. When someone tries to rescue a dog from a frozen lake and they end up dead, it's probably brave *and* stupid.

"I couldn't sleep after Andrea died. I used to come out here. Used to park the car in here back then, used to have a nice garden, kept my seeds on the shelves there, and my hose. It would have been so easy. I thought about it.

"One night I unraveled the hose and opened up the car. But I heard a voice. Do you know what it said?"

Al shakes his head, he has absolutely no idea, but he'd be surprised if the voice inside Brother Rimmer's head said, "Stupid twat."

"A scripture, from Ecclesiastes. One I learned as a boy in Sunday school: *'To every thing there is a season, and a time to every purpose under heaven. A time to be born and a time to die; a time to plant and a time to pluck up that which is planted. A time to kill, and a time to heal; a time to break down and a time to build up.'* It was the Lord, telling me to keep going.

"Anyone can be brave for five minutes or an hour or two. The bravery no one talks about is the hardest bravery of all. When you get up in the morning even though you'd rather be dead, that's brave. When you *build* instead of *breaking down*. No one gives you a slap on the back for it, no one tells you your salvation's assured, but it's brave. The morning after I heard the voice, I moved the car out of the garage and I bought the wood. It gave me something to do, something to look forward to. And when the handcart was finished I decided to let the Primary use it. They had to do a lot of pioneer activities back then. I watched them pulling it around, singing their little hearts out as they made circuits of the parking lot, and I felt *brave*."

Al sort of understands what Brother Rimmer is saying. If you're good at something you can use it as a distraction, as a way to keep going when something bad happens. But why the hell would anyone keep going for a handcart?

"I was going to have you mow the lawn, but you looked like you needed something to *do*. And with the Second Coming getting closer by the day, I might get some use out of this old girl yet." Brother Rimmer stands up and pats the handcart. "Sometimes the bravest thing you can do is to keep going," he says. "When I saw you standing on my doorstep, I thought you looked like you needed to hear that, Alma Bradley."

WHEN IT'S TIME to go, Brother Rimmer gives Al a tenner for his mission fund, which makes him feel like shit.

"Will you come again next Saturday?"

"Yes."

"Good lad."

Al unlocks his bike from Brother Rimmer's front gate and cycles home. The car isn't in the driveway so Dad must still be at the Work Day. He chucks his bike in the shed and grabs a football for keepie-uppie practice: left knee, right knee, shoulder, head, shoulder. He's not sure how to let Dad know that Brother Rimmer's tenner won't be going in his mission fund—he'll have to hide it and hope Dad doesn't ask whether he got paid. It's hardly a *brave* approach, but there's no acceptable way of disagreeing with Dad. Matty sometimes disagrees with Steve, Al has seen them shout at each other and it doesn't ruin anything, Steve just laughs and calls Matty a cheeky git. Dad never expects disagreement because everything he thinks is backed up by the Church and no one is allowed to disagree with the Church. Al isn't sure why, but saying "I'm not saving up for a mission" would be the same as saying "Fuck off, Dad, I hate you."

No one has ever asked if he wants to go on a mission, everyone just takes it for granted. As soon as he could talk, people were beginning sentences with "When you go on your mission," and he had to dress like a missionary on Sundays and sing "I Hope They Call Me on a Mission" and "I Want to Be a Missionary Now" in Primary. The idea of leaving Mum and not talking to her for two whole years used to frighten him. She noticed and whispered, "Don't worry" and, "You don't have to go if you don't want to" when people mentioned it. But as he got older she stopped the whispering and looked at him sadly instead.

Nana and Granddad give him £10 on his birthday. He's not allowed to spend it. It's for his mission fund. Granddad wants the money back if it's not spent on a mission; Al would like to give it back now and save Granddad the bother. Zippy gets money but she's allowed to spend it, and Issy used to spend hers too. Granddad says missions aren't important for girls 'cause their priority is to get married. Girls get fivers and boys get tenners. But a fiver in the hand is better than an invisible tenner any day.

Al puts the ball down, dribbles to the back door, and positions it for free-kick practice. It's sometimes tempting to behave like a twat in order to manage everyone's expectations and give them the pleasure of saying "I'm not surprised" when he turns out badly. What he's done today could land him in deep shit—if anyone finds out he'll look like a proper thief. Maybe the brave thing is to swap the money back, maybe it's to go upstairs and tell Mum about the microwave—who knows? What if Brother Rimmer's stash has nothing to do with the Second Coming and he needs it in real life? What if telling Mum the truth only makes things worse? How can you be brave when you don't know what the brave thing is? He jogs back toward the hedge to fetch the ball and is thumped by the hurt of missing Issy as he half-expects her to emerge from behind a tree to retrieve it. He doesn't know what's brave or stupid, he'll have to work it out. In the meantime he'll do what Brother Rimmer said and just keep going.

– 15 –

Top-Secret Boy

Monday mornings are good because after assembly it's News time and everyone gets to write about what has happened to them that week. Jacob missed two Mondays in a row last month—one when Dad let everyone have a day off after Issy died, and the next one when it was her funeral—so he had a lot of News to catch up on last week. He drew a special picture of Issy being dead in the living room. It was too difficult to draw her lying down, so he drew her sitting up in the coffin, smiling. He wrote his News below the picture.

Issy died and I went to her fewneral.

Mrs. Slade said, "Well done," and stuck one of her special *"Mrs. Slade thinks I am a STAR"* stickers underneath his work.

There's only one really interesting thing to put in his News this Monday but he can't because it's a secret. He chews his pencil and tries to think of something else to write.

It's been a mostly boring week. He went to Early Drop-off Club and After-School Club on Tuesday, Wednesday, Thursday, and Friday. Dad says he'll be going every day this week too unless Mum feels better. School, school, and more school. It's starting to feel as if he lives here. He glances around the table at the other children's work.

George Hindle has written, "My Dad won totil wipe out on saterday." Last week George Hindle said his big sister is Cheryl Cole. Everyone knows George is a big fibber. Jessie Sinkinson hasn't done any writing yet. She is drawing a huge picture of the cinema and all the people in the audience look the same. She draws this picture every Monday because her News is always that she has been to the cinema. She might be fibbing, but Jacob isn't sure because she often gets into trouble for telling the truth. Sometimes she says, "This is boring" in assembly in a loud voice and she said, "You look horrible" when Mrs. Slade had her hair cut short.

Jacob thinks for a bit longer and then he decides what to write. Once he has finished he gets up and takes his book over to Mrs. Slade's desk to show her.

My Mum is like sleeping bewty.

"That's lovely writing!" she says. "Well done, Jacob. Do you think you could write one more sentence and draw a picture? Come back and show me when you've finished, there's a good boy."

He goes back to his place and adds another sentence. Then he draws a picture and colors it in with felt tips. He hurries back to Mrs. Slade's desk and presents his book. Mrs. Slade reads his work and looks at his picture.

My Mum is like sleeping bewty. She has been in bed for a week.

"Oh, is your mum not very well? Poor Mum! Is this her? You've drawn her in a lovely, big, special bed, just like a princess!"

"It's my bunk bed," he says. "She's on the bottom bunk. That's where she is."

"Oh." Mrs. Slade looks surprised.

"But Dad says she isn't lazy," he adds quickly.

"Oh no, I'm sure your mum isn't lazy, Jacob. Everyone gets ill sometimes."

"Do you?"

"Oh yes." Mrs. Slade nods.

"Do you stay in bed all day and cry?"

"Well, not usually. But if I was ill . . . or very unhappy, then I might. How about you, Jacob? Are you feeling ill or unhappy?"

"Nope," he says. "I'm fine." And he is. He knows a secret and it's going to make everything better.

"If you ever feel sad, you know you can come and talk to me," Mrs. Slade says, and Jacob nods, even though he doesn't want to talk to her or any of the other grown-ups who are suddenly anxious to chat. "Go and find a book to read until break time. And, Jacob, you can tell me about anything that's been happening at home, if you need to," she says.

He nods again, fetches the *Big Book of Fairy Tales* from the library corner and sits down next to Jessie Sinkinson, who is drawing identical smiles on every person in her cinema. He opens the book and pretends to read, but he is really thinking about his secret.

BECAUSE IT'S AUTUMN, things are dying everywhere. The geese know it and they're on the move, flying over the house and the school playground toward the marsh and the beach, cackling as they go. Daddy-longlegs flies are blowing everywhere at break times—there were so many last week that Jessie Sinkinson was allowed to stay indoors because she throws a tantrum if an insect so much as touches her. There were dead flies on the windowsill in the boys' bathroom, and in his bedroom, right next to Issy's toy box, was a big, dead spider, all folded up like a hairy umbrella.

Last Monday when Jacob got home from school, Issy's glasses case was on the kitchen table next to Mum's handbag. The case was empty, so he thought it was probably OK to take it. He was late home because Mum had forgotten to pick him up. He wanted to take the glasses case up to his room but Dad was in there with Mum and Dad sounded cross, so he decided to put the case in a safe place, which ended up being his school bag.

After dinner he popped back up to his room to collect the dead spider. Mum was in Issy's bed with the covers over her head. He tiptoed in, picked up the spider, and tiptoed out. When he got downstairs he took Issy's glasses case out of his school bag and dropped the spider in it. He'd been thinking about the dead bird from the garden. It had been small, but he wondered whether it might be easier to resurrect a *really* small animal. He couldn't decide if a spider was the right size so he had a look around the house for some more dead things. He found a fly in the bathroom and a beetle on the back step that wasn't dead, at first. The collecting bit of the job was exciting. That afternoon Mrs. Slade had begun their class project about Egypt. She'd made hieroglyphic worksheets and she talked about pyramids and mummies and a special book of magic spells to bring a dead person back to life, *The Book of the Dead*. He liked hearing about *The Book of the Dead*. If Issy had died in Egyptian times, he could have put a book of spells in her coffin to help her get resurrected. He slipped the fly and the slightly squashed beetle into her glasses case—his Box of the Dead.

That night Mum slept in Issy's bunk. He was glad. He'd been finding it hard to sleep suspended over Issy's bed; it felt as if he was sleeping above a deep, empty space and sometimes, when he woke in the heart of the night and the dark was silent, he worried he might tumble into the emptiness like Alice in Wonderland, falling down and down and down. Sometimes the veil between real life and his dreams was as filmy as a net curtain and he wondered if Issy was in the room, if she could see him in bed, if she was watching all the time, like Heavenly Father, and he made sure to hide his head under the covers when he picked his nose, just in case.

By Wednesday he wished Mum would go back to her own room because she kept crying in the night. The first time, he got out of bed, patted the bump of her hip through the duvet and said, "Shush, shush," like he'd seen her do to Issy when she was little. It worked, and he climbed back into his bunk feeling clever and pleased with himself. But soon she was crying again and this time he didn't know what to do to make it better. It made him want to cry too, so he slipped down the ladder and along the hall to Dad. "Can I get in your bed?" he asked and Dad mumbled something that didn't sound like no, so he crawled in on Mum's side. Dad was a noisy sleeper; when he breathed it sounded like he was blowing up balloons, but at least he wasn't crying.

ON THURSDAY NIGHT Dad went Home Teaching and Jacob agreed to play football with Alma because he'd been crying. But football was boring and when he found a dead wasp Jacob hurried into the house to fetch the Box of the Dead.

Afterward, he made sure Zippy was watching TV and Alma was still playing football before pulling a chair up to the kitchen countertop, flipping open the lid of Issy's fish tank, and plunging his hand into the water. Mrs. Slade said Egyptian people liked to be buried with their pets so they wouldn't be lonely. Jacob knew he shouldn't kill bigger things than insects—and Mum didn't even like him to do that—but it was OK to kill Fred because first, if he prayed very hard and Fred was resurrected, it would prove that Issy could come back too, and second, if Fred was completely dead and couldn't be resurrected, at least he would be able to keep Issy company.

It was hard to get hold of Fred. He was very swimmy and Jacob couldn't quite grip him as planned, so he just grabbed his tail and held him in the air above the water while he twitched and squirmed.

When Fred was dead, Jacob plopped him back in the water—he was very slimy and Jacob didn't want him to make a mess of the Box of the Dead. He wiped his hands on his school trousers and said a prayer, copying the special, powerful words he'd heard Dad use when he gave people blessings.

"Dear Heavenly Father, by the power and authority of the Melky-is-ick priesthood please bless this sick and afflicted fish to be resurrected. Please help thy Spirit to be with us and—"

The back door opened. "What're you doing? Reckon you'll get closer to heaven by standing on a chair?"

"Go away, Alma."

"What're you praying for?"

"Not telling."

"What? Is it a *secret* prayer?" Alma laughed and started to sing the words of a hymn in a high, silly voice. *"Pray in secret, day by day!"*

"Go away."

" 'Tis solace to my soul to know God hears my secret prayer."

Jacob ran out of the kitchen but Alma pranced after him, singing in his high, silly voice; he wouldn't shut up, so Jacob went upstairs to his room and got his pajamas on. Mum was wrapped up in Issy's duvet, facing the wall.

"Hello, Mum," he said. "The geese are flying out to the marsh. They're doing their flying in big arrows, taking turns to be in the front, just like last year." He paused so she could join in, but she didn't say anything, not even "Oh" or "That's nice." He waited a little while longer before he went down the corridor and got into Dad's bed. He said one more prayer, then he closed his eyes very tight and tried to make the morning come quickly.

FRED WAS STILL dead on Friday morning. No one noticed because they were too busy. Jacob watched him floating on top of the water and tried not to mind, but when Dad said there weren't any Shreddies left, he cried.

In assembly he pulled his sweater over his face because the Reception class did their harvest poem, without Issy. He put his head down on the table in math when he had to answer a problem: *"Simon has 16 sweets. He decides to give half of the sweets to his sister. How many sweets does Simon's sister have?"* At break time he found a really big dead daddy-longlegs for the Box of the Dead, but George Hindle stood on it and it stuck to the bottom of his shoe. Jacob cried and Mrs. Slade said he could stay indoors with Jessie Sinkinson at lunchtime and sit outside the staff room drawing pictures with the new felt tips.

"Why are you here?" Jessie asked.

"My sister's dead."

"I know. Mrs. Slade told us when you were off. She said we weren't allowed to talk to you about it in case you got upset, but you got upset anyway." Jessie stuck the felt-tip lid to her tongue and pulled it off with a pop. "Did they drop your sister in a big hole or did they burn her?"

"In a big hole."

"Did you see her when she was dead?"

"Yes."

"Where?"

"At my house."

"Were you scared?"

"No."

"Was there blood and guts everywhere?"

"No."

"What are you drawing?"

"Geese."

"Why?"

"I like them."

"Why?"

"They've got special wings that make them do gliding. They can go up and down and fast and slow. And when they fly it's—it's a bit like a miracle."

"Oh."

"What are you drawing?"

She looked at him like he was thick. "The cinema."

By the time Jacob got home from school he'd forgotten about Fred and so it was a ginormous surprise to go into the kitchen and see him there, all fishy and alive! He pressed his face to the tank and as he watched he felt like he did when he saw his presents on Christmas morning and couldn't work out how Santa Claus managed it. Fred glided back and forth, all boggle-eyed and completely not dead, and Jacob raised both hands in the air and shook them above his head, just as he'd seen Alma do when he scored a goal. "Yes, yes, yes!" he cheered.

· · ·

Jacob flicks through the *Big Book of Fairy Tales*. There are some ace stories, but his is better.

George comes back from the library corner with *The Sports Car Guide* and drops it on the table.

"Fairy tales are for girls," he says, pointing to a red car with doors like wings. "My dad's got a Ferrari. He lets me drive it on the weekend. Bet your dad hasn't got a Ferrari." The red car looks small and Jacob is glad Dad doesn't have one because there's no way everyone would fit in.

"Bet you didn't drive a Ferrari on the weekend," George says. "Bet you stayed home and watched boring telly and your dad drank beer and shouted and called you a right pain in the arse."

"I went to church," Jacob says. "My dad doesn't drink beer and he'd never shout at anyone."

Sundays smell of Mum's perfume and the brown stuff she wipes on her face that smells damp and muddy. Yesterday didn't smell like Sunday. Jacob didn't want to go to church without Mum but Dad said put your best foot forward which meant stop complaining and do as you are told.

Primary was ace. Sister Anderson did "Here We Are Together" in singing time. It took ages to go around the room and include everyone's name—some people went too fast and there was lots of laughter when things got jumbled up. Afterward there was enough time for the first five verses of "Follow the Prophet." Everyone marched up and down the corridor, trailing Sister Anderson, singing, *"Follow the prophet, follow the prophet, follow the prophet!"*

Dad had forgotten to pack the Sunday bag, so Jacob had nothing to play with during Sacrament Meeting. Dad let him borrow his scriptures—thick as a brick and twice as heavy, with wafer-thin pages like the crispy toilet paper at school. Jacob flicked through the scriptures. At the end of the Bible bit there were some color maps of where Jesus lived. They were quite interesting and they had little red arrows on them. Zippy said the arrows showed the journeys different people had taken. One map said "The Third Journey of Paul" and Jacob thought if there was a map about his journeys it would be very boring: "The Three Hundredth Journey of Jacob (to school)."

Yesterday at church it was Testimony Meeting. Testimony Meeting usually happens on the first Sunday of the month, but when it's been General Conference, Testimony Meeting is moved back. Its proper name is Fast and Testimony Meeting. Fasting is when you don't drink or eat anything for twenty-four hours and the money you would have spent on food goes to the church to help the poor. Mum says seven is too young to fast, even though Dad did it. Jacob will miss breakfast when he's eight and he'll fast properly when he's twelve. Alma calls Testimony Meeting "Starve and Cry Meeting" because people go up to the pulpit to say their testimonies and while they're talking they sometimes cry. Alma says they cry because they're hungry but Dad says it's because they're feeling the Spirit.

When it was time for testimonies Jacob put Dad's scriptures down and walked up to the pulpit. Brother Stevens got the big step out so Jacob could climb on it and be seen by the congregation. He arranged one hand on each side of the pulpit, just like Dad, and then he bore his testimony.

"I know the Church is true. I know Joseph Smith was a prophet. I know the Book of Mormon is true. I know we have a prophet on the Earth today. I know families can be together forever."

A testimony is like a list of what you know. Although Jacob knows plenty of other things, like math, reading, bike riding, and how to tell stories, these things are not part of his testimony.

"I love Primary and my teacher, Sister Anderson. I love my dad and my mum. I know miracles do happen. In the name of Jesus Christ, Amen."

It was the first Testimony Meeting since Issy had died, so lots of people mentioned her. Dad thanked everyone for all of their help and kindness with food. Sister Valentine said she was happy to be a member of the true Church and then she cried. Zippy didn't cry but her voice wobbled as she said it was important to keep the commandments and easy to say the wrong things when you're upset. Brother Rimmer waddled to the pulpit to tell everyone that Alma Bradley was helping him with a very important project and Alma's face went bright pink. The room went very quiet when Sister Anderson said Issy had appeared to her in the Temple. Jacob knelt on the pew and looked at the congregation. Several people were wiping tears from their eyes—they didn't look hungry so they were probably feeling the Spirit. Sister Campbell got up next and said she'd been grateful for the opportunity to sacrifice her dinner and give it to the Bradleys. Alma made a sort of snorting noise and even Dad, up on the stand, seemed to smile with his eyes until Sister Campbell said she hoped Sister Bradley wasn't going *inactive*. Zippy made a hissing sound and Alma looked as if he'd like to swing Sister Campbell round the room by her braid but it was OK because Brother Stevens jumped up and reminded everyone that Bishop Bradley was a great guy and Sister Bradley had a terrible cold. Brother Campbell said he'd challenged all of the young men to bear testimony and promised that once they'd said the words they'd start to believe them. He extended a special invitation to Alma Bradley to bear testimony. Alma spent the rest of the meeting looking at the floor.

After church, Dad interviewed everyone who lined up outside his office and then he counted the tithing money. When it was finally time to go home their car was the only one left in the parking lot.

"Can we go to the cemetery on the way home?" Jacob asked, even though he knew it wasn't on the way.

They had to drive past loads of massive statues to get to Issy's part of the cemetery. When they got to the right spot, Alma wouldn't get out of the car.

"What's the point? She's not here," he said.

Jacob carried Dad's scriptures with him as he followed Zippy and Dad along the grass. Issy didn't have a headstone yet, there was just a bit of a bump in the ground where the earth had been put back. Some of the flowers from the funeral were there, all soggy and rotten brown. Dad said the ground had to settle before headstones are put in, which made it sound like the grass and the soil were wrapping themselves around Issy's coffin—Jacob hoped they weren't getting too comfy.

There wasn't much to do at the grave. They looked at the ground and the rotten flowers, at the golf course behind the cemetery with its greens that stretched up to the dunes and the clouds that would eventually meet the sea on the hidden horizon.

"Right, let's go home and get something to eat."

"I'll come in a minute."

Dad nodded and carried on back to the car with Zippy. Jacob lifted the scripture case, holding it against his tummy like a baby. Under its zip were thousands and millions of powerful, magical words. He didn't know which words were the right ones, but he hadn't known on Friday either, so maybe it didn't matter. He closed his eyes.

"Dear Heavenly Father, by the power and authority of the Melky-is-ick priesthood please bless this sick and afflicted girl to get resurrected. Please help thy Spirit to be with us and watch over us and . . . um, thank you very much. In the name of Jesus Christ, Amen."

When he opened his eyes he watched as a big puff of wind gusted along the golf course and swayed the grass. It rolled into the cemetery and when it reached him he could smell the sea. He couldn't see the sea, but he knew it was definitely there, behind the dunes. And although he couldn't see Issy either, it felt like she was there too.

THE BIG BOOK of Fairy Tales has got some good illustrations, way more interesting than cars, but Jacob is only *pretending* to look at the pictures, he is *actually* imagining what it will be like when Issy comes back. Everyone will be so happy. Zippy will hug her and Alma will drag her outside for football practice, Dad will do a big, thankful prayer, and Mum will get up and make the dinner. After dinner, Mum will do bedtime stories and put the clothes away in the right places. He will sleep in his own bed, Issy will sleep in the bunk beneath, and they will all live happily ever after. The end.

BOOK FOUR

In the World
Ye Shall Have
Tribulation

OCTOBER

— 16 —

The Dangers of the Dark

The air smells ill, like stale breath and sweat, and Zippy wonders when Mum last had a shower.

"I need you to get up and do something, Mum."

It's not much to ask, is it? But she has avoided it up to now, suspecting she might be ignored.

"I've got to borrow your wedding dress. Do you know where it is?"

Mum doesn't even move. The back of her head is poking out of the duvet, slick with grease. She is disgusting.

"Sister Stevens is doing a special activity at Youth. It's one they do in Utah. Everyone has to wear their mum's wedding dress and you're supposed to write a letter about your wedding day for me to read out. Dad says I've got to go."

She would like to kick the bunk bed and remind Mum about her divine responsibility to home and family.

"Are you going to write the letter for me, Mum?"

She counts to ten in her head, wondering whether Mum is planning to lie there like a reeking walrus until she dies.

"So *I'll* write about how you met Dad and what your wedding day was like," she says. "I'll just make it up, shall I?"

ZIPPY HATES THE attic. It's accessible by stepladder, through a small hatch in the ceiling, just outside her bedroom. The pitch of the roof is low, which means there's room to stand up properly only in the middle of the attic. It isn't completely dark because there's a small skylight, but the roofing felt is black, and thick cobwebs lace the corners. She tries not to think about enormous spiders while concentrating on standing in the right places.

Dad said he'd find the dress but he forgot and he was on his way out to some meeting or other when she reminded him.

"Don't you think I've got enough to worry about at the moment?" he said.

She isn't even sure what she's looking for. Dad thinks it's in a white bag. So far she has found trash bags of Christmas decorations, spare bedding, and blankets. She edges farther away from the little hole in the floor and the comforting glimpse of the stepladder, prodding stuff that has been heaped on each side of the narrow path of boards.

When she hears the creek and the clank of metal she edges back toward the hole in the floor to see Alma carrying the stepladder down the stairs.

"Very funny! Bring it back, NOW. Come here, you idiot. I HATE you, Alma."

She wants to sit down, but she's worried about falling through the ceiling, so she hunches over and rests her hands on her knees. Everything's awful: Adam isn't talking to her; Lauren's probably going to do something *diabolical* with slimy Jordan Banks; Issy is *dead*—the word hurts each time she thinks it—and Mum's going mental. Things are happening that wouldn't have happened if Issy was alive; life is diverging from its true path, like it does in the story they tell at church where a tiny mistake—a minor, one-degree miscalculation—sends a ship hundreds of miles off course. She shouldn't be here; if Issy was alive, she wouldn't be. But she is. She's stuck in the attic, searching for a horrible meringue dress with a load of giant cobweb-making spiders.

AFTER DAD HAS come home from his meeting, rescued her, and sent Alma to his room, Zippy closes her bedroom door and opens the big white bag. It has *Bridal Emporium* written on it in fancy gold letters and it clips closed at the top and bottom. She unfastens the clips and the dress slides out onto her bed. The material is thick and streaked by little bumpy lines. It isn't white anymore, it's a funny sort of color, almost coral, and huge—like one of those toilet-roll covers that old ladies crochet. She spreads the fabric across the bed, noting the ugly puffball sleeves and the old-fashioned thickets of roses on the shoulders and waist.

Zippy slips out of her jeans and T-shirt. The dress rustles as she steps into it: cool, silky, and soaked in the smell of the attic. Three layers of petticoats plump the skirt out like a lampshade. She looks laughable; it's too big—even when it's zipped up it sags at the front and she has to fold her arms across her chest to counter the gape. There are special shoes wrapped in tissue paper: pointy-toed, spiky-heeled things, covered in the same material as the dress.

Sister Stevens says everyone will parade along a Wedding Runway. Zippy shuffles up and down her room, practicing. The dress rustles as she walks. She stops, closes her eyes, and swishes the material while she pictures Mum walking into the sealing room at the Temple and kneeling down to hold hands with Dad across the altar—something that's hard to envisage because she has only seen pictures of the inside of the Temple in church manuals. She keeps her eyes closed; this time she imagines a nicer dress, a bright bouquet, string music, and Adam waiting at the end of the aisle in the chapel. Armed with the right feelings, she edges onto her chair, flattens the puff of the dress, and begins to write Mum's letter:

"The day I married Ian was the happiest day of my life . . ."

THEY WAIT IN the corridor for the Big Reveal. Sister Stevens has been at the chapel all day, decorating. She has taped tissue paper over the rectangular windows in the hall's double doors to prevent peeking. With the exception of a few mums, every female is dressed as a bride.

The boys pass in a cloud of Axe body spray with Brother Campbell, noisy and annoyed because there's nowhere for them to play basketball. "Here comes the bride," one of them sings. Alma joins in as he passes: "All fat and wide." Zippy scowls; she hasn't forgiven him for the attic. Adam passes too, but he isn't singing and he doesn't look at her. He probably thinks she's going to pounce on him and force him to the altar. She twiddles the skirt of Mum's dress. No one else's dress is as dark. Even Sister Campbell's ancient dress—lacy, like net curtains, with batwing sleeves and a high collar—is bright white.

Sister Campbell adjusts her veil and strokes the white scrunchie she has twisted around the bottom of her braid.

"You're not very white, Zipporah," she says, pointing for emphasis. "But then I suppose your mum was a convert, wasn't she?"

"She got married in the Temple. She was worthy."

Sister Stevens flashes her bright American teeth at Sister Campbell. "It's real silk. That's why it's gone dark. I think it's beautiful."

Sister Stevens is telling kind lies. *Her* dress is beautiful. She bought it from a special shop in Utah that sells only modest dresses. It's got sequins all over the bodice and the skirt is a floaty cloud of net. Sister Valentine is wearing a lovely A-line dress with diamanté-dotted sleeves.

"Whose dress did you borrow?" Zippy asks.

"Oh, I didn't borrow it. I hired it."

"From a bridal shop?"

"It was such fun trying dresses on and deciding which one I liked best."

"But—but, do the people at the shop think you're getting married?"

"Oh, probably," Sister Valentine says, and although she giggles, her forehead and eyebrows knit as if she's worrying about what to say when she returns the dress.

"Right, girls." Sister Stevens claps her hands to shush everyone.

"I'm about to open the doors. Are you ready? Steady? Let's get married!" She dashes ahead of everyone to switch on a CD player and "Pachelbel's Canon" begins to play.

The hall has been decorated with pink and white streamers. Chairs have been arranged on each side of a central aisle, all the way down the basketball court. At the end of the hall, next to the stage, there's a table covered in a frilly white cloth. Sister Stevens has made a three-tier wedding cake. She's modeled icing flowers and a miniature bride and groom. Along the edge of the stage are enough bridal bouquets for everyone.

"Line up at the bottom of the Wedding Runway, girls. Parents and leaders, take a seat." Sister Stevens picks up several of the bouquets and bustles down the aisle with them. "Here you are. Here, take this one. Hold it like this. You can't walk down the aisle without flowers." She hurries back to the stage to collect more bouquets. "Here, here. You all look *so* beautiful. Isn't this exciting?"

Sister Stevens says everyone must take turns walking down the aisle. The watching parents turn in their seats and smile while she comments over Pachelbel.

"Emily Murphy is wearing her mom's dress. Emily's mom got married in 1990. Emily is wearing a full-length veil and carrying a bouquet of roses."

"Katy Hewitt is wearing her cousin's dress. Katy's cousin got married for *Time* in the chapel and for *Eternity* in the Preston Temple later that same afternoon. She honeymooned in the Lake District."

The parents clap politely as each girl reaches the end of the aisle and sits down on one of the empty seats at the front.

Dad turns in his chair to watch as Zippy swishes down the makeshift aisle. She feels like a twit—of course she wants to get married, but she doesn't want to play pretend in front of all these people.

"Zipporah Bradley is wearing her mom's dress. It's made of silk. There are nine silk roses on the sleeves and back. Zipporah's mom got married to our very own Bishop Bradley at the chapel and, later that day, in the Preston Temple."

Zippy sits down in the front row and turns to watch the other girls walk down the aisle. When every bride is seated, Sister Stevens talks about the importance of marriage. She reminds everyone that marrying outside the Church is like marrying outside your culture or race, which makes Zippy think of Dad—who, to all intents and purposes, did just that. Mum had been a member of the Church for only a year when she and Dad got married. What did she really understand about the Church after just a year? What does she understand now? Not enough, clearly, or she wouldn't be lying in bed like a hysterical Jane Austen mother.

Sister Stevens presents the brides with a bundle of specially made handouts. Then she gives a presentation about imagining the person you will one day marry.

"Think of him as a real person," she says. "Make a list in your journal of the qualities he will possess. Think about him often. Isn't it exciting to think that he is somewhere in the world at this *exact moment?*"

Each bride is invited to stand in front of the assembled audience and read the letter written by her mother. When it is Zippy's turn, she is suddenly nervous.

"The day I married Ian was the happiest day of my life." The letter was very hard to write. Mum's past is inaccessible; Zippy can't imagine what it was like for her to grow up without the gospel, never experiencing the true and lasting happiness only Church members enjoy. Her wedding day must have been amazing. Not only did she get married, but she went to the Temple for the first time too. It seems quite possible that on that day, Mum was the happiest she'd ever been.

". . . I was so glad to be worthy to go to the Temple. I had always led a good, clean life, and kept *all* of the commandments, even before I knew about the Church."

Zippy looks up, to see how her letter is being received. Sister

Stevens nods encouragingly, but Dad doesn't. His eyebrows are raised and his mouth is tight.

". . . When I walked down the aisle in the chapel and saw Ian waiting for me at the pulpit, I thought it was the most wonderful moment of my life. But I was wrong. The most wonderful moment was later, when I knelt across the altar at the Temple and held his hands as we were sealed for Eternity."

There's a wistful sigh in the hall that comes mostly from Sister Valentine and is belatedly echoed by some of the mums. As Zippy sits down everyone looks at Dad, hoping to catch him looking pleased and embarrassed, but he just looks uncomfortable.

During the next letter, President Carmichael pops his head round the hall door and motions to Dad, who whispers, "Excuse me" to Sister Stevens as he leaves the hall.

After all the letters have been read, Sister Stevens announces a musical item. Sister Campbell plays an introduction on the piano and Sister Stevens sings a song about families being together forever. When the second verse begins, Zippy decides she's had enough. She gets up, swishes across the hall, and slips through the double doors. She hurries down the corridor, turns left toward the fire exit, changes her mind at the last moment, and slips into the end classroom. She doesn't turn on the light.

The door closes of its own volition and she swishes to the far corner and slides her bottom onto the edge of a table. The petticoats and layers of net puff the wedding dress up, and when she tries to smooth the material, she realizes she is still holding Sister Stevens's handouts: "Dating Decisions" and "The Young Women's Wedding Guide." There is just enough light for her to make out the words.

The "Dating Decisions" handout is a single sheet divided into four headed sections: 1. Avoid the Dangers of the Dark, 2. Beware the Hazard of the Horizontal, 3. Remember the Perils of Privacy, 4. Modesty Is a Must. At the bottom of the sheet, Sister Stevens has added an extra, handwritten warning: Beware of the naughty B's— never show your breasts, back, bottom, or belly.

"The Young Women's Wedding Guide" is bigger. There are several pages and spaces to fill in.

> I think my future husband will have _____ hair, _____ eyes
>   and be _____ tall.
> I think I will be _____ years old when I get married.
> I will have _____ bridesmaids. (Write your bridesmaids' names
>   below.)
>
> _____
> _____
> _____

Zippy realizes something very sad as she examines "The Young Women's Wedding Guide": Issy won't be her bridesmaid. When she has absorbed this new loss, she carries on reading.

> Here is a picture of the kind of wedding dress I would like to
>   wear. (Stick a picture from a bridal magazine below.)
> I would like to get married in the month of _____ and have
>   _____ children.
> My future children. (Write your future children's names below.)
>
> _____
> _____
> _____
> _____
> _____
> _____
> _____
> _____
> _____

On the last page there's a photograph of the Temple and Sister Stevens has printed some words underneath.

I believe the most important single thing I will do is marry the
   <u>right</u> person, in the <u>right</u> place, by the <u>right</u> authority.
I promise to marry a worthy priesthood holder in the Temple.
Signed _____ (Write your name here.)

The door opens and Adam slips into the shadows. "I saw you walk past," he says. "You looked like you were headed outside."

Zippy's heart thuds. She looks down at the dress and grabs a handful of material to show why she stayed indoors. He joins her in the corner of the room and leans against the table, arms propped behind him, legs stretched out. They stare straight ahead at the light that steals through the small window in the door, illuminating the edge of the room. Eventually she speaks.

"It was a joke, what I said about getting married at the party. I didn't mean it."

"Yeah," he says.

"So, are we—are we OK, then?"

"Yeah."

"Good."

"You look like a massive fairy."

"I know. I feel like an idiot."

He turns and has a proper look, which makes her hot and twitchy and glad of the dark.

"It's not that bad, actually. I like you in it."

He *likes* her in a *wedding dress*. "Liar," she accuses, hoping he'll say it again.

"Do you want to get married?"

For an impossible, wonderful moment, she thinks he is asking if she wants to get married *to him* and she is so overwhelmed she can't form the words to accept.

"Sometimes I do," he continues, "just because it's what they're all expecting. But other times I don't."

"Oh." She catches her happiness and swallows it. "Marriage isn't just a Church thing, you know," she says. "People outside the

Church get married too. It's not like baptisms for the dead or Temple garments—there's nothing weird about it."

"They don't dress up and have make-believe weddings. They get married later, when they're like thirty or something. Don't you ever think about *not* doing what everyone's expecting you to do?"

Of course she thinks about it, but she doesn't have any intention of breaking the commandments in real life; that would be awful. When she reads books, she eggs the characters on, encourages them to do all sorts of things she wouldn't dream of doing herself, things that would see her excommunicated and disgraced. Perhaps it's OK because the characters in her books are nonmembers; they haven't received the greater light, which means that they, unlike her, are exempt from condemnation. Dad would say that it's important to avoid even the *appearance* of evil; he wouldn't approve of some of the books she reads, he'd say just *thinking* about breaking the commandments is morally wrong, but he doesn't mind that the scriptures are full of people doing things you shouldn't even think about, like King David ogling Bathsheba in the bath.

"I think about it," she says. "But *I* wouldn't . . . when I read *Jane Eyre* I wanted her to live in sin with Mr. Rochester."

"Why?"

"It was complicated, he had this mad wife in the attic, so he wasn't free to marry Jane, even though he loved her and—"

"No, I mean why is it OK for Jane what's-her-name to live in sin?"

"It's just a story, Adam."

"Let's say this Jane woman was real and she wanted to get married but there was a mad wife in her boyfriend's attic. What would you say then?"

"If her boyfriend couldn't get divorced, I'd tell her to live in sin."

"What if *you* had a boyfriend who couldn't get divorced? What then?"

"I wouldn't be in that position."

"That's such a cop-out."

"OK, I wouldn't live in sin."

"Why not? Why's it OK in stories, but not OK for you?"

"The clue's in the 'sin' part."

"You've divided yourself into two bits. An obedient bit and a normal bit."

It's such a relief to talk to him again, he's the only person in the whole world she can talk to with her whole self, but she wishes he'd stop trying to poke holes in things.

"Isn't Brother Campbell going to wonder where you are?"

"Nah, he's gone into the hall to help with your activity. While he's gone we're supposed to be making a list of the things our mums need to teach us before we go on our missions: ironing, cooking, washing, sewing on buttons . . . He's been asked to talk to you lot about how it felt to marry Sister Campbell for Eternity, in the Temple. I reckon it felt like a life *and* death sentence."

They laugh together, and things are instantly better.

"So what're you doing in here by yourself, then?"

She swings her legs backward and forward a few times before answering. "I don't know."

"Come on."

"They were singing 'Families Can Be Together Forever.' I didn't want to cry in front of everyone."

"Sorry."

"My dad left, I think your dad wanted to interview him or they've gone to visit someone. So when I got a chance, I left too. I feel like a big doofus. I mean, look." She slides off the table to stand and face him. "Other people have got lovely dresses. Sister Valentine hired one specially and Sister Stevens has sequins all over her top." She moves her hands across the sweetheart neck of Mum's dress as she speaks, to illustrate the position of Sister Stevens's sparkles. "But Sister Campbell's got this weird dress with pointy sleeves and she tried to say my dress isn't white because Mum's a convert."

When she notices Adam isn't listening, she follows his eyes and realizes he is looking down the front of the wedding dress where it gapes, ogling her bra and the crests of her chest. His mouth is half open and his tongue snakes along his bottom lip. Even though he knows she is watching him, he doesn't avert his gaze. It's like he can't, and she isn't sure what to do. She doesn't want to be *"walking pornography,"* so she lifts a hand to rearrange the front of the dress but he keeps staring, as if he's been hypnotized. She tries to break the spell.

"I'm so glad no one from school can see me like this."

Finally he looks away, at the closed door. When he looks back he meets her eye. "I think it's fine for . . . friends to kiss each other occasionally, don't you?"

She should say no, what with the Dangers of the Dark, the Perils of Privacy, and her accidental contravention of Modesty Is a Must. He's only just started talking to her again and she doesn't want to spoil things—everything went weird the last time they kissed. But it would be so nice to be wrapped up in a warm pair of arms, his arms in particular.

"Will you hug me first?" she asks.

"OK."

He pushes himself up from the table and folds his arms around her. She closes her eyes and rests her head against his chest; he is lovely and warm and she experiences an unexpected bolt of missing Issy, followed by the memory of dressing her with Mum and how cold her skin was, how inanimate and empty.

"Can I kiss you now?" His voice rumbles in his chest and its vibrations travel through the wedding dress and into her skin.

"In a minute," she says. If she listens carefully she can hear the motor of his heart as it pumps the blood around his body. There is something about being held like this that is almost as moving as listening to "Families Can Be Together Forever."

"Now?"

"Just a bit longer. Please."

"How much longer?"

"Another minute." She closes her eyes and listens to his body. She squeezes him hard, bursting with feelings; if he would only say something nice she would let him open her up and reach past the crate of her ribs to hold her heart.

"Fifty-seven, fifty-eight, fifty-nine, sixty."

His arms drop and he leans forward to claim her lips. They kiss for a while and then he moves his head so he can put his mouth on her collarbone. She should probably push him away, he hasn't even asked her to be his girlfriend, but she leans her head back because it feels so nice. It's lovely to be liked, to have another person stamp his mouth all over your skin and kiss your sadness better. He rests his hands on her waist, just above the fabric roses, and then he moves his lips lower. His mouth is warm and soft, and his chin is just a little bit scratchy. Goosebumps are erupting on her arms and legs, he is making her feel lovely, and it will be even nicer when he uses his mouth to say the words that will make her feel loved.

He moves his lips lower, nudges the gape of her dress with his chin and kisses the top of her chest, which is definitely a sin. She is breaking the Law of Chastity and even though it's not a massive sin, not yet at least, it's big enough that she is going to have to confess it and repent if she wants to get married in the Temple. She'd like him to stop, but she doesn't know how to ask without spoiling everything. She has learned about chastity in terms of not letting anyone do anything *to* her; no one has ever mentioned how she might feel or what she might want. And she wants *this*, with him, but later, when it's not a sin. He cups her bottom with his hands and she can feel his *thing* through the bunch of her dress, which isn't supposed to happen and is entirely her fault for not finding the right words to stop him. She is still searching for the right words when the classroom door bursts open.

"Zipporah! Oh dear . . ."

Adam springs away, but it's too late. Sister Valentine is standing in the doorway like the ghost of Temple weddings yet to come.

"Oh dear," she says again, waving her arms, swatting at an invisible fly. "You shouldn't—you mustn't—the Law of Chastity . . . that, what you were doing, was *wrong*."

Zippy can't look at Adam, so she concentrates on the diamantés on Sister Valentine's sleeves.

"We need to keep a better eye on you. Come on." Sister Valentine grasps Zippy's hand and pulls her to the door.

"We've got some old copies of *Unveiled* and *Modern Bride* and we're going to choose our favorite dresses. Then we've going to eat cake and take photographs. And then"—she turns to give Adam a fierce look—"we're going to choose honeymoons."

WHEN ZIPPY HAS helped Sister Stevens tidy up and carry all the wedding paraphernalia out to her car, she sits in the foyer outside Dad's office with Adam and Alma while Dad and President Carmichael finish their meeting. On her lap are the marriage handouts and a Polaroid photograph in which she is standing next to the wedding cake, trying to smile.

"Do you want to play footie in the hall?" Alma asks Adam.

"Yeah. In a minute."

"Cool. Got a ball?"

Adam reaches into the sports bag at his feet and pulls out the sponge football they use indoors. He throws it to Alma, who dribbles it down the corridor. As soon as the hall door swings shut behind Alma, Adam speaks.

"I'm sorry."

"At least it wasn't Sister Campbell."

"True. She's a nightmare." He clasps his hands together and cracks his fingers. "And don't worry, I won't tell anyone I did *that* first."

"What?"

He points in the direction of her chest, as if she is the owner of a pair of mountains he's just laid claim to with an Adam Carmichael flag.

"I'm not worried." She shuffles the handouts. "There's no prize for being first. It's not a race, you're not the winner."

"Being first is important to some people."

She'd like to tell him he's wrong, but the Law of Chastity is all about being the first. Yet she can't help wondering whether it's more important to be the last, because if something happened—if Adam made a mistake with someone else—she thinks she'd be able to forgive him, as long as afterward it was just the two of them, for Eternity.

"To go where no man has gone before," he continues.

"Stop joking."

"Well, it's a Church thing, isn't it?" He clears his throat and straightens an imaginary tie. "Respect girls who respect themselves."

"Right. Thanks."

"No, I didn't mean—I was being Brother Campbell. We didn't, we only . . . you're not going to tell your dad, are you?"

She imagines telling Dad about what she allowed to happen and how it would make him feel with Issy, Mum, and everything.

"You won't, will you?" he pushes.

"I should confess."

"You haven't *got* to. Wait a bit, 'til you're older. Wait 'til you're eighteen and you know whether you want to keep living like this." He strokes the spread of Mum's dress and shakes his head. "Everything's so small right now."

"Our lives *seem* small, but they're bigger than we can imagine. Eternity's a long time."

"That's not what I meant. Anyway, there'll probably be a different bishop by the time you're eighteen and you can confess everything, all at once. It'll be easier."

"*All at once?* I haven't got anything else to confess."

"You will."

"I'm definitely not going to do anything with anyone else."

"You will. You know you will. You're . . ."

"What? What am I?"

"Hot to trot."

"What?"

"You went from zero to sixty in—"

"I didn't do anything. I just stood—"

"Aw, come on, don't pretend you weren't into it."

"I should've said something and I shouldn't have been by myself with you in the dark. It's my fault about the dress too." She crosses her arms over her chest, just to make sure. "If I die and I haven't repented, I won't be with Issy again."

"Course. Sorry." He rubs his hands along his thighs. "I didn't think. Can you just not mention me?"

She nods. She will be extremely careful. And it's mostly her fault anyway, for tempting him with her chest.

"What're these?" He lifts the papers out of her hands, leaving the photograph in her lap. " *'Beware of the naughty B's—never show your breasts, back, bottom, or belly'*—this is awful." He laughs and nudges her. "They forgot to include balls."

She glances at the photograph and remembers what he said in the classroom—*"I like you in that"*—and while he leafs through the handouts, chuckling quietly, she drops it into his bag.

When the office door opens, Dad and President Carmichael step out and Adam passes the papers back.

"Ah, Zipporah, just the young lady," President Carmichael says. "Can I have a word? You don't mind if I just borrow your office and your daughter for a moment, do you, Bishop?"

Dad shakes his head. He looks rumpled and tired. Zippy leaves the handouts on the seat next to Adam and crosses the corridor to the office. It must be the Holy Ghost that has made President Carmichael ask to speak to her at this precise moment while she is wrestling with right and wrong. Priesthood leaders have the spirit of discernment, they can see right into people's souls and they know when people have sinned and whether or not they are lying. She flattens the dress and squeezes through the door. President Carmichael follows her and points to the empty chair opposite the desk. He waits for her to sit down. His suit isn't shiny at the elbows like Dad's and his shoes are those expensive ones with little holes and patterns all over them. He's still sort of handsome, even though he's middle-aged. And he looks a lot like Adam sometimes, especially when he smiles.

"How are you?" he asks as he sits.

"I'm OK, thanks."

She can't decide whether to confess. It might be easier to tell him than Dad, but what will he think of her when he finds out? Will he remember what she has done, forever? Will he hold it against her and make sure Adam never marries her?

"It's been a difficult time. How are you coping?"

"OK, yeah."

He looks at her and it's like he's switched on his discernment; she knows she needs to confess before the Holy Ghost tells him what she has done.

"Zipporah, I'm getting a sense that . . ."

She takes a deep breath. "I've done something. With a boy." As soon as the words leave her mouth she feels like she's going to throw up.

President Carmichael doesn't flinch. "Ah," he says, as calmly as if he suspected as much. "Well, I'm sure it's nothing to worry about. Can you tell me what happened, so I know how serious it is?"

She tries to think of a way to say it that doesn't involve the words "chest," "breasts," or "boobs," but she can't, so she just sits there, lips pursed, like an enormous toilet-roll-cover doll.

"I'll ask you some questions and you can answer yes or no," President Carmichael offers. Something inside her shrinks, but Zippy nods her head and tries not to look embarrassed.

"So, um, did you, were all of your clothes on?"

"Yes," she says.

"And were you dressed modestly?"

"I was, but well, I—then I . . . no," she says.

"You girls don't realize how difficult you make it for young men. Boys miss out on your . . . loveliness if you show them more than they're meant to see—good lads will avert their eyes, but boys in the world will look."

She folds her arms across her chest and stares at the desk.

"Were you lying down?"

"No."

"Good. Was it something that involved your bottom half?"

Her bottom half—the shrinking feeling intensifies. "No."

"Good. Your top half, then?"

"Yes."

"And the boy's hands?" She shakes her head.

"Oh, right, I see. Oh, um, his mouth? Yes? That's it? That's everything?"

Zippy nods. She feels filthy. She has committed one of the diabolical crimes that Sister Campbell talked about during Standards Night.

"So, I think we can refer to what happened as petting, that's what they call it in the 'For Strength of Youth' pamphlet, isn't it? It's a bit of an old-fashioned word, but I'm sure your mum and dad, and Sister Campbell, have explained it to you."

Zippy hates the word. What happened was not *petting*. She has not been *petted*, like an animal at the zoo or a little dog.

"Zipporah, you need to remember that boys your age—actually it's an unfortunate fact that applies to males in general—are frequently after only one thing." President Carmichael leans back in Dad's chair and makes himself comfortable. He seems perfectly at ease, as if he has said what he is about to say lots and lots of times. "Girls need to be careful—*you like him; you love him; you let him; you lose him*—that's what happens. It'd be such a shame to throw away an Eternity of happiness for five or ten minutes of pleasure. I like to think of chastity as a race. Runners spend a lot of time preparing. They train to make sure they're absolutely ready. You're preparing now, aren't you? You're getting ready for the blessings of marriage, in that pretty dress. Sometimes, despite all their training, runners do a false start. They jump the gun and take off before they're ready. It's such a shame when that happens because all their preparations have gone to waste. Don't jump the gun. Your family would be so disappointed. You won't, will you?"

She shakes her head.

"You're very sorry?"

"Yes."

"I suggest you explain it to the Lord in your prayers tonight and ask for His forgiveness." President Carmichael starts to stand up.

"But, aren't you going to tell me I can't take the sacrament, or—"

He sits down in Dad's chair again. "Your mum and dad would notice if you didn't take the sacrament. It wouldn't serve any purpose to upset them, especially at the moment. You're a good girl, I'm sure you can work this out with the Lord. The boy, is he your boyfriend?"

"No, he isn't . . . I think he—we might, one day—"

"Well, there's no point, is there? You won't be getting married until you're, oh, eighteen at the earliest, so having a boyfriend now would be dangerous, especially a nonmember—it could never go anywhere except the places where these things aren't supposed to go." He digs around in his suit pocket. "I've got some missionary pass-along cards—here, give him this."

Zippy accepts the card; there's a picture of a Temple on it and a link to the Church's website.

"Eternal marriage, that's what you want. Associate with worthy priesthood holders. I always thought that maybe, one day, you and Adam . . ." He winks as he pushes himself up out of Dad's chair.

She stands and bustles to the door, anxious to get out, get home, and shed Mum's ridiculous dress.

"Oh, and Zipporah?"

She pauses, hand poised on the handle.

"How's your mum?"

He is determinedly casual and she suddenly realizes he didn't suspect a thing. *This* is the question he has been waiting to ask, the reason he brought her into the office to begin with.

"She's not feeling very well."

He stares at her for a moment, as if he is trying to see past her pupils and read the truth of the thoughts behind.

"Do you think she would like a visit?"

"No."

"That's what your dad said. Is there anything you want to share with me? Anything I can help you or anyone else in the family with?"

"No."

"If you think of something, you can speak to me. You know that, don't you?"

"Yes."

"Grieving affects people in different ways."

"I know." She opens the door, even though he looks like he hasn't finished talking.

Dad is waiting in the corridor where she and Adam were sitting earlier, leaning forward with his head in his hands. She taps him on the shoulder and he sits up quickly.

"Right," he says. "I'll go and tell Alma and Adam to wrap it up and we can get going."

IN THE CAR on the way home Dad tells her off. "You shouldn't have written that letter for Mum, Zipporah. She wouldn't have said any of those things. You can't presume to speak for someone like that."

"What else was I supposed to do?"

"You shouldn't have written it."

Dad's failure to answer the question makes her angry.

"I don't know why she won't just get up. She's got responsibilities. She's got *children*."

"What did President Carmichael want to talk to you about?"

"He just wanted to ask if we're all OK."

"And you said?"

"I said we're fine."

"Good girl."

Dad doesn't pretend to be Brigham Young as he pulls into the driveway. He doesn't say, "This is the place." He just yawns and sighs.

Mum's dress swishes as Zippy walks up the stairs. When she reaches her room she kneels next to her bed beside the prayer rock and *Persuasion* and she closes her eyes, folds her arms, and explains. She uses Sister Campbell's "walking pornography" defense to excuse Adam and she also apologizes on his behalf, in case something bad occurs before he gets round to it. What happened between them was lovely, but it was *wrong*. The whole point of coming to Earth is to take the test of life and she has made a great big mistake in her test—a filthy, diabolical mistake. A tear lands on the bodice of the dress and another few slip down its front. The tears are mascara-stained—she will ruin Mum's dress. Good, none of this would have happened if Mum had been there tonight. Serves Mum right.

— 17 —

Listening

The morning noises are late, the front door hasn't slammed shut, and the house is full, even though it's after nine. Claire can't get up, she won't have her grief trampled by their busyness and chat and occasional laughter. Yesterday was Sunday—they left for church around 9:30 and didn't get home until 3:30—so today is Monday, and they shouldn't be here.

Slam. The front door shuts finally but the sound is followed by Ian's feet on the stairs. He has taken to saying goodbye in the mornings and goodnight in the evenings. He is very solicitous, addressing her as he would an elderly relative.

"I'm just going across to the park with Jacob. Alma's gone to play football with Matty, and Zipporah's meeting Lauren in town."

He's wearing ordinary clothes, jeans and a T-shirt; it's unusual to see him dressed normally—even on Saturdays there are meetings to attend and people to visit and he must wear a suit. Then it dawns on her—half-term. They are going to be here all week, stomping over her sorrow with their noisy feet and loud voices.

"I'll be back in about an hour."

She listens for the final slam of the front door. After it bangs shut she slides her legs out of the bed and stands. The room wobbles and she holds onto the bunk and closes her eyes for a moment. When everything is straight again she steps out onto the landing.

There are wet towels on the bathroom floor, the window is shut, streaked by condensation, and the windowsill is puddled. She doesn't address the mess. She sits on the toilet and afterward, when she is washing her hands, allows herself a look in the mirror. She is wearing her grief honestly. It has spread all over her face; unwashed skin and hair, unplucked eyebrows, unbleached upper lip—she is coming undone.

She wanders along the hall to her own room. The bed is unmade and Jacob's pajamas are on the floor. One curtain is open, the other is closed, and the single-glazed window is soaked. Ian promised the windows would be done first when they moved in, he said he'd find a company that could do them on the cheap, but he's never got round to it and the house is cold in the autumn and winter. Wind squeezes through the gaps in the wooden frames. Last year she used to turn the heating on for an hour at lunchtime. It meant she and Issy didn't get too chilly in the afternoons and it also ensured that the radiators were cool again by the time Ian got home from work. He moaned about the energy bill but never asked whether she had been helping herself to extra heat, and she didn't feel obliged to confess. It was just a small, harmless deception. The thought puts her in mind of something else Ian doesn't know and she walks to her side of the bed, bends down, and opens the bottom drawer. Her Temple garments are jumbled—Zipporah has been doing the washing; Ian popped into Jacob and Issy's room one night to tell her this, as if he expected it to rouse her and make her feel guilty. It didn't, and she doesn't.

Her grief has grown so big it has ballooned past every other feeling. She rummages through the white, silky pile. Garments must be treated with respect at all times—they aren't supposed to touch the floor—but she drags them out of the drawer until it is emptied and she is blindly patting its bareness. She shakes each item in the heap; floaty camisole tops and knee-length bottoms, symbols of the covenants that bind her to Ian and the children forever, absolutely nothing concealed in their silky folds.

Someone has taken her money. She opens the top drawer and pulls out bras, socks, and flesh-colored tights. Nothing. She empties Ian's drawers next: garments, socks, handkerchiefs. No money. One of the handkerchiefs is bunched and lumpy. She unfolds it and discovers Issy's broken glasses. The bridge is snapped, both lenses are cracked, and there is a scrape on the outside of one of the stems.

She remembers an afternoon during the summer holiday. Ian was at the hospital with the Andersons and she'd taken the children for a walk up the pier to play on the Victorian arcade machines. The children had all won something—a lollipop, a long chew, a packet of Refreshers. On the walk back down the pier they noticed donkeys being led out of a horse trailer on the beach below. Issy jumped up and down, begging and bartering, desperate to have a go. "It's *only* three pounds and I've wanted to go on a horse my *whole life*," she pleaded as they approached the steps down to the parking lot. Alma laughed and said they were just donkeys and he would buy her a real horse one day, when he was rich. Issy stamped her foot, tore off her glasses, and threw them to the ground. They made a cracking sound as they hit the concrete at the top of the steps and she looked surprised, as if she couldn't quite believe her own daring. Claire retrieved them. There was a scrape on the outside of one of the stems. Zipporah picked Issy up, even though she was getting too big to be carried. If Claire had known, she'd have paid for Issy to ride the donkeys all day. She wraps the glasses in the handkerchief, stuffs the rest of Ian's things back into his drawers, and wonders where to look next.

She has been saving ten pounds a week for nearly two years. She buys cheap, store-brand groceries and secondhand clothes, cuts out coupons, and takes down hems. And it's been worth it to feel the cylinder of cash growing and to know it is there, should she need it.

When Ian first told her about tithing, it seemed like a nice idea. Typical Ian, she thought, thinking of others before himself, giving away ten percent of his income to the Church. It didn't matter so much when they first got married, they managed, and every time something unexpected happened—a tax rebate, a bargain, the donation of secondhand furniture from Ian's parents—he said the windows of heaven had been opened, and it felt like that in the beginning.

She assumed the donations would be flexible after they had children, that it would be OK to pilfer a bit back, when necessary, to
pay for new shoes, the car battery, or a broken-down washing machine. But it wasn't; they couldn't go to the Temple if they didn't
pay tithing. Not because of the money, Ian explained, the Church
didn't need their money; it was to do with obedience. *Will a man
rob God? But ye say wherein have we robbed ye? In tithes and offerings.* She didn't want to steal from God, did she? She thought
about it and said she wasn't sure whether keeping something that
belonged to you was the same as stealing. He assured her it was,
and although he explained it very patiently, he looked worried and
she was scared he might be wondering if he'd made a mistake in
marrying her, so she said she was happy to pay tithing, but perhaps
they could cut back on their other offerings: Fast Offering, the Hu-
manitarian Fund, the Mission Fund, the Perpetual Education Fund,
and the Book of Mormon Fund. However, it turned out that these
were also nonnegotiable. The prophet had asked Church members
to be *generous* and Ian was determined to be obedient, and very
generous.

If Ian found the money he'd say something. He'd probably ask
why on earth she was hiding so much cash in the house; he wouldn't
be confrontational, he's never confrontational.

"Guess when I last had my hair cut," she said during the summer holiday.

"I don't know," he replied.

"Two years ago."

"Good grief, Claire, I've never said you can't get your hair done.
Go, if you want."

"It costs fifty pounds."

"Well, you don't need it done, it looks fine to me."

"I'm going gray, see? Here and here."

"I don't care."

"I know."

"That's not what I meant."

She gets so much a week. It's the way Ian's mum and dad did it and it worked for them. Ian would be bewildered and hurt by her hoarding; he'd want to know exactly what she intends to do with the money, a question even she can't answer. Sometimes she imagines spending every last penny on herself—booking the personal shopper in Debenhams, coming away with bags of clothes, new earrings, a tinted moisturizer, and a brand-name mascara that doesn't clog her eyelashes. Other times she pictures the money growing exponentially over the course of several years until there's enough to pay for double-glazed windows or a proper holiday.

One of the children must have helped themselves. Jacob wouldn't dream of it. Alma might, but he has no reason to rummage through her drawers. It has to be Zipporah, she thinks as she shuffles up the stairs. Zipporah's bed is also unmade, but the curtains are open. Claire roots through the drawers and wardrobe. She shuffles papers and lifts books from the desk—*Tess of the d'Urbervilles, Jane Eyre, Wuthering Heights*—her own old editions; she remembers feeling deeply invested in each denouement and wishing, in the way of teenage girls, for a similarly passionate and extraordinary life.

Her hands are trembling as she heads back down the stairs. Over the years she has heard other mothers chatting in the playground about what they would do if they won the lottery. She can't play, of course, but the roll of money has sat in her drawer like a ticket to *something*.

There are dishes in the kitchen sink and crumbs on the floor. A cup of tea, that's what she'd like: a cup of tea in a mug to cradle and sip. It's been more than seventeen years since she's had tea; just one cup would be enough to disqualify her from the Temple. She used to drink tea with her mum in the mornings before school, usually in the kitchen, once she was dressed and ready, but sometimes, for a treat, Mum would wake her with a cup and she'd drink it while Mum sat on the end of the bed and talked to her about school. They did a lot together after Dad left, especially in the beginning when it seemed like they were just passing time until he came back, measuring out the wait in cozy chats and cups of tea.

She opens the fridge then closes it; she doesn't want to eat. Every so often she gives in and grabs a cookie, but when she thinks of Issy lying under the mulching, autumn-heavy soil, each bite feels like a betrayal. Her stomach growls and she ignores it. There is something intoxicating about the subjugation of the self. She feels it every month on Fast Sundays when her brain, high in the nutrient-free atmosphere at the summit of her body, becomes airy, almost weightless; by the time she has gone twenty-four hours without food or water it feels as if she could step outside herself and float all the way up to heaven. She feels similarly buoyant whenever she is required to be obedient to an incomprehensible commandment; there is something horribly appealing about the idea that someone— God, the prophet, Ian—knows exactly what is best and if she obeys their dictates with exactness everything will work out. She has practiced obedience as a precaution up to this point, as a means of ensuring everything will turn out all right in the end. But things can never turn out right now. The children will traverse life without their little sister. Issy will miss everything: She won't be an auntie or a wife or a mother. The fact that they will be reunited sometime within the next hundred years doesn't make everything better, no matter what Ian thinks.

She trundles back up to Issy's room, climbs into the bottom bunk, and wraps herself in Issy's covers. She is empty and exhausted; sleep comes easily.

She dreams she is on the beach with Issy. It is sunny and windy, always windy. The tide is out and the beach is spattered by leftover saltwater puddles that appear to be racing toward the pier as the wind blows. The parts of the beach that aren't puddled are muddy, rippled by the tide and spliced with razor shells. Issy is wearing wellies. Her dark hair is blowing in the breeze. Claire is watching her bend down to examine the shells when the wind whips up, the sunlight switches off, and she can hear the sudden roar of the sea. She looks away from Issy to the horizon. The sea usually slinks in on its belly, but it's approaching at speed, standing on roiling hind legs, a skyscraping bulwark of water. She grabs Issy's hand and tries to drag her away. There's no high ground and the gooey sand sucks at their wellies. "Run, Issy, run!" she shouts, even though she knows it's hopeless and she is already anticipating the slam of the water and the tearing apart of their hands.

Claire is woken, sweating and panicked, by a knock at the bedroom door. She catches her breath, hoping whoever it is will go away, but Zipporah steps in, flushed and rosy-cold from the walk back from town.

"Mum, can I talk to you?"

Claire's throat is gluey, unaccustomed to words, and her heart is pounding. She swallows and explores the dry lining of her mouth with her tongue, which feels fat and sticky.

"I've done something . . ." Zipporah closes the door behind her and leans against it.

Claire coughs, swallows again, and her heart begins to slow.

". . . something wrong. I've prayed, but I can't, I can't stop thinking about it." Zipporah taps the door with nervous fingers.

"I know." The words come out like a growl. She has slipped so far inside herself that it's hard to return to the surface and speak.

"How?"

"You must think I'm stupid." Her voice scuffs the back of her throat and she coughs again.

"Of course I don't. I didn't mean to, I was, I just wanted—"

"I would *never* have done such a thing." She coughs again as she pictures Zipporah putting the washing away, rummaging through the drawers, finding the money, and pocketing it. She imagines her walking around town with Lauren, *spending* the money that has been so assiduously saved.

Zipporah tucks her hair behind her ears and bites her lip. "I wanted to ask whether you—you say *never* but I wondered if in the past you might have . . ."

"I had too much respect for my mother."

"I didn't mean to do it. If you'd come to the wedding activity with me, I wouldn't have—"

"You've got a lot of nerve." Sweat is cooling on her forehead; she wipes her face with the blankets and turns away.

"Mum! I'm trying to talk to you."

The door slams and Claire stares at the wall. She wonders how much of the money is left. The initial shock of its loss is wearing off and she finds she cannot care as much as she did; there are bigger losses to bear. *"Lay not up for yourselves treasure on earth"*—her treasure is in heaven, she had no choice in the laying up of it, and now her heart is there also. She examines a little hole in the wallpaper where Issy must have picked the woodchip and she traces it, running her fingers over the ghost prints of Issy's fingers.

WHEN SHE WAKES again it's dark outside, she is bone tired and doesn't remember dreaming. Zipporah's voice floats up the stairs, wisping under the door, alternating with another—breathy, high, and anxious: Sister Valentine.

". . . Bishop Bradley? . . . talk to your mum . . ."

Zipporah says, "No," and then something about the Andersons; perhaps Brother Anderson is in the hospital again and Ian has gone to visit him.

". . . Family Home Evening tonight . . . shouldn't have come but . . . need to speak to your mum . . ."

Zipporah makes excuses. Claire can't distinguish every word, but she can hear her voice rising as she attempts to deter Sister Valentine.

"No, I don't think Mum would—you can't . . ."

There are footsteps on the stairs and Sister Valentine clearly asks, "Have you repented?" Claire can't make out Zipporah's murmured reply but if she has confessed to stealing the money she must be sorry, which is something.

"Mum." Zipporah knocks. "Mum, it's Sister Valentine." She opens the door and Sister Valentine squeezes past her.

"Oh, Sister Bradley, I'm so sorry to disturb you, I really am, and on a Monday night. I know you'll be having Family Home Evening when Bishop Bradley gets back, so I won't stay long." She steps farther into the room. "I'm so sorry you aren't well. You look terrible. Do you mind if I—can I just talk to you for a moment? It's all right, Zipporah, you can leave us to chat."

Sister Valentine sits on the floor next to the bed, so close Claire can see the jam-packed pores of her nose.

"That's better, I can see you properly now. I'm wondering, what—what exactly is wrong? We haven't seen you at church for weeks. Is it serious? Only, I had—I had a dream, and then I heard you were ill and I wanted to come and see you, because of the dream."

It's hard to keep up with Sister Valentine. There are too many words all at once and Claire can't be bothered to make the effort to decipher their meaning.

"I dreamed I was getting married, in the Temple."

Sister Valentine is so close that Claire can hear the assembly of her words, the way they are dipped in spit before she speaks them.

"I never imagined I'd be one of *those* women—nearly thirty and not married. I've tried. I go to the Single Adult activities but the men are old, or—I don't mean to be rude—a little bit strange. There aren't many single men in the Church in their thirties. I don't want you to think I'm fussy about age—I wouldn't mind an older man, but there aren't many in their forties or fifties either."

A little globe of spit flies out of Sister Valentine's mouth and lands on Claire's cheek. She wants to wipe it away, but that would be rude. She can feel it drying on her skin as she looks up at the bunk above her. Thirteen wooden slats alternate with exposed slices of the underside of Jacob's mattress. She wonders what exactly Sister Valentine dreamed—she hasn't even been to the Temple yet, she is probably imagining it all wrong, just like she did.

"... and when Bishop and Brother Stevens came Home Teaching, they agreed it was probably a sign that I'm going to get married in the Temple."

No one told Claire about the Temple before she went. They told her irrelevant, subjective things—"It was so *special*," "It was the best day of my life"—but they didn't tell her anything important. No one said she would have to take all her clothes off. The old ladies who worked there seemed to float along the corridors in their floor-length white dresses and slippers, every step silenced by thick carpets. They handed her a sort of sheet to wear with a hole in the middle for her head. She sat in a small cubicle, legs crossed and shivering, while an elderly stranger lifted the sheet to dab oil onto her bare stomach and chest while muttering a series of blessings. The words were beautiful but Claire couldn't listen with her whole self because she wanted her clothes back. Afterward, when it was time for the marriage part of the ceremony, her short-sleeved wedding dress was deemed inappropriate and she had to hold out her bare arms while the whispering old ladies covered them with temporary sleeves; they wrapped a triangle of material around her neck to conceal her collarbones and throat, and when she finally knelt across the altar with Ian she was wearing several extra layers—robes, an apron, and a special veil that tied under her chin with a length of ribbon. There was no exchange of rings, they made no promises or vows to each other, and there were different words for men and women: Ian *"received"* her and she agreed to *"give herself to him,"* which bothered her for weeks afterward. She couldn't talk to anyone about it because what happened in the Temple was too sacred to discuss, so she wrote a polite letter to the prophet, asking if he wouldn't mind explaining. The letter was returned opened and unanswered to Ian's dad, who was the Bishop at the time. "The brethren are busy men," he said. "Some things can't be *told;* they have to be *learned,* line upon line, precept upon precept." She apologized. It was silly to get caught up in the details; it was the promise of Eternity that was important.

"... marriage for Eternity or you can't enter the highest degree of the Celestial Kingdom and have eternal increase and I've always wanted children. I think I'd be a good mother . . ."

She wishes Sister Valentine would go away and let her sleep. There is a cobweb on the ceiling just above the wardrobe that's blowing in an invisible breeze like a wispy pendulum, almost hypnotizing.

"The thing is, Sister Bradley, and I didn't tell Bishop Bradley this, but the thing is, and I hope you don't mind me telling you—I'm sure you won't mind, I feel like we're friends—it's just that, in my dream, I was getting married to *him*, to Bishop Bradley."

The cobweb must be lighter than air or it would surely break. Perhaps it will multiply and there will be a white, swaying meadow on the ceiling.

"And then I heard you were ill and I, well, I wondered if it's *serious*. I thought if you were, if you *are*—seriously ill, I mean—it might be of some comfort to you to know that I'm here and in the event, in the event of any unfortunate thing, I would—I *will* be so happy to *help*."

There is a sudden thrumming in Claire's ears as she becomes aware of the seriousness of what's being said.

"... been thinking about it, and I've realized I *could* love Bishop Bradley. And you too," Sister Valentine adds hastily, "like a sister. And the children. Zipporah and I—we've already shared so much. And I'm sure with time the boys and I—little Jacob and Alma—I know they like my cooking and, well, I'm sure."

Claire has no words for this. She wonders if she is supposed to die in order to make way for Sister Valentine's revelation; has she failed the test so badly that she deserves to be bankrupted, her assets stripped and given to another woman? Is she supposed to let Sister Valentine help herself to the family, to Ian? In the event of her death, Ian would probably do it. After a suitable period of mourning he would remarry and he'd pick someone from church, a woman who otherwise didn't have much hope of marrying in the Temple. He would decide to love this other woman in the same single-minded way he loves her. It's a horrible thought, one she has done her best to banish since Ian's mother revealed that eternal marriage is, at its very heart, polygamous.

". . . like children—I love them. And it's not too late for me to have some. I've got a good eight years at least, I think . . ."

The spot of spit has dried now. Claire lifts her hand and rubs at it, but she can't erase its stamp.

"Anyway, Sister Bradley, I wanted you to know. I thought it might give you some comfort." Sister Valentine gets to her knees and uses the bunk to heft herself up. "You look so tired and pale. And you never—you never said what's wrong."

Claire thinks for a moment. "I'm sad," she croaks.

"Oh . . . is that—is that all?" She sounds disappointed. "Well, you look terrible. If you're more ill, and you just don't know it yet . . ."

"Thank you."

Sister Valentine steps out of the room and closes the door behind her. Claire rolls over and stares at the picked wallpaper. It would be lovely to drift off to sleep and wake up in heaven, with Issy—"*Where your treasure is, there will your heart be also.*" Ian is always saying this life is short and God's time passes differently—quicker, somehow. Would it hurt so much to leave the family behind and fly through the next forty years with Issy rather than linger through them out here? She can't leave deliberately, of course, that would be a sin. But she might leave accidentally or fortuitously. Ian would cope, he'd give comforting Family Home Evening lessons about pioneer trials and keep everyone going. Each morning she lies in bed and hears the sounds of the gap she would leave—the voices and the breakfast noises, the carrying on. She cups a hand over her heart and collects its beats. She isn't ill, not at the moment. That could change, though. She rubs at the spot where Sister Valentine's spit struck her. Everything could change.

— 18 —

Gobby Little Shite

Al is a coward. He hasn't been to the bank to swap the fifties for tens 'cause he's dreamed about the money every night since he took it. Last night's episode was replete with smells, sounds, and feelings so horrifyingly real that they were bonded to the inside of his head when he woke up.

He dreamed he was pulling the handcart across America—the burned money was worthless, leaving them with no access to other forms of transportation. Brother Rimmer lay in the back of the cart, half dead with exhaustion. Having finally crossed the Rocky Mountains, they reached a gate manned by Brigham Young. Al tried to speak, but each time he opened his mouth Brigham Young shouted, "This is *my* place!" Al begged and pleaded but Brigham Young wouldn't open the gate and that's when the flesh-eating Armageddon zombies teemed down the nearest mountain: Brother Rimmer's screams have been ricocheting around his head all morning.

Al zips up his hoodie and strokes the pocket. It's been only five minutes since Dad left. "Look after your brother," he said as he split for the hospital to see Brother Anderson. He's spent hours there this week, even though he promised to take Jacob to the beach and the penny arcade at the end of the pier.

When Dad's been gone for ten minutes, Al sneaks out the back way. He's got no intention of looking after Jacob, he's far too busy. He gets his bike out of the shed and wheels it round to the front of the house. As he lifts his leg over the bike frame, Sister Anderson pulls up in her car and rolls down the window.

"Alma, dear! I hate to be a nuisance, but is your dad home?" she calls.

"He's gone to see Brother Anderson."

"Oh, I hoped I might catch him first. I'm going shopping." Someone beeps their horn at her, but she isn't at all bothered. "Your dad said he'd sit with Brother Anderson while I catch up with a few things. I've been meaning to tell him something, but with Brother Anderson being so ill, I keep forgetting. And as I was passing . . ."

"Well, he's not here."

"Can you give him a message, Alma, dear? In case he's gone when I get to the hospital?"

"All right."

"I'm a bit concerned about Jacob. Something happened in our Primary lesson on Sunday. He said—this sounds silly, but he definitely said it—he said his goldfish was *resurrected*."

Al stares at Sister Anderson's puffy pink cheeks and her fluffy hair, at her bright red lips and the way she's somehow managed to smear a bloody, Halloween line of lipstick across her top teeth. He hates her for telling tales on Jacob, for blocking the road as if she owns it, and for coming to the house to speak to Dad when he is already at the hospital.

"I'm sure Jacob wasn't telling lies," she continues. "He's a good boy. I'm sure he *wishes* it happened, but he needs to learn the difference between make-believe and real life."

Beep-beep. Al watches as the cars that have formed a line behind Sister Anderson take advantage of a break in the traffic to get round her by driving on the wrong side of the road. She doesn't give a shit, she's perfectly happy to block the way.

So what if Jacob lied about the fish? What does it matter? Why shouldn't he get in on the miraculous-story gig? Everyone else is bullshitting about spectacular visitations and answers to prayer.

"So you'll remember to tell your dad?"

He nods, and then he can't help himself. "Sister Anderson?"

"Yes, dear."

"You reckon you saw Issy in the Temple."

"Yes, I did," she says.

"I'm sure you weren't telling lies."

"Sorry?"

"But you need to learn the difference between make-believe and real life."

"I beg your pardon?"

He puts both hands on the handlebars and pedals away. He totally *owned* Sister Anderson, he rained on her parade and shat on her stupid story; there's no way she saw Issy, no way. He lifts his butt off the seat to gather speed and then he races all the way to Brother Rimmer's house, laughing into the wind.

AL SITS ON the edge of the pink velvet sofa, grateful to see Brother Rimmer alive and intact, despite the annoying racket.

Clackety-clackety. Clink-clink-clink.

"It's a dying art, spoon playing. Andrea used to love this, she used to beg me to do it."

Clackety-clackety. Clink-clink-clink.

Brother Rimmer slaps the spoons against his hand and thigh and grins as if he's on one of those dancing programs on TV, trying to make the audience like him. "Give us a tune on the spoons, Dad— that's what Andrea used to say."

Clackety-clackety. Clink-clink-clink.

Al doesn't want to know about poor, dead Andrea. Just hearing her name makes him wonder whether she drowned on the beach in the olden days before the marsh took over and the sand was golden, or somewhere else: one of the sluices out on Churchtown Moss or the lake in the park across the road from home.

"I can teach you, if you like."

Clackety-clackety. Clink-clink-clink.

"Nah, it's all right, thanks," he says.

Clackety-clackety. Clink-clink-clink.

"It'd be no trouble. I don't charge for lessons!"

"No thanks."

"Good opportunity for you to develop a talent."

Playing the spoons is beyond pointless; Brother Rimmer would have been better off learning to swim, Al thinks. Brother Rimmer smacks the spoons along his belly and across his chest in a rousing finale and Al claps a couple of times, eliciting a gratified bob of the head.

"Shall we go out to the garage now?"

"Not yet, I'm puffed." Brother Rimmer lowers himself onto the cushioned swivel chair. "Anyway, I've got something to show you first." He turns on the computer and types something into the Internet search bar. "Wait 'til you see this," he says. "Just you wait! Wait . . . wait . . . wait . . . There. Look!"

Al stands so he can see over Brother Rimmer's shoulder. "It's a picture of a tree," he says.

"It's an apple tree."

"Yeah."

"Blossoming in *October.*"

"Oh, right."

"It's a sign of the times. The seasons'll get all mixed up before the Second Coming. Prime piece of evidence for any Second Coming detective right there! Could be any day now. What does the Lord say? *'Behold, I come quickly.'*"

Al cups one hand over his mouth to catch a snigger.

"Don't just stand there like a bump on a log, come closer, have a proper look." Brother Rimmer clicks on another tab and opens a site called Follow the Signs of the Times. The home page is boardered by flames. He clicks on the "Questions" tab and a list appears.

Is it true that the Second Coming will happen after a year without rainbows?

How soon after the Second Coming will Christ declare the Mormon Church his Church?

Is it true that God is the literal, physical father of Jesus Christ?

"You can learn anything you want here," Brother Rimmer says. "Pick one thing. Go on."

Al sighs. "That one," he says, pointing at the middle of the screen.

"*Where are the three Nephites?*" Brother Rimmer reads. "Right then, let's find out, shall we?" He clicks on the question and a whole page of text appears. "Now this is very interesting, Alma Bradley. What do you know about the three Nephites?"

"I've heard of them," Al says. "I'm meeting my mate to play football at one o'clock, so I need to—"

"When Jesus visited America, after he was crucified, three of his Nephite apostles asked if they could stay on Earth until he came again. And Jesus said yes, which was nice of him. Look here, listen to this: '*The three Nephites are still on the earth today, ministering to all nations, kindreds, tongues, and people.*'" Brother Rimmer swivels his chair slightly to look at Al, who makes a feeble attempt to appear interested.

"Isn't that smashing? And do you know what? When Sister Rimmer was alive, she had a very special experience." Brother Rimmer sits like one of those nodding dogs people stick in the back windows of their cars. Al can see he is supposed to ask about the special experience, but he doesn't. After a few moments Brother Rimmer gets fed up with waiting and carries on anyway.

"It happened on the highway. On the hard shoulder of the M58. One of her tires blew out and she had to pull over. It was before cell phones and the Interweb. Sister Rimmer didn't know what to do, so she prayed for help."

Al stuffs his hands in his pockets. Not another stupid story where someone gets their prayers answered.

"Eventually, another car stopped to help. Three men got out. They put the spare tire on for her and then they drove away." Brother Rimmer's eyebrows flex, as if to say, "Ta-dah!"

Al shrugs. He can't believe Brother Rimmer thinks three ancient, undead Americans changed Sister Rimmer's tire—he may as well credit the three little pigs.

"The three Nephites. First thing we thought of. Can't say for sure, of course. But that's what we reckoned—our very own miracle. Sister Rimmer told everyone in Testimony Meeting. She was right proud." Brother Rimmer swivels back to the computer screen and minimizes the page. "It's a comfort, isn't it? To know the Lord's looking out for you. He's a personal God and no problem's too small to turn over to him."

Al wonders why the three Nephites went for a roadside-assistance miracle when they could have rescued Andrea. At least the miracle was practical—a changed tire is more useful than a bleeding statue or a potato chip shaped like Jesus.

"Can we go out to the garage now?" he asks.

"All right then. You're keen, aren't you? Good lad."

SANDING THE WHEELS is tricky and time-consuming. They are huge, higher than Al's waist, with twelve thick spokes. Brother Rimmer sits in his high-backed chair, arms resting on the mountain of his belly.

"Won't be long now," he says. "A few little repairs and a couple of coats of varnish."

Al slides his spare hand between the spokes as he rubs the wood. "How do you make wheels, then?" he asks.

"You start with the hub." Brother Rimmer points to the middle bit of the wheel. "You drive the spokes into the hub with a sledgehammer. Then you attach the wheel. It's divided into four fellies, they're like quarters, and they join up to make a circle. Once that's done you measure around the outside of the wheel with a traveler so you know how much steel you need to hold it all together. You have to heat the steel and hammer it round the wheel while it's hot. You cool it with water and the steel shrinks tight. No need for screws or anything. There's other ways, of course, but I wanted to do it like the pioneers did."

"Did you need special tools?"

"Oh yes. I used to have a workshop in the industrial park. I did

a bit there, in between jobs, and I brought sections back here to
work on. Used to carry bits and pieces backward and forward in the
car—just about squeezed the axles in. Had to use the trailer once in
a while, though."

"How long did it take?"

Brother Rimmer puffs his cheeks up, then blows the air out.
"Best part of two years, I should think. After work and Saturdays.
Never on a Sunday, of course."

Al wonders if the project lasted for two years because that was
how long it took Brother Rimmer to feel better about Andrea. It
seems like a long time, until he thinks of Issy; he can't imagine a
time when he won't miss her.

"How are you getting on?" Brother Rimmer asks.

"Just finishing off this spoke."

"No, I mean, how are you?"

"Fine." Al gets his head down and rubs the spoke vigorously.

"That's what I thought." Brother Rimmer sighs. "Well, I don't
know about you, but I could eat a buttered frog." He holds onto the
arms of his chair and rocks himself upright.

"You carry on and I'll fetch cake," he says.

As soon as Brother Rimmer leaves the garage, Al kneels on the
wood-dusted concrete floor and flicks the rusty clasp of the little
toolbox. He lifts out the *Ensign,* the old-fashioned teddy bear, and
the handkerchief and puts them on the floor.

He has to swap the notes back. There's nothing brave about
taking money off a daft old bloke with a dead daughter. He runs his
finger along the edge of the envelope and flicks it open. The damaged notes are almost corrugated; he takes them out, unzips the
hoodie pocket, and swaps the money over slowly, as if he hasn't
quite made up his mind, enjoying the luxury of pretending there's
still a choice to be made.

The slam of Brother Rimmer's back door makes him jump. He
stuffs the envelope back into the toolbox, chucks the other stuff on

top, closes the lid, and zips his pocket shut as he gets off the floor. He's dusting his knees as Brother Rimmer pushes at the garage door.

"Come and help with the tray. That's it. Now put it down there." Brother Rimmer sits heavily and holds out a hand for his Barleycup and cake.

Al passes a mug and a plate of Victoria sponge to him.

"Eat up, then."

It's good cake. One glance at Brother Rimmer is enough to reveal he is a man who likes good cake.

"You'll be off on your mission before you know it," Brother Rimmer says in between mouthfuls. "You've got, what—four years? It'll fly by. Any thoughts about where you'd like to go?"

"No."

"Hawaii. That's what people always say. Hawaii and the Bahamas. Come on, you must've thought about it."

Al tries not to think about it whenever possible, but he can see Brother Rimmer isn't going to give up until he names a country.

"France."

"What do you want to go there for?"

"The European Championships are in France in 2016."

Brother Rimmer laughs. "You won't be watching football on your mission."

Al gets up and starts sanding again. He won't be going on a mission at all, but if he tells that to Brother Rimmer he won't get paid.

When he's finished sanding the wheel, Brother Rimmer gives him another tenner. "You're back at school next week, aren't you? So you can come a week on Saturday."

"Yes."

"All right then. Be a good lad, now."

"I'll try."

"Don't try, *do*."

• • •

BROTHER RIMMER'S HOUSE is only a five-minute bike ride from the footie pitch. Al arrives just before 1 P.M. There's a big gate and a tree-lined path. He cycles down the path, even though there's a "No Cycling" sign. When he gets to the field he jumps off his bike and leans it against a tree. The grass is wet even though it hasn't been raining. There are empty chestnut shells and soggy leaves around the outline of the pitch, which has recently been repainted. He kicks the empty shells, thinking about the money while he waits for Matty. At the far end of the field there's a sandy area with some swings and a slide. Two big lads are mucking about with the swings, flipping them over and over and over until they're too high for anyone to sit on. He thinks he recognizes them, reckons they used to be in Year Eleven.

Meeting up with Matty to play football has been the best thing about half-term. Matty doesn't talk about Issy. He just carries on as if nothing has happened. It's nice to pretend everything's normal, even though afterward, when he remembers it isn't, things often seem extra crappy.

A flock of Canada geese chase through the sky in arrow formations, screeching to one another as they head for the marsh. He stops and watches them pass.

When Matty arrives he leans his bike next to Al's and dashes onto the field. He's brought his new Premier League ball. It's light and soft. It's got a nice feel, and Al thinks he might buy himself one, next season, or the season after, once he's thought of a way to sort out Mum's money.

They jog down the pitch, passing to each other. When they reach the far end, near the park, Matty goes in goal and Al practices free kicks. Then Al goes in goal so Matty can practice. They concentrate on their feet, hands, and eyes—they don't need to talk to each other. It's perfect, until Matty misjudges a free kick and the ball flies over the top of the goal and into the little park.

Al expects the lads mucking about next to the swings to thump it back, but the taller lad, whose hair is shaved so closely to his head that he almost looks bald, drops his cigarette, picks up the ball, and starts to head out of the playground toward the alley between the houses that back onto the field.

"Oi," Matty shouts. "Oi! That's my ball!"

Al runs. He remembers the lads on Queens Drive and how everything was fine once they started playing together. He calls to the lads. "Do you want to play?"

They turn round. "Do you want to play?" the shorter one mimics.

"How about a kick-about, two on two?"

"If you want the ball, come and get it."

The lad with the shaved head holds the ball up. He's got wicked acne—his cheeks are bubbling with pus. When Al steps closer, he chucks the ball in the air and catches it again and again.

"Congratulations, you can catch." Al gives the lad a slow hand-clap and Matty nudges him.

"You're a gobby little shite, aren't you?" the shorter lad says.

"Give us the ball."

"Come and get it."

Matty swallows hard; he looks like he might be about to cry. A ring of anger warms the ache in Al's stomach, like a gas flame. He's going to go apeshit if the lads don't give the ball back.

"Aw, look. He's going to cry." The shorter lad points at Matty and wobbles his bottom lip up and down with his finger. "Aw, did-dums," he says. "Do you want your mum?"

"Bet he does. Mummy's boy."

"I reckon his mum's gross. Ugly enough to make an onion cry."

"Shut up and leave him alone. It's not your ball. Give it back."

"Do you fancy his mum, then?"

"Oh, fuck off." Al experiences a pleasant rush of disobedience as he swears.

"I reckon he does, poor sod." The shorter lad looks pityingly at Al. "Do you like fugly old women?"

"Fuck. Off."

"He likes fugly old women 'cause his mum's one—a great big fugly whale. So fat and lazy she's got her own postcode." Spotty-Face throws the ball up high and catches it with a grin.

Al thinks of Mum—who is *not* lazy or fat—and the simmering ache in his stomach begins to burn.

The shorter lad laughs and his mate, showing off now, carries on. "She's so lazy she sticks her arse out the window and lets the wind wipe it."

That's it. When Spotty-Face throws the ball in the air again, Al lunges at him, shoving him in the chest as hard as he can. The lad lands smack on his butt.

Al grabs the ball. "Run!" he says to Matty.

"Come here, you little shit."

Al doesn't look round. He runs alongside Matty, as hard as he can, the ball held under one arm like a rugby player. Moments later, he hears two pairs of feet pounding the grass behind them. Is this brave or stupid? He can't tell. He keeps running, all the way across the football pitch. The lads are unfit, they smoke. He can hear one of them coughing behind him.

When they reach the edge of the field, Al and Matty tear down the path to the trees where they left their bikes. Al unzips his hoodie far enough to stuff the ball down his front and they jump on the bikes.

"You look like you're, ha ha, like you're, ha ha, bloody preggers, Al."

"Shut up and ride."

They push off and pedal hard. Once their feet have got some traction and their tires have made a few rotations, they're away and there's no chance of being caught. Al isn't angry anymore. He's just avoided having his head kicked in. And he's done it all by himself, without any supernatural help, just his own brain and legs. Another swarm of geese arrows above the park, cackling madly, black against the sky like animations. He looks back over his shoulder. The two lads are clutching their knees as they catch their breath between coughs.

"Fuck off, you wankers," he shouts. "Fuck off!"

– 19 –

Happy Are Thy Men, Happy Are These Thy Servants

Ian flops into the car and fastens the seat belt. The windshield is streaked with rain and he's soaked from the walk. The glass steams up and he closes his eyes. Just a moment's rest, he thinks.

The car has been parked in the supermarket parking lot all afternoon. There's a risk of getting booted, according to the signs, but it costs £3 to park at the hospital and this week alone he's saved £18 by ignoring the big yellow warnings. It occurs to him that parking in the supermarket in defiance of the warning signs may be an act of dishonesty. *"Are you honest in your dealings with your fellow men?"* is a question he must answer satisfactorily in order to be worthy to enter the Temple. Is it dishonest to park illegally? Probably. Lying to everyone about Claire is dishonest too, but he can't think what else to do. Eyes closed, he fumbles to adjust the seat, sighing as it reclines. Just five minutes' peace and quiet, that's all.

He is woken by the sound of his own snores. When he tries to sit up he is held in place by the seat belt. He checks his watch and groans—he's been asleep for more than an hour. He unclips the belt and adjusts the seat, then wipes a circle in the steamed-up window with the cuff of his suit jacket. It isn't raining anymore, the wind is blowing tides into wide puddles, and people are fighting it as they push shopping carts across the lot. He turns the key and switches on the fan to clear the windows properly.

There's something exhausting and stultifying about sitting next to a hospital bed and there's a heaviness, a melancholy quality to the air that, given recent events, means it's difficult for him to be there at all. No one has thought of it, and he doesn't like to say. Brother Anderson is not particularly forthcoming at the best of times, but during today's visit he was virtually mute and Ian had to resort to delivering a running commentary on the weather as it blustered past the window. At least the weekend starts tomorrow and Brother Stevens can take his turn at the hospital. "It's so lucky you've got a week off, Bishop," Sister Anderson said when she realized it was half-term. "I hate to be a nuisance but it's like an answer to prayer." Ian bristled but he was trapped by scripture: *I was sick and ye visited me . . . inasmuch as ye have done it unto the least of these my brethren, ye have done it unto me.* Would he go and visit Jesus in the hospital? Of course he would. Should he go and visit Brother Anderson in the hospital? Of course he should.

As soon as the windshield is clear, he refastens his seat belt and begins the drive home. Jacob will be waiting. He has promised to take him to the beach and he will keep his word, even though it will be cold and incredibly windy there this afternoon.

It hasn't been much of a holiday for poor Jacob. Before Issy, when things were normal, Ian could help people and not feel the slightest bit guilty about being away from home. But it's suddenly difficult to balance the scales of service. Alma isn't prepared to do his bit and it's not fair to expect Zipporah to do everything. When he was called as Bishop he was promised the family would be blessed if he did a good job; if he put the Lord first, everything else in his life would fall into its proper place. He still believes this, he does. And if he can just keep going until Claire gets back to normal, the blessings of his service will be made manifest, he is certain of it. No one needs to know what is happening at home. If people find out, President Carmichael might decide that early release is the best option—a failure so enormous Ian can't countenance it. In fact he's aware of only one occasion when a Bishop was released early and he remembers how awful it was.

Bishop Davie was released when Ian was twelve. He'd served for only two years, which was strange because bishops usually serve for at least five. Ian was aware of whispered exchanges between his mum and dad and there was a funny atmosphere at church for a few weeks. Then Bishop Davie disappeared. His wife and children kept coming to church at first, but it wasn't long before they disappeared too. Ian overheard Mum saying that Sister Davie couldn't cope with the shame.

Several months later Ian was shopping with Mum and they saw Bishop Davie. Of course, he wasn't "Bishop Davie" anymore, but Ian didn't know his first name and couldn't think of him as anything else.

Mum grabbed his arm. "Quick," she said. "He might see us." Ian was supposed to turn round but he couldn't help staring at Bishop Davie. He'd grown a beard in the months since he'd been released and he looked tired. When she thought Bishop Davie wasn't looking, Mum tried to march Ian away, but it was too late.

"Sister Bradley!"

Mum had to stop. She pretended to be surprised. "Ah, *Keith*," she said, which sounded all wrong. "We haven't seen you for ages."

"I'm still around and about, Sister Bradley."

"We've—we've missed you at church." Mum kept glancing at Bishop Davie's cart as if she was expecting to find something awful in it, so Ian stared too. It was full of normal things. He couldn't see any coffee, tea, or beer—nothing that gave a clue as to why Bishop Davie had been released.

"Well, we still live in the same house, Sister Bradley. There's no need to miss us. I think Sister Davie might appreciate—you're always welcome to visit."

Mum said they were late for something and pulled Ian away. In the car on the way home she told him *Keith* was an adulterer. There'd been a woman at work—that was the problem with having women in the workplace. *Keith* had confessed to the Stake President immediately, which went in his favor, of course. There'd been a Church court. Mum knew this because Dad was on the High Council. Sister Davie had begged for leniency because she didn't want anyone to know. She said if *she* could forgive her husband, it was no one else's business. But *Keith's* punishment was excommunication. Mum explained that *Keith* wasn't a member of the Church anymore, he wasn't married for Eternity or sealed to his family, and he couldn't serve in the Church until he had repented properly and been rebaptized. That was why he had to be released as Bishop.

Ian stops the car and then reverses into the driveway.

Bishop Davie's release is the only early release he's encountered. He pulls the handbrake up. Whatever happens, no matter how sad Claire is, *he* can't be released early, especially while Mum and Dad are away. They would be horribly disappointed at his failure to lead the family through a crisis. *"No other success can compensate for failure in the home"*—that's what Mum would say, and she's right. Heavenly Father must have already known what was going to happen when He inspired President Carmichael to put Ian's name forward as the next Bishop, therefore there must be some greater purpose, some special lesson in all this.

When he walks through the front door, Jacob is sitting on the stairs.

"I'm so sorry. I'll just get my boots. You fetch your coat and we'll get going."

"It's all right, Dad. I'm just going to stay here."

"Oh, it's not too late. If we go now we can have a good walk and a bit of a splash-about before it gets dark."

Jacob has got a coloring book balanced on his knee and Issy's pink pencil case sits on the stair beside him. "No thank you," he says. "I'm just going to stay here."

"But you wanted to go. You always go to the beach with Mum in the holidays."

"Mum's in bed."

"And she'll get up as soon as she feels better. In the meantime you'll have to put up with me." He pulls a funny face and when that doesn't work he bends down and starts to unlace his shoes.

"I just want to stay here, Dad."

Ian steps out of his shoes and pads up the stairs. He lifts Issy's pencil case and sits down next to Jacob. "What's so good about sitting here, then?" he asks.

"I can see through the glass in the door. I can see who's coming."

"Well, I'm here now. You don't have to watch out for me anymore." How sad that Jacob has been waiting for him like this. He'd like to say something to make it better, but he has already apologized. He puts his arm around Jacob and squeezes. "Shall we go upstairs and ask Zipporah what she's going to make for dinner?" he asks.

"You ask her, Dad. Then you can come and tell me if you like."

"Oh, all right." Ian stands. He feels humored. "I'll just check with your sister, then, shall I?" he says.

Jacob resumes his coloring. He doesn't reply.

THEY HAVE PASTA mixed with tins of tuna and mushroom soup for dinner. Pasta in one form or another is all Zipporah seems able to cook.

"Can we have something different tomorrow?" Alma asks.

"Yeah, if you want to cook it."

"Why don't they teach you how to cook at Youth? It'd be better than dressing up and pretending to get married."

"Why don't they teach *you* how to cook?"

"Stop it," Ian says. "If you can't say anything nice, don't say anything at all."

"That'll render Alma mute for the rest of his life."

"I said stop it. Fetch Mum's plate and take it upstairs."

"There's no point."

"There's every point."

Zipporah disappears with the plate and they hear her sighs and huffs as she trudges up the stairs. Alma smirks and continues eating, barely chewing before he swallows. Jacob picks at his food. Ian knows he should ask Jacob what's wrong but what if it's something unfixable?

Zipporah is on her way back down the stairs when the doorbell rings and Ian decides to leave it to her. He hopes it's a double-glazed window salesman or a Jehovah's Witness—someone she can get rid of without his help.

There are voices in the hall, then Zipporah calls, "Dad, it's President Carmichael and Brother Stevens."

Ian gets up from the table and rubs his face hard with both hands, trying to arrange it into a welcoming expression. "Come on," he says to Jacob and Alma. "Come and say hello."

The three of them spill out into the hall, where President Carmichael greets them.

"Good evening, Bradleys! How are you? Brother Stevens and I just wanted to come and see if you're all right."

Ian swallows and glances at the stairs. "Come in and sit down," he says, pointing to the living room. "Make yourselves at home." He grabs Zipporah's hand as she passes. "See if Mum will come," he whispers. "Tell her I said please."

She shakes her head at him. "She won't."

"She has to. Do you want people to think there's something *wrong* with her?"

He watches Zipporah head back up the stairs and then joins the others in the living room. President Carmichael and Brother Stevens are wearing their suits, which means they have come on official Church business. They have arranged this. He wonders whether they did it on the phone or in person, whether they met to discuss him, whether his name is on a meeting agenda under a list of *concerns*. "What can I do for you both?" he asks.

"We just wanted to make sure everything's OK."

"Well, it is!"

"That's good to know." President Carmichael clasps his hands together. "Are you having family prayer and daily scripture study? It's important not to let these things slide when you're facing trials."

"I, well—we try." Family prayer and scripture study have always been Claire's responsibility. "Could do better, must try harder," he jokes feebly.

"Brother Stevens has brought the Visiting Teaching Message with him, for Claire. Sister Stevens made it, specially."

Brother Stevens holds up a homemade card. It has a pink ribbon glued to it and there is writing on the front.

Ian stretches out his arm, but Brother Stevens doesn't pass it over. "What does it say?" He hasn't read any of the *Ensign* this month. "What's the Visiting Teaching Message for October? I haven't got that far yet."

"Bless you, Bishop, for *ever* reading the Visiting Teaching Message since it's just for the sisters—trust you to go the extra mile! This month's message is *'Do Not Doubt.'* Sister Stevens has written a quote from it right here: 'Women who recognize that their strength comes from the Lord's atonement do not give up during difficult and discouraging times.' "

Ian's stomach swoops. He needs to tell Zipporah to keep Claire upstairs. What on Earth was he thinking?

"That is so true," he says. "Excuse me, I just need to—"

"Dad, wait, watch this—can you do the elephant song, Brother Stevens?" Jacob asks. "Go on, please!"

"Oh, I don't know, I—" Brother Stevens is bashful, his round cheeks pink.

"Please!"

Jacob's pleading moves Ian. Here is something Jacob wants, something that might make him feel a little bit better. "I'd like to see this elephant song too," he says and settles back into his seat.

"Oh, Bishop!" Brother Stevens laughs. "I do it with the kids if I'm helping out in Primary. It's just me kidding around. I kinda—"

"Please!"

"OK, OK!"

Brother Stevens gets up and hunches over. He lifts one arm out in front of him, like a trunk, and starts to sing in a deep, tuneless

voice. "One elephant began to play upon a spider's web one day."
He lollops around the middle of the room in an awkward loop. "He
found it such enormous fun that he called for another elephant to
come."

"Pick me, pick me," Jacob calls.

Brother Stevens lumbers up to Jacob and tickles him with his
elephant trunk. Jacob giggles, gets to his feet, and joins in the song.

"Two elephants began to play upon a spider's web one day . . ."

President Carmichael leans around the lumbering elephants.
"Where's Claire?" he asks.

"She's in bed. She's still not well. In fact, I should check on her."

"She isn't in bed, Dad."

Alma points to the doorway and Ian hardly dares to look. The
singing stops and he turns in his chair. Claire is standing in front of
Zipporah. She looks startled and slightly mad, hair askew, her
nightie grubby and scrunched like an old tissue.

President Carmichael stands. He extends his hand toward Claire
but she doesn't step forward to shake it.

Jacob rushes up and hugs her. "Mum," he shouts as if he hasn't
seen her for months.

Claire pats him, absently. Her legs poke out of the bottom of her
nightie like dolls' legs: shiny and improbably white. Zipporah is
standing behind her, mouth flat, throat bobbing. It looks like her
hand may be resting on Claire's back, and Claire's fixed expression
reminds Ian of a ventriloquist's dummy.

Brother Stevens steps forward with the card. "Here, Sister Bradley.
Ashlee made it specially for you. It's the Visiting Teaching Message."

Claire doesn't say thank you, she just holds the card and stares
at it, as if she can't remember how to read.

Ian hurries to the doorway. "Let's get you back to bed," he says.
He puts his arm around her but it's as if she's frozen to the spot
and he almost has to push her along the hall. When they reach the
stairs he pulls the Visiting Teaching card out of her hand. Then

he tugs her and she shuffles after him, like a toddler. As he reaches the top of the staircase he hears President Carmichael say, "Your mum looks terrible, Zipporah. What on Earth's wrong?"

When they get to Issy's room Claire's steps become more purposeful and Ian stands on the landing and watches as she crosses the room and crawls back into the bottom bunk. He waits until she pulls the covers over her head, then he folds the card in two and slides it into his trouser pocket.

"Mum's not lazy," Jacob is saying as Ian approaches the living room. Zipporah is still standing in the doorway and he has to squeeze past her in order to sit down.

"Of course not," Brother Stevens replies in his loud, emphatic American voice. "Your mom is kinda sick right now, huh? And I'm guessing you guys could use some help."

"We're fine, thank you," Ian says.

"Aw, come on, Bishop. We're here on behalf of the Lord, as His servants, and I'm sure He'd want you to know that accepting service is as important as giving it. How about I tell Sister Stevens to organize some more Relief Society meals?"

"Yes!" Alma thumps the air with both fists.

Brother Stevens grins at Alma and they high-five each other.

"How long do you think you need, Bishop? Has Sister Bradley had a blessing? Do you think a blessing might make her feel better?" Brother Stevens's voice drops to a whisper, which Ian assumes is for the sake of the children, though they can still hear. "Is she, do you think—she seems kinda *depressed*?"

Ian looks at the children, at President Carmichael, and finally at Brother Stevens. *"Are you honest in your dealings with your fellow men?"*—the question pops into his head as he tries to think of a reply. What *is* wrong with Claire? She's not grieving properly. She isn't behaving like a pioneer. She's lying down on a shoulder of her life's path and he doesn't know how to make her get up again. He can't say any of that.

"She's so . . . tired," he says. "She can't—she can't sleep."

"Aha." Brother Stevens is pleased with the answer. He nods his head. "Sleep deprivation—it's been used as a kind of torture, hasn't it?"

"She'll be a lot better when she can sleep properly." Ian is aware of Alma's hard gaze and the anxious bunching of Jacob's brow. He doesn't even look at Zipporah.

"There's great purpose in the struggle of life," President Carmichael says.

Brother Stevens nods and Ian forces himself to join in.

"I'll tell Ashlee about the food as soon as I get home," Brother Stevens promises. "Can we have a prayer with you before we go, Bishop?"

WHEN ALMA AND Jacob are in bed, Zipporah approaches him.

"Dad," she says, and he knows what it's going to be.

"What?"

"I think Mum should go to the doctor's."

He bristles, has to stop himself from saying it's none of her business.

"I told her you said she had to get up. I asked her to get dressed and she didn't—she wasn't listening properly, it was like she couldn't even hear what I was saying. I tried to stop her from coming downstairs like that, but I couldn't."

"Things will get better."

"How?"

"It's time for you to go bed."

"Maybe she should see a counselor."

"No. It's not . . ." He can't put his hope into words or explain his faith that if they just carry on and keep to the path, Claire will pick herself up, dust herself off, and rejoin their trek to salvation. "If you take something to pieces it's harder to stick it back together."

"What does that mean? You can't take people to pieces."

"It's time for you to go to bed."

"But, Dad, Mum's upstairs. And no one's helping her." Zippo-rah pauses. "She's ill, and it—it reminds me of Issy."

Ian puts his arms around her. "Everything will be OK," he says.

AT NIGHT, AFTER the children have gone to sleep, he has started to talk to Claire. Sometimes she doesn't say anything, other times she says things he doesn't understand. Last night he told her about the pass-along cards.

"I don't know how I'm going to get rid of them," he said. She said something that sounded like "Rumpelstiltskin." When he asked what she meant she said, "Spin the straw into gold, Ian," and he didn't want to ask again in case it didn't make any sense at all.

Tonight, the plate of rubbery pasta is still on the floor; he can't tell whether any of it has been eaten—she may have had a mouthful or two. He nudges the plate to one side and sits on the floor next to the bed. The bed is becoming Claire's bed but it's not hers, it's Issy's, and he feels a thump of frustration at her refusal to vacate it.

He tells her he visited Brother Anderson again and starts to ex-plain what it was like sitting in the hospital, then stops, uncertain as to whether he is being insensitive. He remembers falling asleep in the car but he decides it's best not to mention it. He wants to say something about her appearance downstairs in front of President Carmichael and Brother Stevens but he doesn't know how to broach it, and since there's no point in asking about her day, he quickly runs out of things to say. While he searches for more words, he re-alizes she hasn't moved at all since he sat down next to the bed. He tries to mimic her stillness. The tension it takes is surprising. His neck hurts after a few seconds and it occurs to him for the first time that she may blame him; she may not see the bigger picture, may not recognize that what has happened must be the Lord's will, and re-grets and what-ifs are futile.

"Are you angry with me?"

Finally her head moves. "You blessed her to live. And she didn't."

Her words hurt. "Sometimes live means *'live unto the Lord,'* Claire." The words don't taste right, they sound half baked and inadequate.

"Sometimes to live means to die—is that what you're saying?"

"That's what it says in the scriptures." He can hear weakness when he says it and he is worried that her anger may be stronger than his conviction.

"I don't blame just you," she says.

"You mustn't blame Heavenly Father."

"Well, I do."

"Please don't," he begs. He would rather she blamed him than God. Her eternal salvation isn't dependent on faith in Ian Bradley.

"And I blame myself."

"That's ridiculous, Claire. It's not your fault."

"I went *shopping*. I cooked sausage rolls and played musical chairs while she was dying. She was upstairs. All by herself."

He hears the approaching tears in the wobble of her voice and he extends his hand and slides it under the covers, feeling about until he finds one of hers. It is limp and unresponsive, but he holds it anyway.

"You said . . . you said that . . ." She tries to swallow a sob, but it jumps straight back out of her mouth. "You, you said she'd get better, when you gave her the blessing. You said she'd get better if I had enough faith, you said it. But I didn't have enough faith. I knew she was dying."

"That's OK," he says. "You knew. *'To some is given the word of knowledge'*—that's what it says in the scriptures; you knew before I did. That's OK. It's no one's *fault*."

"What's the point of blessings then, Ian? What's the point?"

He is about to answer when he realizes her question is about more than blessings. "You know the point of everything," he says. "To come to Earth and gain a body. To be tested and found worthy." She sighs and closes her eyes. He squeezes her hand. "It's—it's been weeks, Claire. You can't stay here forever. It'll be Christmas before we know it. The children need you."

She opens her eyes. "Do you think this life is a short time?" she asks.

"Oh yes," he says. "The blink of an eye."

"A very short time?"

"Yes."

"So when someone dies it seems like a long time to the people left behind, but it isn't a long time at all."

"That's right." He knew she would understand eventually. He squeezes her hand again. "It's just moments."

"You'd be OK if *anyone* died, wouldn't you?"

"Yes," he says with more confidence than he feels. "With the Lord's help and an eternal perspective I'd be OK. But it's unlikely that anyone else will die soon. Is that what you're worried about? Is that what all this is about? Statistically it's very unlikely. I can work it out if you like, if it'll make you feel better."

"No, no, it's OK." She pulls her hand away from his and reaches out to touch his face. "You're all right, aren't you?"

"Yes," he lies, turning to kiss her palm. She doesn't move her hand so he grasps it and rubs it against his cheek. "I mean, I miss you." He laughs—it sounds like something he should say on the telephone or write on the back of a postcard. "I'd like it if you'd come back. Any time soon would be good." He tries to smile, to offer some encouragement. "But I'm all right. Everyone's all right."

"And you'll be all right no matter what happens, won't you?"

Although he is beginning to realize the answer to her question is no, he doesn't want to disappoint her. "Yes, I'll be fine."

He looks at her bare face. Her skin is oily and gray. She smells of sweat and bed, but he doesn't care. These past weeks have been so lonely. Her hand is a stroke of consolation and a reminder of sex. He turns his head to kiss her palm again and she just watches, so he kisses the heel of her hand and then her wrist. She doesn't turn away as he edges closer on his knees, already thinking about undoing his belt, about squeezing into the bottom bunk, squeezing into her. She isn't saying no with her eyes. She isn't saying anything. He leans under the roof of the bunk and kisses her cheek. It feels slick and buttery. He lets go of her arm. It drops onto the pillow. He places his hands over her breasts. They are smaller. She is thinner. He gets up and closes the door. Then he hurries back to the bed and peels Issy's duvet away.

Claire's nightie is bunched around her waist and he can see the poke of her hips through her Temple garments. One of Issy's teddies lies in the bed beside her. He places the little white bear on the floor and then he grasps the roll of Claire's nightie and slides it up to her armpits. He does the same with her garment top.

Her belly is crisscrossed by silvery stretch marks. She usually covers herself with her hands if he tries to look too closely, despite his insistence that he doesn't care about the snags that lace her skin, but she doesn't cover herself today. She's the only woman he has ever seen naked and, even now, he is sometimes struck by the fact that he is allowed to look at all of her and experiences a burst of gratitude as he removes her clothes. He pushes his hands along the bumps of her ribs until he reaches her breasts. They seem sad, punctured. He covers each breast with a hand and pumps, as if he might reinflate her, but when he lets go they shrink back into slack pockets.

If he can make her feel something else, he thinks, something besides her grief—if he can just wake her up a bit. They've never gone this long without sex. Even after the children, things were always back to normal within a month, and it's not as if he can take care of it himself.

He stands and unfastens his belt. He lets his trousers fall and kicks them off, steps out of his garment bottoms and folds them carefully. He doesn't bother removing his shirt or his socks. He kneels back down, he'll stop if she gives him the slightest sign, but she just lies there, bleached and cadaverous, arms flung back against the pillow. He hooks his fingers into the waistband of her garment bottoms and pulls them all the way down. She smells briny and sour. He folds the garment bottoms. Then he parts her legs and climbs onto the bunk. He leans over her, on all fours, taking care not to bang his head on the slats. She looks past him with empty eyes. There are goose bumps on her arms and he can see the knot of bone where her humerus and ulna lock. There is something about the lay of her limbs that reminds him of chicken wings and he is startled by a sudden remembrance of his mother, each Sunday morning before church, holding an inert, raw bird under the kitchen tap as she rinsed its insides.

He closes his eyes and kisses Claire's jaw and her neck. He doesn't try her lips. Her skin salts his mouth and as soon as he's inside her, he knows he isn't going to last long enough to wake her up or make her feel much of anything. The warmth surrounding his penis, the friction of her indifference—it's too much. He stops moving, holds his breath for a moment, tries to retrieve the image of his mother holding a decapitated chicken, but it's no use.

"Sorry . . . sorry . . . uh, uh . . . sorry." He pants his apology into the hollow where her neck meets her shoulder and it blows back at him, hot and wet.

He climbs off, one hand cupped around his seeping penis, the other supporting his weight.

"Sorry," he says again.

He hurries to the bedroom door and opens it carefully. The landing is empty and he steps quickly into the bathroom. When he has washed himself in the sink he picks up a washcloth, runs it under the hot tap, and tiptoes back to the bedroom. He kneels on the floor and wipes the trickle of semen from between her legs. She looks straight up at the roof of the bunk. He isn't sure whether she is shocked or just vacant. She didn't ask him to stop. But she didn't say he could.

"I'm sorry," he says. "I just, I'm . . ." She isn't listening properly. "I didn't think to—are you—have you been taking your pill?"

He waits for a moment, scared, then hopeful. Another baby might bring her back to herself. Issy can never be replaced, never. But another child might raise Claire from the bed.

She doesn't reply and he can see that she has used up all her evening words. He puts the washcloth down on the carpet and gently slides her legs back into her garment bottoms. He tugs her top and nightie back down and then he lifts Issy's bear off the floor and places it beside her.

"I love you," he says.

When he picks up the washcloth it is already cold and a sluggish trail of semen glistens across its folds.

– 20 –

Lying Boy

Assembly is always best when Mrs. Slade does it. She asks lots of questions and everyone thrusts their hands up and makes little bursting noises in the hope that she will pick them. Today she is holding a bag and it looks like she is going to do something fun.

"What night is it tonight?"

There's a sound like wings as more than a hundred arms part the air.

"Yes, Kyle?"

"Halloween!"

"That's right. Halloween's usually in half-term, isn't it? But not this year."

Mrs. Slade talks about Halloween. She gets a funny mask out of her bag and asks for a volunteer to wear it. Then she produces a pumpkin-shaped bucket and talks about trick-or-treating safely with big brothers and sisters or mums and dads.

Jacob has never been trick-or-treating. Two years ago, when he was really small, Sister Stevens did a Halloween party in the parking lot at church and it was completely ace. It was called Trunk or Treat because car boots in America are called "trunks." All the children walked from car to car saying, "Trunk or treat?" and the *trunks* were open like mouths and full of *candy*, which means sweets. Last year there wasn't a party because Halloween was on a Sunday.

Today is Monday—Family Home Evening. Jacob will suggest that they all go trick-or-treating later, after Dad has given the lesson.

There are some old costumes in the wardrobe that Mum made for dressing up and World Book Day. He can wear one of them and maybe it will be all right for Zippy to take him out, just once around the houses that ring the park.

"Who knows what the day after Halloween is called?" Mrs. Slade asks. Hands shoot up again. "Yes, Abigail."

"The first of November?"

"That's certainly true, but I'm thinking of something else. The day after Halloween is called All Saints' Day. And the day after that, the second of November, is All Souls' Day. It's a day when everyone used to pray for the souls of people who'd recently died. They used to believe that everyone who died wandered about the Earth until All Souls' Day, when they finally moved on to the next world." *All Souls' Day*—Jacob's never heard of it, never. It must be one of those things they do at school that they don't do at church, like Advent, Lent, and Harvest. Sometimes it's hard to work out how all the different bits of both worlds fit together. Once, he thought that the word "penis" was part of church because he'd never heard anyone at school say it—they said "dick" and "willy." He asked Mum about it and she laughed and said he could say "willy" too, if he liked.

"All Souls' Day." He whispers the words to himself so he doesn't forget them: "All Souls' Day. All Souls' Day. All Souls." *All* Souls— that means Issy too, doesn't it? All Souls' Day, when people who've died move on to the next world . . . *or come back to this one.*

AT NEWS TIME Mrs. Slade asks everyone to write about What I Did at Half-Term. George Hindle writes, "I went to the Norf Pole and saw 100 pengwins." Jessie writes about the cinema. Jacob writes:

I waited on the stares for sumthing to happen.

Underneath the words he draws a side view of a staircase with him sitting on the top. Mrs. Slade says it's an unusual thing to have done during the holidays and she asks if he would mind telling her what he was waiting for.

"It's a secret," he says.

AFTER LUNCH, JACOB takes the Box of the Dead out of his desk. He flicks it open and touches the dry, curled-up dead things. None of them came back to life. Nothing happened, despite all his prayers, all his practice. But Fred came back to life, the prayers worked for him. Jacob isn't sure why, maybe there's something special about fish; fish are in the Bible, Jesus feeds them to people, the disciples catch them, and Jonah is swallowed by a big, whaley sort of fish. There must be special rules for fish.

George Hindle pokes him in the back as he closes the glasses case. "What's that?"

"Nothing." He shoves it back in his desk.

"Mrs. Slade, Mrs. Slade! Jacob's got a load of dead stuff in his desk!"

Mrs. Slade is fiddling with the SMART Board. "Sit down, George," she says.

"But, Mrs. Slade, Jacob's got—"

"No I haven't." Jacob's words are loud and he feels the lie spread straight to his face, where it burns his cheeks.

"George, that's enough. Stop making up stories and sit down, both of you."

George glares at Jacob. "Pants on fire," he whispers as they sit.

Jacob looks away. Lying is wrong. He has to tell the truth to Mrs. Slade or he will be in trouble with Heavenly Father. What's the best way for him to tell her that there *really are* dead things in his desk? He can't decide. She will be so disappointed in him. She'll think members of the Church are liars and one day, when the missionaries knock on her door, she won't want to learn about Jesus. She'll say, "Jacob Bradley is a member of your Church and he tells lies." And then she won't be able to go to the Celestial Kingdom and it will be completely his fault.

. . .

AFTER DAD HAS collected him from After-School Club, Jacob goes up to his room and says hello to Mum. She's awake, but she doesn't say anything back. He looks in the wardrobe. There's a furry Dalmatian costume, a fairy dress, a Victorian child's outfit that's just an old school uniform with some holes cut into it, and a Harry Potter cloak with a red-and-yellow scarf Nana knitted. He decides on Harry Potter. He ties the cloak over his school uniform and wraps the scarf around his neck. There isn't a wand so he goes downstairs, takes a piece of paper out of the printer, rolls it over and over, and finishes it off with some sticky tape.

It's dinnertime when the bell rings. Dad opens the door and Sister Stevens is there, wearing a Cookie Monster onesie. She says, *"Coo-kie,"* in just the right voice and then she says, "Happy Halloween." She's holding a big pot and there's a lovely, meaty smell wafting out of it. She says it's a special cowboy casserole for pioneers and she hands it to Dad. Then she dashes back to her car and returns with a pie and a shopping bag.

"Pumpkin pie," she says. "Especially for Halloween. And *coo-kies.*" She does the voice again and everyone laughs.

"How's Sister Bradley?"

"She's a little better," Dad says. "Thank you for the food, it looks wonderful. I'm sorry you had to come out to deliver it on a Monday."

Sister Stevens tells Dad not to be silly. She says something about man not being made for the Sabbath, but the Sabbath for man, which, she thinks, also applies to Mondays and Family Home Evening. Dad nods, thanks her again, and closes the door.

As they turn to head down the hall Jacob glances up at the stairs and thinks of Mum, who is not *"a little better."* Then he hurries to the table with the others and they all stuff themselves with cowboy casserole, pumpkin pie, and *coo-kies* until there's hardly any space left for sadness.

. . .

AT THE END of the Family Home Evening lesson, which is about patience, Dad asks, "Any questions?"

Jacob likes to think of really difficult questions because it makes Dad happy to answer them: questions like, if you got baptized on the same day as other people, and you were the last one in the font, would you get dirty standing in the water that had washed away their sins?

Today he asks another hard question. "Is it ever OK to tell lies, Dad?"

"No, Jacob, it's not. Always tell the truth."

"Even if you're going to get into trouble?"

"Yes."

Maybe he will have to tell the truth to Mrs. Slade . . . but then he thinks about Dad and the way he keeps pretending Mum is just a little bit tired. "Is it OK for you to tell lies about Mum?"

"Jacob!" Zippy's eyes go all googly and she shakes her head at him.

"No, it's a fair question," Dad says and he thinks for a moment. "I was wrong. I think maybe it is OK to tell lies in certain, special circumstances. Abraham had to lie to the Egyptians. He had to tell them that his wife, Sarah, was his sister. He was worried the Egyptians might kill him if they knew the truth."

"Talk about moving the goalposts," Alma huffs.

"No one's going to kill you for telling the truth about Mum, though, are they, Dad?"

"No, but sometimes you can't tell the whole truth, even if you want to; sometimes there are valid reasons not to be one hundred percent honest, but it doesn't happen often."

Maybe it was OK to lie to Mrs. Slade about the Box of the Dead, then. It might be one of those times when it was best not to tell the whole truth, even though he wanted to. He tries another question.

"Can I go trick-or-treating?"

"I don't think so."

"But I've got my costume on and everything. Someone could

come with me," he suggests, remembering what Mrs. Slade said about safety.

"Mum could go with you," Alma mutters. "She could be a zombie; she wouldn't even have to dress up."

"I beg your pardon? Would you like to say that again, out loud?" Al shakes his head and Dad glares at him. "I don't like Halloween. I don't think it's conducive to the Spirit."

"Everyone does it in Utah," Zippy says. "Sister Stevens thinks it's great."

"That's not saying much—Sister Stevens thinks everything's great."

"Alma Bradley, if you can't say anything nice, you know what to do. I'm not prepared to accompany any of you while you knock on the neighbors' doors, bothering them."

"Save that for the missionaries."

"*Enough*, Alma."

"Did you get anything for the trick-or-treaters, Dad?" Jacob asks.

"No."

"We have to give them something—"

"Look, I've got more important things to worry about than buying sweets for other people's children. You'll have to give them a cookie."

Alma snorts. "It's not like we've got any nice cookies since Mum stopped doing the shopping. And they're not getting any of Sister Stevens's cookies, no way. 'Trick or treat'—here, have a Rich Tea biscuit! Ha ha! That's so bad it's hilarious."

"There's an easy solution," Dad says. He gets up, tugs the curtains closed, and turns off the lights in the living room and the hall. Then he goes outside and returns holding the doorbell battery.

"But, Dad, I *really* wanted to go trick-or-treating." Jacob stands up and waves his paper wand at Dad, as if it might charm him into saying yes.

"Come here," Zippy says. "Come on." She takes his hand and

leads him out into the hall. She opens the front door and gently pushes him outside onto the step. "Knock," she says and then she shuts him out.

Jacob stands on the step in the deep dark. He turns round to face the road and the park. The dark is cool and velvety; it collects between the street lights, right at the tips of the trees where Issy might be floating about, waiting until it's precisely the right time and the right day to come back.

He knocks.

Zippy answers. "Yes?" she says.

Alma is standing behind her, holding the bag of cookies.

"Trick or treat?"

Alma gets a cookie out of the bag and extends his hand but at the last minute he pulls it back and stuffs the whole cookie in his mouth.

"Oh, for goodness' sake." Zippy takes the bag off Alma while he laughs, shooting crumbs over the hall carpet.

"Here you are, Harry Potter."

Jacob takes the cookie and waves his wand—"*Wingardium Leviosa!*" He pretends the cookie is flying up to his mouth and copies Alma by stuffing it all in at once. Then he comes inside and Zippy locks the door.

When it's time to go to bed he takes his costume and school uniform off. He leaves them on Mum's dressing table and he steps into his pajamas. Dad comes up and Jacob manages to talk him into reading a story from the big fairy-tale book. After Dad has finished "Hansel and Gretel" he asks, "What's the moral of the story?"

Jacob isn't sure. "Is it to do with not stealing food?"

"I think it's a lost-and-found story," Dad says. "When good people get lost, someone always finds them."

Dad says this so emphatically that Jacob wonders if it's a rule.

Dad says, "I hope so," and then he says goodnight.

After Dad goes downstairs Jacob gets up and puts the Harry Potter cloak back on. If he was a real wizard he would use magic.

He'd talk to Issy in photographs, he'd fight battles and make her soul shoot out of the end of his wand so he could talk to her again. He sits on the big windowsill, where he can look out over the park. He tucks the curtain behind him and shivers because the air next to the window is cooler than the air in the bedroom. The front door is locked and the whole front of the house is dark; he hopes Issy isn't trying to get in. He rests a cheek against the icy glass. If she looks carefully, she will see him sitting there, watching out for her. The autumn leaves on the trees across the road seem blacker than the sky behind them. Every so often there's a breeze and the leaves part to show a slice of path or a line of light from one of the lamps that surround the lake. He is sleepy but he keeps watching, murmuring the words of a Primary song to keep himself awake.

Sing your way home at the close of the day.
Sing your way home; drive the shadows away.
Smile every mile, for whenever you roam,
It will brighten your road,
It will lighten your load,
If you sing your way home.

He wakes up in Dad's bed. It's dark, but it's morning. He can hear cars on the road outside and he lies still for a moment and watches as their lights stroke the walls.

He feels around his neck; he isn't wearing the cloak anymore, Dad must have taken it off. Dad is still asleep, breathing heavily. Jacob slides out of his side of the bed. He tiptoes to the door. The cloak is on the dressing table with his school uniform. As he passes he picks it up and sneaks out onto the landing. He fastens the cloak around his neck, sits down on the top stair, and waits.

Zippy is up first. "What are you doing?" she says.

"I'm waiting."

"Oh. Shall I wait with you?" She sits on the step next to him and puts her arm around him. "You're nice and warm," she says.

Jacob wriggles out from under her arm.

Dad gets up next. He wanders down the corridor scratching his tummy. "What are you two doing?"

"We're waiting," Zippy says.

"It might be a good idea to do it somewhere else so people can get up and down the stairs."

Alma stumbles out of his room, eyes half shut. "You woke me up! I could've had another ten minutes. What's up?"

"We're waiting," Jacob says.

"What for?"

"It's a secret. But I *can* tell you something, something completely ace that you'll never guess." They look at him and he can see they're listening. He rearranges his cloak.

"So, guess what."

"What?" Alma says.

"No, guess."

"I've no idea."

"Come on."

Zippy has a go. "You got a certificate at school?"

"No."

"You got picked for the School Council?"

"No. Way better than that. Way, way better. Issy's fish got resurrected." He nods at them. They don't look impressed, so he nods harder, until the stairs go all swimmy.

"Oh yeah," Alma says. "I heard about that."

"What *are* you talking about?" Dad rubs his cheeks with the palms of his hands and it makes a scratchy sound.

"Sister Anderson was going on about it last week when she came."

"What? When did she come? Never mind—what makes you think the fish was resurrected, Jacob?"

"It was dead before I went to bed. I prayed it would come back to life and when I got home from school the next day it was *alive*."

Dad sighs. "Oh, Jacob."

Zippy wraps her arm around him and this time he doesn't shuck if off. They don't believe him. He can't understand how they can go to church week after week and talk about miracles, and faith, and the resurrection, and believe it all but not believe *him*.

"You can think the fish was resurrected if you like," Alma says. "If it makes you feel better you can think it. Brother Rimmer thinks all sorts of stuff and it makes him feel better, so why shouldn't you?"

Dad looks sad. "That's not exactly right. There's no point in believing something that's not true, even if it makes you feel better."

Alma does a long, mean laugh, which Dad talks over.

"Jacob, when the fish died, I went to the shop and bought a new one. I didn't want you to be upset about Issy *and* the fish. I didn't realize you already knew the fish was dead. I'm sorry."

"What did you have to tell him that for? Now you've made things even worse." Alma stomps to the bathroom and shuts the door.

"Never mind, Jacob," Zippy says. "Let's have a sing. Shall we do your favorite?" She begins to sing "Here We Are Together" all by herself, not realizing it's a rubbish idea until she gets near the end. "There's Mum and Dad and Zippy and Alma and Jacob and . . ." She stops singing and squeezes him hard and he lets her; she's not as soft as Mum, but she's better than nothing.

It's still All Souls' Day tomorrow, isn't it? That hasn't changed. He tries to cheer himself up but it's as if there's a little magnet stuck in his throat and every fragment of unhappiness and gloom, every ache of missing Issy is racing toward it.

"Oh dear," he says. "Oh dear."

He is lost, like Hansel. All his breadcrumbs have been eaten, and he doesn't know how he will ever get Issy home.

BOOK FIVE

———

A Day
of Miracles

NOVEMBER

– 21 –

Dreaming

Claire wakes in the night to the sound of crying. She thinks it's Issy and kicks at the duvet, pushing herself up on weak elbows. Then she remembers. The sound comes again—Jacob. She hears the low rumble of Ian's voice. More cries and more Ian. Maybe it's just a bad dream.

"Everything will be all right"—that's what Ian will be saying. *"You'll see Issy again in about eighty years' time. Cheer up. It's not long, not really."*

She stares up at the dark, comforting shadow of Jacob's bunk. When she wakes in the night it almost feels like she is in a cave and the slatted roof limits the geography of her hurt, keeps a lid on things as she waits out this standoff with God. All she wants is a moment, a reassuring glimpse, something to counter the yearning that worsens with every inhalation. She is not the first to require such a sign—the disciple Thomas doubted and was allowed to see with his own eyes.

She rolls onto her side. Her tongue is swollen and the tide of her mouth is out, its roof is rippled by dry corrugations. When she swallows, her tongue runs aground. She closes her eyes and falls into a sleep that is deep and bottomless. But after a time, the darkness splinters, light glints through the breaks, and Claire dreams she is walking along a beach with the Lord.

— 22 —

Happy Is the Man That Feareth

Ian stands in the hall outside Issy's bedroom. A little hammer of tiredness knocks against the uppermost rim of his eye sockets, acid spurts from his stomach like a geyser, and his thoughts are fuzzy. What to say? He is losing faith in the power of his own words. Perhaps he could sing a hymn. She likes hymns—"Cast Thy Burden Upon the Lord" or "Come, Ye Disconsolate," something like that, perhaps. Or a poem. She likes them too—she used to read whole books of them, years ago. A poem pops into his head—one he's heard so many times at funerals: the one about how death is nothing because it's just like slipping into the next room. He glances at the door. Watching someone you love slip into the next room is *not* nothing. Perhaps the poem gets better; he tries to remember the other words, something about whatever we were to each other, we are still . . . call me by my own familiar name, speak to me in the way you always used . . . He can't recall the rest. In any case, he doesn't have the time to wait in the hall until he is blessed with the right words, not on a school day.

He edges Issy's door open. Claire is lying on her side, facing the wall. He tiptoes across the carpet, kneels on the floor next to the bed, and listens to the slow blow and draw of her breath.

He rests his fingertips on the top of her arm.

Speak to me in the way you always used.

"Please come back. I love you," he whispers.

— 23 —

Fight, You Faggot

What a shitty morning. Al can't wait to get away from everyone.

"I've got to go early," he says as he grabs one of Sister Stevens's leftover cookies. He's even got an excuse ready—some History homework he needs to discuss with Matty—but no one cares enough to ask.

He hurries out to the shed. It's chilly and still a bit dim but the geese are already mucking about, chasing one another, squawking like loonies, and he can see it's going to be a nice day 'cause the sky is clear and glassy. He stuffs an old football into his backpack, sticks his headphones in his ears, and grabs his bike.

He's dog-tired, but his feet find the rhythm of the music as he cycles along the quarry-tile pavements. Once his lungs get going, the cold air inflates and wakes him.

He had a totally crap night. He was woken by Jacob's crying in the early hours and had to jam his pillow over his head to block it out. He couldn't get back to sleep properly for ages and then, when he was finally dozing off, it was time to get up.

Jacob blessed the food at breakfast time. "And please bless us all to stay at home today," he said. "Bless us not to have to go to school—"

Dad interrupted and finished the prayer, which got Jacob crying again.

"Ask and it shall be given to you," he whimpered, pointing at the painting on the kitchen wall. "With God all things are possible."

Dad snatched Mum's crappy bird picture off its nail and put it facedown on the countertop. "Prayer isn't like a Christmas list," he said. "You can't just ask for any old thing and expect to get it."

This made Jacob cry even more, and when it began to look like Zippy might join in, Al decided it was time to leave.

He pedals through the gate to the footie pitch past the "No Cycling" sign, and down the tree-lined path. When he reaches the grass he brakes hard, skids, jumps off his bike, and leans it against one of the nearly bald trees. He shucks off his backpack and hangs it from the handlebars. Then he retrieves the football and stuffs his school blazer in its place.

He jogs onto the field, carrying the ball under one arm. The grass is wet and there are heaps of leaves at the edges of the pitch. His shoes are immediately soaked and he wishes he had his boots. He drops the ball and dribbles it down the field toward the goal near the little park. When he reaches the edge of the box he glances up and smacks the ball into the top right corner of the goal. That's better. He jumps up and down on the spot for a moment and his shoulders start to loosen. He undoes his top button and lowers his tie, wishing someone was there to fetch the ball for him as he jogs to the goal: Issy—the thought smacks into the net of his imagination before he can save it. He pauses to sniff, wipes his nose on the back of his hand, and rubs his eyes while he's at it—it's bloody freezing, no wonder they're watering.

He pulls his iPod out of his trouser pocket and turns the volume up until the music fills his whole head—"*I need a dollar, dollar, a dollar that's what I need*"—not a single rude word in this whole song and appropriate words too. He grins and dribbles back to the edge of the box, where he repositions the ball. He kicks again, aiming for the top left corner. The ball hits the post and he hurries to retrieve it.

He sees the lads only when he turns round. They're jogging

toward him—they must've come from the alley between the houses that back onto the field—and they're smirking, already closer to him than he is to his bike.

There's no one about, but someone is bound to come before long. People walk their dogs on the field. Give it ten minutes and there'll be shitting dogs everywhere. Al picks up the ball and squeezes it to his chest.

"All right, *fucking wanker*?" Spotty-Face calls. "Where's your little friend?"

Al flicks the headphones out of his ears and tucks them into his pocket. He wishes he hadn't been quite so cocky as he cycled away the other day. He wonders if he should run round the back of the goal and at least get the net between them. But there are two of them. They'd just split up and catch him in the middle or chase him round and round like something out of a cartoon.

"All on your own today?"

When Spotty-Face gets close he shoves Al in the chest, the way footballers shove each other when they're warming up for a fight over a foul or a dodgy penalty decision. Al rocks like one of those wobbly kids' toys, but he doesn't fall.

The lad laughs and shoves again. This time Al staggers and regains his balance. He falls only after the third shove, when he drops the ball and stumbles to one side, saving himself with a well-placed hand.

The shorter lad nicks the ball. "Get up and fight, you faggot."

He doesn't know how to fight. Not properly. He's done the shoving thing before on the playground, but teachers have always stepped in and saved him from having to follow through. Spotty-Face lifts his fists and goes all springy at the knees. His mate drops the ball, making fists too.

It's not like a proper fight on TV. Al tries to throw punches, but his arms aren't fast enough. He moves more like a windmill than a boxer, and while he's flailing, their knuckles sneak past his defenses and clout his head and his cheek. Fists don't bounce, they smack, and Al is surprised at how little spring there is in the space between his bones and his skin. He keeps thrashing, makes contact with something—it feels like an ear—and is rewarded with a thump in the mouth. He gasps as his top teeth puncture his lip. He wishes he was brave, but he's scared and hurting.

"Hey, stop it."

The voice belongs to an adult and it's coming from somewhere behind him. The relief sends Al all bendy; his arms droop and he has to sit down. As soon as his butt hits the grass, one of the lads kicks him. He grasps his thigh and he rolls onto his side.

"Leave the boy alone."

Two more kicks. One near his kidney, the other somewhere else, he isn't sure where 'cause the pain in his back is roaring.

"Stop it," the same voice calls, closer now.

The lads jog away, toward his bike. He watches as they grab his backpack from the handlebars and empty everything onto the grass. He breathes carefully, trying to keep rhythm with the pulse in his back as Spotty-Face picks his blazer off the ground, frisks it, and empties the pockets.

When the pain slips past its peak, he starts to feel other things all at once, in a big rush—the wet grass soaking into the butt of his trousers, the pain of the second kick—to his calf, it turns out—and the lump inside his lip that's beating like a small heart. He touches his mouth with the tips of his fingers and they come away bloodied. Spotty-Face waves something he has pulled out of the blazer pocket. He and his mate tussle over what they've found, jostling and shoving each other—Al can't think what could possibly be of any interest to either of them.

"Leave his stuff alone," a different voice calls.

"Mind your own fucking beeswax, Granddad."

Al finally looks over his shoulder. Three old men are shuffling toward him—one of them has a dog, a daft dog in a little red coat. He turns back, rests his head on his knees, and watches the lads wrestle.

"I've got my phone," one of the old men calls. "It's got a camera. I can take a photograph of you."

The lads go all out in a final scrap. They tear at something and shout at each other before they run away.

"Are you all right?"

Gloved hands reach out and tug at Al's elbows and shoulders.

"Come on, lad. That's it. There you go. Let's get you on your way to school."

He struggles to his feet. His knees are slack and his trousers are stuck to his butt. There's no way he's going to school with a wet butt and wobbly legs.

The men surround him. They tap his back and shoulders and shepherd him toward his bike, muttering to him and one another.

"Poor lad."

"I've been on the end of some hidings in my time."

"Me too."

"You're not hurt badly, are you?"

Al shakes his head and runs his tongue over the burst in his lip.

"If we'd been able to move a bit faster . . ."

"I've not been able to move quickly since the nineties."

"The 1890s?"

"Very funny."

Three men. Three really old men with skin like battered leather. Purple noses and massive ears, flat caps, parkas, mad eyebrows like dog's whiskers—they're ancient and there're three of them. Al's breath catches in his throat and he is assailed by a spluttery sort of laugh—he's been rescued by the three fucking Nephites, it's a bloody miracle! The three Nephites, last seen changing a tire on the M58, are here in the park, demonstrating that the Lord is looking out for him. There's clearly no other explanation—ha ha! Wait till he tells Brother Rimmer.

His backpack is on the ground next to his bike and his best football cards lie beside it—Luis Suárez shiny, and Steven Gerrard Man of the Match—torn to bits. His house key rests in the grass beside a couple of empty candy wrappers, his football sits next to the trunk of a tree, and alongside a small drift of leaves he can see one half of his emergency fiver. That's the icing on the crap cake. Not the pain in his back or his bleeding lip, not his earlier thought about needing someone to fetch the ball and the subsequent, inevitable ache of missing Issy, but the money and the way it's not even been stolen, just ripped—ruined.

He cries. He tries to do it quietly, tries so hard it sounds like he's panting, and the little dog in the red coat thinks it's a game and dances about, licking his shoes.

A gloved hand rubs a wave of static along his head.

"Come on. There's a good lad. There's nothing wrong that can't be mended."

The man crouches slowly, creaks, like he needs a squirt of oil in his hinges, and picks up the torn note. Al stares at it. He's in a horrible amount of debt, all kinds of it: the kind Dad goes on about, the kind that has to be settled with payments of goodness and devotion, and the other kind, the real kind—all the money he's borrowed or stolen or whatever it is he's done.

"Here's the other half." Another gloved hand waves money at him.

Al pulls his school tie out from under his sweater and uses it to wipe the tears sliding off his jaw.

". . . to the bank, all right, lad? Are you even listening?" He shakes his head and wipes his nose on his sleeve.

"You just take it to the bank. The money."

"But, but—it's ripped."

"Yes. Are you listening, lad? They'll give you a new one."

"A n-new what?"

"A new fiver."

"They'll give me, they'll—really? You're n-not joking?" He makes a noise that's a cross between a laugh and a sob, it sounds a bit like a bark, and the little dog joins in and Al notices that there are other people about now, a lone dog walker and a woman jogging through the alley. He lifts the bottom of his sweater and buries his face in it.

"Come on."

The old man tugs at the sweater and Al emerges, still breathing the rhythm of his tears.

"I'm not joking, lad. Take the pieces to the bank and they'll give you a new one."

"Is it—is it a special fiver?"

"Do you think he's all there?" The old man looks to his friends, points at his head, and taps his temple a couple of times.

"What if, what if it got dead wet? And what if—what if there was a sort of hole burned into it?"

"It's not wet or burned, it's just ripped. Have a proper look. Did those lads knock you in the head?"

"Would the bank replace it—would they?"

"Well, yes. I expect they would."

"That's incredible!" He doesn't know what to do with himself. He feels all balloony, as if he might float above the park on a cloud of relief and join the geese in their mad, follow-the-leader games. If he has tipped Mum over the edge, he can winch her back with a trip to the bank.

The old men return his smile, pleased that he's pleased.

The little dog catches the excitement and jumps up to rest its wet paws on Al's school trousers.

"Down!" One of the men puts his hand in his pocket and the dog removes its paws from Al's leg and sits dead still. When the man pulls his hand out of his pocket, fingers pressed together, he isn't holding anything, but the dog waits, certain there's a reward in the offing.

Another of the men chuckles and says, "That's dogs for you, lad. Just like gamblers. They try harder if they don't get rewarded the first time. Go on, lad, you have a go."

Al waits until the dog is back on all four paws, then he stuffs his hand in his pocket and pulls it out slowly, fingers pressed together.

The dog sits and looks up, eyes wide, its little face fixed, pleading, hopeful.

"See? They're funny, aren't they, dogs?" The man stoops to ruffle the animal's head with his gloved hand and when he straightens he does the same to Al. "All better now?"

Al nods.

"You'd best be going then, lad."

Al stuffs his things into the backpack and slides his arms through the straps. He climbs onto the bike, clasps the handlebars, and flicks the pedal into readiness. The old men lift their hands in a sort of saluting wave. He waves back, then he pushes down on the pedal and cycles along the tree-lined path toward the gate. Just before he reaches the gate, he glances over his shoulder and shouts, "Bye." The three Nephites are still waving.

Bride of Frankenstein

Zippy wishes Jacob and Dad wouldn't argue. She'd like to give Dad some of his own good advice: If you can't say anything nice, don't say anything at all.

"Prayers *can* be like a Christmas list, Dad," Jacob insists. "And anyway, Santa Claus is in the Old Testament."

"What?" Dad bangs his hand on the countertop and Mum's painting jumps.

"Sister Anderson told us in Primary. In Zechariah it says, '*Ho, ho, from the land of the north.*'"

"She said *what*?"

Zippy catches Jacob's eye and shakes her head but he carries on.

"She said in Zechariah—"

"I heard you. *That* woman . . ."

"She said it in Primary, so it's true."

"No it's not."

"You're not even *listening* to me, Dad."

"It's not true. Prayers are *not* like Christmas lists, and Santa Claus isn't in the Old Testament."

"But Sister Anderson read it out loud from the Bible, I saw her with my very own eyes."

"It's absolutely not true because there's no such—"

"Dad!"

She smacks her spoon into the side of her cereal bowl and it rings out like the bell at the end of a boxing round.

Dad stops and she thinks she's done enough, but he's too wound up, so intent on being right, that he's forgetting to be kind.

"There's no such thing as Santa Claus."

Zippy gasps. Jacob closes his eyes against Dad's words and when he opens them he looks straight at her. There's a long, gluey moment in which she is unable to respond, but when she realizes it's too late for anything but the truth, she nods.

"Is there such a thing as Jesus?"

"Of course there is," Dad says. "Don't be ridiculous."

"What about Rudolph?"

Zippy takes her bowl to the sink and rinses it.

"And the tooth fairy?"

She listens for Dad's answer as she dries her hands, but he is silent and the kitchen noises—the hum of the fridge, the clanking pipes, the tick-tock of the Celestial Marriage clock—are heavy and cheerless. When she turns, Dad is holding Mum's painting.

On her way out of the kitchen she stops to hug Jacob. She feels the thud of his heart through his school sweater and whispers, "It's OK. We'll do something after school—some coloring. You can come up to my room, it'll be fun." Then she hurries up the stairs and packs her school bag.

On the way back down the stairs she pauses outside Issy's room. She lifts a hand to the door but she doesn't have the guts to push it open.

She leaves the house ten minutes early and traipses down the road to the bus stop, her breath sending swirls of steam into the cold air.

LAUREN IS WAITING outside the school gates, frowning at her phone—it'll be Jordan Banks, he's probably chucked her because she hasn't had sex with him yet. "I can't believe you didn't tell me," she says.

Zippy tries a smile and takes it back when it isn't returned.

"I tell you everything. We're supposed to be best friends."

"We are!"

"Yeah. Whatever. I told you all about Jordan."

"I don't know what you're—"

"And then you go and do this."

Zippy can't think what she's done, but Lauren's expression suggests it's something awful. When she holds the phone out Zippy takes it, hoping to see a joke, a meme, something hilarious they can laugh at in a moment's time. But she sees herself, in Mum's wedding dress, on Facebook. And there are sixteen Likes and a load of comments—thirty-four of them.

She strokes her thumb down the screen.

Michael Lewis #megalolz!!!

Brandon Marshall OMFG LMFAO ☺

Martin Hayes ♪♫ i think i wanna marry you ♪♫

Nikita Hewson totes amazeballs

Lauren grabs the phone back. "You got married and never told me." She scowls and folds her arms.

"No!"

"You're my best friend and I didn't know. I found out on fucking Facebook!"

"No, I—"

"Don't lie. I know it happens—I watched a documentary about it. Are they going to make you leave school? You don't have to, you've got rights."

Zippy's knees are slack and trembly. She opens her mouth but her lips are rubbery and no sound comes out.

"Have you *done it*? What was it like? Did it hurt? I can't believe you haven't told me any of this."

"No! I'm—I don't—" She sits on the school wall. "I'm not married. I was dressing up, it's not real. No one would force me—that's a different religion. I'm not married, promise."

"You're sure?" Lauren sits next to her and looks at the phone again. "It's a horrible dress."

"I know. At church, there was this thing—it wasn't—"

"So why the hell did you dress up like that?"

"We had to. It was just this wedding thing, that's all."

"Not an *actual* wedding?"

"No."

"Why's it on Facebook, then?"

"I don't know—I . . . whose page is it?"

"Have you read the comments? They reckon you've married Adam, by the way."

Zippy snatches the phone back. She scrolls to the top of the page; the photo has been posted by one of Adam's friends, Ethan Taylor. His status reads: **Adam Carmichael** you sly bastard!

She scrolls through more of the comments.

Jack Cox First of many, eh, Adam—that's how Mormons roll, isn't it? Lucky you #whyhavejustone

Chloe Ward minger in a meringue alert!! (jk)

Jade Watson You're not married are you Adam? That's *seriously* fucked up.

"There's something else you should see," Lauren says. She takes the phone back and fiddles with it for a moment.

"Here."

She holds the phone out and there's the photograph again, repeated with a variety of captions.

"Shotgun wedding—case of wife or death."

"He sez 'hi,' she planz wedding."

"I went to my wedding and all I got was this ugly dress."

Zippy looks up from the phone. Cars stop on the yellow zigzags, dropping kids off, even though they're not supposed to; cyclists jump the curb, weaving in and out of pedestrians, and another double-decker bus hisses as it pulls in at the stop just down the road. How many of these people have seen the photograph?

Lauren returns to Facebook. There are more comments now. People are probably checking their notifications as they arrive at school, before they have to switch their phones off and put them away. Soon everyone will have seen it.

"I'm going home." She rubs her cold hands together and makes sure her coat is fastened right to the top.

"What, now?"

"Yeah."

"Don't be daft. I can comment. Let's think of something to explain why you were dressed like that, something that's not religious."

"There isn't a good explanation—not one that'll sound normal, anyway." The cold of the wall seeps into Zippy's thighs and bottom.

"I'll report the photo—I'll say it's offensive and ask Facebook to take it down."

"Everyone's seen it."

"So let's think of something I can say to make them all fuck off and stop making fun of you." Lauren glances at the phone again. "Oh God, Adam's commented."

Zippy digs the fingernails of one hand into the palm of the other and waits for Lauren to read the comment.

"OK, this is what he said: *'Chillax people! It was just a Halloween party. Ur looking at the Bride of Frankenstein—she's well scary! Not married! Get a life—4realz!'*" She slings her arm around Zippy's shoulder and squeezes. "There you are, settled! God, what a drama! Come on."

"I'm going home."

"He only called you the Bride of Frankenstein to shut everyone up. You can't just go home. What'll your mum say?"

"Nothing."

"As if. She'll give you the third degree."

"No she won't."

"Oh God, don't look now, it's Adam."

Zippy looks. President Carmichael has stopped his Jag on the yellow zigzags and Adam is climbing out, bag slung over his shoulder, phone in hand.

"You should ask him how the picture got on Facebook. And he should make a groveling apology for being such a knob. He's coming over." Lauren drops her arm, stands, and rearranges her school bag. "I'll see you in a bit. I'm glad you're not married—it was freaking me out."

Zippy stands as Adam approaches. She looks at the pavement when he starts to speak.

"Do you know about the photo?"

Head down, she nods. "Why did you do it?"

"I didn't! I don't even know how . . . Did *you* put it in my bag?"

His shoes are dirty. He'll have to clean them better when he goes on his mission. She rummages in her coat for a tissue.

"What did you do that for? I didn't give it to Ethan, you know," he says. "He must've found it when he was getting the ball out of my bag the other day. He'll have done it for a laugh. I'll get him to delete it."

She finds a tissue and pulls it out of her pocket.

"And I'll get it back for you, if you like."

She doesn't want the photo. It was meant to be for him; he said he liked her in the wedding dress. If he keeps it, he'll be able to look at her dressed like a bride. She doesn't need a prop to help her imagine marrying him, but he might find it useful to have the photo—Sister Campbell says men are *"visual creatures."*

"It's OK, I don't want it," she says.

"Fine. Neither do I."

"Oh." Her voice sounds small and whiny. "I thought you'd like to . . . well, just chuck it in the trash then."

She crouches and rubs at the dirt on the toe of his shoe with the tissue.

"What're you doing?"

"Cleaning your shoes."

"My mum'll clean them. Don't—get up." He steps back and as she straightens, she finally looks up at him properly.

"What were you going to say? You thought I'd like to . . . what?"

"Nothing."

"Go on."

"Keep it. I thought you'd like to keep it." She fiddles with her coat and rearranges her bag. "Anyway, I'm going now. Thanks for sorting it out." He walks with her and stops alongside her when she comes to a halt at the school entrance. "I'm going home," she says.

"Why?"

"Everyone's laughing at me."

"They're not. They probably feel daft for jumping to conclusions."

"I'm a *well scary* Bride of Frankenstein."

He shakes his head and scuffs his shoe against the pavement. "Better than being a *real teenage* bride. You can't just go home. What'll your mum say? The photo's *stupid*. People will forget about it, it's not worth getting . . . Are you upset because I said I don't want to keep it? Look, what happened this morning shows how lame it is to be going on about marriage all the time. Come on, we'll be late."

He lets his bag slide off his shoulder, unzips it, and drops his phone on top of something glossy, some kind of brochure—a university catalog.

Zippy bends and peels back the bag's lip. "Manchester," she says. "Not far away. Is that where you want to go? Do you think it'll be easy to get a deferral? My dad couldn't get one, he had to apply when he got back from his mission." Adam's reply is too long in coming. Another bus hisses past. A car stops on the yellow zigzags. He looks away and the cold air fluffs their breath into clouds that touch as they dissipate. Zippy aches. It feels as if her hopes are leaking from a small perforation between her lungs, and although each escaping wish is small and ordinary—for Dad to think before he speaks, for Mum to get out of bed in the mornings, for Adam to serve a mission—the hurt as they trickle away is considerable.

"You're not going," she says.

"No."

"You'll change your mind."

"I won't."

"I'll pray for you to make better choices."

"Don't."

"People will think you're unworthy, even if you're not."

"I know. But you can't expect me to do it just to please a load of people I don't care about."

"I'm not *expecting* anything—"

"Zippy, you are." He looks at her properly. "You've got Great Expectations." He smiles and brushes her coat sleeve with his fingertips. "Great Expectations, get it?"

"I'm not expecting things for *me*, it's—I want—it's for *you*. Have you been doing something bad—apart from the kissing and stuff? Have you been looking at porn or reading anti-Mormon things on the Internet?"

"No."

"Your dad will be so disappointed."

"Don't."

"Will he let you live at home?"

"I hope so."

"No one will want to marry you."

"No one at church—so that's about zero point three percent of the population."

She just about manages to stop herself from saying, it's more than a percentage point, it's *me*. "But you'll still come to church, won't you?" she asks. "You can't leave completely."

"You've just done a good job of explaining why I can't stay," he says gently.

"Please stay."

"I don't believe."

She doesn't know what to do. If this was a story in a Church Lesson Manual, she'd give him the Temple picture card from his dad and he'd agree that missions are essential and there's nothing lame about eternal marriage. But the card is sitting on her desk at home and if she tried to give it to him he'd almost certainly laugh and pass it back.

"Do you believe in eternal marriage?"

"Give it a rest, Zippy."

"Either you do, or you don't."

"Not everything's *either-or*. We've been friends for ages and we—we *like* each other. There's no reason why we shouldn't . . ."

She shakes her head, remembering President Carmichael's horrible little saying: *"You like him; you love him; you let him; you lose him."* She won't lose him.

The school bell rings and Adam steps closer to the gate.

"You'd better go."

She watches as he jogs away and then she walks to the bus stop by herself, wondering whether things might be easier if love wasn't inextricably linked to marriage and she didn't have to live every moment in the present *and* the endless future; it's an unworthy thought—there's nothing more important than marrying the right person, at the right time, in the right place. She'll wait for him, hopefully not for as many years as Anne Elliot waited, but still, what's a few years compared with forever? It's just a small sacrifice; she's only giving up something good for something better. It's better to experience the agony now and save the hope for perpetuity, isn't it?

— 25 —

A Bloody Miracle

Al stands on the pedals but the position magnifies the ache in his thigh, so he sits down and decides to take his time. He explores the new contours of his lip with his tongue and thinks about what's just happened. The old men have gifted him a story: He's discovered the password to a club that's excluded him for years; he's pretty sure he doesn't want to join, but he *could*. He could tell people, if he wanted. He pictures himself standing at the pulpit on Fast and Testimony Sunday, describing how the three Nephites came to his rescue. The room would go quiet, people would *really* listen, and they'd know he was someone important and good. That's the whole point of miraculous stories, isn't it? To let people know that Heavenly Father thought it was worth stopping whatever it was He was doing, in order to intervene in your life. Al could hang *everything* on this story—build his testimony on it, like the wise man who built his house upon the rock.

He pedals faster, even though the effort pumps pain into his thigh and shin and his breath rubs against the ache in his back. He sees other kids cycling on the opposite side of the road, cars and buses packed with uniformed bodies, all heading for school. Not him. He's going to get the money out of his hoodie pocket, cycle to the bank, swap the notes, and take them straight to Mum. She'll be stoked; she might even get up right away—it'll be all religious like that bit in the New Testament when Jesus tells the man to take up his bed and walk. Once that's happened, the whole story will be totally epic. He imagines going into Issy's room with the money in his hand and holding it out to Mum. He tries to think of some words to go with the action as he swings onto the pavement and over a pedestrian crossing in order to avoid a red light at the cross-roads. The words come to him as he bumps back onto the road, and he tries them out.

"Mum," he says in an authoritative voice that makes him sound quite a lot like Dad, "throw off your duvet and walk!"

He cycles past the end of Brother Rimmer's road. He doesn't feel the urge to turn around until he gets to the next junction, and he wouldn't normally pay any attention to such an urge, but it's been such a weird morning that he slips down a side road, turns, and heads back. He isn't sure why. All he knows is Brother Rimmer will listen and join the dots together. No doubt most of what he says will be completely bonkers, but Al finds he doesn't mind.

Brother Rimmer opens the door in his pajamas.

"You're lucky, I've just stuck my teeth in," he says. "What's happened? Are you all right?"

"I wanted to tell you something."

"You'd better come in, then."

He follows Brother Rimmer down the hall, past the Blu-tacked pictures of the prophets, and into the kitchen. Brother Rimmer hefts a bag of peas out of the freezer and wraps it in an orange tea towel. "Hold that against your lip. Reckon you can manage a bacon sandwich?"

Al lifts the peas away to say, "Yes please."

Brother Rimmer doesn't put the bacon under the grill. He fries it in a frying pan with a big lump of butter. Then, when it's ready, he dips bread in the fat, folds it around the bacon, and smacks his lips.

They eat standing up in the kitchen. Al takes small bites and chews with his back teeth. There isn't a radiator, but Brother Rimmer's got one of those electric heaters that blow like a hair dryer and Al stands with his back to it so his trousers can dry.

After they've finished eating, he tells Brother Rimmer about being attacked by the lads and rescued by the three old men; he doesn't mention the money.

Brother Rimmer says the story is the best thing he's heard in ages. He can't be sure whether the men were the three Nephites, largely on account of the dog, which doesn't feature in any of the reports he's heard. However, it's possible they may have decided to get a pet. After all, it must get a bit lonesome and boring, wandering the Earth until the Second Coming. Either way, he reckons it's a sign that Heavenly Father is looking out for Alma Bradley—most likely a miracle, in fact. And because he says it so seriously and thoughtfully, Al can almost believe it; when it comes down to it, a miracle is just an unexpected but welcome change—water to wine, dead to alive, crap to brilliant.

On the way out, Al pauses next to a picture of Brigham Young, whose sour expression is partially obscured by a lawnlike beard.

"There's something else I should tell you," he says.

"Go on then, lad. Spit it out."

"That money you've got in the garage."

"Oh yes?" Brother Rimmer's eyebrows flex.

"You should take it to the bank. It's not safe. Anyone might steal it."

"Not *anyone*, it turns out. You're a good lad, Alma Bradley." He holds the front door open as Al climbs back on his bike. "Go carefully now," he calls. "Don't do anything daft—you've had your miracle today!"

– 26 –

Big Boy

It's quiet in the car. Dad doesn't play the Tabernacle Choir CD and he doesn't talk. When he pulls up outside the school, he switches off the engine and says, "I've learned something over the years, Jacob. The answer to some prayers is no."

They walk up the path together. Jacob says goodbye and Dad says, "I'm tired," which feels like, "I'm sorry," even though the words are different.

He sits by himself in Early Drop-off Club. There's no point in talking to anyone. Issy hasn't come back, even though it's All Souls' Day.

He wanted to tell Dad a story in the car but he wasn't brave enough. The story is true, at least that's what Sister Anderson said. It's about one of the apostles who kept rabbits when he was a little boy. One day, when the apostle was seven, his favorite rabbit escaped. He looked for the rabbit but he couldn't find it. Then he said a prayer and immediately a picture came into his mind and he went to the exact spot he had imagined and found the rabbit. This showed the apostle that Heavenly Father responds to the small, simple prayers of *everyone*.

Jacob thinks about the rabbit story and what Dad said about answers to prayers in the car. There should be stories where the answer is no. There should be stories where children pray for lost rabbits that never turn up and then people might get used to it and know what to do next; he doesn't know. He has prayed and blessed and waited, he's done everything you have to do to get a miracle. If he can't bring Issy back, the only way to see her again is to be good for his whole, entire life, which means he's got to fix his lie.

IT'S BUSY IN the classroom. People are putting their lunch boxes on the cart and chatting as they open their bags to retrieve reading books and spelling lists.

Mrs. Slade hangs her coat and scarf over her chair.

"What a chilly morning! Who can smell winter coming? Let's get ready. Hurry up, everyone."

Jacob opens his desk. The Box of the Dead is just Issy's glasses case now. There's nothing special or magical about it. He picks it up and peeps inside. The dead things are getting smaller. Their legs are folded tighter. Perhaps they would disappear altogether if he just left them there. But he can't. He told a lie and he has to repent. He carries the case over to his table and sits down. He feels a bit sick. He knows Mrs. Slade likes him, he can tell by the way she says his name; it sounds like "Jay-cub," and her voice goes up and down just like it does when she says the word "lovely." But she won't like him once she finds out he's a liar.

"Why've you got that out?"

Jacob ignores George. In just a moment Mrs. Slade will write three sums on the board and there'll be five minutes to answer them before the bell rings for assembly. As soon as everyone is working on their sums he will go over to her desk and explain.

George pokes him in the leg. "What're you doing?"

"Get off."

"Give us a look in there."

"No."

"Go on." George slides his hand across the table, wraps it around one end of the glasses case, and yanks.

"Get. Off."

"Make me."

Jacob stands, George follows, and they're suddenly doing a

tug-of-war in front of everyone while Mrs. Slade writes sums on the board. A few people start giggling and Mrs. Slade turns round.

"Sit down please, boys."

Jacob slides a nail into the lip of the glasses case to get a stronger grip. George pulls harder, and then the case flicks open and a litter of insect skeletons flies to its final resting place beside Jessie Sinkinson.

Mrs. Slade runs. She glances at the insects on the table and bends down to lift the big, umbrella-shaped spider off Jessie's lap. She puts it with the other dead creatures and that's when Jessie starts to scream, her mouth so wide that Jacob can see the dangly bit at the back of her throat.

The screams jab fright into his tummy, they remind him of Mum howling at Issy's funeral, of the coffin sliding into the earth and mud splatting onto its white lid, and of every other sad and disappointing thing that has happened since. He sits down, clutching the open case. Another teacher rushes into the room and tells everyone to stop staring and line up for assembly while Mrs. Slade kneels on the floor next to Jessie and says, "Shush, shush." Every time Jessie pauses to take a breath, George hisses, "I *knew* Jacob Bradley kept dead things in his desk. I told the *truth*."

"Go to assembly with the others, George. And, Jacob, please don't cry. It was just an accident."

There are splashes on the table. Jacob rubs them with his finger. Jessie's voice is loud and strong like a burglar alarm and it seems even louder as the classroom empties and there's more air to fill.

"Shush, shush." Mrs. Slade slides her hand across the table and brushes the insects away from Jessie and onto the floor. "Jacob, there's no need for you to cry," she says.

He can't stop the tears, it's like someone's switched a tap on in his eyes. "Issy's *never* coming back, my mum won't get up, and there's no such thing as Santa Claus."

George pokes him in the shoulder. "You're a liar, Jacob Bradley, a big, fat liar."

"George, go to assembly. Now."

"Pants. On. Fire."

"Now."

George hurries away. He'll be in trouble later and that should make Jacob feel better but he just feels tired and old, as if he has been awake for his whole life.

"Why don't you go and wait in the corridor, until Jessie calms down?" Mrs. Slade says.

He does as he's told and waits by the door to the classroom, beside the display of Egyptian pictures and drawings. He realizes that all the tears he could have cried but didn't because he was busy bringing Issy back to life haven't gone anywhere, they're still inside him. He tries to swallow them but it's hard and in the end he thinks "better out than in," which is what Mum used to say when someone did a burp. Thinking of her makes more tears come and he watches them splash on the corridor floor.

Once Jessie's screams have settled into an unhappy sort of hum, Mrs. Slade comes out and puts her arm around his shoulder.

"What are we going to do with you, Jacob Bradley?"

She makes him sit on a chair in the corridor, outside the bathroom, right where you have to wait to be picked up if you've been sick. Then she goes to the office to telephone Dad's school. It smells of wee and disinfectant by the bathroom, and when people walk past on their way back from assembly, they leave lots of space because they don't want to catch sick germs. But he hasn't been sick; he's been sad, which is actually much worse.

His eyes are sore and he feels all crackly and dry inside, like a bag of potato chips. He wonders when he will be allowed to come back to school—you have to wait twenty-four hours if you've been sick. If he has to wait until he is completely happy again, he might be off for quite a while. He clasps Issy's glasses case in both hands and rests his head against the corridor wall. As he closes his eyes, it occurs to him that all *this*—the Box of the Dead and George and Jessie and the insects—is an answer to prayer.

— 27 —

He That Is Happy
Shall Be Happy Still

Ian is doing percentages with Year Eight when Dave Weir knocks on the door.

"Can I have a word, Mr. Bradley?"

Ian hurries down the aisle between desks and steps out into the corridor.

"Firstly, everything's OK, mate. Everything's OK."

The terror is instantaneous. "What is it?"

"There's been a call from your son's school. He's fine, but they want you to go and pick him up. I'm covering—what're you doing?"

"Which son? Why do I need to pick him up if everything's OK? Has he had an accident on his bike?"

"I don't know, sorry. Swing by the office on your way out, they'll fill you—"

"Percentages." Ian feels for his car keys and realizes his things are still on the floor next to the desk.

"Percentages?"

"That's what I'm doing."

"Oh God."

"Top number divided by bottom number, times one hundred. It's all up on the SMART Board—click on MyMaths—I'm sure it'll all come back to you." He dashes into the classroom. "I'm needed elsewhere and Mr. Weir's going to supervise the rest of this lesson." He grabs his bag and coat. "Thank you, Mr. Weir."

They tell him it's Jacob in the office, they say he's fine but Ian can't believe them. He breaks the speed limit and runs two red lights. He'll repent later.

Mrs. Slade is waiting in the foyer. She says perhaps Jacob came back too soon. She suggests a few days off, maybe a week, to give him a chance to *come to terms with things.*

"Mr. Bradley, you should know he thought his sister . . . he didn't realize . . . he thought she was coming back," she says, and Ian feels horribly ashamed of Jacob, and himself, and the whole family for failing to set a good example. He thinks back to the Family Home Evening he gave after Issy died; he thought he'd covered everything but perhaps he didn't.

Jacob is sitting on a small plastic chair in the corridor, leaning into the wall, eyes closed, Issy's glasses case in his lap. Ian resists the urge to pick him up and carry him to the car. Instead, he is jolly.

"Oh dear, never mind, you big silly billy. Come on, let's go."

He heads for the cemetery. Jacob doesn't say anything when he realizes they aren't going straight home. He just sits quietly, clutching the glasses case.

Ian pulls up near Issy's grave. The sun is higher now and it's not as cold as it was first thing. They cross the grass and stand side by side looking at the ground.

"We'll have to choose a headstone before too long," he says. "What do you think Issy would like?"

"Something with animals on it. And birds. And purple writing."

"It would be good if we put something on it to let people know about the Church. Something about how families can be together forever. Lots of sad people come here; they could do with hearing about the Church."

Jacob taps him on the arm.

"Yes?"

"We're sad, Dad."

"We are. But not as sad as nonmembers would be."

The ground seems flatter, as if it's beginning to settle around Issy's body. He watches Jacob test the mound with the tip of his shoe and disturb a few clods of soil. "When we die, our spirit leaves our body," he begins.

"Do you think Issy is a skeleton yet?"

He remembers what Jacob's teacher said and resists the temptation to say Issy isn't actually there anymore—one step at a time. "I don't know."

Jacob holds his hands up and inspects them. "How does all your skin come off when you die?"

"I don't know that either."

He watches as Jacob drops his hands into his pockets and begins to nudge the ground again.

"Dad?"

"Yes?"

"Issy's going to be dead for my whole, entire life, isn't she?"

"Yes."

"That's sad, isn't it?"

Ian can't trust his voice. He nods.

"Dad?"

"Yes?"

"I know I'll see her again and everything, but I'll be grown up by then, so it's not that good, is it? We were going to get grown up together, and now I'll be getting grown up by myself."

Perhaps if he was a better Bishop, a better father, he would know what to say.

"Dad?"

"Yes?"

"What about the presents?"

"Sorry?"

"At Christmas. Do you hide the presents?"

He thinks for a moment. "I'm afraid that's classified information. If I told you I'd have to . . ." He realizes too late that the joke is in bad taste.

"You'd have to what?"

"Hug you."

"Is there anything else?"

"What do you mean?"

"Any more secret stuff? You might as well tell me."

"Well, don't tell your mum—I'll be in enough trouble as it is when she's all better and she finds out—but the tooth fairy and the Easter Bunny . . ."

"I thought so. But everything else is true?"

"Everything except Santa Claus in the Old Testament. I'll be having a word with Sister Anderson about that."

"Are you going to tell her off?"

"No, I—the Bishop shouldn't . . . Do you know what? I think I might."

"But not too much. She got me an ace birthday card. It played a tune and everything."

"OK, not too much." He takes Jacob's hand. "Let's go home."

Here We Are Together

Zippy sits on the floor outside Issy's room. Once she's had a chance to organize her thoughts, she'll go in and talk to Mum and Mum will listen properly and remember she still has a daughter.

When the key turns in the downstairs lock, she jumps and scrambles to her feet. But it's only Alma. "What are you doing?" she calls as he steps into the hall, and then it's his turn to jump.

"What are *you* doing?"

He looks up and she notices his mouth. "Are you OK? Who did that to you?"

"I'm spectacularly OK." He races up the stairs. "This is a game-changer! The tide has turned." He pushes past her and dives into his room.

"Whoop-de-do," she mutters. He's such an idiot but he's hurt and she's supposed to be being kind. To everyone. "So what happened?"

"Hang on."

She can hear him rummaging. It sounds like he's chucking stuff about, making a mess. He comes out onto the landing holding something.

"It was just these lads, at the field. They gave me a bit of a battering. Back soon," he says.

"What're you up to?"

"It's a secret."

"First Jacob, now you. Have you been secretly resurrecting stuff too?"

"Something happened this morning—you could say it was a bit of a miracle . . ."

She rolls her eyes.

"OK, so it probably wasn't, but have you ever wondered why miracles happen only to weird people or people we don't know, like the prophet? Why they don't happen to normal people? You believe in miracles, but you don't expect them, do you?"

"What are you talking about?"

"Why are you home, anyway?"

"I need to talk to Mum."

"Good luck with that."

"I'm not going anywhere until she talks to me."

"You can't *make* her."

"I've got all day."

"Better get started, then." He reaches for the door.

"Stop." She puts her arm out in front of him, like a parking barrier. "Just hang on." She waits, her throat full. "OK." She gives the door a gentle push and it rolls open.

The bed is empty. Mum is gone.

THE FRONT DOOR is unlocked. Ian hesitates. His guts are watery—he doesn't think he can stomach any more surprises, but Jacob wriggles past and opens the door to reveal Zipporah and Alma, arguing in the hall.

"But Mum's an adult."

"You know exactly what I mean, Alma."

"She can go out whenever she wants."

"I didn't say she can't, it's just that she's—"

He steps into the house, primed to ask what on earth they're doing, why they're home from school, when he notices Alma's swollen, bloody lip.

"What's happened?"

"I was in a scrap with some lads at the field."

"Are you—did they hurt you anywhere else?"

Alma nods and lifts his trouser leg to reveal a purple knot on his calf; he untucks his shirt and turns round and Ian can see the beginnings of a bruise on his lower back, shaped like the toe of a sneaker.

"They got my thigh too, but I'd better keep my trousers on."

"Yes, you'd better." Ian lifts his arms but they fall back to his sides. He has forgotten how to touch Alma. He tries again and as he raises his arms and reaches out, he can almost see the dividing line he has drawn between touching and not touching, between approval and acceptance. "Come here, you," he says.

Alma edges closer and ducks, ever so slightly, enough to demonstrate reluctance but not enough to escape the embrace. Ian wraps him up. He's all angles and bones, sharp and spiky, awkward, irreverent, and *his*.

Alma pulls away, red-faced and tongue-tied, and Ian turns his attention to Zipporah. "And why aren't you at school?"

"Everyone's here, Dad!" Jacob says. "I prayed for it this morning and now everyone's—"

"Mum's not here."

Zipporah's words don't make any sense. Ian waits for her to continue, and when she doesn't, he hurries up the stairs in an effort to understand.

"She's not there," Zipporah shouts after him. "We've looked."

He pushes Issy's door open. The bed is empty. He looks around. There's nowhere else an adult could hide, but he searches anyway: in the wardrobe, under the bunks.

He steps out onto the landing. "Claire, where are you?"

"She's not here, Dad." Zipporah follows him up the stairs. "We've looked everywhere."

"Claire!" He dashes from room to room, he won't believe until he has seen it with his own eyes. He even checks the garden, Zipporah tagging along all the while.

Back in the kitchen, he finally concedes the point. Claire has gone. But she'll be back. Maybe she needed some fresh air; she's probably walking around the park as they speak. It's just a matter of waiting until she comes back. Perhaps she feels better and her disappearance is, in fact, a good sign.

"Her wellies aren't here, Dad."

"She's probably gone to the beach, then. Let's try not to worry," he says as he opens the top cupboard, finds the antacid medicine, and swigs it straight from the bottle.

"Dad?"

"Yes?"

He fills a glass with water and knocks it back to get rid of the taste.

"I had a look for her nightie because I wondered, after the other night with President Carmichael and Brother Stevens, whether she would think to get changed."

He puts the glass down on the countertop, slowly, and watches the remaining water sway, then settle. "And?"

"I can't find it . . ."

He looks up. Zipporah is chewing her lip.

"I think . . . I think she's still wearing it."

The telephone breaks the hiatus and Jacob runs to answer it. "It's for you, Dad," he says.

Ian thinks it's Claire, which makes no sense because she doesn't have a mobile, but he thinks it anyway and that makes it particularly disappointing—no, infuriating—when he puts the phone to his ear.

"Oh, Bishop Bradley, it's an answer to prayer that you're home—I tried your mobile but you're not good at answering it during the day, are you? I hate to be a nuisance but Brother Anderson wants to come home and he's just not well enough, his blood count's—"

"I'm sorry."

"—a bit low and I don't think he—"

"I'm sorry."

"Thank you, Bishop—and I don't think he—"

"No, I'm sorry because I'm busy." His voice trembles; he's setting a terrible example as the children look on. "I can't come, I'm not a doctor. Brother Anderson needs to listen to his doctors. I have to go now, goodbye." He ends the call and puts the phone down on the counter.

Zipporah and Alma don't move but Jacob takes his hand. "Don't worry. Even Jesus got cross sometimes. Shall we go and look for Mum now? I haven't been to the beach for *ages*."

He glances at the phone and then at the children. "Yes, come on. We'll all go. Together."

As soon as they get in the car, Dad says, "Let's have a prayer."

Zippy, Jacob, and Dad bow their heads and close their eyes. Dad speaks quietly and humbly. He says *"thank you"* for his many blessings. He says *"please."* Please this, please that, just as he must have done when Issy was dying.

Al stares at Dad in the rearview mirror. His forehead is creased and he looks like he's on his best behavior—like the little dog in the park: arms folded, eyes squeezed shut, hoping for a reward, convinced if he's good one more time, he might actually win something. And although it's tempting to make fun of him, Al closes his eyes and pulls the same face, just in case.

Dad drives past the park, toward the coastal road. Jacob looks out the window for Mum. Her wellies are pink, so she will be easy to spot. Dad doesn't slow down when he turns onto the Bumpy Road and it feels as if the car might take off as it gallops over the bumps.

"Faster, Dad, faster!" Jacob calls.

No one is walking along the Bumpy Road, there's just the marsh and the birds. At the end of the Bumpy Road, Dad turns right and pulls into the parking lot, where there are a few other cars and some cocklers' vans. Jacob can see a couple of dog walkers on the path that cuts through the marshy bit of the beach. He thinks he can just about see a pencil line of sea, but he can't see Mum.

Dad pulls the handbrake up and stares through the windshield. "Where is she?" he says, tugging off his tie and unfastening his top button.

After the marshy bit ends, the beach stretches on and on. Jacob tries to spy Mum. He has spent all these weeks praying for huge, difficult things. Finding Mum shouldn't be difficult; she's bigger than the apostle's rabbit and much more important.

Dad drops his tie in Zippy's lap and scrambles out of the car, but he doesn't head down the path to the sea; instead, he jogs in the opposite direction and crosses the road.

"He's going the wrong way!"

"No, look, he's just asking that man . . ." Alma points. Dad talks to a bird-watcher. They wait as he borrows the man's binoculars and scans the horizon. Dad gives the binoculars back and sprints over the road. He runs through the parking lot and past the warning sign at the start of the path; he isn't running in the embarrassed, careful way grown-ups usually run, he's running properly, palms flat, arms slicing. Past the cocklers' vans and the dog walkers, down the incline to the track that runs through the marshy grass.

"I can't see her," Zippy says.

"Shall we—" Alma begins.

Zippy and Alma open their doors and step out of the car. "You can run fast, can't you, Jacob?" Zippy asks.

He nods and follows.

"Ready, then?"

"Yes," he says. "Mum's good, isn't she?" Zippy and Alma agree that she is.

"I know something about being good," he says. "If you're good and you get lost, someone you love comes and finds you."

Footprints
in the Sand

NOVEMBER

The sea licks its way along cuts and grooves in the sand, trickling into oozing cricks that curl behind Claire and slink toward the shore. She mustn't look back in case like Lot's wife she betrays her hesitation.

Earlier, it seemed possible that life might continue where her dream left off, that He may appear and make a concession, offer an accord: a kind word, a glimpse of Issy—Claire isn't fussy, she'll accept crumbs. But now she is beginning to doubt whether He will come, and if He doesn't and there is only sand and sea and the bare curve of the horizon, if that is all there is, perhaps she'll find a path to Issy anyway.

As she walks, her breath beats with the pulse of the waves. A flock of starlings swoops overhead as she refastens her coat and inhales the sea smells: oil, rot, seaweed. And she waits.

It's cold and she's terribly tired but she fixes her eyes on the horizon, countering the chatter of her teeth with the murmured words of a hymn: *"Jesus lover of my soul, Let me to thy bosom fly, While the nearer waters roll, While the tempest still is high."* Her tongue is thick, her mouth drained and sticky.

She waits, plastering the cracks in her conviction with hope; she *hopes* He will come—it's nearly the same as believing, isn't it?

Standing here, she could almost believe the world is flat and it doesn't seem at all unreasonable to think if she just stepped into the water and swam far enough, she might fall off its edge and into heaven.

The sea seeps over furrows and swells into puddles: rolling, rushing—He isn't coming. The realization has crept up on her like the tide. Of course He isn't coming. No one is coming.

She readies herself. Turning will betray a longing for something other than Issy—sleep, bed, home, the children, Ian—she can't say, and the possibility of other wants surfacing feels like a betrayal. The wind sifts salt over her; she tastes it on her lips and feels it crusting her cheeks.

She turns.

While she was waiting the water has swept along rifts in the sand and arced around her. She is stranded on a boggy island, surrounded by dark, charging sea: not deep yet, only knee height, certainly no more than thigh height. As the tide unfolds, her island will shrink and sink and she will have to make a choice. There is only one set of footprints and they are her own. No one has walked beside her. No one has carried her.

She can't see the coastal road or the parking lot, but she is aware of the sweep of the beach and the distance she must cover before she reaches safety. And when she turns to check the incoming tide she sees how she still might drift out of this world and into the next.

A large bird, a heron perhaps, swoops overhead, its wings spread like a cloak. She follows its movements as it tracks back, plunges, and lands beside her on backward-facing legs. She keeps as still as she can, lets her hair whip across her face, and clenches her pocketed hands in an effort to control her shivers. The bird looks old and wise, like something out of one of the fairy tales she used to read to the children. The wind ruffles its spiky blue-gray feathers and its long neck unfurls like a question mark. It has no brows to vary its expression or soften the scrutiny of its searching stare; it's only a bird, but it's looking at her intently, as if it has caught the wave of her thoughts.

The bird lowers its head and its long beak points at the sand while its yellow eyes continue to hold hers. It seems like the dip of its neck is an expression of sympathy. Maybe it is also a mother, and, for the first time in weeks, she experiences the feeling of being observed, attended, and appreciated.

The bird's presence is the sort of faith-bolstering detail Ian would gratefully note, a Tender Mercy, and she wonders whether the Lord, too busy to offer reassurance in person, has sent this messenger in his stead. She tries to ask, but her voice scrapes her parched throat, and when the dry crackle sounds, the bird takes a couple of running steps on its impossible legs, spreads its wings, and soars away, skimming the water as it ascends. If she wasn't so exhausted, perhaps she could also fly.

Tiredness presses on her shoulders and knees. It's becoming hard to hold her body upright. Her hands are numb, and when she looks at them, the skin is almost transparent, which isn't surprising because she has been disappearing for some time. Her thoughts are lagging and it feels as if she may be dissolving, breaking into a scatter of notions and impressions. Her eyelids shutter and she knocks back yawns, thirsty for sleep . . . so many stories about sleep: Once upon a time there was a princess who slept for a hundred years; once, five foolish virgins napped while the bridegroom tarried; once there was a little girl who was not dead, but sleeping.

The island is shrinking and it's as if her body, expecting to be vacated, is switching out the lights before she leaves. She isn't cold anymore and the sea sounds far away. She closes her eyes and experiences the airy weightlessness she associates with fasting, the heady retreat to the summit of her body, and for a moment her arms span, her fingers quill, and she can see herself as if from above, stranded on an island in the mud flats, surrounded by gray water—head bowed, nightie flapping like a flag. She scans the horizon, dredging the line where the sky skims the water, and there is nothing but the spare spread of the sea and bare heaven.

Soaring on an updraft, she spirals and looks back at the shore. On the other side of the swirling water, a man in a white shirt and dark trousers runs at the tide, three smaller figures arrow after him: A hurtling boy is followed by a young woman towing a scampering child.

She wheels back to consciousness, assailed by the stinging wind and whirling sea. She has been so very lost; she has watched and prayed and waited. And while she has waited, her family has come.

Indistinct cries sail on the wind—they could be avian or human; she defers judgment, twists away from the sounds to review the horizon. And as she acknowledges the permanence of the uninhabited skyline, she detects the germ of a feeling that isn't sadness, but something else: a coalescence of the fear of being caught and the comfort of being found. The wind carries more cries, words now. She will not answer yet. Instead, she imagines they are echoes of the many memories that ghost the beach: iterations of kite flying, shell collecting, crab catching—slivers of an irretrievable past that will always exist here.

"Claire!"

"Mum!"

The sea is reeling and she wonders whether she has left it too late. She digs the toe of one wellie into the heel of the other and extends her arms, balancing with none of the elegance of the heron as her foot emerges. The empty wellie drops and is joined seconds later by the other.

Damp seeps between her toes, crawls up her socks, and as this secondary cold banishes tiredness, it occurs to her that the contrast between the bare horizon and the promise of the shore marks the difference between heaven and earth.

The waves rock inexorably closer. Lacy spume swamps her toes; the tide licks and retreats, licks and retreats. She waits for the inevitable surge, watches as its expanding arc is held high, until it heaves like a long exhalation, pitching past her knees. The nightie tangles her legs. She staggers then straightens, standing fast as the island is buried. And as the last of her lonely, waterlogged footprints melt under the rush of the tide, she turns to face home.

Acknowledgments

I'd like to thank my Ph.D. supervisors, Ailsa Cox and Robert Sheppard, for their ongoing support and friendship. I'd also like to thank the members of Edge Hill's Narrative Research Group for valuable feedback and Edge Hill's Postgraduate Research Bursary Fund for funding an Arvon Course. Special thanks to Amanda Richardson and Jenn Ashworth for reading draft chapters, and to Sarah Franklin for reading and critiquing the final draft.

Thank you to Jo Cannon for help with medical details and Tony D'Arcy-Masters from the Southport Offshore Rescue Trust (Southport Lifeboat) for answering numerous coastal questions. Thanks to Dialogue—a Journal of Mormon Thought for publishing an early version of "Miracle Boy" as a short story.

A huge thank-you to my agent, Veronique Baxter; my editor, Jocasta Hamilton; and everyone at Ballantine Books.

Finally, love and thanks to my lovely children—wearers of smelly football boots and tellers of terrible jokes. And to Neil, for everything.

ABOUT THE AUTHOR

CARYS BRAY was brought up in a devout Mormon family. In her early thirties she left the Church and replaced religion with writing. She was awarded the Scott prize for her debut short story collection, *Sweet Home*. *A Song for Issy Bradley* is her first novel. She lives in Southport, England, with her husband and four children.

#IssyBradley
@CarysBray

ABOUT THE TYPE

This book was set in Sabon, a typeface designed by the well-known German typographer Jan Tschichold (1902–74). Sabon's design is based upon the original letter forms of sixteenth-century French type designer Claude Garamond and was created specifically to be used for three sources: foundry type for hand composition, Linotype, and Monotype. Tschichold named his typeface for the famous Frankfurt typefounder Jacques Sabon (c. 1520–80).